Also by Julian Stockwin

Kydd
Artemis
Seaflower
Mutiny
Quarterdeck
Tenacious
Command
The Admiral's Daughter
Treachery (US title: The Privateer's Revenge)
Victory
Conquest
Betrayal
Caribbee
Pasha
Tyger
Inferno
Persephone
The Baltic Prize
The Iberian Flame
A Sea of Gold

JULIAN STOCKWIN

Invasion

HODDER

First published in Great Britain in 2009 by Hodder & Stoughton
An Hachette UK company

This paperback edition published in 2019

7

A CIP catalogue record for this title is
available from the British Library

Paperback ISBN 978 0 340 96117 9

Typeset by Palimpsest Book Production Ltd,
Falkirk, Stirlingshire

Printed and bound in Great Britain by
Clays Ltd, Elcograf S.p.A.

Hodder & Stoughton policy is to use papers that are natural, renewable
and recyclable products and made from wood grown in sustainable
forests. The logging and manufacturing processes are expected to
conform to the environmental regulations of the country of origin.

Hodder & Stoughton Ltd
Carmelite House
50 Victoria Embankment
London EC4Y 0DZ

www.hodder.co.uk

Let us be masters of La Manche for just six hours — and England will have ceased to exist!

—Napoleon Bonaparte, Paris, 1804

Chapter 1

'Mr Kydd, how dare you, sir? To think to approach me in my own headquarters, demanding a hearing in such an impetuous manner.' Admiral Sir James Saumarez stood upright at his desk, clearly outraged. 'I'll remind you, sir, that you narrowly escaped court-martial by your contemptible actions and must be satisfied with a dismissal.'

Commander Kydd held his impatience in check: at long last he had the evidence to prove false the accusation that had led to him being removed from command of his beloved *Teazer* and his first lieutenant, Christopher Standish, given the ship. 'Sir, I beg leave to place before ye – this.' He handed over a small, folded piece of paper.

Saumarez inspected it, then flung it down with contempt. 'Mr Kydd! If this is a brazen attempt to implicate *me*—'

'No, sir, it is not. Those are the secret orders I found within your reg'lar instructions as made me act as I did, an' which—'

'It's nothing but a crude forgery! And not in the proper form as you must well allow.'

'Sir, I acted in good faith as I've never seen secret orders afore. I couldn't produce it for ye in your investigation as it was stolen from me, but now I can! If you'd be so good as to hear me out . . .'

Saumarez's expression remained stony but he sat reluctantly, and as Kydd told his story, the admiral's anger was replaced first by bewilderment, then dismay.

It was a sorry tale: driven by envy and resentment at Kydd's successes, a more senior captain had arranged for false secret orders to be inserted into Kydd's main instructions that had him clandestinely retrieving a chest ashore. After a tip-off by an anonymous informer, a formal search was made of HMS *Teazer* on her return and the chest was found to contain smuggled goods. The upright and honourable Admiral Saumarez had seen no option other than to remove Kydd, the ship's captain, from his command.

Still standing, Kydd produced a second sheet of paper. 'And this is Lieutenant Prosser's confession, sir. He agrees to testify against Commander Carthew as principal in the matter.'

'Thank you, Mr Kydd,' Saumarez said heavily. 'If this is true, it is a particularly sad circumstance, imputing as it does an appalling transgression against common morality on the part of an officer of my command. It were best I should bring this matter to a head without a moment's delay.'

The admiral rang a bell and ordered his flag-lieutenant, 'Commander Carthew, *Scorpion*, and Lieutenant Prosser, *Teazer*, to attend me here within the hour.' Then he turned back to Kydd. 'You'll oblige me by remaining, sir, while I establish if there is a case to answer.'

* * *

Carthew entered the room, his dress uniform immaculate. When he caught sight of Kydd he recoiled.

'Sit, if you please, Mr Carthew – there,' Saumarez said, indicating the place opposite Kydd.

'Mr Prosser, sir.' The flag-lieutenant ushered in a haggard-looking officer who stared doggedly downwards. Carthew was clearly disconcerted to see him.

'Now, this should not take long, gentlemen,' Saumarez began. 'Mr Kydd has laid before me evidence of a conspiracy that resulted in the loss of his ship and his good name. We are here to—'

'Sir!' Carthew flung a murderous glance at Kydd. 'Surely you're not to be swayed by anything this proven blackguard has said! He's—'

'Mr Prosser,' Saumarez said flatly, ignoring Carthew, 'do you recognise this?' He handed across a paper.

'I do, sir,' the man said miserably, in barely a whisper.

'Did you or did you not give Mr Kydd to understand that it was part of his orders from this office?'

'I did.'

Carthew turned pale.

'Under whose instructions?' Saumarez continued.

'Mr Carthew's, sir,' Prosser muttered.

'This you will swear in court?'

After a tense silence he replied, 'I – I will.'

Saumarez took a sharp breath. 'You shall have your chance to rebut in due course, Mr Carthew. I find that this matter shall go forward in law.

'You, Mr Prosser, may consider yourself under open arrest. Mr Carthew, your case is more serious and I can see no alternative but—'

Carthew's chair crashed to the ground as he leaped up,

chest heaving, crazed eyes fixed on Kydd. 'You – I'll see you in hell—' With a panicked glance at Saumarez, he pushed wildly away.

'Commander! Return at once, sir!'

At the door Carthew knocked aside the flag-lieutenant and ran down the stairs.

'Stop that officer!' Saumarez roared.

Kydd leaped to his feet and followed. Shocked faces peered out of offices at the commotion. The sound of footsteps stopped, and when Kydd reached the main entrance Carthew was nowhere in sight. 'Where did the officer go?' he demanded of a bewildered sentry.

'Well, an' I was salutin', like,' the man said. Even a hurrying officer still required the stamp and flourish of a musket salute, with eyes held rigid to the front in respect.

Two marines with ported muskets appeared. 'Too late. He's gone,' Kydd snapped, and returned to Saumarez. 'Nowhere to be found, sir.'

'Then I take it he's absconded. Flags, do alert the provost. He's to be returned here without delay.' He turned to Prosser. 'You, sir, will hold yourself in readiness to make deposition concerning this lamentable business. Now leave us.

'Mr Kydd,' Saumarez began gravely, 'I'm faced with a dilemma. By his actions Commander Carthew stands condemned, and will answer for it at his court-martial, as will Lieutenant Prosser. I am concerned that you, Mr Kydd, do see justice. In fine, a public disgrace – losing your ship – should at the least deserve a public restoring. Yes, that must be the right and proper thing to do.'

Kydd's pulse beat faster. Could it be? Was he to step aboard *Teazer* as her captain once again? He tried to appear calm.

'Yet at the same time there is something of a *moral* difficulty.'

Kydd's heart felt about to burst.

'I believe you will have already considered the grave consequences of your assuming command of *Teazer* at this time, and it does you the utmost credit, sir,' Saumarez went on.

Fearful of betraying his feelings Kydd dropped his eyes.

'Therefore I shall relieve you of any responsibility. In my opinion the claims of natural justice outweigh those of position and advancement.'

Kydd was struggling to make sense of what was being said.

Saumarez pondered, then continued, 'Conceivably the circumstances should properly be construed as the unfortunate relinquishing of command, which, in the nature of the sea service, must from time to time occur.'

So he was *not* going to be allowed to take back *Teazer*!

Saumarez saw Kydd's stricken face and hastened to console him. 'Pray do not allow your natural human feeling for a brother officer to affect you so, sir. Consider, in leaving command Mr Standish must in any event revert to lieutenant. He is an acting commander only and therefore the mercy is that, by this happenstance, he is spared being sent ashore as unemployed.'

Kydd's mind whirled. He certainly did not want the arrogant prig back as his lieutenant after the contempt he had shown for him when he had become a privateer captain. 'I – I do see that, sir,' he managed, 'but I have concern that the hands might not show proper respect, he being reduced back to lieutenant an' all.'

Saumarez reflected for a moment. 'Oh, quite. Then you shall have a new lieutenant. I see no reason to delay matters. The sooner this sorry affair is concluded the better for all.

I shall draw up your letter of appointment immediately, Mr Kydd.'

Having allowed Standish a couple of days to set his affairs in order and send his gear ashore, Kydd now stood proudly on North Pier watching *Teazer*'s gig stroking towards him from where she lay at anchor in the Great Road of St Peter Port. Hallum, his new lieutenant, waited behind him.

The boat approached and at the tiller Midshipman Calloway fought hard to keep a solemn face. 'Oars!' he snapped. Obediently they stilled as the gig swung towards the pier.

'Toss oars!' As one, each man smacked the loom across his knee and brought it up vertically. The gig glided into the quay; the bowman leaped nimbly ashore and secured the painter. Calloway snatched off his hat with a huge smile.

Kydd looked down into the boat: Stirk at stroke, Poulden next to him, others, all beaming.

As was the custom, Hallum descended first. 'Bear off!' Calloway ordered. 'Give way t'gether!'

It had happened. At last Kydd was on his way to reclaim his rightful place. Beside him, Hallum nodded agreeably and both took in the lovely ship until the gig was brought smartly around to the side-steps to hook on. Conscious of the men lined up on deck, waiting, Kydd straightened his gold-laced cocked hat a second time, then clambered aboard.

There before him was the ship's company of HMS *Teazer*. With Hallum standing respectfully behind him he drew out his commission and read himself in as captain. Instantly, his commissioning pennant broke out proudly on the mainmast truck.

'Mr Purchet.' He acknowledged the boatswain, whose smile split his face from ear to ear. Kydd went on to greet individually those he had come to know and respect in times past. 'Mr Clegg. An' how's our little Sprits'l, can I ask?'

The sailmaker grinned and whispered shyly, 'Why, he's a berth in m' cabin, Mr Kydd, an' nary a rat shall ye find in th' barky.'

'Mr Duckitt.'

The gunner removed his hat and shuffled his feet in pleased embarrassment. 'Our metal's as good as ever it was, sir,' he muttered.

Kydd's eyes found others and the memories returned.

The rest of the Teazers were assembled forward, their faces leaving no doubt about their feelings that their old captain had been restored. Kydd had *Teazer* back and the future was up to him. He turned to address the men. Legs abrace, he took off his hat and opened his mouth, but a lump in his throat stopped the words. He drew out his hand-kerchief and spluttered into it until he had regained his composure. Then he began, 'Teazers. It's – it's with . . .' It was no good. He wheeled on the boatswain. 'Mr Purchet, this afternoon a make 'n' mend for all hands!' In the storm of cheering that resulted he took refuge in his cabin.

It was bare and unkempt, with an alien smell. Standish had cleared it completely and, without furnishings, it looked immense. Kydd gave a bleak grin. After his dismissal from his ship he'd been reduced to the life of a wandering vagrant, sleeping in a sail-loft until he had achieved handsome riches through privateering. Standish's petty act was meaningless – with his new-found fortune he could easily purchase replacements.

There was a well-remembered knock on the door. 'Come, Tysoe!' he called happily, and stood to greet his old servant.

The man entered discreetly, his nose wrinkling in disdain at the sight of the forlorn cabin.

'Aye! Well, we've a mort of work to do in seeing this'n all shipshape – but there's none better, I dare t' say, as I trust to take it in hand.' In the absence of his sister Cecilia's womanly touch, he could safely leave it to Tysoe to go ashore and make the necessary purchases.

A murmuring outside resolved in to the anxious features of Ellicott, the purser. 'We should set th' books straight now, sir,' he said, holding a pack of well-thumbed papers.

'We will,' Kydd promised. He knew the reason for the haste: Standish had no doubt fudged the signing-off on some accounts. Ellicott feared that until Kydd signed them into his charge he, as purser, would be held responsible for any deficiencies in the boatswain's store, gunner's allowance and so forth.

Before Kydd started on the paperwork, though, there were a few things he must attend to first. 'Is the ship's clerk in attendance?' he asked carefully. It was a delicate matter: his friend Renzi had been acting in that role while Kydd was captain but had given up the post and gone ashore with Kydd when he had been dismissed from his ship. But if the new one was . . .

'Larkin, sir,' Ellicott said apologetically, ushering an elderly seaman inside.

'You!' Kydd said in surprise.

'Aye, sir,' Larkin mumbled. Kydd was taken aback: he knew him to be a fo'c'sleman with an unusual attachment to poetry. In the dog-watches it was his practice to copy out verse from books in large, beautifully formed copperplate. Clearly he had been 'volunteered' for the task by the previous captain.

'This is no task for a prime sailorman, Larkin,' Kydd said briskly. 'I'll see if Mr Renzi is at leisure to relieve ye, an' then your part o' ship shall be fo'c'sleman again.'

The man beamed.

'So, Mr Ellicott, I'm your man in one hour.' He turned to Tysoe. 'Now then, I'd like t' hear as how you think we should best fit out the cabin. Then ye're to step off an' secure it all. Oh, an' at six bells ye'll find Mr Renzi on North Pier with his books. He'll want hands to bear a fist in swaying 'em aboard.'

In the afternoon the men settled to their make-and-mend, a time set aside for leisure and attention to sea-worn clothing or the crafting of a smart step-ashore rig. It was also a fine opportunity not only to make discreet survey of how his ship had fared out of his hands but as well to bring Hallum to a closer appreciation of *Teazer*'s character. It would be a welcome respite, too, from the welter of paperwork that Ellicott seemed intent on drowning him in.

Hats firmly under arms, the two officers strolled along the deck forward. In favoured positions on the gratings, against the sunnier bulwark or simply sprawled out on the planking, men got on with the serious business of gossip and yarn-spinning while they skilfully stitched away. They fell silent as Kydd approached but, in the custom of the sea, off-watch this was their territory, and once the two had passed they resumed chatting.

The Teazers seemed in good heart; Kydd knew the tell-tale signs of disaffection and saw none. He had a suspicion, however, that much of their contentment stemmed from the prospects of a proven prize-taker being in command – but who knew what lay ahead?

Kydd went to a carronade and lifted the lead apron protecting the gunlock bed. The weapon gleamed with attention from lamp-black and linseed oil, but when he peered more closely he saw that the fire-channel between vent and pan shone with equal lustre. The gun had probably not been fired since his own time.

Further forward there were other giveaway signs of a ship that had been prepared more for a flag-officer's inspection than war, but with growing satisfaction he noted there was nothing wrong with *Teazer* that a good first lieutenant could not bring to order in quick time.

As dusk fell Renzi came aboard, Kydd's closest friend and one to whom he owed his present felicity. It had been Renzi who had uncovered the truth behind the conspiracy to ruin him, but he had not wanted to go into details. From long experience Kydd knew not to press his friend until he was ready to talk.

'M' very dear Nicholas! Let's strike your dunnage down and my apologies to ye, the ship being all ahoo like this. We'll sup together tonight.'

It was a brave showing. The great cabin had a dining table in the form of a grating on mess tubs, tastefully concealed beneath borrowed wardroom linen and quite passable in the golden candlelight.

'I fear it could be short canny t'night,' Kydd said, as they entered. 'Tysoe has been ashore an' not had time for my cabin stores.' It was a small price to pay for his return to his ship.

'Shall you . . . ?' Renzi hesitated before the carpenter's canvas easy-chair – or was it to be the boatswain's stout high-back, which was said to be proof even against the frenzied movement of a fresh gale?

Kydd settled into the boatswain's chair and nodded to the awed purser's steward, tasked with the honours of the evening in Tysoe's absence. A light claret was forthcoming, glasses charged, and the two friends toasted their new situation with feeling.

'Nicholas, you must have something in your philosophies as should prepare a man for fortune's sport,' Kydd remarked.

Renzi shook his head with a smile. 'As to that, dear fellow, who can say? Let us seize the hour and reck not the reasons. The workings of Fate are not to be comprehended by mortals, I'm persuaded.'

Renzi looked gaunt, his eyes deep-set and lines in his face adding years to his age. Kydd regarded him with concern. At their lowest ebb, Renzi had travelled to Jersey and found menial employment with a titled foreign émigré. 'You've suffered, m' friend. That rogue y' prince has worked ye near to death! I've a mind to say—'

'Let it rest, brother,' Renzi said firmly. 'I've a notion that the certainties of the daily round in dear old *Teazer* will set me up in prime kelter before long. What piques my curiosity at this time is whether my good friend Tom Kydd will be changed at all by wealth.'

Kydd laughed. 'Aye, it's a grand thing not to worry at laying out for a new coat, or an evening with the ladies. But you should know as while I have m' prospects, that scrovy prize-agent has his fee an' then there's y'r pettifoggers who feel free to take their fill o' guineas afore ever I see 'em. I'm t' settle a fair sum on my parents, I've decided, but the rest I'm putting away. Not in a bank as might fail, but the Funds. Consols at three per cent.'

'You'll want to prettify *Teazer* handsomely, I believe,' Renzi murmured.

'The ship'll have her gingerbread, it's true, and m' quarters are to be congenial. Topping it the swell at sea is t' no account, though – t'would soon turn me soft as a milkmaid. No, Nicholas, your friend'll not be changed by his circumstances.'

'I'm gratified to hear it, brother.'

Kydd grew thoughtful. 'There is a one more matter – one o' delicacy.'

'Oh?'

'I'd surely want to see my dear friend right in th' article o' pewter as—'

'Thank you, but my needs are few and my modest income sufficient unto the day,' Renzi said, with finality. 'Your riches were honestly gained and by your own hand. Do rejoice in them. If – if I should come by some misfortune, you can be assured that I shall indeed remember you.'

A cautious knock sounded on the door. 'Come!' Kydd called.

It was Hallum with some papers. He took in their dinner setting and made to leave, but Kydd motioned for him to join them at the 'table'. 'Pray don't stand on ceremony, Mr Hallum. Here, where is y'r glass, sir? Oh – I'm forgetting my manners. This is Mr Renzi, a philosophical gentleman takin' passage with us, for the sake of his studies. He's obliging enough to act as our ship's clerk while aboard.'

Hallum was mature with a hint of grey about him and an air of deliberation. 'From *Diomede*, I believe?' Kydd prodded. It would have been something of a shock for him to be told with just hours' notice to move from the tranquil backwater of the old flagship to a prime fighting vessel like *Teazer*.

'I am, sir. I'll have my baggage aboard tomorrow and then be ready for duty.'

'Have ye had experience in a sloop?'

'As a midshipman before the war, yes, sir.'

'An' where was that?'

'In Leith,' he said uncomfortably. 'Scotland.'

'Any interesting service?' Kydd asked encouragingly.

The man appeared to be considering what to say. 'A frigate, *Pegasus*, for two years in the North Sea in 'ninety-eight.' He looked at Kydd as though seeking approval for his disclosure.

'North Sea Squadron?'

'Er, no, sir. Timber convoys from the Baltic, mostly.'

Kydd nodded pleasantly, privately reflecting that if this was the extent of his 'interesting service' then his time in *Teazer* was no doubt set to prove an eye-opening experience.

Several steaming dishes arrived. 'Do tell, Mr Hallum – from what part of the kingdom do you hail?' Renzi asked politely.

By the first remove it was discovered that Hallum's family was noted in Suffolk for its sea connections and that he himself had made several trading voyages to Norway as a youngster. Over the port Kydd had a measure of his lieutenant: solidly reliable but with little ambition and less imagination. 'Then let's raise a glass to *Teazer* an' her company,' he said warmly. 'I've a fancy we're in for exciting times. The admiral says as how he wants to put us to the test right quickly.'

Chapter 2

Kydd sighed deeply as he took in the understated splendour of his great cabin – its dark polished bulkhead across at the forward end and the brightness of whitened sides and deck-head, which seemed to increase the apparent area to a gratifying size. With a black-and-white chequered floor covering and a deeply polished table in the centre, it was almost intimidating, and Tysoe moved about with a lordly air in his silent ministrations.

On deck the whole sweep of the interior of the bulwarks was now a rousing scarlet with black and gold finishings about the scrollwork. The yards were a deep black against the varnished masts and Kydd had willingly parted with the necessary funds to ensure that the band of yellow between the gunports was shown at its best by a liberal mixing of white pigment in the paint. The carronade tompions had been picked out in crimson and green, and from the sweet intricacies of the miniature stern gallery aft to the dainty white figurehead forward, with flecks of blue and gold, *Teazer* had never looked so bewitching.

Kydd was keen to see his ship, now in all respects ready for action, back where she belonged – at sea. In the weeks since he had been restored to his post Carthew had not reappeared and therefore preparations for a court-martial could not begin. Prosser had been allowed to resign his commission and leave, in return for making full deposition of his evidence.

It was, however, not in the interests of the service to keep a fine ship at idleness and *Teazer*'s orders duly came. They were short and to the point: a cruise eastwards from Alderney along the north coast of the Contentin peninsula, past the port of Cherbourg and as far as its natural conclusion at Pointe de Barfleur.

All the east–west coastal traffic from northern France must proceed that way and a Royal Navy presence athwart its passage would effectively bring it to a halt. Kydd would be sharing the task with lesser fry – a gun-brig and a cutter.

It was gratifying to have the master, Dowse, and their local pilot, Queripel, back in earnest conclave as they deliberated over their mission. Saumarez insisted that all non-native naval vessels in his command carry a permanent local pilot, as well as the usual ship's master. Given the treacherous nature of the waters of the area, Kydd had quickly seen the wisdom in this requirement.

'Mr Queripel,' he said, 'y'r opinion of this coast, sir.'

'Not easy, sir, not a-tall,' the man replied carefully. 'Th' charts, they doesn't tell the half of it.'

'How so?'

'All along this seaboard,' he said, indicating the whole north-facing coast, 'steep-to an' bold mostly, but deceitful, sir, very deceitful. See here, Cap Lévi. Coast trends away t' the nor'-east an' you'd think to weather the cape a cable or two clear, but that would be to y'r error, sir. Straight to th' north, a good two mile out – a wicked long rocky shoal below the waves a-waiting for ye.'

Queripel continued, 'An' that's not all. Should the tidal stream meet wi' a contrary wind, why, then ye gets the Raz du Cap Lévi, a dangerous race as can set any good ship t' hazard.'

'Aye, y' tides,' Kydd murmured.

'Tides? Why, y' same Cap Lévi at spring tides sees a east-going stream o' eight hours but a west-going f'r four hours only at a fierce rate o' knots. An' with y' Saint-Pierre shell bank roilin' an' shiftin' down where no man's eye c'n see, an' your Basse de Happetout, why it'll—'

'Thank 'ee, Mr Queripel,' Kydd said. 'It's my intention to stay as close with the land as will make it a sore puzzle f'r the Frenchies to think to pass us by,' he added firmly. The whole coastline, though, seemed to be wilfully arranged as a snare and trap for English sailors. 'Your best charts, Mr Dowse – an' don't spare the expense in their getting.' The illicit French productions to which he was referring could be purchased ashore – at a price.

The next morning when *Teazer* weighed for the north an air of expectancy was abroad. It was a hard life in a small ship on such a coast but there would be much satisfaction in action against the enemy – and the chance of prizes.

Laying Guernsey abeam, *Teazer* shaped course to clear the Casquets to starboard where the helm went over and they eased to the south-westerly for the long coastwise patrol to the east. The forbidding rocks, with their characteristic three-part lighthouse, were left astern, and the bare green of Alderney, the most northerly of the Channel Islands, came into view.

With a fair wind on her quarter *Teazer* showed her breeding. One of the myriad uninhabited islands was coming up, distinctive with its generous frosting of bird droppings. Kydd drew out his watch and calculated their progress. A cast of the log confirmed it – eleven knots and a half.

Past Alderney there was clear water for the eight miles to the north-west tip of France but almost immediately Kydd felt *Teazer* dip and sway as the notorious Alderney Race surging from the south took her full on the beam, the waves tumbling on themselves in their hurry to emerge into the Channel proper.

The dark mass of land ahead was France. Kydd's duty was clear: to take, burn, sink or destroy by any means the forces that so threatened England; no consideration of prizes or personal ambition must stand in the way. 'Keep your eyes open, there!' he roared up at the foretop lookout. Cap de la Hague was approaching fast in the fair wind but once round the larger mass of the peninsula, the wind under the land would drop and the ship would take longer to respond to anything they came up with.

'Th' Grunes, sir,' Queripel warned, as they neared the rocky outliers.

'To clear 'em?' Kydd grunted. It would not do to stay safely distant out to sea while the French crept along furtively close inshore.

'I'd not be happy under a mile, Mr Kydd,' Queripel answered.

With an offshore wind and a favourable tide they could take risks. 'Let's have it eight cables,' Kydd said. The French chart had La Petite and La Grande Grunes at no more than seven. Queripel said nothing.

They approached the bleak shore, and as they eased to sail along it the lookout hailed to point out something in the sea.

It was a wide and lazy surface eddy over some sinister submarine hazard that they wouldn't have noticed had the water not been so calm.

An accusing glance from Queripel told Kydd that these were the Grunes and he turned to the first lieutenant. 'Mr Hallum, we're going coastal now. The people to their stations, if y' please.'

With the boats in their davits free of their gripes and ready for lowering, a hand on the fo'c'sle with lead-line ready coiled, the watch-of-the-hands alert and in no doubt about their duties for emergency manoeuvres, there was little more they could do to alleviate the deadly danger they were in by sailing so close.

Two or three miles ahead the first anchorage of note was marked. Queripel mumbled that it was a contemptible place with a sizeable rock awash the very entrance, but Kydd would not leave anything to chance.

The south-westerly that had been so briskly bearing them from Alderney had now died to a gentle breeze in the lee of the cliffs and *Teazer* moved along at little more than walking pace. All depended on what they saw when they passed the headland. In the small bay anything might be at anchor, prey or predator, but they could not meet every hidden inlet closed up at battle quarters: they must trust to quick reactions and correct judgements.

The bay was innocent of any vessel, merely a sweep of sandy beach between two nondescript headlands set amid an appalling sprawl of rocks scarring the sea out to a dismaying distance. The visibility was good and the winds safely offshore – but what would it be to cruise here in adverse weather, Kydd wondered.

Around the far headland the coast fell back; it would stay

trending away to the east-south-east until the port of Cherbourg, ten miles further on and mercifully less set about with reefs and hazards. They remained under easy sail – there was no point in haste: the patrol was for a period of days on station and then they would return.

Teazer settled to routine, the age-old and comfortable rhythms of the sea that the Royal Navy had evolved to a fine art. 'Hands to supper' was piped, as eight bells signalled the start of the first dog-watch. In noisy conviviality the grog tub was brought up and the spirit mixed for issue to all messes before their evening meal.

Kydd kept the deck out of sheer contentment. Cherbourg came into view; over there, one of Napoleon's arsenals was dedicated to the crushing of England and yet, he reflected, *Teazer* was sailing by unchallenged with a merry crew enjoying their evening.

The port was well defended by fortifications, which Kydd had no intention of provoking. He knew that small English cutters of shallow draught were lying off the harbour and that their sole purpose was to keep watch on significant movements there. If necessary they could alert Saumarez's heavy frigates within half a day.

Kydd kept well away and, towards dusk, had made the far side of the port. Earlier he had noted a cryptic marking on the French chart that had piqued his interest: Pointe du Brick and within, a tiny bay, Anse du Brick. '*Brick*' was French for 'brig' and, who knew?, it might have a more subtle meaning. He intended to anchor for the night close in, under full view of the enemy shore, thereby retaining his clamping hold on the coast.

'Is this wise, sir?' Hallum murmured. 'At our moorings we'll be at the mercy of any of superior force.'

'Aye, this must be so,' said Kydd, 'but ye'll observe that nothing can get by without we know it.' No vessel of size would risk a close-in passage at night and by dawn they would be well on their way.

In the fading light they found their place, little more than a deeply wooded cleft in impassable terrain with a neat beach at its foot. The hand-lead told of rapidly shoaling water so *Teazer* went to two anchors with a precautionary kedge to seaward. It left them in an admirable position to pounce on any vessel trusting to the cover of darkness to slip by into Cherbourg.

The quiet of the night enfolded them; the delicate scent of woodland was borne out on a gentle breeze and the faint *maaaaa* of a goat sounded to one side. Only the soft slap and gurgle of the current along *Teazer*'s sides intruded and about the deck men spoke in low voices in respect to the stillness.

It was a bold, even impudent move – but it had a weakness that might prove fatal. If the wind shifted foul in the night they might find themselves trapped against the shore, unable to claw off, helpless against the gunboats that would be quickly called from Cherbourg once their plight was discovered.

The night was quiet and the wind had held, if anything backing more southerly. At dawn *Teazer* weighed and stood out for the north but almost immediately there was a heavy thud and smoke from a fort on a small promontory.

'Surprisin' t' see 'em awake,' growled the boatswain, shielding his eyes from the first rays of the day as he tried to make it out.

'Fort Lévi,' Queripel said.

'An' they should've held their fire until we were under their guns,' Kydd said contemptuously. 'Bear away, if ye please.' They skirted around the impotent fort while he considered the next hazard. 'We'll keep inside the Septentrionale,' he told Dowse, leaving Queripel to mutter on his own. It was hard on the man but this was the only way they would be in any real position should enemy craft chance by.

Once Cap Lévi was rounded and they resumed eastward, Queripel came up to Kydd and offered, 'If ye'd keep east b' south five mile, there's an inside passage only th' fisher-folk takes as will see us through t' Barfleur.'

After they had angled across near to the low, marshy coastline, *Teazer* found herself easing between the land and a near-submerged cluster of dark, granite rocks, the highest with a strange-looking twist of iron atop it. 'Th' Chenal Hédouin the Frenchies call it,' Queripel said, 'on account of—'

'Aye, well, do keep a weather eye on y'r channel, then, Mr Queripel. I don't want to leave *Teazer*'s bones here,' Kydd said tightly. He suspected that only a small number of the countless crags under the surface were showing trace of their existence.

Now within less than half a mile of an endless dun-coloured beach the country's remote nature was plain: low, marshy, a reedy lake. They were far from the civilised world. Eyeing a projecting knot of rock on shore, Queripel said, 'Now east b' north, sir.'

Teazer altered more to the northward until she was just abreast a large lake, at which point the helm went over again and they found themselves heading between a sullen clutch of offshore rocks and a flat headland sprawling out to sea with a lighthouse that was a good seventy feet high.

'Pointe de Barfleur?' Kydd asked doubtfully. Surely they had not reached the end of their patrol area so quickly.

'Aye, sir,' Queripel said, with satisfaction. They emerged suddenly into the open sea. It was masterly piloting, Kydd conceded, grateful for the Channel Islander's years of merchant-service experience on this coast in the peace.

He took in the calm glitter of an unbroken horizon. This was now the Baie de Seine, and at its opposite shore was Le Havre and with it the Seine river down from Paris. It was an utterly different land, and the start of the line of ports stretching away that Bonaparte was using to assemble his invasion fleets. Those would be the desperate business of the legendary Downs squadron under Admiral Keith, daily hand-to-hand struggles as small ships like *Teazer* were thrown at the enemy flotillas in epic engagements before Napoleon's very eyes.

They themselves had seen nothing – one or two fishing luggers, lobstermen and tiny craft; no sign of the armada that was threatening England. But they had reached the limit of their cruise: it was time to return.

Renzi came on deck, blinking in the sunlight. He glanced in puzzlement at the open sea with the coast at their backs, then at the sun. 'Either the land has shifted in its axis or the celestial orb has taken leave of its senses,' he mused.

'Neither.' Kydd chuckled. 'This is the termination of our patrol line. Y' see the Baie de Seine ahead but, when wind an' tide permit, we wear about and return.'

Renzi gazed intently at the French coast.

Concerned that his friend was still fatigued from his labours in Jersey, Kydd said softly, 'Not as if you're to miss a fine sight, Nicholas. The coast here is dull enough country, you'll believe.'

Renzi turned to face him. 'Ah. Then this is . . . ?'

'Pointe de Barfleur.'

'Barfleur?'

'The town is a league down the coast.'

'Quite.' Renzi brightened, 'Then . . . would it be at all convenient should we sight the same?'

Kydd responded to the sudden animation in his tone. 'Why, yes, m' friend. The breeze backing more southerly by the hour, a little diversion will find us with a fair wind for our return. An' t' tell it true, I'd be happier then with th' tide on the make.'

Hauling their wind, *Teazer* made sail southwards and Barfleur was sighted, a small but prosperous-looking village with a squat church in a tight little harbour, but otherwise undistinguished. The quarterdeck officers were respectfully standing to leeward, allowing the friends their privacy.

'The Edward III of Capell's Shakespeare mentions this place warmly, I believe.' Renzi looked about. 'Then there must be under our keel at this very moment the last sad relics of the *Blanche Nef*.'

'Erm, which is?'

'I will tell you, dear fellow. On a dark night in the year 1120, the *White Ship* sailed from Barfleur for England, with the only son of the most puissant Henry the First aboard. The mariners, in a merry state, neglected to consult the state of the tide, with the dolorous consequence that the ship ran fast upon a rock and was lost. Only one was saved – and that was not the King's son.'

'A cruel tragedy.'

'It was – but worse for England. At Henry's soon passing in grief, his daughter Matilda's crowning as Queen of England was disputed by his nephew, Stephen. The realm was plunged into years of an anarchy that only a medieval world can produce.'

Kydd nodded. 'Aye, but this is y'r centuries past. We're now to consider the invading of England herself, no less!'

'Then what more apposite place than this little town I cannot conceive of, brother,' Renzi said drily. 'It was from Barfleur, of course, that in 1066 William the Conqueror did sail to seize England, the last successful invasion of our islands, I believe.'

Further historical musings were cut short, for Kydd had found it necessary to give the orders that saw *Teazer* go to exercise of her foretopmen while they stretched further down the coast. As anticipated, the wind's backing produced a useful southerly, and by the time the ship reached Pointe de Barfleur again it was fair for the return, a near perfectly executed cruise, were it not for the complete lack of action.

They rounded the point and took up by the wind on the larboard tack for the inshore passage, handing in the sheets in a smart and seamanlike manner that brought a grunt of satisfaction from *Teazer*'s commander as he considered whether to anchor in the lee of Cap Lévi for the night—

A disbelieving cry of '*Saaail!*' came from the maintop lookout. 'Two points on the bow, a – a brig wi' some . . .' He tailed off in perplexity but threw out an arm to starboard.

Kydd leaped for the main-shrouds and shaded his eyes as he peered out at a confusing scene – numbers of vessels of different sizes crowding together, about four or five miles off. The largest was a brig-o'-war with distinctive red ochre sails and quite as large as *Teazer*. It was being circled by a smaller vessel, a topsail cutter, and had three open craft of puzzling form close astern. Kydd fumbled for his pocket telescope. It soon became clear that they had come upon a drama which could have only one meaning. 'Colours, Mr Hallum!' he roared.

Their white ensign flew aloft as he jumped to the deck to meet the expectant faces of the quarterdeck. 'Frenchy invasion barges! Three of 'em being towed by a brig-o'-war as is fighting off a cutter!'

After a short delay the cutter responded with the correct private signal to *Teazer*'s challenge. She would be one of a number of game little ships that were making life uncomfortable for the gathering invasion fleet and had come upon these three barges probably being towed to the next port. No doubt they had been new-built at Barfleur and, thinking that *Teazer* was continuing south, had been gulled into taking the chance of slipping out.

The cutter had found she had not been able to take on the bigger ship but had been snapping at its heels. Now the tables were well and truly turned. Against two determined men-o'-war the brig stood little chance – and fleeing into the land was no longer an option, for *Teazer*, in her inshore passage, was waiting.

Caught under two fires the brig did its best. The barges' tow lines were thrown off and, ignoring the cutter, the brig circled round to confront *Teazer*'s onrush, but as its crew hauled on the braces it slewed suddenly and stopped. Then the foretopmast tumbled.

'He's taken a rock!' Hallum crowed, watching the confusion on the hapless vessel's deck.

'Boarders, if you please,' Kydd said sourly, as their prize slowly settled. On the opposite side he could see that the cutter was hove to and already had a boat in the water. 'I'll take 'em m'self,' he muttered and, with a token force of men, set out for the brig.

The vessel had driven up a ledge of rock and was fast aground, but the slight swell was lifting the after part, then dropping its dead weight again and again in a cacophony of cracking timbers. Closer to, Kydd could see that this was a merchant brig converted to appear fierce and protective: the guns were 'quakers' – false wooden cannon at the gunports meant to intimidate. The crew were crowded together on the highest part and appeared to await their fate with resignation.

Kydd had the boat brought alongside to the main-chains and swung himself lithely on deck. At the same time a lieutenant from the cutter boarded from the opposite side. 'My bird, I think!' the officer said with a dazzling grin. He was absurdly young, and it was difficult to take offence. Kydd smothered a cynical smile. Any naval ship in sight at the time of a capture could demand a share of any prize-money.

'Kydd, Commander, *Teazer* brig-sloop.'

'Oh, sir – Clive Leveson-Wardle, lieutenant-in-command, *Linnet* cutter.'

'Well, now, Mr, er – L'tenant, do ye take possession o' this vessel, sir, as you've *half* a right t' do so? An' I'd not linger, sir. I fancy she's not long for this world,' Kydd said, knowing that any talk of prizes was now merely academic.

By this time the brig lay ominously still and unresisting to the waves, hard upon the rocky ledge just visible below in the murky depths.

Kydd crossed to the little forward companionway access to the hold and opened the door. There was an unmistakable dark glitter and the hollow swash of water below. The ship's bottom was breached and it had flooded, then settled on the ledge, which it would never leave.

'Th' barges, sir?' The boatswain, his cutlass still drawn, nodded to where they were being secured by the cutter.

'Ye're right, Mr Purchet,' Kydd said, with a quick grin. 'They'll serve.' He returned to the young lieutenant. 'Sir, I'm taking ye under my command,' he said. 'Your orders are to send a party o' men to recover as much o' what she carries as ye can an' stow it in the barges.' It would go some way to making up for the loss of the brig.

'I understand, sir.'

'An' then to take 'em under tow until ye make your offing and shape course for Guernsey. I'll send help when I can.'

'Er, it's that I see soldiers in them there barges, sir,' the boatswain said uncomfortably.

'All th' better,' Kydd said briskly. 'No doubt they'll kindly bear a hand in return for they're saved from the briny deep.'

Kydd surveyed the activity with satisfaction. The cutter's master's mate had had the sense to disarm the soldiers before boarding each barge and, with marines borrowed from *Teazer* to act as guards, they were brought alongside one by one for transshipment to *Linnet*.

He looked down curiously at one of the strange craft. It was the first he had seen at close quarters of the thousands he had heard were being built and assembling in the invasion ports.

This must be a *péniche*, designed for landing the maximum number of soldiers in the minimum time. Over three score feet long and twelve feet in the beam, the open boat could probably cram aboard sixty or seventy troops and all their equipment. It had provision for stepping three masts, a simple lug rig. No doubt a howitzer or mortar could be mounted forward.

And this was the smallest of the flotilla: there were others

27

much larger that could take horses and field guns, still more that were big enough to warrant the same three-masted square rig as a frigate and with guns more than a match for *Teazer*.

'Sir? I heard 'em say among 'emselves like, they'm new-made in Barfleur an' hoping t' take 'em to Cherbourg.' It was one of *Teazer*'s Guernseymen, with the Breton tongue.

It was a chilling sight, so close to the reality of Napoleon's menace. Notwithstanding Kydd's seaman's instinct, which was telling him that, fully loaded, they would be pigs to sail, the thought of them in uncountable numbers crowding across the Channel to invade England was a fearsome prospect.

There was little more he could do. He called the lieutenant over. 'I'm continuing m' cruise to the west. I'll leave the marines for the prisoners and expect ye to haul off before dark. Good voyage to ye, sir.'

In the late afternoon they had reached the western end of the inshore channel without further incident and Kydd was looking forward to supper with Renzi, who had been locked away for hours in his tiny cabin restoring acquaintance with his philosophical studies after his labours in Jersey.

He turned to go below, then stiffened: a distant sound, like the mutter of thunder. Guns!

He strained to hear, but there was no more. He might have imagined it – but one or two about the deck had paused, like him.

'Mr Calloway!' he called. A younger man's ears would be sharper. 'Did ye hear guns?'

'Aye, sir, I did.'

'I thought six-, nine-pounders?'

'Could be twelves, Mr Kydd.'

Some frigates mounted twelve-pounders as main armament, and if he went to see what it was about, Kydd knew he might find himself turned upon by one of unanswerable force. His duty was plain, however. 'Clap on more sail, Mr Dowse.'

As near as he could tell it had been somewhere in the open sea beyond where Cap Lévi marked the abrupt turn south into the bay of Cherbourg, so he decided to press on directly after reaching the cape.

They passed the sprawling point and met deep water once more. Stretching out for the west, *Teazer* lengthened her stride in relief that the treacherous shoals were left behind, and in half an hour's fast sailing she had made her sighting: right in the eye of the sunset, and as close to the veering southerly breeze as practicable, it was a substantial vessel. If it saw them it gave no sign, crossing their bows steadily on the starboard tack some three miles or so distant, making directly for Cherbourg.

With the light fading, it was difficult to discern details – until two things made all plain. The first was that the ship was barque-rigged, so it was not a man-o'-war. And the second was the two flags that fluttered at her mizzen – the French national flag triumphantly over the English ensign. She was, therefore, a British merchant ship taken recently by the enemy vessel whose guns they had heard. The French, with the safety of the port so close, were flaunting their prize.

It was galling – in front of their eyes a valuable British ship being borne off to France. Kydd felt for the luckless crew, now prisoners destined to rot in one of Bonaparte's prison-fortresses. 'Be damned to it! I'll not see 'em in chokey!' he burst out, but he was not clear how this could be prevented. *Teazer* was still on the same larboard tack, leaning into it on a course parallel with the distant depths of the bay, while the barque was already on the opposite tack and set fair to make Cherbourg in one reach.

Firing on the vessel was out of the question and the time needed to tack about in chase would probably hand the Frenchman an unbeatable lead. They could hope for a wind-change in the fluky conditions nearer the coast, but the breeze was holding strength, now veering slowly to the south-west.

Kydd saw the plain stern-quarters of the barque pulling steadily away and gritted his teeth. Either way they stood to lose the chase – unless . . .

It was without question that he had the finer ship. But how much better? 'Mr Purchet, bowlines to th' bridle, an' sheet in on all courses until ye hears 'em sing.' He was going to make a race of it; a long board deep into the bay, a flying stay about to the other tack and direct chase in the hope that he could head the other ship before it made port.

Word got about quickly. Soon the decks were crowded with tars, each with his own opinion of how to get the best from their fair bark, some all for an immediate tack and lunge, others urging extremes of sail spread.

The boatswain was cautious. 'Sir, ye'll want a slip-rope an' toggle on the bowlines, I'm thinking.' Their purpose was to tauten the leading edge of the major sails to allow the helmsman to ease in right up to the wind. Purchet was suggesting a way to cast them off rapidly and take up on the other side when they tacked about.

'Aye, make it so,' Kydd agreed, as he considered the next move. *Teazer*'s trim was fine. He made a point of checking whenever possible for it had a surprising effect on perform-ance: if the ship had a tendency to come up to the wind – if she was ardent – this had to be counteracted by the opposite rudder, which necessarily caused a degree of turbulence and drag to the detriment of speed.

He crossed to the helmsman, Poulden, probably the best timoneer aboard. 'Does she gripe?' he demanded. He had not sensed any giveaway lurch to windward when the bows rose.

'Not as who should say, sir,' the man said stolidly.

They were making excellent speed. The seas were fine on the bow, and without the need to punch through them, there would be no slowing to their progress. However, the barque was well past and into the bay, making a fine show of it with royals now spread.

It was time for vigorous measures. *Teazer* did not carry fancy sail – he could set the foretopmast stuns'l in these conditions, but bonnets and drabblers would impede rather than assist. No, this race would be won if he tuned his ship like a violin.

'I'll have ye swift in the cat-harpings,' he told the boatswain. He considered for a moment, then turned to the master. 'Take the larbowlines an' see to the bracing, Mr Dowse. Each yard to be braced in half a point more'n the one below it.' The resulting slight spiral would take into account the stronger winds to be found aloft.

'Aye aye, sir.'

'An' set hands to th' lifts, the yards to be agreeable as ye can to the horizon.' At their lively degree of heel so close-hauled, this would restore the sails' natural aspect rather than bag the wind to the lee side.

'Sir.'

There was more to think about: too great a press of sail might bury her forefoot or thrust her to leeward. Paradoxically it was often better to reduce sail to increase speed – that foretop-gallant, for instance? He gave the order to Dowse to make it so.

It was exhilarating sailing. Never had *Teazer* been urged like this, the sea hissing and seething past, all sail drawing to perfection in the spanking breeze and glorious sunset.

Kydd stood by the wheel, every nerve at full stretch, sensing the exact angle of the wind on his cheeks, listening intently to its thrum on taut rigging and the creaking, high-pitched then low, from deep within the ship as the waves passed under her keel. Any of this might change and be the first warning of sudden calamity in the straining spars and rigging.

'Mr Hallum? Stations f'r staying.' This was the trickiest part: putting about to the other tack. If they fumbled it, all would be over. And they needed more than a workmanlike manoeuvre. They had to make it a lightning move that had them over on their new tack and sails fully drawing with not a second's delay.

Kydd snatched a glance at the barque, now significantly closer to Cherbourg and safety. He was going to play it out to the last card. 'I have the ship, Mr Dowse,' he said formally, to the sailing master.

'Aye, sir.' There was no resentment in his tone: he understood that it was for his own protection – any failure in timing or execution could not now be blamed on him.

'Stay by me, if y' please,' Kydd added quietly.

Hallum approached to report that stations for staying ship were now complete: lines thrown off from the belaying pins and faked along for running, every part-of-ship readied and tense – waisters, fo'c'slemen, topmen, each a part of the whole. Just one false step could bring them all down.

'Ready about!' Kydd roared, and looked over the side.

They were slashing along as fast as he had ever seen her stretch before.

'Ready . . . ready . . . Ease down the helm!' Carefully, spoke by spoke, Poulden began the fateful turn. This was not the time for a sudden showy spinning of the wheel and abrupt angling of the rudder over, which would result in spectacular white foaming and a sudden slowing in impetus as the drag came on. Instead *Teazer* kept her speed on, allowing time for the jib sheets to be eased and, behind Kydd, the mainsail boom hauled amidships to keep the sail full until the last moment.

'Helm's a-lee!' Forward there was instant movement as the fore-sheet was let go, together with the sheets to the head-sails, and *Teazer*'s bow began to swing into the wind, the sails slatting busily. Checking away the top bowline and lee fore-brace they heaved around. Kydd saw the motion and bawled, 'Rise tacks an' sheets!'

The mainsails had lost their taut straining and their lines were manhandled to clear the nettings and other gear as *Teazer* nosed into the wind. 'Haul in! Mainsail haul!' Kydd bellowed.

Hand over hand the mainyard was braced around at a furious pace, the fore remaining on the old tack. As *Teazer* rotated through the wind's eye this levered round the after part of the ship. The fore as well took the wind aback but on the opposite tack, pushing the bows away on to the new course.

Everyone knew the stakes. It was the synchrony of movements that held the key, and *Teazer* responded nobly. 'Haul of all!' Kydd ordered exultantly – the main would fill and draw just as fast as the new weather tack and lee-sheets could be brought in. The fore was braced around smartly and, with a brisk banging and flapping, the sails caught. *Teazer* leaned to her new course, the men frantically at work to get in every foot of their hauling.

It was done – and beautifully. Kydd grunted, satisfied. His ship was as capable as she was pretty.

As they settled to their rushing passage he looked across at the barque. It was now on the same board and, although it was ahead by a considerable margin, the game was far from over. Their prey was clawing as close to the wind as it could, while *Teazer*, thanks to Kydd's patient and careful estimates, lay to the wind with every sail drawing optimally.

'We're fore-reaching,' the master admitted, eyeing the other vessel. Their tracks were converging and *Teazer* was coming up on the barque with every minute. Kydd found himself clenching his fists, frustrated that there now seemed little more that could be done.

The boatswain cleared his throat awkwardly. 'Er, sir, when I was a younker I seen a trick once.'

'Oh?'

'Th' lower yards, sir. T' increase th' traverse.'

A square-rigged ship could lie only about six points to the wind, for the big spars swinging across the ship would come up against the mast stay and shrouds, a natural limit. Kydd glanced at the big mainyard above them, immovably up against the mainstay at the extremity of its traverse. 'I'd like to know how, Mr Purchet.'

'Why, sir, we slacks off th' truss-tackle as gives us play, an' then cants down th' weather yard-arm while we swigs off on th' cat-harpings all we can.' This would allow the yard to slide up and into where the shrouds were at their narrowest – at the cost of the set of the sail.

From his memory of studying for his lieutenant's examination

34

Kydd recalled the double tangent rule: the tangent of the angle of the wind to the yard should be twice that between yard and keel. This ensured that even a little achieved would see the effect multiplied. 'We do it, Mr Purchet,' he said. It would be tricky work: with sails drawing hard, the truss-ropes held the big spar against the mast. To slacken them deliberately . . .

With both main- and fore-course cocked up at an angle they sheeted in once more.

'Half a point, I'd say,' the master said, clearly impressed.

While this was not dramatic, it would amount over the miles to several ship's lengths further to weather. Could it make the difference? Kydd eyed the distances. The object was to point higher into the wind yet retain a faster speed, culminating in an overlap at any distance to windward with the chase at his mercy under his lee. Should they end even yards to leeward it was certain to get away.

Dowse assumed position next to Poulden and monitored closely the flutter at the edge of the main. It could so easily change to the sail taken violently aback. 'Be ye yare at th' helm, son,' he said quietly, aware of the tender situation. 'I'll bear watch.' Together they worked to bring the racing sloop to within a knife's edge of the wind.

'Luff 'n' lie,' Dowse murmured, and Poulden inched over the wheel. 'Dyce!' he ordered. 'An' nothing t' leeward.'

Teazer flew. In the gathering dusk she seemed to reach out after the fleeing barque, every man aboard watching forward and feeling for the gallant ship now doing her utmost for them. If the chase ended triumphantly, the epic pursuit would be talked about for years to come.

In the further distance the sullen dark mass of northern France lay across their path, with the lights of Cherbourg dead ahead and their prey now visibly nearer, as though it were being hauled closer on a rope. It was evident that before long a convergence would take place.

In the last of the sunset they were finally within cannon shot of the vessel to windward. Kydd spared a fleeting sympathy for the unknown captain, who must now be seeing the stone quays of the entrance to the harbour, but then he thought of the prisoners soon to taste freedom. 'Place us within hailing distance, Mr Dowse,' Kydd said – but suddenly the situation changed utterly.

The barque fell away to leeward in a tight turn, wearing about to place itself directly before the wind – away from the safety of Cherbourg and back towards where they had come from. It caught Kydd completely off guard and it was some time before they could throw off the gear they had rigged for the chase against the wind.

It was a meaningless move: there was no friendly port to the north or anything except the endless desolation of rocks and reefs before Barfleur and there was now no question but that *Teazer* was the swifter. The barque had made good distance by the sudden wearing but *Teazer* was closing rapidly, the wind astern allowing any course she chose. When the other ship veered towards the shore *Teazer* did likewise. At this rate it would be over before they made Cap Lévi even though the Frenchman had put up a fine show.

Then, half a mile short of the cape and with *Teazer* only a few hundred yards astern, the vessel sheered towards the land and, in the gathering darkness, rounded to and calmly let go her anchor. Incredulous, Kydd was about to give the orders for a final reckoning when the mystery resolved. In a flurry of gunfire, bright flashes stabbed from the squat fort on the promontory above. In the gloom he had overlooked Fort Lévi. The guns were of respectable calibre and quite capable of smashing *Teazer* to a ruin well before he and his crew could secure their prize. It was all over.

Circling out of range, Kydd knew he should give best to the Frenchman now sheltering under the guns of the fort and move on. But his blood was up and he would not give in. Boats after dark – a cutting-out expedition! The French would imagine that he would give up and sail away during the night and therefore would wait patiently for morning before making for Cherbourg – but they would be in for an unwelcome surprise.

The night was moonless, impenetrably black and relatively calm; perfect conditions. The fort obliged by carelessly showing lights that were ideal navigation markers and Kydd set to with the planning.

He reviewed his forces: the barque would be manned by a prize-crew only and should not present a serious difficulty for a prime man-o'-war's boarding party. The main object was to crowd seamen aboard in sufficient quantity that sail could be loosed and set before the fort could react. Too few, and with three masts to man, there would be a fatal delay. So it must be every boat and all the hands that could be spared.

There would be two main divisions: the armed boarders as first wave over the larboard bulwarks and the seamen to work the ship over the starboard. It was essential to have the best men in the lead, those who would not flinch at mounting the rigging in the dark and with the initiative and sea skills to know what needed doing without being told.

'Mr Hallum, are ye familiar with the barque rig?'

'Er, no, sir.'

'Then I'll take command in the boats.' There were no barque-rigged vessels in the Royal Navy and although the major difference was only in the fore-and-aft-rigged mizzen Kydd felt it was probably asking too much of this staid officer. And, of course, he himself had made a voyage to Botany Bay as the reluctant master of a convict-ship barque in the days of the last peace.

There was no point in delay. Divisions for boarding were quickly apportioned and equipment made ready – cutlasses, boarding pistols, along with a fresh-sharpened tomahawk for every fourth man to use in slashing through boarding nettings and the like.

Faces darkened by galley soot, the Teazers awaited Kydd's order. He peered into the blackness once more: nothing to see, no sound. They could wait for the last moment before moonrise just before midnight, but little would be gained by sitting about.

'Get aboard!' he whispered. Men tumbled into the boats silently, nesting their weapons along the centre-line and taking up their oars.

The pinnace left the comfort of the ship's side, lay off in the inky blackness and waited for the other boats to take position. 'On me,' Kydd called, in a low voice, and the small flotilla set off for a point somewhere to the south of the twinkling lights of the fort where the barque must lie.

They pulled in silence, rags in the thole pins to muffle the clunk of oars and nothing but the swash of their passage to disturb the night. He'd spell the men before they—

Away to the right but frighteningly close, a scream in French – a boat out rowing guard! A musket banged into the night and another. Then a deeper-voiced command had the French boat's crew pulling for their lives – directly away.

Keyed up for a desperate clash at arms, Kydd couldn't understand why they were running. Then he saw. Starting as a wisp of flame, which mounted quickly then cascaded down in a flaming mass, bundles of straw had been lit and thrown over the walls of the fort. More fell and their flaring leaped up until the dark sea was illuminated by a pitiless red glare with themselves utterly revealed at its centre.

'Turn about!' Kydd bellowed, to the boats behind him. 'Go back!'

Disbelieving, they hesitated. Then the guns of the fort opened up and the reason for the guard-boat's departure was apparent; it had hastily cleared the field of fire for the artillery and now the cannon thundered vengefully into the night at *Teazer*'s fleeing boats.

Kydd flopped wearily into his cabin chair, his face still smeared with soot. 'Be damned t' it!' he muttered. 'To be beaten after such a handsome chase. At the least we got away with our skins.'

Renzi was in the other chair, looking grave. 'It seems the Revolutionary Army does not know much about night firing over sea, Tom. You were fortunate.'

'Aye – but the Frenchy captain was a canny one. No codshead he – I should have smoked it.' He frowned, and added sorrowfully, 'I should so have liked to set the English crew free, Nicholas. It's a hard enough life they face now.'

Renzi nodded, staring down. Then he lifted his gaze to Kydd. 'There's conceivably still a prospect of a successful outcome, should we be so bold.'

'A direct assault on 'em by daylight? I think not. If I'm seen to hazard men's lives on a merchantman it's to be understood as I'm prize-takin' to the neglect of my orders.'

'Quite. But I'm not referring to courage before cannon and blade, rather the devious application of cunning and deceit to attain the same object.' At Kydd's puzzled look, he continued, 'A stratagem as may secure your ship without need for overweening force, that asks the enemy to allay his fears and put down his arms . . .'

'Nicholas, ye're being hard to fathom. Are you saying we should creep up as they're not looking, then—'

'Not at all. Heaven forbid we should think to skulk about like your common spy,' Renzi said, with a shudder. 'What crosses my mind is that we could perhaps turn our recent experience to account and . . .'

As dawn's early light stole over the little bay *Teazer* crept around Cap Lévi once more, her crew quietly at quarters and Kydd on her quarterdeck, tense and edgy. If Renzi's stratagem failed they would be sailing to disaster and it could only be his responsibility.

The bay opened up and the barque was still there. Now at two anchors it was heaved around ready for a rapid departure – and then *Teazer* had come on the scene. For now she lay watchful but at any moment . . .

All depended on the effectiveness of the ruse. *Teazer* eased slowly into full view; a trumpet call sounded distantly from Fort Lévi but there was no hint of alarm.

Boldly, *Teazer* continued on course, set to go on her way southward past the barque, yet still there was no clamour of the call to arms – could that be because she was being lured onwards? They rounded the last of the point, which now took them within range of the fort's cannon. And nothing.

Where was the cutter? It should be . . . but then, coming up fast, *Linnet* rounded the cape and, sighting *Teazer*, opened fire on her with six-pounders. *Teazer* answered shot for shot in desperation – encumbered with three invasion craft towing astern, she was in no position for rapid defensive manoeuvres.

Was it working? No point in wondering now. They were committed. On Kydd's order a string of random flags jerked uncertainly up *Teazer*'s signal halliards but the wind was blowing them unreadably away from the French.

It was time. 'Y' know what to do, Poulden,' he told the helmsman. The wheel went over – and *Teazer* headed directly for Fort Lévi.

The response was immediate. A gun cracked out from the highest turret but it was only to draw attention to the welcoming three-flag hoist. 'By heaven, an' we've carried it off,' Kydd breathed, and glanced up at the ruddy ochre sails that had done their work so well.

Kydd had counted on the French having word passed of a brig with red sails due from Barfleur towing valuable invasion craft and, obligingly, he had provided one. That it was being harried by the Royal Navy was only to be expected, of course, and that it was seeking protection beneath the guns of the fort was equally understandable.

Confident that no French soldier could be expected to know the difference between two similar-sized brig-rigged ships, Kydd took *Teazer* in, gliding along the foreshore before the fortifications until, at precisely the right position, they hove to, preparing to anchor. Under threat of the shore guns the cutter abandoned its attack and hauled off – then seemed to have second thoughts and, curving round once more, placed herself in a daring show of bravado squarely alongside the barque that had been captured earlier by the French.

Kydd played out the agreed scenario: the position this foolish brig captain had chosen to heave to in just happened to mask the fort's field of fire. Horrified by the cutter's audacious attack, he failed to notice the frantic signals from the fort and sent his men tumbling wildly into the boats and crossing to the barque's rescue. Meanwhile the cutter's men swarmed aboard in attack from the seaward side.

The brig's men scrambled over the other bulwarks and soon were fighting for their lives with the cutter's fierce crew – but any cool observer might have been puzzled at the surprising increase in the number of men racing up from below . . .

To all ashore it must quickly have become clear that the brig's gallant rescue attempt had been in vain; by some means sail was got on the barque and, cables slipped, it headed for the open sea.

But the brave souls in the brig were not going to let it get away – the invasion barges were hacked free and the ship turned seaward to chase after them. Under full sail the ships raced away until at last they had disappeared over the horizon.

'Well, upon my soul, sir!' Admiral Saumarez sat back in amazement. 'It does you the utmost credit. When balked of your capture you turned to guile and artifice to accomplish what main force could not. To be quite frank I'd not have thought it, er, in your nature, Mr Kydd.'

Fighting down the urge to give Renzi his due – he had been insistent that his role was not to be mentioned – Kydd responded, ''Twas easily enough done, sir. The moon rose just after midnight, an' by it we sighted the wreck an' stripped it of fore 'n' main topsails. The cut o' the canvas wasn't pretty but it sufficed an' *Linnet* we found floggin' gamely along. She seemed eager enough for the adventure. The rest, well . . .'

'You're too reticent, sir. Did you have a stiff opposition on boarding the Frenchy?'

'That's the pity of it, sir. They yielded t' *Linnet* as we came over th' bulwarks, so we needs must fight among ourselves.' He chuckled as he recalled goading the Linnets to have at the Teazers in order to keep up the pretence, and the bewilderment this had caused among the French.

'When we released the crew of the merchant ship from below they loosed and set sail tolerably quick.'

'No one can doubt that at this moment they are drinking your health in a bumper, Mr Kydd,' Saumarez said drily. 'A pity the French got back their invasion craft, I suppose.'

'For that, sir, ye can rest easy. The men took along the bungs for keepsakes, leaving 'em t' sink.'

This left Saumarez speechless. Then he laughed and clapped Kydd on the shoulder. 'You've had a grand cruise, that's not to be denied.'

'Thank 'ee, sir.'

The admiral's expression turned thoughtful. 'And it leaves me in something of a dilemma.'

'Sir?'

Saumarez crossed to the window and gazed down on the harbour scene. 'This is a quiet station, as you know. Due mainly to the enterprise of officers of initiative such as yourself the enemy are kept cowering in their harbours and I should be grateful that one of your quality is under my command.' He turned back and regarded Kydd gravely. 'Yet I cannot help but reflect that two elements converge that are in themselves unanswerable. The first, that the kingdom lies under a menace unparalleled in its history and in stern need of its most able warriors. The second, that your continued presence here will render it near impossible to achieve a distinguished action and hence preferment. In all conscience, I believe that your recent ill-usage deserves better.

'Mr Kydd, with great reluctance I'm going to have you and your ship released to the very forefront of the struggle. The Downs Squadron.'

Chapter 3

Holding back his excitement, Kydd peered from the window of the coach as it crossed the bridge and ground up High Street past well-remembered sights from his youth. Renzi had been anxious to visit London so this time Kydd had journeyed to Guildford on his own.

They approached the Angel posting house, the coachman cracking his whip to clear a path for the Portsmouth Flyer as it wheeled round and clattered into the courtyard. The snorts of the horses echoed in the confined space and their pungent aroma lay on the air as Kydd descended and went inside. He had taken rooms at the Angel as he didn't want to burden his mother.

There was a wondering unreality about it all: while *Teazer* was undergoing refit in Portsmouth before joining the Downs Squadron, he had snatched a week to go home for the first time since the beginning of this war of Napoleon. Now he was back in the place where he was born and had grown up. Soon he would be greeting his parents – and with such a tale to tell . . .

With a deep breath he stepped out into High Street. The noise and smell instantly transported him back to the days of his youth and his eyes sought out the sights: the big hanging clock on the hall opposite the Tunsgate market, the Elizabethan alms-house – and before it the little wig-shop where he had once worked. It was now a print-seller, the shop front filled with luridly coloured patriotic sheets.

That a war was on did not seem apparent. The business of the town was cheerily going forward with hardly a reminder of the titanic struggle gathering strength out at sea.

Things were the same – but different.

As Kydd strode up the street not a soul noticed him but he had now been away for some time. Towards the top he took the little path past the sombre Holy Trinity churchyard to School Lane.

Several years ago, with his father's eyesight failing and the wig trade in decline, Kydd's family had summoned him home in despair. He and Renzi had restored the family fortunes by establishing a small school run along naval lines. The enterprise had thrived, with Jabez Perrott its fierce and strict boatswain keeping order and Mr Partington its keen young headmaster.

Kydd wondered if his sister Cecilia would be at home. Since securing a position as a companion to Lady Stanhope she had travelled the world. Kydd knew Cecilia would love to hear his tales as a rakish corsair, even if the reality was a little different. His voyages as a privateer captain had been successful, though, and he hugged to himself the anticipation of revealing his surprise to the family.

The trim school-house came into view; above it a blue ensign floating – Kydd smiled at the thought of the boatswain's face when he told him those were the colours he would fly in Admiral Keith's Downs Squadron. The school was neat and clean, and sounds of dutiful chanting issued from the classroom with the aroma of chalk dust and ink. Kydd crossed the little quadrangle to the residence.

'Thomas! It's you!' his mother squealed in delight at the door. 'Do come in, son. Ye'll catch a death if y' just stands there!'

'Who is it, Fanny?' The querulous enquiry had come from his father, frail with years and now completely blind.

'It's Thomas. An' how fine he looks in his new cream pantaloons an' brown leather boots.'

'Is Cec here?' Kydd asked.

'No, dear. She's in America somewheres wi' th' marquess an' lady,' Mrs Kydd said proudly. 'Have ye brought that nice Mr Renzi wi' ye?'

Letting the warmth of the homecoming wash about him, Kydd settled in the best armchair next to the fire while the wide-eyed maid proffered a hot caudle against the cold and chairs were brought up for everyone to hear his tale.

'So ye was a privateer, son. That's nice. Was it scareful a-tall, you wi' all those pirates about on th' boat?'

He was sparing in his account of battles and omitted any reference to the tragic loss of his fiancée Rosalynd, but he made much of the thrill of the chase and exciting tempests until he saw that the old couple were visibly tiring. 'How is the school, Ma?' he asked politely.

Jabez Perrott, the one-legged sailor who had been working in a Guildford bookshop until offered the position of school disciplinarian, was summoned to report, which he did most willingly and with the utmost dignity. He was a grave, upright figure who had taken to wife a respectable widow and become a man of repute at chapel.

Dinner was announced: Kydd took the place of honour at the other end of the table from his father and nodded to Mr Partington, who respectfully asked about his sea career. He was lodging at the house but it seemed he had an understanding with a certain young lady and his hopes for connubial bliss were well advanced.

The unreality crept back. Each had found their place in life and, in a quiet way, had prospered. He, on the other hand, had experienced so much that to tell of it could only invite incomprehension of a world they could not be expected to understand. He was possessed of means beyond any of their imaginings and of memories that could never really be shared; there was now an unbridgeable distance between himself and his folk.

It wasn't meant to be like this, his homecoming. He glanced about the room, saw the darted admiring glances, heard the shy chatter, the awkwardly addressed conversation. Perhaps it was because he had been away for so long that they were unsure of him – but in his heart he knew this was not so.

After the cloth was drawn and he was left with his parents he would bring out his surprise. With rising elation he waited until he had their full attention. 'Ma, Pa, I've somethin' to tell ye!'

'Aye, son?' his mother said quickly, clasping her hands over her knees in excitement. 'Is she pretty a-tall?'

A shadow passed over his face. 'No, Ma, it's not that. It's – it's that I've done main well in the article o' prize-takin' and it's to tell y' both I'm now going to see ye into a grand mansion – a prodigious-sized one as ye both deserve.'

Mrs Kydd looked at him with some perplexity. 'Thomas, dear, we're comfortable here, y' knows.'

Kydd looked at her fondly. 'Aye, that's as may be, but here's the chance to live like the quality in a great house wi' rooms an' grounds an' things . . .'

'A big house'd be a worry, dear.'

'No, Ma! There's servants as'll take charge of it for ye. An' then, o' course—'

'Not now, Thomas, love.'

'Ma! Tomorrow I can talk to the—'

'Listen, dear. We're happy here. It's all we need an' don't f'get, y'r father's eyes might ha' failed him but he knows his way about here. A great big place, why, we'd *all* get lost. Not only that, but what would I put in all them rooms?'

Taken aback, Kydd could only say, 'Ye'll soon be used to it, Ma. Then ye'll—'

'No, son,' his father said firmly. 'Pay heed t' what your mother just said. We stays.'

'Yes, Pa.'

'But thank 'ee most kindly for thinkin' of us in that way, son.'

'Yes, Pa.'

His mother brightly changed the subject. 'I've jus' remembered. Mrs Bawkins always has us t' tea on Thursdays. Would ye like t' come an' say hello?'

It was the best room in the Angel but Kydd did not sleep well. He took his breakfast early and, as he watched High Street come alive through the quaint windows of the dining room, tried to shake off a lowering dissatisfaction.

He started to walk to his parents' home, then realised it would be too early for them and turned back down the hill. The previous evening had not been what he had looked forward to and his parents' refusal of his offer had given him pause to think.

Guildford was just the same – or was it? The tradesmen were out in the old ways, their cries echoing in the streets as shops were opened and the town woke to another day. But it seemed subtly different.

He reached the bottom of the street and the bridge over the river Wey where the road led to the south and Portsmouth. He wanted time to reflect so he wandered down to the towpath, its curving placidity stretching away under the willow trees.

He had just turned thirty. Was it now time to take stock of his life? By any measure he was a success. He had left Guildford a perruquier and returned a well-to-do sea captain, with experiences of the wider world that any man would . . . But he had returned to Guildford expecting it to be as it always had been . . . He now saw that *it* had not changed, *he* had. Those very experiences had given him perspectives on the world that were very different. They had not only broadened his horizons but made it impossible to go back.

He stopped still. Guildford was of the past, not the future. It was no longer his home . . . but what, then, *did* he call home? Many men and most women of his age had settled in their ways and begun to raise a family. Was it now time for him to cease adventuring and put down roots somewhere? Guildford? The country? He had a not inconsiderable fortune and must be a most eligible bachelor. A stab of pain came at the thought of the death of his fiancée Rosalynd – but he had a duty now to his future.

The thoughts flowed on. Put down roots? Where? And as what? A gentleman of leisure whose glory days were past? No! Quite apart from the peril under which his country lay at the hands of the French, he knew that he was a man of the sea and belonged there. So was that what he must call home? He would not be at sea for ever and it was the expected and natural thing for any officer to acquire a property for the time when he swallowed the anchor and returned to the bosom of his family.

Since he had left Guildford, sea adventures had followed each other in exciting succession and his attention had been largely on the present. Perhaps now was the right time to consider where he was going with his life – and who he was.

There was no point in denying that he was a natural-born sailor who had the gift of sea-sense and tactics, and from long ago he had not been troubled by fear in battle: his end was just as near by land as sea, and duty was a clear path in war. No, there was no doubt that the probability was, given a reasonable run of luck, that he was destined for yet greater honours. Even to the dignity of post-captain? It was not impossible now, for with Napoleon Bonaparte declaring himself Emperor of the French there was no prospect in the near future of peace and unemployment.

His heart beat faster. To be made post – the captain of a frigate and later even ship-of-the-line, and firmly set on the path that led to . . . admiral!

It was not impossible, but there were many commanders and few post-captains. It would take much luck and, of course, interest at the highest level, which he did not have: he did not mix in the right circles. He must re-enter the society he had turned his back on when he had chosen Rosalynd, a country lass, over an admiral's daughter. That much was clear. A chill of apprehension stole over him at the thought of facing patrician gazes again, the practised swift appraisal and rapid dismissal.

But it had to be acknowledged that he was now a man of substance. He had no need to be intimidated by those grander than he. His situation was quite as fortunate as theirs, probably more so than that of some, and he could validly expect to step forward and claim his place among them.

The thought swelled. He could afford the trappings, need not fear lacking the resources to keep up with them in whatever pursuit the occasion demanded. He would be treated with politeness and deference, would be allowed and *accepted* into their company. He would make friends. He would be noticed.

It was a heady vision but to become a figure in society it was not enough to dress modishly. To be accepted he must comport himself as they did, assume the graces and accomplishments of gentility that Renzi had been so at pains to instil in him when he had first become an officer. He had no desire to be thought quaint, which meant he should quickly acquire the requisite elements of polish such as an acquaintance with the classics, musical accomplishments and, remembering Cecilia's exasperated comments, gentlemanly speech.

Was that so hard? If he was to achieve a credible finish then, with his other advantages, he could pass for one of them. Of course, there was the difficulty of his origins, his family, but was this not the way the great families of the day must have started? Northern iron-masters, Liverpool shipping lords, rising merchants of the City of London were all now laying down estates and being honoured in a modern world that was making way for men who were reaching the heights by their own efforts.

Damn it! He would be one of them and take his place among them by right. And if it took the hoisting in of a few ancient tomes and working on his conversation, so be it. He would meet his future squarely and seize any opportunity with both hands.

Suddenly impatient, he began to walk back quickly, letting his thoughts race. Above all, he had the means to see it through: if he was right about his prospects, then the sooner he was equipping himself for his destiny the better. It was going to happen. There would be a new Thomas Kydd.

Feeling surged. But did that mean he was turning his back on Guildford, the place of his birth, that until now he had called home? No. He would put this world gently but firmly to one side. It was just that it was no longer the centre of his universe.

He hurried along the last few yards to the school-house gate, lightness of spirit urging him onward. 'Good mornin', Ma,' he said happily. 'Y' say Mrs Bawkins is entertainin' this afternoon?'

Teazer was delayed in her refit. A humble brig-sloop had no claim to priority in a dockyard that was at full stretch keeping the vital blockading ships-of-the-line at sea and she was left for long periods in forlorn disarray, her crew in receiving hulks and her officers bored.

Kydd lost no time in taking rooms ashore. Not for him the noisy intimacy of the Blue Posts at Portsmouth Point, he could now afford to stay where officers of rank were to be found, at the George in Penny Street. And there he began the process of refinement.

It was vexing that Renzi was in London, out of reach for advice, but on the other hand this was Kydd's own initiative and he would see it through. He went first to the largest bookshop; the assistant had been studiously blank-faced as he asked for suggestions as to what primers gentlemen found most answered in a classical education.

He left with a clutch of books and hurried back. The Greek

grammar was hopelessly obtuse and required him to learn by rote the squiggly characters of the alphabet before ever he could start. It could wait for later. The other looked more promising; an interlinear copy of Caesar's commentaries on the campaign in Gaul, the Latin on one line, English on another. At least it was about the manly pursuit of war, not the fantastical monsters and gods of antique Greece.

'*Omnia Gallia in tres partes divisa est . . .*' Did he really have to get his head round all this? Or could he learn some of the more pithy sayings and casually drop them into the dinner-table conversation to the pleased surprise of all? That sounded much the better idea.

In the matter of polite discourse there could be no hesitation. He would be damned as of the lower orders by his own words just as soon as he opened his mouth in company. Since the days of Cecilia's patient efforts on his speech, he had slipped back into his comfortable old ways.

No, this required an all-out effort – and he must apply himself to it this time. Resolved, he gave it careful thought. This was not to be learned casually with others or from books, he needed professional assistance. In the Portsmouth Commercial Directory he found what he was looking for.

'Mr Augustus DeLisle?' he asked politely, at the door of a smart Portsea terrace house.

'It is, sir, at your service,' the rather austere gentleman answered with a slight bow, appraising Kydd's appearance, then bestowing on him a professional smile.

'Th' language coach as can be engaged t' fit a gentleman for converse even at the Court o' St James?' Kydd persisted.

'The same,' the man said with a sniff. 'You should know that I count most of the noble houses of Hampshire among my satisfied clients and—'

'Are ye available for immediate engagement, sir?' Kydd asked abruptly.

'Why, at such notice—'

'I've ten guineas to lay in y'r hand as says it'll fadge.'

'Er, very well – but be aware, sir, I cannot abide the fugitive aspirate, still less the cruelly truncated participle! You shall bring along your child and he will—'

'Not a younker, sir, it's t' be me.'

'I – I don't quite understand you, sir,' the man said uncertainly.

'M' name's Kydd, and I want t' speak wi' the best of 'em. Ye've got me half a day, every day until I can stand up an' be taken for a lord.'

'Every day?' he spluttered. 'My young masters usually attend but twice a week and—'

'M' time is limited, sir,' Kydd said impatiently. 'I'd be thinkin' ye a rare 'un if I sees ye refuse half a year's fee for a few weeks' work.'

The refit ground forward in the dockyard but the day came not so many weeks later when *Teazer* was released and became inhabited once more by her rightful denizens. She stored, watered and took in an overseas allowance of powder and shot, the Downs Squadron being considered so active a station as to warrant a maximum loading.

There was no time to be lost: Admiral Keith needed every vessel that swam in his crucial command, and Kydd was determined for *Teazer* to play her part.

'Er, I have to report, ship ready for sea, sir,' Hallum said awkwardly.

Kydd grunted. It was now common knowledge about the ship that their clerk was still at large, adrift from leave. A letter of recall had been sent to him, which had been acknowledged, but he had not appeared and it now seemed that the ship would sail without him.

It was no use. They could not delay. Kydd sighed heavily and went on deck, searching vainly for a hurrying figure on the dockside. 'Single up!' he ordered. All lines that tethered them alongside were let go save two. Away from the wharf, dockyard work-boats attended for the sloop to warp out, and in *Teazer* there was the age-old thrill of the outward bound.

Sail bent on, men expectantly at their posts, Kydd reluctantly gave the command. 'Take us out, Mr Dowse.'

Ropes splashed into the murky water and *Teazer* was ready to spread her wings. Colour appeared at the signal tower. 'Our pennant, "proceed", sir,' squeaked their brand new midshipman, Tawse, wielding the big telescope importantly.

'Acknowledge,' Kydd said heavily. With the ebb tide *Teazer* loosed sail and left to meet her destiny.

The narrow entrance was difficult and needed concentration. They passed the rickety jollity of Portsmouth Point close abeam, then King Henry's tower on one side with Haslar and Fort Blockhouse only a couple of hundred yards to the other, and they were through.

'*Haaaands*, t' the braces!' Constrained by sandbanks close to larboard and the Nab still to round before clear water, there was little room for manoeuvre.

'He's there, sir!' screamed a youngster, wildly pointing shorewards. A sharp-lined wherry was putting off hastily from the Sally Port on a course to intercept.

'It's Mr Renzi, right enough,' confirmed Purchet, after snatching at the telescope.

Without hesitating, Kydd rapped, 'Heave to, Mr Dowse!' It was madness in the fast current and sandbanks past the entrance to be not under way . . . and close astern a heavy frigate was coming down on them at speed. With the wind large there was no other way than to wheel about awkwardly and place the fore aback, but Kydd was not going to lose Renzi.

The frigate plunged past with an energetic volley of abuse from her quarterdeck. The wherry stroked out manfully and at last hooked on at the main-chains. While *Teazer* paid off before the wind, willing hands hauled Renzi in, his bundles of books needing more robust hoisting.

'I do apologise, sir,' Renzi said formally.

Kydd, still in his quarterdeck brace, frowned but said nothing.

'We lost a wheel before Petersfield and—'

'Mr Renzi! I rather feel that in this instance you might have been topping it overmuch the *cunctator*, as it were.'

Renzi was transfixed with astonishment at his friend's cultivated words. The Latin *cunctator* – delayer – was indeed appropriate, an allusion to the tactic used by the Roman commander in the war with Hannibal, an attempt to deny the enemy a battle. 'Why, thank you, sir!' He wasn't about to let Kydd get away with this one, whatever the reason for its mysterious appearance.

'Thank you?' Kydd said, crestfallen.

'For the compliment, of course, dear fellow. It was by this very tactic that Quintus Fabius Maximus may have shamed the Roman Army but it undoubtedly won him the war and his nickname.'

The open Channel won and a fine westerly in their sails, by evening there was chance to sup together.

Renzi opened politely. 'Er, at the risk of impertinence I

cannot help but remark the elegance of your speech, its genteel delivery, the—'

'Quite simple, Renzi, old chap. I've given it a deal of thought. And it seems to me, the only way to move forward in this world is not to *kick against the pricks* . . .' a flash of smugness was quickly smothered '. . . but be agreeable to the customary forms of civility and breeding when in genteel company. In fine, if I'm to enter in on society, then I'm to be like them. And you have m' word on it, enter in I will!'

'Then you have my most earnest admiration, Tom – er, Kydd, old trout. So recently shunned by society and cast into the very depths, yet you hold no grudge, no antipathy towards those who—'

'It's past. I have a bright future now and I'm going to take it with both hands and do what I have to.'

'Are you certain that—'

'M' dear friend. Since coming into my fortune, I stand amazed at the boldness and presumption as can be found from having a pot o' gold at your back! I cannot fear the rich-dressed when I'm rigged the same, or stand mumchance while they talk wry, when I can, just as well.'

'There are other—'

'You must believe I've not trifled away my time, m' dear Renzi. There's quantities of professional gentlemen in Portsmouth who do rue our sailing, and I have a stand o' books in my cabin as will keep me amused for voyages to come.'

'I honour you for it,' Renzi said.

'You'll oblige me by maintaining a quality o' discourse while about my person.'

'I shall endeavour to do so,' came the sincere response.

'Then m' course is set. Tysoe, do attend to Mr Renzi's glass, if you please.'

The Downs! A fulcrum for the torrent of shipping that came and went around the corner of the North Foreland into the Thames and the mighty maw of London, where hundreds of ships of all flags might be lying anchored, waiting for a favourable wind to take them outward bound down-Channel, or inbound to the north, or across to the Baltic. The ten-mile stretch of the Downs was bordered five miles offshore by the notorious Goodwin Sands, since medieval times a fearful hazard, but this acted both as a shelter and a barrier. It was the point at which the Channel was at its narrowest, a bare eighteen miles from Dover to the French encampments at Cap Gris Nez. The last Kydd had seen of it had been as the master of a convict ship bound for New South Wales. After the desolate shingle spit of Dungeness, it was the wide sweep of bay that was the foreshore of the smugglers' haunt of Romney Marsh, then the rising crags of Folkestone turning into the soaring white splendour of Shakespeare's cliff, Dover, and on to the rounding of South Foreland.

In the bright early-morning light the massive chalk ramparts seemed to Kydd to stand four-square and proudly defiant against England's foes, marching away north in impregnable array. *Teazer* closed within half a mile of them to round the foreland and make the southern reaches of the Downs. The vista of countless ships at anchor was opening up before them now: coasters, East Indiamen, colonial traders from far distant parts of the globe, an impressive multitude stretching for ten miles of open water. But Kydd had eyes only for the naval anchorage, that of the legendary

Downs Squadron standing so valiantly at the forefront of England's defence.

There. Across the anchorage. He would never forget her, ever: the seventy-four riding to two anchors, her lines old-fashioned but graceful. It was *Monarch*, the flagship. After the bloody battle of Camperdown not so many years before, Kydd had, in her, become one of the very few who had taken the incredible journey from before the mast as a common seaman to the quarterdeck as a king's officer.

He let Hallum take *Teazer* inshore to moor while he took his fill of the sight. It seemed odd but only *Monarch* and two other minor ships-of-the-line were present, three frigates further distant and a number of sloops. Where was the battle squadron, if not with their commander-in-chief?

They would know soon enough. Tysoe had out his dress uniform and, buckling on his handsome sword, Kydd returned on deck to board his gig. Poulden, his coxswain, and the entire boat's crew were smartly turned out in matching blue jackets – he was determined to be noticed in the new command.

'*Teazer*!' blared Poulden, importantly, in answer to the hail as they drew near to the flagship. A side-party could be seen assembling and Kydd's heart swelled. He mounted the side of the old ship slowly, letting the moment touch his soul.

It was the great cabin he remembered; but Admiral Lord Keith, his commander-in-chief, was before him and this was no time for lingering sentiment.

'Do sit down, Mr Kydd,' the august being said absently, taking papers from his flag-lieutenant and flicking his eyes down them. The lieutenant collected others, and, with a glance at Kydd, left the cabin.

'I do bid ye welcome to my command, sir.' The Scots brogue seemed to be one with his austere presence.

'Thank you, sir.'

He held up one particular paper and intoned mildly, 'You've had some adventuring since last we met.' His cold eyes rose to meet Kydd's.

'I've – that is to say, it's been interesting enough for me, sir.' The last time they had met was in the previous war when Keith had been forced to give Kydd orders to lay up *Teazer* and resign his command in the retrenchment following the announcement of peace – but he had also bestowed that precious captaincy in the first place.

'I'll have ye know, sir, that the Downs is a far different duty from what ye're used to.' He paused significantly. 'No more than six leagues distant, Napoleon Bonaparte and his hordes lie in an encampment ready to lunge at us across the water. Our duty is plain, sir.'

'It must be!' Kydd responded strongly.

'Is it?' Keith said pugnaciously, leaning forward. 'I will say this to you, Mr Kydd. If any captain returns from sea with a prize at his tail without he has an explanation, I promise I will break him.'

'Sir.'

'In these perilous times the first duty of a sea officer is the ruin and destruction of the enemy forces, not the pursuit of private gain.' Keith leaned back slowly. 'That said, there's everything in your record to encourage me to believe your service here will be a credit to the Royal Navy. When you return you may depend on an active employment.'

'When I return?'

'This is the most complex and fast-moving station in the realm. I will not have my commanders in any doubt about the strategics and dispositions of the situation in which they sail. You will this day take coach for London – the Admiralty – and within the span of a week acquaint yourself most thoroughly with the details of what faces us. Is this clear?'

'Er, yes, sir. My ship?'

'Your ship will relieve another here *pro tem*. Are ye in doubt of your premier, sir?'

'Mr Hallum? No, sir,' Kydd said hastily. 'A most reliable officer.'

'Your orders will be ready for your return. Good day to ye, Mr Kydd.'

The capital was crowded, noisy and smelled as pungently of sea-coal smoke and local stenches as it always did, but Kydd was not of a mind to care. The hackney carriage creaked and swayed as it bore him towards the Admiralty Office in Whitehall, the jarvey swearing sulphurously at any who dared cross him while Kydd gazed from the grimy window.

He had left Renzi with Tysoe at the inn: he smiled to himself at the pathetic excuses Renzi had contrived at short notice to accompany him but was secretly pleased. It would not be all a duty visit and he had never before been with his friend in London.

They lurched from Cockspur Street into the broad reaches of Whitehall and came to a stop by the colonnaded screen of the Admiralty. Kydd paid off the jarvey and hastily pushed through the admiring throng outside and into the courtyard. He raised an arm in acknowledgement of the patriotic cries that rang out at the sight of his uniform and hurried inside.

Through the high portico the doorman showed him to the captains' room – but this time it was not as a penniless commander begging for a ship in the days of the last peace but as the captain of a front-line man-o'-war about to be informed of the grave strategic questions that faced his country. There were other commanders in the room; they looked at him enviously as the first lord's second secretary came down to spirit him away.

Earl St Vincent was in the Board Room, seated at the long table beneath the legendary wind-gauge. A vast mass of papers was spread forth and he was flanked by several dour-looking men not in uniform. They did not rise or attempt to leave.

The first lord, however, got to his feet and returned Kydd's civil bow. 'So your flag-officer wants ye to hoist aboard an understanding of our situation,' he said bleakly.

'Aye – er, yes, sir.'

'Right and proper, too,' St Vincent growled, sitting again heavily. He had aged since Kydd had seen him before, his thick-set figure bowed and stiff. This was the man who had taken it upon himself to root out the gross inefficiency and corruption of the royal dockyards, standing alone against the powerful timber cartels. In a bluff and uncompromising sea-dog fashion he had faced down the political storm that resulted. 'The Downs command – you'll be seeing as much action as ye'd wish, sir,' he said with a wintry smile. 'As it's rightly said, "The frontier of Britain is the coastline of the enemy." Do your duty, sir, and England need have no concern for its fate.'

An elegantly dressed post-captain appeared at the other door and waited diffidently.

'I've no time to attend to ye myself,' St Vincent said, with an ironical glance at the seated figures. 'Captain Boyd will see to the matter. Good fortune be with ye, Mr Kydd.'

'Thank you, sir.' But the old earl had turned back to the grey men and he was dismissed.

'Boyd, late of *Bellona*. And . . . ?' He was a post-captain of one of Cornwallis's major ships-of-the-line and had probably been moved closer to the centre of power to acquire the necessary experience before elevation to flag rank.

'Kydd, brig-sloop *Teazer*,' Kydd said defensively, at Boyd's languid and polished manner.

'Joining the Downs from where, Mr Kydd?' the officer said distantly, as they walked together.

'The Channel Islands, for m' sins,' Kydd said, as lightly as he could.

Boyd raised one eyebrow. 'A sea change of note,' he said drily. 'You've seen active service, no doubt.'

'The Nile – and Acre following,' Kydd said, with a touch of defiance.

Boyd stopped. 'Did you really, by God?' he said, suddenly respectful. The droll affectation fell away as he resumed walking. 'Then you'll relish the Downs – no end to the sport to be had there.'

They entered a small office and a worried-looking lieutenant glanced up from his desk. 'Do carry on, Dukes,' Boyd told him testily, then asked Kydd, 'You have somewhere to stay?'

'The White Hart in Charles Street.'

Boyd nodded, then crossed to gaze out of the window. His office overlooked the vast parade-ground behind Horse Guards, the army headquarters further along. Distant screams of sergeants and the regular tramp of soldiers in formation drifted up in the warm sunshine. He turned back to Kydd. 'The volunteers. Always at their marching up and down, I see. Now, Mr Kydd, I rather think you'll need me to provide something a trifle more useful than I can at short notice. Shall we say tomorrow at ten?'

'At ten would be most civil in you, sir.'

'Oh, and it might be politic to present yourself at the Admiralty reception tonight,' Boyd added. 'A Russian who thinks to mount some expedition that has our interest. Carriages at six – swords and decorations, I'm afraid.'

'No, sir. Mr Renzi has not yet returned,' Tysoe informed him.

Kydd sighed and took an armchair. His friend could be anywhere in the vast, seething city, after some musty book or arranging to meet a savant – just when he needed re-assurance before an important social occasion, both formal and diplomatic. Idly, he picked up the morning newspaper. A theatre scandal occupied all of three columns and trading figures for the stock exchange were neatly summarised on the right, but by far the majority of articles were in some way connected to the war.

One piece dealt at tedious length with a review by the Duke of York of the Medway militia battalions. A breath-less editorial alerted the faithful readers to the dangers of a Baltic embargo on ship timber. Another item reported that the conveyance of a trade minister of Spain, said to be very soon an enemy state, had been set upon by a mob and lucky to escape with his life. The pretext had been a punitive increase on duty for imported Spanish wines. Hardly his fault, Kydd thought wryly.

He turned to the next page and stared in surprise at a detailed picture of a vast platform of heroic dimensions, fit to carry a regiment of men and horses and held aloft by a dozen fire balloons of the kind that the Montgolfier brothers had demonstrated before the French Revolution. In earnest words, the newspaper reiterated its promise to keep its readers informed of the plans of Napoleon Bonaparte to deploy such craft in great numbers for the invasion of Britain – ten thousand men and guns to cross the water as fast as a galloping horse, then descend from the skies in irresistible numbers, visiting upon Britain what the continent had already suffered.

It was pointed out gravely that if any would doubt it they had only to recall the historic first flight across the Channel by Jeffries and Blanchard, which had occurred all of twenty years before.

Kydd paused. He had no idea of the practicality of the scheme but if it were true then the Navy would be helpless to defend the shores as the giant platforms sailed across overhead to invade. It was a menace as unanswerable as that which he had heard from a garrulous army officer in the coach, that Bonaparte was employing his idle army in Boulogne to dig a tunnel under the Channel.

Kydd tried to dismiss a mental picture of battalions of crack grenadiers suddenly pouring out of the earth in the pretty countryside of Kent to overwhelm the local volunteers. Yet who could say it was impossible? At one wheelbarrow of earth from each man every twenty minutes, with a quarter of a million men, it would not take so very long to tunnel the eighteen miles. Bonaparte had been preparing his invasion now for more than a year; the tunnel might be nearing completion at that very moment.

'How's this, sir? As some might say, a brown study?' Renzi had returned unnoticed and came to sit in the other chair. 'Here, old fellow, I have something for your diversion.' He slapped down a few garishly coloured prints.

Kydd picked up the top one, entitled, 'A correct View of the French Machine Intended to Convey Their Soldiers for the Invasion of England'. It was a gigantic raft and had what appeared to be windmills spaced along its sides. To give point to its size, troops of horses were galloping about its decks.

'Most ingenious,' Renzi murmured. 'The mills may be turned into whatever direction the wind deigns to blow, and being in train each to a paddle-wheel, we have a means of locomotion for a vessel to enable it to proceed on any course it wishes. One may assume even directly into the wind's eye,' he added thoughtfully.

Kydd perused the next, a French print of a vessel, *La Terreur d'Albion*, of extraordinary length and with an obligatory Liberty cap in bloody red atop an enormous forward turret, and what seemed to be an iron skeleton flourishing the grim reaper's scythe on the after one. In gleeful detail a legend explained that the turrets were machinery towers, and inside a series of paddle-wheels would be powered by a great number of horses, whose combined strength would urge the craft to speeds unmatched by the noblest of English frigates.

Kydd's eyes met Renzi's in sombre reflection before he picked up the next. This was of a flat, lozenge-shaped raft fully seven hundred feet across with a central citadel and powered by a giant lateen sail on a swivel, itself five hundred feet long. It was soberly estimated to be capable of trans-porting thirty thousand troops. Other prints depicted man-carrying kites, unsinkable hide-covered cork boats and other bizarre contrivances.

'And today I heard of a weapon of terror that would chill the blood of any man,' Renzi said. 'It is a species of clockwork balloon.'

'A what?'

'An automaton aloft,' Renzi said. 'Set forth, it requires no man aboard to control it. A deadly craft of the skies which, when commanded by its mechanism, soullessly rains down fiery destruction on the cowering wretches beneath.'

'It . . . Surely they'd never . . .'

'I'm desolated to say that it appears to be true, my friend. At the Royal Society's rooms I was privileged to view an experimental French balloon captured only this last month. It is raised aloft not by the fire of Montgolfier but a cold miasma of Lavoisier's "hydrogen", which, of course, will never need tending by man in order to retain its lifting powers.'

'Then . . .'

'Yes, dear fellow,' Renzi said quietly. 'It would seem that very soon war will be visited on every creature promiscuously. Skill at arms will be of no account in this new—'

'It'll never happen,' Kydd retorted. 'Can't you see? England would never stoop s' low as to use such, and for the French, why, they'd hold back for fear we'd pay 'em back in their own coin. No, they'd not dare.'

'Bonaparte is soon to be crowned the Emperor Napoleon but, mark me, he won't rest until he's master of the entire world.'

At Kydd's look of disbelief, Renzi continued darkly, 'You don't understand the man. He holds his country in a vile subjection while he destroys and plunders, but the world sees only his glory. The France of Versailles and the Encyclopedists no longer exists, for inside the country . . .' He trailed off.

Kydd felt unsettled. 'Strong words from a man o' letters, I'm persuaded,' he said, then added, 'Where did you hear all this?'

Renzi gave a twisted smile before he spoke. 'Dear fellow, I do believe I must trust you. May I have your word that nothing of what I'm about to tell you will go any further?'

'Why, er, yes, o' course, Nicholas.'

'Very well. Your understanding of my occupation in Jersey is that I was a species of secretary to an exiled royalist prince. This is, in fact, true, inasmuch as Commodore d'Auvergne is indeed the Prince of Bouillon and awaits a restoration of his fortunes. However, the greater part of my duties was to support and assist in his real vocation – an unremitting clandestine war against the tyrant conducted through a network of brave souls opposed to his rule.

'In that cause, I had occasion to treat with spies and agents as they came and went in France as, indeed, once I was obliged to do myself. You must believe me when I say that this has given me insights of a personal nature into the character of Bonaparte's imperium that trouble me greatly.

'You will be startled to learn that secret police are being deployed by him for . . .' Renzi went on to recount what he had learned of the true state of the tyranny that he had played his part in trying to overthrow, the paradoxes that lay at the heart of the most rational nation in civilisation, which had been torn apart by a bloody revolution and was now being forged together again at the will of one man for one purpose: his own personal vainglory.

Kydd felt growing disquiet; he had never seen Renzi so intense on a subject.

'So you were a – a spy then, Nicholas,' Kydd said uncomfortably, shocked to discover that while he had been roaming the seas as a successful privateer his friend had been hazarding his life for higher principles.

'A spy, yes, but in a particular service – the desperate plot to kidnap Bonaparte that came close to ending this war but unhappily terminated in the most hideous consequences to those involved. You should know I find the practice of spying odious and utterly incompatible with the condition of gentleman, and I pray most earnestly that I shall never again be so employed.'

Kydd slumped in his chair. If Renzi thought that this was much more than simply the latest war with the French, there was every reason to take fear that some of the rumours and agitations at large were true, and the peril to England that much more serious than he had thought. Later, no doubt, when he was ready, Renzi would divulge more about his time in Jersey. He had come back shattered and must have endured much.

It was a glittering affair and, with a mixture of exhilaration and trepidation, Kydd entered the grand room with Boyd. The hundred or so guests were in every mode of fashion and elegance, their stars and ribbons in a breathtaking show of splendour under the chandeliers.

'It would oblige me, sir, should you point out the Russians to me,' Kydd murmured in his best speech, bowing civilly to a passing couple.

'I'll do better than that, Kydd. Come – meet Rezanov. He's to be their new ambassador to Japan,' Boyd replied suavely, ushering him across the room. 'Ah! Sir, may I present Commander Kydd, a distinguished officer in His Majesty's Navy? He did confide to me that it would gratify him immensely to make the acquaintance of one so soon to make such an historic circumnavigation. Mr Kydd, the Kammerherr Rezanov.' A compact but striking man with a neat black beard regarded him dispassionately as Boyd excused himself and left.

'Your servant, sir,' Kydd said, bowing low.

'A sea officer of note, I believe,' Rezanov said mildly, in barely accented English.

'Why, er . . .'

'Mr Kydd, you bear the Nile medal and I have no doubt that your presence at this gathering is not altogether fortuitous.'

'Sir, modesty forbids me a reply,' Kydd said smoothly, inwardly exulting at the successful deployment of his new-found urbanity. 'But I do confess, I'm curious to know the objectives of your expedition.'

Rezanov's eyebrows shot up in astonishment, then he eased into a smile. 'Very well, sir. You speak directly – and I will tell you. By direction of His Imperial Majesty the Tsar, our prime concern is to discover new routes that will enable us to supply our colonies in Russian America.'

Russian America? Kydd supposed he must be speaking of the frozen reaches of the American continent to the north-west.

'You will have no conception of the difficulty we face at the moment – it would astonish you to learn that we expend the lives of four thousand horses a year in the traverse of Siberia with supplies, and alternate means would be very welcome as our interests extend southward.'

Kydd was out of his depth: if the Russians were entering from the north and, the Spanish were to the south, where did this leave the United States and Canada? He reached for more familiar ground. 'A voyage of that length, sir, is a great thing. Your ships are well found, at all?'

'From Kronstadt to Sitka Island? It certainly is an enterprise to remark, but as to our vessels, you may rest easy – both the *Nadezhda* and the *Neva* are recently purchased from the Royal Navy, Mr Kydd. For your further questions, I believe you shall speak now with the commander of the expedition.'

Kydd bowed in acceptance and was taken to a knot of officers in haughty discussion. 'Kapitán, this is Commander Kydd,' Rezanov snapped at a young but intense-featured officer in the centre. 'Mr Kydd, Kapitán-pérvogo Ivan Krusenstern.' He bowed smartly, with a crisp click of the heels, and was gone.

'My best wishes for your success, sir,' Kydd said to the officer, as graciously as he could. 'Mr Kru – er, I understand you're sailing in one of our ships,' he said slowly, hoping the man had sufficient English for polite converse.

'O' course, Commander. Ye'll recall *Leander* o' the Nile as was?' It was passing strange to hear the robust idiom of an English fo'c'sle coming from an exotically dressed Russian. 'She's now th' good ship *Nadezhda* an' I'm t' see her where y'r Captain Vancouver once led.' He saw Kydd's surprise and added dismissively, 'Oh, I've done a mort o' service wi' the King's Navy afore now.'

'Why, er, to be sure,' Kydd said, taken aback. 'I do recall *Leander*, Mr Krusenstern, as I was at the Nile myself. A fine ship and gallant!'

Krusenstern beamed as his eyes flicked to Kydd's medals. He leaned across to shake Kydd's hand. 'So ye were, b'God! An' 'twas a thumpin' fine mauling ye gave 'em that night, cully!'

The circle of officers about them fell back at the sudden comradely friendliness and Kydd grinned. 'A thunderin' hard enough mill f'r all hands, as I c'n tell ye! An' for y'self, a world cruise, why, ye'll have yarns enough t' tell at every dog-watch f'r years t' come.'

'Aye, well, it's aught but a tradin' matter,' Krusenstern said guardedly, taking Kydd aside. 'An' th' mutinous dogs o' Tlingit tribesmen on Kodiak needin' our attention.'

They started walking alone together. 'But belay th' tough yarns, we've a tight barky or two, and our pel-compass an' y'r Taunton's artificial magnet as'll see us through all a-taunto. A right rousin' voyage it'll be . . .'

The two seamen disappeared happily into the throng.

In the morning it seemed that Boyd had got together his appraisal of the situation, but before they began he told Kydd that it was noted he had conducted himself in a most satisfactory manner. 'To cut out Krusenstern from under the eyes of the ambassador by talking sea-cant was a most ingenious stratagem. You should look to more of the same in the future, I dare to say.'

'Er, the Kapitán Krusenstern, he claims service in the Royal Navy?' Kydd asked.

'He has, and others too. Since Tsarina Catherine's day they've had many of their best men serve with us for a spell. First-class training, they believe.'

'Any . . . active service?'

'If by that you mean a whiff of powder-smoke, then most definitely. Odd thing, though, this Ivan seems to prefer the company of the foremast hands to the officers when ashore. A hard-drinking cove, you see, your Russian.'

As they mounted the stairs to the upper floor of the Admiralty Office Kydd tried to reconcile his excitement at the pomp and glitter of a diplomatic occasion with the nervous, febrile atmosphere of a London trying to make light of the dreadful threat of imminent invasion. The frightful images of the prints, and Renzi's revelations, had stayed with him. 'Should we take fear o' those fantastical invasion machines, do you think?' he asked hesitantly.

At first Boyd did not reply. Then he said thoughtfully, 'It's as well never to underestimate the Corsican, Kydd. He knows how to sow fear and panic by lie and invention. To believe every word of the *Moniteur* would be to credit the tyrant with ten times more victories than he has, but we must accept that there are those to which we are compelled to accede.'

They reached a discreet door and Boyd found his keys. As he selected the right one he added soberly, 'I suppose it is possible that many of these horrors are rumour and deceit, but the French are a logical and inventive people and there may well be substance in them. I really can't say.'

The key rattled and the door opened on a darkened room. Boyd crossed to a single shuttered window and threw it open. Daylight through the bars revealed a single bare table and chairs. What resembled a ship's chart locker, with its array of flat drawers, stood along one wall.

Kydd was motioned to the table while Boyd closed and locked the door, then sat opposite. 'Mr Kydd,' he said, with chilling gravity, 'what I have to tell you this morning is privy information whose disclosure would cause panic and riot if known by the general public, yet it is necessary for you to learn of it should the worst happen. Do you understand?'

'I do, sir.'

'Very well. Let me begin by admitting to you that never in the history of this realm has England lain under greater menace of invasion and consequent extinction as a nation. Our country cherishes the liberty of individuals and as such we're ill-placed to maintain great armies. Most of our land continues its daily round much as its forefathers did, with little to tell that a war rages on the continent.

'King and Parliament are amicable but the people will not stand for oppression. On the contrary side, France now is subject to the resolve of one man who is able to focus the entire resources of his nation to one end. An invasion. And he is so pledged to invade this country I do not well see how he can avoid it. Therefore we must stretch every sinew in our defence. There are volunteers, the militia and our army, all of which combined are greatly outnumbered by Napoleon's battle-seasoned legions.'

Kydd stirred restlessly. 'Sir! You discount the Navy as our—'

'If,' said Boyd, heavily, 'by any means, the French get ashore there are plans.' He opened a drawer, extracted a large map and spread it out. 'Our best intelligence now is that Bonaparte intends to descend on the closest part of England to the coast of France.' His finger stabbed down at the shoreline of the Downs. 'In fact, just to the south. Dover Castle is an ancient but still formidable fortification, which must be subdued, but see here . . .' Kydd recognised the flat and barely inhabited Romney Marsh a few miles on to the south. 'It's wide open to a massed assault on a broad front and I fear it will prove a forlorn hope to expect our militia and volunteers to move up quickly enough to meet a sudden descent.'

Kydd frowned. What possible chance did those inexperienced amateurs have against the hardened troops that had stormed over Europe to victory after victory?

Boyd continued remorselessly. 'Thus it would seem not impossible to conceive that a landing would be met with a rapid success . . .'

Kydd went cold. 'Did the – will the King—'

'His Majesty is under no doubt of his duty. Glenbervie, of the Household, tells me he sleeps every night with his camp equipage and accoutrements to hand, to the evident anguish of the Queen. In course he will not be suffered to take the field. In the strictest confidence I have to tell you that the Bishop of Gloucester has prepared his palace for the evacuation of the King and the Royal Family across the Severn at Worcester.

'In addition, Sir Brook Watson, the commissary general, has instructions in the event of the imminent loss of the capital to make ready thirty ox-wagons for the transport of the nation's entire gold reserves to be deposited with the King at Worcester under the same guard.'

To speak of such things! To hear and consider the destruction and conquering of his country of birth. It was a thing of horror for Kydd.

Boyd continued, 'At Woolwich the arsenal and artillery stores will be taken, as will the Purfleet Ordnance Board powder magazines, to Weedon in Northamptonshire. There is in construction there a vast military complex which will act also as a seat of government in the event of—'

'This is hard to bear, sir!' Kydd blurted. 'Surely—'

'—the fall of the capital. It is by way of being astride the Grand Union canal and well placed for the conduct of a protracted campaign.'

Kydd tried to gather his wits. 'The – the common people, sir. How will they, er, what might be done to . . . ?'

'They have not been overlooked. Plans have been drawn up for their preservation. Here. These instructions have been lately sent to every town and village in the south.' He extracted a leaf and passed it over.

Kydd read. 'The Deputy Lieutenants and Justices . . . the following directions . . . in case of an Alarm of the Landing by the Enemy . . . for the removal of women and children, aged and infirm to a place of general Military Rendezvous . . .' It went on to direct how a village was to be sectioned by responsibility, how carts were to be numbered, marked and covered such that those with a ticket of the right form might be conveyed away with provisions following. Males of the village over the age of twelve had duties of driving livestock or firing deadstock, nothing of value to be left for the foraging army.

Clergy and other worthies would act as shepherds and superintendents, and it was trusted that on the receipt of an alarm, regularity, sobriety and seemliness would characterise the comportment of the villagers. More followed in the same vein, calm, ordered and clear, but underlying all was awful reality: that the defences of England had failed and a hostile army was at last to take vengeance for centuries of humiliation.

'Sir. The Navy is ready. We've fleets o' the finest battleships as are poised to fall on the invading—'

'Just so, Mr Kydd.' Boyd sighed, and sat down wearily. 'As you shall see later, our squadrons are outnumbered by a margin and are wide scattered. While we have the greatest confidence in them, and recognising Bonaparte faces formidable difficulties, I'm supposing they are overborne and the enemy is able to reach our coasts. In that melancholy eventuality the last service the Navy can do its country is for the small ships to throw themselves before the armada in sacrifice in the hope that the time so dearly bought might—'

He was interrupted by a timid knock at the door. 'Sir, the volunteers?' his lieutenant asked.

'Ah, yes. We'll be down presently.' He moved briskly and scrupulously barred and shuttered the room.

'Volunteers?' asked Kydd, as they clattered down the stairs.

'Do you have any objection?' Boyd said cuttingly. 'The Loyal London Volunteers. These men may well be hazarding their lives in the very near future. To attend a parade seems little enough in return.'

'A parade? In that case, sir, o' course I'll be present,' Kydd hastened to say.

Mollified, Boyd went on, 'It's a duty to be performed by those in the Admiralty who can from time to time be spared, as you must count yourself.'

They left the rear of the Admiralty and emerged onto the great expanse of the parade-ground. Opposite, two long lines of redcoats stood motionless. Kydd's mind, though, was on what had been passed on in the office. Of rumours he had had his fill, but he had been shaken to hear the final dissolution of his country discussed in such clinical terms.

A stand was erected on one side, flags of all kinds proudly aloft and flanked by a guard in different regalia. 'Be so good as to make a countenance, sir,' Boyd hissed icily. 'There are those who look to us for assurance in these times.' His own demeanour was pleasant and confident and he stepped out forcefully, Kydd quickly falling in beside him assuming a like pose. They mounted the stage, nodding to the other officers in uniforms of every possible description, and sat nonchalantly. A corpulent and red-faced general puffed on to the central dais, and to the left, with a spirited whirl of drumsticks and crash of cymbals, a band stepped out.

Kydd was in no mood to enjoy the spectacle. As each rigid line passed he mechanically rose and removed his cocked hat with the rest but his mind was elsewhere: to seas far over the horizon where, without a shadow of doubt, the destiny of England was to be decided – not here with these well-meaning amateur soldiers.

At last it was over and they could return. Inside their little room again, Boyd's expression tightened as he pulled out a long map covered with ciphers in red and tiny scrawled notes. He studied it for a moment. 'This is our situation as of this morning. The disposition of our major fleets need not concern you – the Brest blockade with Cornwallis is holding, Nelson is in the Mediterranean and the North Sea Fleet is watching over the Dutch.

'What is of more intimate concern is the disposition of Bonaparte's forces.' He glanced at Kydd, as if weighing what he should say. 'I will not hide it from you, since it is you who must oppose them. The number of line-of-battle ships he has to command is many and will be still greater if Spain moves against us, as it must surely do, but these are matters of high strategy and change from day to day. You will want to know more of what faces your own part of the field. In fine, it is the forefront of the battle. The invasion Grand Army is massing with three corps – Marshals Davout, Soult and Ney, if you're interested – with more than a hundred thousand picked troops ready to embark for the first assault, the Emperor Bonaparte himself to take command. For this, as you will know, he has been fast assembling the largest invasion flotilla in history with specialist craft only some of which we have knowledge of.'

Kydd stared at the map. The dense-packed notations on the French side seemed endless, stretching away down the coastline. Across the Channel – so very close – a single line of dots and squares was brought right up against the line of the sea.

'You will be informed about the details of these vessels later. Take it from me that they are in their thousands and under the direct command of Admiral Bruix, a most experienced and canny officer. They have been in the building at every boatyard and river port on the coast and are being assembled at the main ports. To the north of Cap Gris Nez we have Calais, Dunkirk, Gravelines and so on to Ostend and Flushing, to the south Wimereux, Ambleteuse, Boulogne and Étaples, of which Boulogne has by far the largest concentration.

'Now, Bonaparte is no sailor. He believes the Channel is a ditch to be crossed as in any other military operation, but he will find it very different. However, he is the devil incarnate in the arts of war and is vigorously pursuing great works to assist his cause. For instance, at Boulogne he is creating an embarkation quay a mile long and an artificial basin capable of floating a hundred vessels. He is not to be underestimated – some say he is mad, but it were folly to take him so. With his immense resources, and a surprise by your infernal devices or a feint at Ireland, he could be across in the space of a tide or two only. No, sir, make no error, we're under the greatest peril that ever was . . .'

'Then what is *our* force, sir?' Kydd said evenly.

'Stand fast the main battle fleets, we have three lines of defence against the immediate prospect of invasion,' Boyd replied. 'The first is of sloops and gun-vessels, and it is the inshore squadron of Admiral Keith's Downs command against the French coast,' he added drily. When Kydd held silent he continued, 'The second is of heavier metal and consists of frigates and older sail-of-the-line and it is in with the English coast to contest any landing in the south-east, as well within the Downs command. The third may be found in every creek and estuary from Hartland Point in north Cornwall to Great Yarmouth on our east coast. By this I am referring to the Sea Fencibles, who at this moment are some twenty-five thousand strong and manning some eight hundred vessels of, er, all kinds.'

'Then . . .'

'Quite. The first line of defence must be our strongest. There is no doubt but that you must brace yourself for the hardest-fought struggle this age. I do wish you well in this, Commander.'

'Sir.'

'We'll go on to the details now. Signals, chart emendations, the invasion craft and their characteristics as known, rendezvous positions – there's much to take in. First we shall look into the new signal book . . .'

Kydd was troubled and apprehensive. The mass of operational particulars had done nothing to lessen the effect of Boyd's first words, that this was a situation of such dire consequence as had never been faced by his country before. Now, knowing the details, he was only too aware of the knife edge of chance factors that could determine the future of the world. As head of the entire military strength of the kingdom, the Duke of York had nevertheless solemnly pronounced that, 'The fate of the nation is in the hands of the Navy.' And he must be right: the war was as much the Royal Navy's to lose as Napoleon's to win. A faint-hearted admiral, a deceitful piece of intelligence to send a fleet in the wrong direction, any or all could ensure Bonaparte got the unfettered hours he needed.

Returning to the White Hart, Kydd found his chair and sat quietly, eyes closed, letting the tensions drain. In two days he would return to the Downs and take *Teazer* to war. Would she come through? Would he? The only thing that was certain was that the immediate future would test both himself and his ship to the limit. Half a million Frenchmen under arms opposed by just a few thousand storm-tossed seamen in worn ships . . .

'Do I intrude, brother?' Renzi's gentle voice interrupted his thoughts.

'Oh, er, not so much, m' friend,' Kydd said, opening his eyes. 'Renzi, there's a matter I need to talk to you about, if y' will.' It was coming out too stiffly but he had to say it. 'That is, it touches on the future, you see.'

'Why, certainly,' Renzi said, sitting.

'I've – it's been an . . . interesting week. And now I'm much clearer what is to be facing us.'

'And what is that, pray?'

'If Bonaparte crosses, it's nothing less'n a fight to the finish – the last extremity, if you catch m' meaning.'

'If he crosses.'

'The invasion fleet is ready – near a hundred thousand men in the first assault. Only the Navy to keep 'em off. The first line o' defence is ourselves, m' friend, up against the French coast. If they break through us and launch their monstrous flotilla there's precious little to give 'em pause before they're flooding ashore.'

'If I may be so bold, dear fellow, might I observe that this agitation of spirit is quite unlike the Tom Kydd of yore?' Renzi said lightly, but his eyes were sombre.

'You've not heard what I have,' Kydd retorted grimly, then caught himself. 'No, m' point is this, that shortly *Teazer* is sailing into, um, uncertain times. It's possible we'll need to stand against Bonaparte's whole armada – and, m' dear friend, I'd rather I had no distractions, if you understand,' he said firmly.

'Am I to apprehend . . . ?'

'Nicholas. It's a hard enough thing that I must place *Teazer* athwart their bows. It's hard, but it's necessary. What is not so is that I put the life of a learned scholar to hazard.'

'Are you—'

'Hear me, if you will. You must agree there's clerks a-plenty to be had, but not such a one who's as well a philosophical gentleman, one whose work mankind will soon surely set a value to.' Kydd faced Renzi squarely. 'Nicholas, I'm asking that you take y' books and remain ashore until this business is concluded.'

'That will not be possible,' Renzi said immediately.

'Pray why not?'

'Grant me that my sense of duty is as . . . consequential as your own. And for all that there is little enough I can do for my country in its extremity. All I ask is that I be allowed to continue in my post of duty to the satisfaction of my conscience.'

'It – a time might come that—'

'As we agreed in the beginning, if the ship is in imminent danger of boarding or some such, you may rest assured I will take up arms to defend it. As to the value of my carcass to posterity, you will allow me to be the judge of that.'

'Nicholas, this is not—'

'Dear chap, there is nothing further to discuss. Rather, your attention should be better reserved for the item addressed to you, so recently brought by messenger.' He found a slim packet and handed it over.

It was a substantial sized invitation of stiff pasteboard and edged with gold. A ducal crest was prominent. With it was a hastily scrawled note from Boyd, indicating that he had been able to contrive an invitation for Kydd before he left to an evening of entertainment and fireworks at the estate of the Duke of Stanwick further up the Thames in the country.

A duke! This was far beyond anything Kydd had experienced before and despite his anxieties he felt a quickening

83

of excitement. It was generous of Boyd to think of him. At this level there would be the wealthy and famous, statesmen and nobility, and before going to war, he would at least taste the heady delights of the highest society. 'Nicholas, you must come o' course,' Kydd said impulsively, giving him the card.

Renzi studied it carefully. 'The Duke of Stanwick. At such an eminence you will not lack for fine victuals or the company of ladies of quality, I believe. An evening assembly – it will be by the river in as elegant a landscaping as Mr Repton has ever achieved.'

'Then I'll send to Captain Boyd to say—'

'I thank you, no.'

Kydd drew in his breath sharply. 'At times I find you a mort hard t' fathom, my friend. Here I am asking you to enter in on society again—'

'Again?'

Kydd hesitated only a moment. 'Nicholas, we've been particular friends for a long time. And, please believe me, I've tried to understand, but why it is you've never talked about your family, always kept mumchance concerning your real past, no letters from home, no visits. You're a gentleman o' the first rank, that's plain to any simkin. And on Jamaica I met your brother as is the same. His name is Laughton, so this is yours as well. I know something of the moral feelings that made you turn your back on 'em and go to sea as a foremast jack – but you became a king's officer and can be proud of it, return to your family with honour. Why do you not?'

Renzi sat as still as a statue and did not speak.

'Your family is wealthy, you told me so yourself. So why, then, do you top it the poor scholar? Why do—'

'It is a matter for myself alone, how I conduct my own affairs,' Renzi snapped. 'This is not a subject I wish to pursue.'

Kydd lifted his head and said softly, 'But I rather think we must, sir.'

'Wha—? Your presumption on our friendship is astonishing!'

'Nicholas, if you are to marry my sister one day I'm bound t' satisfy myself on the particulars. No, wait, let me finish. There are those who'd say that any in your circumstance must surely have offended the family honour in a grievous way, and been cast out to fend how they may. I'm not in their number, but I'm most . . . curious as to why your family has so deserted you and why you're so . . . shy of showing your face in society.'

Renzi looked away, then returned Kydd's gaze steadily. 'I can see how it must appear. There is good and proper reason for this, I can sincerely assure you.'

Kydd said nothing.

'Very well.' Renzi sighed. 'If you must. It's easy enough said. I'm the eldest, the heir presumptive. After a disagreeable *contretemps* with my father concerning my unwillingness to give up the sea, he has seen fit to disown me so the estate passes to another. Thus I'm to find my own way in the world, you see.'

'And o' course this is why you cannot—'

'Not at all. My father's character is not unknown to society and no doubt there is ready sympathy to be discovered, but the chief reason for the discretion you have observed is my profound disinclination to come upon my father in a social situation. He is often to be found in London for the season – but I seem to feel secure within the purlieu of the Royal Society.' He smiled thinly.

'Er, it seems hard t' say, but might I ask,' Kydd said awkwardly, 'if you are – if it can be said you're of noble birth?'

'Certainly. My father is the fifth Earl Farndon, of Eskdale Hall in Wiltshire. It cannot escape you that had matters passed in another vein then in the usual course of events, at my succeeding to the title Cecilia might rightly look to the style of the Countess of Farndon, wife of the sixth Earl, and mistress of Eskdale Hall.'

Struck dumb with the revelation Kydd could only wait for Renzi to resume.

'As it is, I shall endeavour to earn her respect and attention with my philosophies, which I am sanguine will bear fruit within a conscionable time. I, er, feel it, um, inappropriate to apprise her of what can never be and most fervently trust and hope she will be satisfied to be – Mrs Renzi.'

For the first time Kydd had full measure of the truth of his friend's moral compass, the deep well of conviction from which he found the strength and courage to see through his logical decisions to their conclusion, and he was humbled.

'Nicholas,' he said, in a low voice, 'as t' that, I c'n tell ye – er, you – for a certainty she will be satisfied, m' very dear friend.'

In the early-summer evening the mist-hung Thames was enchanting, the darkening waters a-glitter with the red of the flaming torches set at the edge of the grassy slopes before the stately hall.

'Your Grace, Commander Kydd of the Royal Navy, shortly to take ship for the French coast.'

Amiable words from the elderly duke, gracious attentions from the duchess, a sweeping curtsy and thoughtful gaze from the eldest daughter, then into the throng, bowing to right and left, making agreeable conversation in the excitement of the warm evening.

Kydd worked his way to the long table of refreshments. A full orchestra arrayed just beyond struck up with a grandiose 'Rule, Britannia' at which he found himself immediately occupied in acknowledging the civil bows in his direction.

Boyd passed, in conversation with an imposing lady whose pearls alone would have been sufficient to buy *Teazer* complete with her crew. She glanced across to Kydd and drew herself up. 'Boyd, is this one of your young men?' she asked imperiously.

'Indeed it is not, milady. This is Commander Kydd of *Teazer*, sloop-of-war.'

'Do you introduce me then, sir,' she commanded.

'Mr Kydd, please meet Lady Musgrave, Dowager Marchioness of Winchcombe.'

'Enchanted, m' lady,' Kydd said with a well-practised leg. 'A fine evening.' He rose to meet a quizzical look.

'A handsome blade indeed. And I vow quite wasted, floating about on all that sea. Tell me, Mr Kydd, are you in London for the season or . . . ?'

'I'm desolated to say, ma'am, but Mr Bonaparte has quite spoiled my plans. I'll be back aboard to sail very soon.'

'A tiresome and disagreeable fellow, your Bonaparte. I say, Canning,' she called to a distinguished gentleman nearby, 'what are we to do with this Napoleon Bonaparte? He's quite ruined Mr Kydd's season.'

'Why, Lady Musgrave, surely the young gentleman is best placed of us all to chastise the fellow.' The man gave an exquisite bow and returned to his conversation.

'Ah – quite. A political can always be relied upon to conjure some words to sport with.' She held up her lorgnette. 'Now, Boyd, I've decided Mr Kydd will escort me tonight. Be off with you!' She took Kydd's arm and they moved away together.

The orchestra was playing a spirited 'Britons Strike Home', and followed with some delicate Purcell. Kydd was swept up in the charged atmosphere, part excitement and part defiance at the fearful danger they were all facing.

Dusk fell, more lights were brought and the hubbub increased. Kydd met statesmen and nobility, ladies of quality and young bucks of the fancy in a dizzying whirl. And with more champagne it was becoming difficult to tell which was the greater reality – this fantastic gathering of jewelled splendour under the torchlight or the private knowledge that he was a sea captain about to go forth to defend his country.

At one point, nibbling at a sweetmeat and listening to a somewhat racy account of a country weekend, he happened to look at the black river sliding silently past and over to the opposite bank. As his vision adapted to the darkness, he saw that hundreds of people were silently standing there, watching. It was unnerving. Were these the common folk come to see the quality on show in their finery? Was he really one of them? With a guilty surge he realised that tonight he must be numbered among the well-born. Indisputably he had now won a place at the highest levels.

He gulped at the heady realisation, but before he could dwell on it there was a tap of the lorgnette on his arm. 'You're not paying me attention, Mr Kydd.' But the frown turned to a smile and she confided, 'A charming picture, is it not? I do so adore these outside entertainments.'

Kydd bowed. 'It is an evening I will not soon forget, m' lady,' he said, with perfect sincerity.

'The best is yet to come – and I do believe that now is the time.'

Mystified, Kydd tried to look knowing but she laughed. 'Mr Handel's music for the Royal Fireworks, silly!' The orchestra began the noble, dignified piece, and Kydd felt peculiarly elevated.

There was general movement to the water's edge. At the bend of the river he saw a procession of boats coming, some with lights strung around the canopy, each with oarsmen in striking uniform keeping perfect stroke. These men need have no fear of the press-gang for they were in the livery of the Worshipful Company of Watermen.

A sudden *whoosh* startled everyone as a rocket soared up from a nearby raft concealed in the blackness of the river. It was the signal for others and, as the music swelled, the sky was lit with vibrant detonations while the reek of powder-smoke drifted down in the still night air.

Caught up with the spectacle Kydd's attention was skywards – but a muttered warning from the marchioness brought his eyes down. To his astonishment all conversation suddenly ceased. From his left the lords and ladies faced the river and were taken one by one in deep obeisance, held motionless.

'The King, you fool!' his companion hissed from the depths of her curtsy. Kydd dropped hastily to one knee, too flustered to recall the details of the elaborate court bow. Head still bowed, he tried to glimpse the royal barge in progress. It approached slowly and majestically, and then, by the sharp flash of firework clusters, Kydd caught sight of the person of his sovereign and liege lord, His Britannic Majesty, King George III of Great Britain and Ireland.

Chapter 4

'. . . and two in irons on account of disagreements with the soldiery ashore.' The first lieutenant finished his report, visibly relieved that Kydd had returned. The crew had been restless, keyed up to play a leading part in a desperate resistance to Napoleon's legions. Instead, they had been idle in *Teazer*, anchored all week in the Downs.

'Very well, Mr Hallum.'

'Er, and we're to hang out a signal immediately you're back on board.'

'Make it so, if y' please.'

Kydd lost no time in going below to get out of his dusty travelling clothes and into his comfortable sea rig. *Monarch* did not bear her commander-in-chief's flag indicating Keith was aboard his flagship so he had no need to report. It would give him time to—

'Mr Hallum's compliments, sir, an' boat putting off from *Actaeon*,' an eager midshipman blurted at the door.

Kydd knew he would not have been disturbed unless the boat was heading for *Teazer* and bore someone of significance.

He lost no time in appearing on deck and watched while the gig threaded expertly towards them through the anchored vessels, her ensign at the transom indicating a king's officer aboard.

'Boat ahoy!' Poulden's challenge was answered immediately from the gig. '*Actaeon*!'

'Mr Purchet!' roared Kydd, for this meant it was the captain of the thirty-eight-gun frigate and, as such, he must be piped aboard by the boatswain.

'Charles Savery, sir,' the man introduced himself, after punctiliously saluting *Teazer*'s quarterdeck. 'If we could repair to your cabin . . . ?'

There, he looked about appreciatively at the quality of the appointments. 'Then you've done well in the article of prize money?' he said equably.

'I've been fortunate enough, sir,' Kydd replied cautiously, aware that his appearance was not best suited to greeting a senior post-captain.

Savery gave a dry smile. 'I'm here on behalf of Admiral Keith to enquire your readiness, he being detained on another matter.' The man was large in *Teazer*'s neat little cabin but his round, jovial features were reassuring.

'Sir.'

'He particularly wishes to assure himself that you are in no doubt concerning the operational details of the Downs command. I take it that you have been well informed at the Admiralty of the strategical objectives?'

'I have, sir – and I will confess, t' me it's been a caution to learn what it is that faces us.'

'Yes, as it would to most, I'd agree. However, to details. You know the strength of Admiral Keith's command?'

'Sir. It was told to me as six o'-the-line, thirty-two frigates and some hundred or more sloops.'

'Quite so. You should understand that the sail-of-the-line are old and unseaworthy, each moored permanently to defend estuaries and therefore unavailable to us. The frigates and sloops you will find anywhere from Selsey in the Channel all the way up the east coast to Scotland, and of those to stand directly against Bonaparte's invasion we are disposed in two divisions.

'One, to defend the Channel coast of England, the other before the French coast. Of the latter we are again of two forces: the first, those sloops and cutters in constant warfare against the enemy flotillas, the other in the form of two more powerful flying squadrons based here at a moment's notice to sail. Your orders, which I have, attach you to the one commanded by myself.

'Both squadrons have the same vital imperative: to harass the invasion craft by any means, clamping a hold on the harbours up and down the enemy coast to prevent their leaving and concentrating in overwhelming numbers at the main invasion ports. I have to remind you that there is a deeper duty, Mr Kydd, which is to immediately apprise the commander-in-chief of any intelligence that bears on the deployment and motions of the invasion fleets.'

'Aye aye, sir.'

'And especially should they sail on their enterprise. Neither ship nor man should be spared in the need to raise the alarm.'

'May I know, sir, what's t' be our action here consequent on receiving this?'

'The first intelligence of an invasion fleet at sea is to be conveyed to Deal. There, the shutter telegraph will have the news to the Admiralty in ten minutes. At the same time we have General Craig's flags. These are a chain of posts on church steeples and similar that constantly fly a white flag.

Receiving word of an invasion, they will be replaced by a red, which will be the signal to loose the messengers, picked men whose duty it is to set forth on horseback, fly inland and raise the alarm. At night we shall have beacons of furze faggots on hilltops as will instantly call the volunteers to arms and set in motion the evacuation plans – but the details of that we can leave to the military.'

'Sir.'

'To return to our own operations. You're to maintain at all times sea and ordnance stores conformable to a two-hour notice to sail, and when at alert, a watch of the hands closed up at stations for unmooring, yourself and principal officers on board.'

'At alert, sir?'

'Wind and tide favourable for a sortie, an intelligence that Bonaparte is contemplating a descent. The signal tower hangs out a red warning pennant with a gun – you'll see all this in the orders.'

'I understand, sir.'

'To the squadron instructions. You'll observe that there's little enough on manoeuvres and signals. This is because when we shall be called upon for service it will of a surety be a pell-mell action as will not be of a character to allow the forming of line and so forth.'

Savery spoke calmly, but there was no mistaking the icy determination. 'As well, of course, we are all of different sailing qualities and in this I will be clear. At an alarm, the duty of every captain is to crowd on sail as best he might to close with the enemy, not an instant's delay. How this is achieved is of secondary consideration.'

'Sir.'

'We are all of one band and must rely on each other – in

this you will see each must trust the other in the prime cause. No signals, no permissions, no hesitation. Lay yourself alongside an enemy and you will have fulfilled your duty, sir.'

It was a level of trust in a commander that Kydd had never encountered before: to rely implicitly on a subordinate's tactical judgement, seamanship and brute courage without issuing a direct order, this was what it was to be a sea officer of such a supremely professional navy. 'Aye aye, sir,' Kydd responded. 'You may rely on *Teazer* and her company.'

'Very well. Do complete your stores and, as of noon tomorrow, consider yourself under orders. Er, and it would be my pleasure to see you at our little gathering in the Three Kings at seven tonight. You'll find some of the other captains of the flying squadron there and they'll be pleased to meet you.'

In the early afternoon Kydd went ashore with the purser and Renzi. He wanted to inspect the capability of the King's Naval Yard in Deal and also to see something of the town.

He had read the orders. Keith's were straightforward and to the point, with no duty explicit other than the defence of the realm in so far as it meant harrying the enemy by every means possible. The usual commander-in-chief's Fighting Instructions were almost non-existent, confirming Savery's earlier comments that a grand fleet action was not likely – for the moment.

Savery's orders, too, were sparse, emphasising individual initiative and deprecating caution but with the proviso that the preservation of his ship was a central concern for every captain. Throw himself at the enemy or hold back: it would be Kydd's decision. Kydd realised that Keith's constant fear would be that his forces would be so whittled down by taking the war to the enemy shore that at a sudden invasion breakout they would prove of insufficient numbers.

It was a warm, sunny afternoon and, with the breezy north-westerly a foul wind on the French coast, there was little likelihood of an alert. Kydd walked quietly with the other two to the King's Naval Yard, letting the character of the place seep in.

Deal was a curious place, a town at a seemingly random position along a lengthy stretch of flat shoreline, nestled right up to a shingle beach. It was said to be one of the biggest ports in England – yet it had no harbour.

But there were reasons for its existence there: the lethal Goodwin Sands offshore were also a barrier to Channel storms and the ships that gathered in its embrace, waiting for a fair wind, needed provisions, stores and chandlery. Passengers favoured boarding their ships at Deal, thereby avoiding the tedious river trip to London. With naval forces to support in addition, the town was lively and prosperous.

The King's Naval Yard at one end of the waterfront was impressive, with sawpits, smith's shops, sail lofts and the like. A ship could be victualled for an entire ocean voyage from the brewhouses, compendious storehouses and the bakery producing vast quantities of ship's biscuits. Yet without a harbour – no quays, jetties or wharfs – tons of stores, masts and yards, weighty lengths of new-spun cordage, all had to be taken out to the ships in boats.

This meant that the heavy craft must be manhandled down to the water over the steep shingle, loaded and, after delivery, heaved back up again. At the yard there were eight slipways, oaken balks settled well in with a massive capstan at the top of each. Kydd watched as a three-ton frigate launch was hauled up for repair. Even with thirty men at the capstan and others steadying the boat it was a hard grind.

Their business concluded, the Teazers returned to their ship. Kydd knew he had paperwork to deal with but felt restless. He went to the shrouds and gazed out across the sparkling sea to the hard, clean line of the horizon where the distant sombre headlands of France were stark and clear.

There was now no doubt: the gathering storm that was about to break on England could be stopped by only one agency, the Royal Navy. *Teazer* was at the cutting edge, the furthest forward she could be on the field of battle. And Kydd was her captain.

'Ah, Mr Kydd, come meet this merry band of mariners!' Savery said heartily, stepping back from the fireplace. A half-dozen officers looked at him inquisitively. 'Commander Kydd is new-joined in *Teazer*, brig-sloop, from the Channel Islands,' he boomed. 'Claims he wanted a more *interesting* station.'

There were murmurs of welcome and a shuffling to allow him a sight of the fire.

'This is Commander Dyer, of *Falcon*, ship-sloop.'

A cautious-looking older officer nodded.

'And L'tenant Keane, *Locust*, gun-brig . . .'

The cheerful, red-faced young man winked at him playfully.

'L'tenant Mills out of *Bruiser*, gun-brig.'

The big man grunted defensively. 'Service?'

'Oh, North American station t' begin with,' Kydd said amiably. There would apparently be no standing on ceremony in this company. 'The Med,' he added, 'and the Nile,' he finished lightly.

There was a general stir. 'Doubt we can find anything to top that, Mr Kydd,' said Keane, respectfully.

'I'm not so sure,' Mills said forcefully. 'Boney's down on 'em hard if they don't put on a brave show defendin' afore their own soldiers on the shore. Why, in that mill we has last month off Calais . . .' The talk ebbed and flowed.

The Three Kings, like so much of Deal, was on the edge of the waterfront, its entrance set at right angles for shelter. The naval officers favoured rooms to seaward that looked out over the Downs and, in the strengthening north-westerly, the windows shook and rattled.

Savery glanced out to sea at the miles of bobbing ships and white caps, then suggested, 'Cards, gentlemen? No alarums to be expected in this blow.' There was a general move to the table. 'I do hope the claret is agreeable to your taste, Mr Kydd,' he said, as the cards were cut. 'For our Friday gathering we make it a point that the enemy provides for our wine. Out of a prize, of course.'

Kydd did not shine at cards; his heart was not in it. His memory refused to take note of which had been successively dealt and he was regularly trumped. In this company, however, it was no chore, and gave him an insight into the personalities of those with whom he would go to war.

Savery was cool, precise and deadly, clearly enjoying the exercise. Keane was impulsive but ingenious, while Mills was stolid but infinitely patient, marshalling his assets until he could bang down his winning hand with a colourful oath.

It was an experience more pleasurable than he had expected: there was relief to be had from sharing anxieties and fears with those who were in the same position as him, and he took strength from the sense of brotherliness in adversity, of fellow warriors awaiting the dawn.

*   *   *

97

The following morning the wind still held to a north-westerly but had moderated somewhat. There was no alert at the semaphore tower and Kydd held court with Hallum and Purchet over how best to bring the ship to a knife edge of readiness.

It was the age-old problem in war; men raised to a nervous pitch of skill and expectations, then forced to idleness while waiting for the enemy's next move. Traditional make-work employment in harbour centred around cleaning and bright-work, but nothing could be more calculated to dull the spirit; more warlike tasks, such as attending to the gunner's store, had long since been completed to perfection. With a fine edge on every cutlass, pistols and muskets flinted and tested, shot brought to an impressive roundness by careful chipping with a rust-hammer, there was little more that Kydd could think of to do.

Poulden knocked tentatively at the door. 'Not sure as what t' do with this'n,' he said, holding out a paper. 'Mr Calloway says ye'd be interested.'

Kydd read it and chuckled. 'Why, this is just the medicine for the harbour mullygrubs! Gentlemen, your attention, please . . .' Lieutenant Keane and HM gun-brig *Locust* were issuing a challenge-at-arms to HMS *Teazer* for the honour of hoisting a 'Cock of the Downs' for the better ship.

Locust lay a quarter of a mile to the eastward, moored, like *Teazer*, head to wind. Keane was proposing a contest of boarding – the very proficiency that would be so needed in the near future. Kydd read aloud the challenge: it was to be undertaken from an eight-oared pinnace, the only boat held in common by both sides, the object being to haul down the other's colours in the face of various unspecified discour-agements, then return.

There were some interesting provisos. Boarders were to be fully 'armed' and might not enter at any point between the quarterdeck and fo'c'sle. The winners would be the first to return to their own ship and triumphantly re-hoist their own colours to the masthead. And, to prevent later recrimination, the respective captains would lead the boarders.

'An impudence!' spluttered Hallum. 'They can't just—'

But Kydd had made up his mind and turned to Poulden. 'Mr Calloway is t' hoist *Locust*'s pennant over the "affirmative", if y' please,' he said firmly.

It was well conceived. Distance to cover under oars was equal, as were the number of men carried in the boats. Bearing arms and coming aboard only over the bow or stern meant a boarding under realistic conditions and discouragements would add the necessary incentive to haste.

Recalling Keane's confidence, Kydd grinned. He would be leading the Teazers and it was fairly certain that the young officer had not heard of his own years as a young and agile seaman . . .

With boats in the water in deference to *Locust*'s lack of the new-fangled davits, it needed only the signal to start. *Actaeon*'s gig arrived and Savery, suitably grave as befitted an official umpire, proceeded to an inspection of *Teazer*'s boarders.

'A fine body of men, Captain!' he pronounced. They were not the words Kydd would have used of his crew of desperadoes in every kind of piratical rig clutching their wooden 'cutlasses' and grinning at each other in anticipation.

'Into your boats!'

Kydd settled at the tiller and tried not to beam back at Stirk, gunner's mate, and a seaman who went back to his earliest time at sea. Ready with his grapnel in the bows he snapped. 'Toss oars!' In obedience to the 'rules' oars were thumped down and held vertically as a sign that the boarders were standing by. Savery sighted over at *Locust*: their boat was in similar readiness.

'Fire!' A swivel gun manned up in the maintop cracked out but the sound was almost drowned in the storm of cheering from the spectators. Kydd's urgent roar sent oars thudding down between the thole pins and the boat slewing round to leap ahead, straight as an arrow, for the trim gun-brig.

The Locusts were in view almost at once, her captain crouched, urging on his crew like a lunatic and coming on at a dismaying rate. It was not Kydd's way to shout at men doing their best but he quickly found himself leaning forward and berating them as lubbardly old women and a hopeless parcel of gib-faced mumpers. The resulting expressions of delight seemed to indicate it might have been expected.

As the pinnaces passed each other halfway, yells of derision were hurled across. Keane stood precariously and bowed solemnly to Kydd, who couldn't think what to do other than doff his hat in reply. Then it was the final stretch, the seamen panting and gasping with the brutal effort.

Defenders were spaced evenly along the decks of *Locust* and doing suspicious things with sacks. Like *Teazer*, the gun-brig was flush-decked with a continuous deck-line. Her fo'c'sle was rounded and therefore without the usual beakhead with its useful climbing-aboard points. It had been agreed that boarding nettings would not be deployed as inviting damage to His Majesty's sea stores, so it was a choice between bluff bow or sturdy transom.

Kydd made up his mind and went for the stern. Instantly there was a frantic rush along the decks of the brig to take up position to repel boarders. He snatched a glance behind:

the Locusts were heading at breakneck speed directly for *Teazer*'s bows and there was the same mad scramble forward to meet the boarding. He smiled wickedly – it would be a valiant crew who made it to that hostile deck.

Just a few hundred yards away from their goal he weighed up the angles and distances. With *Locust*'s protruding rudder stock, a side-to approach allowing simultaneous exit from the boat would not be possible. Better a head-on one, with Stirk leading the charge up and over that plain sternwork.

They neared, and he spotted defenders hunkered behind the low bulwark. Just before they made ready Kydd twisted to look behind. At the last minute Keane had put over the tiller, shooting under the bowsprit and at full tilt sped down the length of the ship to end up under *Teazer*'s more ornate stern. Grapnels flew up in a perfectly timed—

'Sir!' Poulden's anxious cry brought him back – *Locust*'s humble stern, with its two small windows, was looming above them but before he could act the boat drove head on into her timbers with a rending thump, sending the oarsmen down in a tangle of legs and bodies.

'Go!' Kydd cried hoarsely, from the bottom-boards but Stirk had already hurled his grapnel and swarmed up the line with a roar. He took the contents of a pail of galley slops full in the face, then bilge-water, flour, slush and the like rained down. Stirk let out a howl, but quickly recovered and fought his way slowly up through the deluge. The Teazers were now spurred on with the prospect of revenge, and as Stirk disappeared over the bulwarks he was followed by the rest, with Kydd fighting through the vile onslaught to join him.

On the neat little after-deck the Locusts were waiting with their wooden cutlasses at point, except one sailor who was taken helpless with laughter at the sight of the enemy. It was too much for Stirk who threw himself at the man and, with a show of strength, wrestled him to the side and up-ended him bodily into the sea.

The decks resounded to fierce snarls and the sharp *clik-clok* of wooden combat, but the Teazers' blood was up and it didn't take long to fight through to the mainmast halliards. Guarded by a ring of vengeful seamen, Kydd rapidly hauled down their colours.

Returning to the boat, some jumped headlong into the early summer sea to rid themselves of their ordure, then hauled themselves dripping over the gunwale. 'Move y'selves,' Kydd urged, taking the tiller again.

They stretched out manfully. The contest would not be over until their own colours had been restored. The Locusts, however, were already two-thirds back, well on their way to victory.

When the Locusts drew abreast Kydd's boat to pass, more taunts were thrown. Keane stood up in the boat and bowed low. It was galling to be treated this way again – Kydd spotted a *Locust* flour-bomb among the mess in the bilge, and as Keane straightened his posture, he received it full on the chest.

It burst with a satisfying white explosion and the young man teetered and fell, bringing down his stroke oar and causing the next man to catch a crab, then lose his oar. The boat came to a stop in hopeless confusion while the Teazers savagely saw their chance and threw themselves at their oars.

It was sweet victory! Captain Savery shook his head at the sight of the seamen who heaved themselves aboard but allowed the Teazers triumphantly to haul their colours aloft once more. A crestfallen Keane was summoned back to witness the award to the victor.

'Sir – sir, I . . .'

'Yes, Mr Keane?'

'It wasn't fair!'

Kydd couldn't help it. 'Fortunes of war, old trout!' he rumbled smugly.

Savery held up the trophy, a handsome red-painted mast vane in the shape of a cockerel. 'Cock o' the Downs. And this I award to the rightful winner with the strict injunction: *in hoc signis vincit*!'

'Under this sign go ye forth and conquer!' murmured Renzi, next to Kydd.

With a satisfied smile Kydd stepped forward to accept the prize.

'Not you, sir!' Savery said, in mock horror, snatching away the vane. 'The Locusts are declared victors this day. Come forward and be honoured, Mr Keane.'

'The Locusts sir?' Kydd spluttered. 'I don't understand – we were—'

'Mr Kydd! I have above a hundred witnesses who will swear they saw you resume hostilities on your opponent even while your colours were struck. This is not to be borne, sir. Yet I dare to say you will be seeking a *rencontre* at another date . . .'

The north-westerly eased and veered overnight leaving a fine summer morning to spread its beneficence abroad. But at eleven, as the wind passed into its easterly quadrant, there was the thump of a gun and the red flag of the alert was hoisted. The wind was favourable for the French.

A hurried muster revealed the absence of the gunner and his mate at the King's Naval Yard and a victualling party at the storehouse. Both midshipmen were dispatched with trusties to find them post-haste and *Teazer* moved to sea watches.

Before noon her complement was entire and the ship ready for sea; lying to a ready-buoyed single anchor, sails bent on to yards, her broadsides primed and waiting. Kydd's eyes turned to *Actaeon*. The first sign of an alarm might be the sudden blossoming of a signal at the halliards and a warning gun. Then the flying squadron would be streaming instantly to sea.

But the day wore on. Was this to be their entire existence, to lie waiting at a split yarn? It could be days, weeks, before the French made their move to sea.

At sunset the men were piped to supper; at least here they would eat well, fresh greens and regular meat from the garden county of Kent. And Renzi was clearly content with his lot: little ship's business to do and a stand of books to devour that would not disgrace a bookseller.

Kydd vowed to find fresh ways to keep the men occupied and in fighting trim, but for now he turned in early and drifted into sleep.

'Sir! Mr Kydd, sir!' called an anxious Moyes. As mate-of-the-watch he was confronted with the old naval dilemma. He had been sent to wake an officer, but if he shook him this might in theory be construed as laying hands on a superior, with all the dire penalties that the act entailed.

Kydd propped himself up in his cot and rubbed his eyes. Moyes was streaming water from his oilskins; it must be dirty weather topside, although the ship's gentle motion did not indicate a blow. 'What o'clock is it?'

'Middle watch, sir, an' *Actaeon* is hanging out three lights with a gun.'

All captains!

'I'll be up directly. Rouse up a boat's crew and have the gig in the water immediately.'

'Aye aye, sir.'

Moyes disappeared, considerately leaving his lanthorn, and Kydd thudded to the deck, shaking his head to clear it of sleep.

'Cast off!' he growled, after they had entered the boat. He had only a sea-coat over his nightdress and maddeningly the light rain trickling off his hat found several ways to penetrate to his sleep-warm body. But he knew there could only be one reason for the urgent summons.

The boat hooked on and he heaved himself up the rain-slick side of the frigate, noting bustle through the open gunports. The ship was fully awake.

Savery lost no time. When all were assembled he snapped, 'An alarm, gentlemen. Sir Sidney Smith has sent urgent word of an invasion flotilla slipping out from Ostend, taking advantage of this nor'-easterly and thinking to join with others in Calais and Boulogne. It must be stopped.'

There were grave expressions on the faces of those who stood about, wet and drooping and in all manner of strange night attire.

'This is no small force. It numbers over sixty craft and, being a joint Dutch force, is defended by the Jonkheer ver Blaeu, who, I might remind you, learned his trade under de Winter at Camperdown.'

Kydd would never forget the ferocious scenes of combat that day – the British had been victorious, but the Dutch had fought like demons showing the old spirit that had seen them lay waste in the Medway the century before.

'They are even now at sea, proceeding down the coast

towards Dunkirk, Ambleteuse – who knows? It seems to be an attempt to overwhelm us with numbers and I expect a stiff fight. There will be no help from Sir Sidney as he is heavily engaged, but he offers to break off and come to our aid if requested.' His demeanour gave little doubt as to the likelihood of this.

'Have we reports of the type of vessel we're likely to find, sir?' said Keane brightly.

'At least thirty, forty gun-vessels – anything from your *chaloupe canonnière* to a full-rigged *prame* to be expected, I believe. Your duty is the same in any case. Now, to business. 'The squadron will sail without delay with the goal of an intercept off the French coast at dawn—'

'We sail in darkness?' Dyer said, in a tone of disbelief. 'The Goodwins are—'

'In these winds we cannot sail north or hazard the Gull passage, therefore we shall go south-about to make our offing. I would have thought it reasonable to stand in that direction for the lights of St Margaret's Bay and thence haul your wind for France?' Savery said irritably.

Kydd's mind raced. If there were clear night waters rather than some eighty or so ships at anchor through which they must pass . . . If the few lights of Deal showing at three in the morning were as well loyally shining at the small hamlet in the great cliffs . . .

'I shall expect the squadron to make rendezvous to the nor'-east of Dunkirk in the morning,' Savery continued. 'Come, come, gentlemen, there's not a moment to lose.' The other business was dispatched rapidly and Kydd returned to find his ship in a scurry of activity.

Teazer slipped her anchor within the hour, the night breeze taking her at some speed through a world of dimly bobbing lights in the pitch darkness with the occasional bulking mass looming of an unlighted vessel.

It was vital not to put the helm over for the reach to seaward too early, for this would bring them to an unpleasant acquaintance with the deadly sands. If left too long, though, it would take more time to beat back up the French coast. And every seaman knew that the slower and more cautious the progress, the more sluggish would be the response at the helm.

Less than an hour passed but it seemed like a lifetime before Kydd felt able to make the move. *Teazer* heeled as she took the wind abeam and struck out into the Channel darkness. It would be entirely by dead-reckoning: a larboard tack for long enough to get them past mid-Channel then a stay about to starboard to put them to weather of the rendezvous when dawn broke.

Log-line, careful sail trim and much discussion of current sets and leeway at different points of sailing: seamanship of the first order was demanded. They were comfortably to seaward of Dunkirk when the first tentative shafts of light from the east promised a fine day to come.

One by one sail was sighted and by full day the squadron was in position: *Actaeon* with the sloops *Teazer*, *Bruiser*, *Falcon* and *Gallant*, with the gun-brigs *Locust*, *Starling*, *Plumper* and others. It seemed a pitiful number to throw before such odds.

They stayed in deep water with the frigate. Then a cutter came racing downwind with 'enemy in sight' fluttering urgently from her halliards in the morning breeze. From directly in the wind's eye a handful of low sails appeared out of the haze. More and more came into sight, then still more, until it seemed impossible there was room for others.

Kydd was conscious of what the chart had shown about

the coast – endless hard sandbanks strung out to parallel the shore as if to ward off marauders, a fearsome threat to any trespasser. There was no point in beating towards. It would be better to let them come, then fall on them somewhere off Dunkirk. He raised his telescope and scanned the oncoming armada. Every kind of rig was there, luggers of all descriptions, brigs, even fully ship-rigged vessels, advancing inexorably in a vast swarm of sail.

Then he saw the invasion craft he had been told about: the long and low *péniche* under a single lugsail, the Swedish-designed shallow-draught *crache feu* type that carried frigate-sized twenty-four-pounders on slides and the various *chaloupes canonnières*, which, while smaller than *Teazer*, were armed with guns of much larger calibre.

The transports were gathered in the centre, seemingly anything that swam, including many of the Dutch *schuyts* used in the rivers and shallows of the Netherlands and ideal for close inshore work.

He wondered what the soldiers packing their decks would think of the ships lying in wait for them. They would know them to be the same ships that had cleared the seas of every French battle-fleet sent against them, that had destroyed and captured their ships as they watched impotently from the beach. But now, seeing the crowds of French and Dutch vessels around them and so few English ones ahead, there could only be one answer: contempt, and the conviction that in the face of such numbers the English ships would just step aside.

There was no indication of faltering among the leaders of the armada. As *Teazer* neared, the throng seemed to take on an order of its own, the larger ships assuming seaward positions to shepherd along the lesser, which were sailing as close to the shore as they could.

Kydd swallowed. Now was the time to manoeuvre round and select where he would direct his charge into the enemy. At this angle of the wind it would have to be somewhere off Dunkirk – but would they simply slip away into the port and wait it out?

The first of the vessels was approaching the port entrance: if he did not make his lunge now it might be too late. Along the decks, long closed up for action, his ship's company looked gravely at him.

'Mr Kydd, sir?' Dowse said quietly, interrupting his thoughts.

'Um – yes?'

'Sir, it's my opinion th' tide's not going t' allow us in, without we know th' ground better.'

'The Frenchy thinks it safe enough.'

'Aye, sir,' the master said patiently. 'He's in a mort deeper water – the Passe de l'Est as goes past th' entrance. A'tween us an' them will be y'r Banc du Snouw, Binnen Ratel, all shiftin' hardpack sand as at this tide-state is shoaling fast.'

Was this why the others in the squadron were still hove to, waiting?

The first enemy vessels reached the harbour's cramped entrance – and passed it. The wily Dutchman in command had known of the inshore passage and taken full advantage of the wind's direction being the same as the ebbing tide; in the protection of the offshore sandbanks he was making fast sailing towards his ultimate destination: Calais and Boulogne.

Now there was a chance: once past, they had to leave the protection of the sandbanks, which did not extend any further. And the little haven of Gravelines on the way was near useless on an ebbing tide, so somewhere off the low, endless sand dunes between Dunkirk and Calais, action must be joined.

The sun was high and warm to the skin when the time came. Careful bearings of the tall, four-square tower in the centre of the town told Kydd and the other members of the squadron when the armada was finally clear of the protecting shoals. First away was *Locust*, her red cockerel brazenly at the main-mast head, with *Bruiser* and *Falcon* close behind then *Teazer* joining the rush in an exhilarating charge straight into the heart of the enemy.

Kydd willed his mind to icy coolness.

The swarm resolved to individuals: the *schuyt*s or the *prame*? The first guns opened up but *Teazer* would hold her fire to make every shot count. The enemy sloops came round to meet them but, surprisingly, showed no inclination to close. Kydd looked back: *Actaeon* was astern – the biggest threat, she must be their target. He grinned savagely. All the better to allow *Teazer* to get among the flotilla.

Locust disappeared in a haze of gunsmoke into the very centre and Kydd made up his mind. 'We take the *schuyt*s and draw the big 'uns towards us. Lets the cutters and gun-brigs have a chance.'

Teazer made for a gaggle of four ahead. White splashes kicked up around her. It was small-calibre: the bigger guns they carried must be on crude slides and could not bear on them. Then a vicious whip of bullets all around him showed that they were making up for it with musketry.

Kydd tested the wind once more – fair and brisk on the larboard beam. 'Bring us astern o' the last,' he ordered calmly. The *schuyt*s maintained course, unsure of his inten-tions, and he was quickly able to reach his position. Swinging round before the wind he tucked in astern of the last, then surged forward to overtake the craft on its shore-ward side.

'Fire!' he barked. The forward half of the starboard guns smashed into it. Screams and hoarse shouts came from beyond the choking mass of powder-smoke and then they were up with the second, and the after half of the guns opened up.

The next in line jibbed in fear at what was bearing down on it. *Teazer*'s helm went over and she plunged between the opening gap to the seaward side and, with a furious spin of the wheel, straightened and passed the next *schuyt*. The same trick again – but this time it was the unused guns of the larboard side that did the execution, taking the next with the forward guns and the last of the four with the rest.

Beside Kydd, Purchet pounded his fist into his palm. Then, in the hellish noise, Hallum snatched at Kydd's sleeve and pointed. Looming out of the roiling smoke and appallingly close, a powerful *prame* as big as a frigate was lunging towards them.

As *Teazer* passed beyond the *schuyt*s the *prame* slewed about parallel to bring its full broadside of twenty-four-pounders to bear – at near point-blank range it would be slaughter, and with *Teazer*'s guns not yet reloaded they could not fire back.

Kydd agonised as he waited for the eruption – his skin crawled as the moment hung – then suddenly he swung round to look in the other direction. As he suspected, a lumbering transport was to leeward; the *prame* dared not open up on *Teazer* while it was in the line of fire.

Light-headed with relief, Kydd tried to think of a way out. They couldn't stay with the transport for ever. It was hard to concentrate as a chaotic swirl of noise and smoke battered in on his senses but the matter was shortly taken out of his hands. With an avalanche of muffled thuds and a sudden rearing of gun-smoke on the other side of the *prame*, the ship-sloop *Falcon* had taken her chance to attack while its attention was on *Teazer*.

The *prame* wheeled about on its tormentor and *Teazer* pulled into the clouds of powder-smoke rolling downwind from the two. Suddenly, with a hideous splintering crash, they were careering along the side of a ship – timbers smashing to wreckage, sails snatched and torn away, ropes parting with a vicious twang in a long agony of collision.

They stopped, two ships locked together in a hideous tangle and, for a moment, a shocked quiet descended. 'It's a Frenchy!' someone screamed, and broke the spell. Kydd fought to keep cool: this was an enemy and it was bigger than *Teazer*. 'Teazers t' board!' he yelled. 'T' me, the boarders!' He whipped out his precious fighting sword and leaped on to the enemy deck where *Teazer*'s bulwarks had been beaten flat.

The French gun crews gaped at him, caught off-balance and dazed by the sudden turn of events. The first to recover was a dark-featured officer with a red sash who snarled in anger and rushed at him, swinging a massive sword. Kydd dropped to one knee with his own blade above his head. The weapons met in a clash, the shock numbing his arm, but his fine Toledo steel held and deflected the blow to one side.

He let the stroke spend itself and, with a dextrous twist, got inside it and thrust out savagely, taking the man in the lower body. With a howl of anguish he dropped his sword and clutched at the skewering blade, then crumpled, knocking Kydd sprawling and tearing it from his grasp.

The *Teazer* gun crews had snatched up rammers, tomahawks, anything to hand and were racing toward the unarmed

Kydd. With an urgent thump on the deck, Renzi arrived first, taking position over Kydd with a boarding pike out-thrust, its lethal point questing for the first to dare an assault.

The Teazers soon had their bridgehead; the disorganised gun crews saw no chance against fully equipped boarders and skidded to a stop. The rush turned to a rout.

More Teazers arrived and the ship was theirs. Trembling with reaction to the near-disaster, Kydd sent parties to secure the vessel and looked about the battlefield. The action had moved away from them: the flotilla was doggedly pressing on towards Calais, and the English, firing wildly, were staying with them.

He looked across at *Teazer*. The wreckage seemed confined to the bulwarks and fore-shroud channels but there was a trail of dismounted guns and, at more than one spot, the dark staining of blood on the decking.

Purchet loped up and reported, 'Spars still sound, sir, but th' standin' rigging t' larb'd is in a sad moil.'

'Get us free, quick as y' like, Mr Purchet. Stoppers and doubling – anything as'll see us under canvas again.'

He looked out at the broader battle scene. *Actaeon* was beset by four large sloops and nearly hidden by towering clouds of powder-smoke but gun-flashes regularly stabbed through from her and, as Kydd watched, a mast on one of the sloops descended and the damaged vessel fell away.

The enemy did not seem inclined to pay attention to the two vessels locked together so they had a chance. The Royal Marines took charge of prisoners while the entire seaman complement of *Teazer* swarmed over the rigging aloft, passing stoppers that joined the severed ends of ropes and adding relieving tackles to weakened sections.

When it was complete Kydd sent Hallum to limp back in

the prize while he considered the state of *Teazer*. At a pinch they could keep to the wind, particularly running large as the flotilla was doing, but effectively they had lost all except one of the larboard guns and were open to the weather and small-arms fire along that side. And they had numbers away as prize-crew.

Kydd watched the receding battle. He had been shaken by the savagery of the fighting, the desperate flinging of their force into the midst of the armada. And the French were far from running: they were staying together to brute it through and add this huge number of invasion craft to their concentrations.

There was no alternative but to do his duty. With Kydd warily keeping an eye on the makeshift repairs aloft, *Teazer* set out after them but well before they were able to overhaul the rear the enemy entered Calais roads and the unassailable shelter of the fortress batteries.

Regrouping beyond the treacherous offshore ground of the Ridens de la Rade the flying squadron hove to; it seemed that the Franco-Batavian flotilla had indeed won precious miles from Dunkirk towards their eventual destination, Boulogne, and all the squadron could now do was to leave a pair of watching cutters and return to the Downs.

Yet within the hour there was movement: incredibly the flotilla was putting out once more. It was no feint: the canny Dutch commander had merely added to their number by drawing in those who had sheltered in the port earlier. Now nearly a hundred sail were issuing out, steadily heading south-west.

It was an audacious and cynical move: they had no doubt reasoned that while the English were occupied in their butchery of the unfortunates, there would be left many more to plough on regardless and make their destination. The simple outworking of time and numbers would ensure that by far the majority survived.

It was still before noon when heavy guns thundered out from the great citadel and no less than five forts. Falling back, but warily pacing with them out to seaward, the squadron waited until the strung-out flotilla was clear of the port and its defences, then one by one selected a victim and once more sailed in to close with the enemy.

Teazer was no longer in the best shape for another deadly action but the stakes were extreme. Therefore, with torn sails and trailing ropes, she set her bowsprit resolutely at the foe – three of the flat-bottomed *bateaux canonnières*, equipped with a stern ramp to take on even field guns and horses. These were therefore of prime value to Bonaparte and worth any sacrifice.

At this point, with fewer sandbanks, the immense sea cavalcade huddled close inshore. It seemed incongruous to join battle before the mussel beds and lowly dunes, and with no larboard guns *Teazer* must work some miracle to come inside them to fight.

But as she made her approach guns opened up – guns that had no right to be there. Shot tore up the sea all around and two heavy thumps told of hits – but from where?

Through his telescope Kydd saw troops of horse artillery cantering up, unlimbering their field guns on the crest of the dunes and blazing away. It was an intelligent use of the immense military machine being assembled but it would only serve while they were close in with the land. Beyond the range of the fortress on the heights of Cap Blanc Nez there were devilish offshore hazards, which the French called 'The Barrier,' that would force the armada miles out to sea.

The guns ashore fell silent as the range widened and the predators closed in. It was close, vicious and bloody work – the invasion flotilla must be stopped and nothing would be spared. The first *bateau* dug in its steering oar and slewed around at *Teazer* – a field artillery piece was tied down with ropes on its clumsy foredeck but when it fired, the ball reduced *Teazer*'s quarterdeck rail to flying splinters, and ended the life of the lively and willing Philipon, an able seaman who had been with them since the Channel Islands.

It was an heroic act by the Frenchman for they could not reload the piece: they must wait while *Teazer* stood off and destroyed them – except that her own guns on that side were useless. The two vessels faced each other defiantly but impotently until Kydd took his ship under the stern of the other and crushed the little craft with a single broadside.

The next *bateau* sheered away cravenly inshore, taking the ground a full mile out in a shuddering stop, the shock canting the long vessel's bow skyward. Tumbling over the side in a panic-stricken flight the crew stumbled away.

A *chaloupe* appeared from the smoke, her eighteen-pounders opening on *Teazer* as soon as she appeared. The shots went wild and it disappeared as quickly as did the *bateau* they had been ready to engage.

The din and acrid reek of powder-smoke drove in on Kydd – where was the next target? For a short time he could see *Locust* hammering away frantically at two *chaloupes* assaulting her but there was nothing Kydd could do for them and smoke drifted across to hide the scene.

An unknown vessel lay stopped ahead, only a single mast left standing. Men swarmed over the wreckage like ants – was it *Bruiser*? They had to take their chances for Kydd's duty was to engage the flotilla and there inshore was another *bateau canonnière* – but beyond lay the dour heights of Cap Gris Nez.

As if to mark the invisible boundary that had been crossed, a plume of water shot up – and another, and more as the ball skipped towards them. It was from the heavy guns on the dark heights of the iconic headland, and the mass of sails quickly converged on its deep-water flanks – it was now all but over.

Held off by the formidable ring of iron, the flying squadron stayed out of range but kept with the armada as it rounded the cape and, with the last of the tide, passed into the safety of the harbours of Ambleteuse and Wimereux, their goal of Boulogne just six miles further on.

It was not yet noon on a beautiful early-summer's day: from first to last the action had taken just a few hours, but now it was time to leave.

Chapter 5

The summer sun was high in the sky when HMS *Teazer* made her way home with the others to find her anchor buoy and pick up her moorings once again. It was still warm and beneficent when Kydd returned to his ship after an immediate conference aboard *Actaeon*.

Teazer was to be stood down from the flying squadron due to battle-damage – much of her larboard bulwarks beaten flat and guns dismounted – and it would be several weeks before she could look to active service again.

Kydd felt the need to stay on deck in the brightness of the day, with the pleasant sight of the town and its bustle, the constant to-and-froing of scores of ships about their occasions – reality, normality. But a captain could not idly pace among the men as they worked. Reluctantly, he went to his cabin and found Renzi at the table scratching away at papers, the interminable loose ends after any scene of combat.

'A hot action,' he said, looking up.

'Yes,' Kydd muttered, slumping into his chair. Only that morning his ship had been plunged into a desperate fight for survival and here she was, an hour or two later, battered and sore but lying to single anchor in sun-kissed tranquillity.

Seeing Kydd's drawn face, Renzi laid down his pen.

Kydd went on sombrely, 'As it was necessary, m' friend.' The sheer savagery of the encounter and the seemingly unstoppable determination of the vessels assembled for their grand enterprise had unnerved him. He had also found himself quite affected by the death of young Philipon, a gay, laughing soul now removed from the world of men, and by the sight of *Locust*'s pinnace on its way past them to land the pitiful figure of her captain, writhing under a blanket and mortally wounded. Later, no doubt, others from the naval hospital would be making their last journey on earth to the austere St George's church in Deal.

'". . . these are times to try men's souls – but he that stands it now, deserves the love and thanks of men and women" . . .' Renzi murmured.

'What?' said Kydd, distracted.

'Oh, naught but the rantings of an unfashionable rogue of fevered times now past.'

Kydd sighed. 'Who is your philosopher, then, Renzi?'

'His name, you may have heard it, Tom Paine.'

Kydd allowed a twisted smile. He had borne the name of the revolutionary since birth, his parents having once heard the great man speak and been caught up in the fiery rhetoric. 'So the villain can conjure some right words, I'm to say.' He sighed heavily. 'But its hard t' take. After as grim a fight as ever we've been in, what've we won? Naught but a handful o' Boney's flotilla. They say that, with this last, he's now above one thousand craft near Boulogne.' So many vessels with but one purpose – and he had seen for himself how powerless they had been against mere scores.

*　　*　　*

119

'Mr Hallum, I've a yen to step ashore. The ship is yours.' Kydd picked up his walking cane and clapped on his tall yellow beaver. Renzi was delayed with ship's business and, anyway, he felt the need to walk alone, to let the calm tranquillity of the land work on his soul.

With a lazy surf hissing in the shingle, he was carried ashore safe and dry by his boat's crew. To the left was the King's Naval Yard, with its Admiralty telegraph to London even now clattering away, and the smoky fumes of the smithy spiralling up behind the high wall.

To the right, a long street faced the beach, the inns and taverns giving way to substantial buildings further on and the bright, hazy prospect of Pegwell Bay in the distance. Kydd struck out briskly, nodding to passing gentlemen and doffing his hat politely to promenading ladies, no doubt passengers from the Indiaman anchored offshore.

He turned inland towards the town proper, entering Middle Street: here, there were courts and passageways with cobbled streets and rich merchants' houses. He strolled on to High Street, with its bustling shops and markets, and his eyes caught a placard in one window:

> *. . . And our brave Sons invite the foe to come;*
> *For they remember Acre's valiant fight,*
> *When Britons put the vaunting Gaul to flight;*
> *Remembering too, Nile's Battle . . .*

He had been at both and felt a stab of pride. Then he noticed a recruiting poster:

Brave Soldiers! *Defenders* of YOUR COUNTRY! The road to glory is open before you – Pursue the great career of your

Forefathers, and rival them in the field of honour. *A proud and usurping TYRANT* (a name ever execrated by Englishmen) dares to *threaten our shores* with INVASION, and to reduce the *free-born Sons of Britain* to SLAVERY . . . The Briton fights for his *Liberty and Rights*, the Frenchman for *Buonaparte* who has robbed him of both!

There was a hard gaiety on the air: women sported martial cockades and children strutted about, every gentleman wore his sword. The markets were thronged, and the street cries, as lusty as ever, suggested that none in this town was about to be affected by the awful forces gathering just a few leagues across the water.

The cheerful hustle lifted his spirits. Restored, he threw a coin to a begging child and returned to the seafront. The view from the shore was impressive: the crowding ships in the Downs and, just visible on the horizon, a sable-brown line that was the Goodwin Sands.

Reluctant to quit his view of the sea he strolled along in the warm sunshine and pondered the peculiar difference to be had in perspectives of it: from the rock-still shore, the land-bound saw the line of white waves acting as a boundary between the two worlds, and beyond, the sea's mystery, with ships disappearing so quickly from man's ken over the horizon to far and unknowable regions.

A sailor's prospect, however, was of being borne along on a constantly moving live quintessence without limit, the land an occasional encounter in the endless oceanic immensity.

His steps took him past the King's Naval Yard and on to Deal Castle. Part of a coastal chain put in place by Henry VIII, under much the same invasion threat, the battlements were small, round and squat. They were from an era when cannon had been changing the rules of war but even today they were manned by redcoats and ready for service.

At the top of the shingle, scores of Deal luggers were drawn up before humble cottages and huts, each of which had a capstan to the front with men working on them or just sitting in the sun with a comfortable pipe and baccy. Kydd wandered up. Every tiny sea-place on England's coasts had its own peculiarities and he was curious to see how the unusual steep shingle landings had influenced the boats' construction.

They were all substantial craft, few less than forty feet long and fifteen broad, long-yarded with a square-headed dipping lug-sail and handy mizzen, and remarkably high-waisted. Most had an iron skeg with an eye at the turn of the forefoot to assist in hauling up, and all were bright-sided, the varnish work on them as winsome as a new-fallen horse chestnut.

Eyes turned suspiciously on Kydd as he crunched through the shingle to take in the bluff lines of one, the *Kentish Maid*. He bent double to catch the rise of bilge. As he suspected, the high gunwale was matched by a broad, flat bottom, ideally suited to coming ashore on a steep beach in anything of a sea.

He peeped over the gunwale. It was simply equipped with a small shelter forepeak; it was easy to sense great strength. The boat stank richly of its sea gear. Caressing the sturdy sides in admiration he was startled when a shrill voice challenged him. 'Oi! Th' young man yonder! I seen ye – what are y' doing wi' that boat?'

A wizened but bright-eyed old man sitting on a pair of shipwreck timbers shook a knobby stick at him. Kydd chuckled and went over to him. 'Why, sir, I'm taking m' pleasure in the sight of as fine a barky as ever I've seen. Elm-built, is she?'

The man squinted at him. 'Then who *are* ye, then?'

'M' name is Thomas Kydd. May I know . . . ?'

'Tickle – William Tickle – an' ye hasn't said as why ye're so taken wi' th' *Maid*.'

Kydd had passed an ancient tap-house on the way. 'Sir, if you'd tell me more o' these I'd be honoured t' stand you a glass o' the true sort in the tavern.'

'No.'

'Well—'

'I likes th' prospects here,' Tickle said, waving his stick at the boats drawn up. 'Go to y' tavern an' get me a jorum of ale an' I'll tell ye all there is t' know.'

Kydd returned with a pot-boy and, leather tankards a-flow with dark beer, he learned from the Deal boatman.

'A hard life, t' be sure,' Tickle began. 'Hovellin' an' foyin' is all we got, isn't it? That an' the other.'

'The other?'

'Gift o' the sea. Free tradin', like.'

Smuggling.

'Er, tell me of your foying, Mr Tickle.'

'Aye, well, it's naught but plyin' for trade wi' the merchant jacks out in th' Roads as wants fresh wegetables, dry provisions, y' knows.'

Kydd nodded. There would be many a blue-water merchantman inbound from a lengthy voyage who would be more than willing to pay over the odds for fresh victuals.

'And we'm Channel Pilots o' the Cinque Ports – Trinity lot gives best t' us, any which wants t' try th' Goodwins in a fog.'

'Hovelling – can't say as I've heard of it afore,' Kydd said.

'Then I guess ye haven't been t' sea much. Where ye from?'

'Um, Guildford, Mr Tickle. The hovelling . . . ?'

It turned out to be as colourful and dangerous a sea trade as any he had heard of in his years of voyaging. Thoroughly at home around the treacherous Goodwins, on fine-weather days the hovellers would hoist their distinctive blood-red sails and occupy themselves sweeping the sea-bed close to the great banks for anchors and ground tackle lost in storms. They would sweat to recover them by art and sea craft and either bring them aboard or sling them beneath and return, storing them in an anchor field close to the King's Naval Yard.

On foul-weather days they would keep close watch on the edge of the Goodwins for signs that a ship was dragging her anchors or had lost one and was nervously eyeing the remainder. A stout Deal lugger would then be launched into the violence to take out a complete anchor, weighing tons, along with heavy coils of cable, and offer it to the anxious captain for a handsome fee. It was seldom refused.

That explained the high-sided construction and generous scantlings of these hardy boats. Kydd could only imagine the fearful effort required to set the boats to sea with such a load.

'Why, thank 'ee, Mr Tickle,' he said, happily back to his old self. 'You've quite explained it all for me. I'm much obliged.' He doffed his hat politely and required the old seaman to accept a small contribution in token of the time he had spent.

'How goes it, Mr Purchet?' Kydd asked, looking doubtfully at the cluttered larboard deck. The King's Naval Yard had done well to have five shipwrights and their sidesmen out to them within two days and their clunking and chipping had sounded ever since throughout the daylight hours.

'Main fine, sir.'

It seemed that their primary concern, the slide on which the carronades recoiled, was simple enough to repair, the design being nothing more than a sliding bed on a longer one and secured by a thick pin. The quarterman shipwright was therefore sanguine that *Teazer*'s armament would be whole again within the week. The bulwarks were another matter, seasoned timber of such length apparently not in ready supply and . . .

Kydd promised to take better care of his command in the future and, in the meantime, offered an earnest by which it would appear the timbers would be more expeditiously acquired. It would be a frustrating wait but in Deal rooms were to be had for sea officers at the genteel end of Middle Street, and Kydd established a presence ashore, where Renzi's valuable work on his treatise could be kept in a place of safety.

'Yes, Mr Hallum?' Kydd said, about to step ashore one morning.

'I'm truly sorry to have to report that a midshipman has not returned from leave.'

Calloway, in the Navy since childhood and as loyal as it was possible to be? Or could it be their first-voyage new reefer Tawse, unable to face another bloody action?

'Who is it?'

'Calloway, sir.'

'He's to wait on me the instant he returns on board.' Kydd swore under his breath. There was no possibility of going ashore until this had been resolved, and when Calloway did return an hour later his captain was in no mood for trifling.

The young man stood before him, pale-faced but defiant. 'I'm sorry, Mr Kydd, It's . . . I overslept, is all.'

'Slewed t' the gills, no doubt.'

'I weren't, Mr Kydd!'

'Then pray tell, what tavern-keeper fails t' shake his customers in the morning as will have 'em back on board in time? Or was it—'

'I was – that is, there's this girl I was with and . . .'

'And?'

'Sally an' I, well . . .'

Kydd waited.

'Mr Kydd!' he burst out. 'S' help me, I'm struck on th' girl! She's – she's right dimber an' says I'm the first she's been with, an' she wants t' be spliced to me, and – and . . .'

Biting back a sarcastic retort, Kydd glared at him. 'For an affair o' the heart you'd hazard your chances at the quarter-deck, let your shipmates down? And if there's to be an alarm . . .'

'We're not under Sailin' Orders,' Calloway said doggedly.

'That's not the point, as well you know, younker.'

The young man's eyes dropped, but he went on, in a low voice, 'An' I'm remembering, too, that time in th' Caribbean, you an' Miss Sukey, Mr Kydd . . .'

'How dare you?' Kydd spluttered. 'An' that was afore I had m' step as an officer,' he added unconvincingly, as though it excused everything.

'Sir, I—'

'Be damned to it! I'll not have m' men out o' the ship at this time. There's a hot war out there, in case y' haven't heard.'

The youngster stared obstinately into space and Kydd nearly weakened, but told him, 'Any seaman in your division as overstays his liberty will be served the same way. It's t' be stoppage o' leave for you, Mr Calloway.'

The eyes turned on him in misery. 'But, Mr Kydd, she'll—'

'If you're not on deck assisting the boatswain in ten minutes, I'll double it.'

After the young man had left Renzi looked up from his papers with a wry smile. 'Miss Sukey? In those piping days of our youth I do not recollect our being introduced . . .'

'I do apologise, old fellow. An unfortunate oversight,' Kydd replied sarcastically. 'And might I ask how your letters are progressing?'

Before Renzi could reply there was the thump of an alarm gun.

Kydd hesitated, but for only a moment. It did not include them, for he had not declared ready for sea, but who could stand idle while others threw themselves into battle? 'We must join 'em,' he said forcefully. The larboard carronades were more or less mounted now and the bulwarks – well, they'd rig canvas dodgers or something.

'Hands t' unmoor ship!' he roared up the companionway, having thrown aside his shore clothing for action dress. By the time he reached the deck the ship was in an uproar.

'Mr Hallum, a muster o' both watches after they're closed up, if y' please.' Who knew how many were ashore?

The first of the flying squadron slipped to sea, a game little cutter thrashing out into the overcast for the French coast, followed closely by *Actaeon*. Others loosed sail and joined them, *Teazer* bringing up the rear, still tying off on the improvised bulwarks. It might have been worse: with a two-thirds complement they could maintain fire on at least every other gun and, with no real need to mount long sea watches, they had a chance.

In hours *Teazer* and the others were hove to before Boulogne and telescopes were quickly raised on quarterdecks. At first glance there seemed no threatening movement. Then, from inshore, a small sloop set course under a crowd of sail direct for *Actaeon*. It would be one of the British inshore squadron that was doggedly watching the huge concentration.

'A baneful sight for English eyes,' said Renzi, who generally kept out of sight until the ship was called to quarters.

His station was then on the quarterdeck to record events for the captain.

'Why, t' be sure,' Kydd responded off-handedly. 'And as long as we don't fall asleep, I dare t' say this is where they must remain.'

He grunted and continued to search with his telescope. It was his first encounter with the menacing sights around this premier invasion port. The prospect was awesome. The pale regular shapes of the encampment of the Grande Armée were spread out in an immensity beyond counting, covering the swelling heights of the hills and valleys around the port as far as the eye could see.

This, then, was the reality, the reason for their being: a tidal wave of the finest troops in Europe arrayed in plain sight against them.

The sloop reached *Actaeon* and passed out of sight around her lee. After half an hour a general signal was hoisted: 'All captains repair on board.'

Kydd wasted no time in complying and convened with the other captains in the great cabin. 'I'll be brief, gentlemen,' Savery opened, his features grave. 'It does appear that the final act is at last upon us. We have intelligence that the Emperor Napoleon Bonaparte himself is at this moment in Boulogne.'

There was a stir of apprehension, which was brusquely cut short. 'This is not the first time he has been here – he likes to show himself to his army and to inspect preparations. This is not exceptional. What is unique and disturbing is that this time not only the Emperor but his *entire* military staff has come. Paris is left without a single marshal's baton!'

This was received in utter silence.

'Marshal Ney is here with his corps as are Soult and Davout. The Grand Army is now complete and I don't have to remind you that tomorrow is a new moon, with spring tides, the winds fair for England and the weather holding. Bonaparte has even sent for his brothers Louis and Joseph, now styled princes, and columns are said to be on the march for Boulogne, to a total of at least twenty cavalry squadrons and sixty regiments.' He concluded soberly, 'I can see no reason for this sudden descent on Boulogne other than . . .'

'Lord Keith has been informed, sir?' Kydd asked.

'Of course. He is making his dispositions, but I fear it will be a little time before we might see any reinforcements. Meanwhile, our duty remains as it always has. Should the Grande Armée sail, we place ourselves between it and England. Do I make myself clear?'

There was a murmur of assent, and Savery finished, 'We have an agent of the first calibre in Boulogne who will attempt to reach me tonight under cover of dark with the final details, which naturally you will share at first light. I wish you well for the *rencontre*, gentlemen.'

It was no longer high strategy or studied tactical manoeuvring that would be needed tomorrow: it would be nothing less than a frenzied fight to the finish, a sacrifice for the very highest stakes. *Teazer* was as ready she could be and everyone aboard knew their duty. While her company was issued a double tot of rum, Kydd and Renzi took a quiet and reflective dinner together.

Later, in the privacy of his sleeping cabin, Kydd drew out his fighting sword. In the flickering candlelight it gleamed with a fearful lustre, the blued Toledo steel blade at a razor's sharpness and the gold damascening catching the light with a barbaric glitter. His hand caressed the ornamentation, a pair of choughs that he had insisted on to remind him of his uncle in far distant

Canada, a noble lion-head pommel chased in gold. Would this blade taste enemy blood tomorrow or must he shamefully surrender it when *Teazer* was overwhelmed – or worse?

Dawn came: there was no news. Instead there was a sight that caused the whole ship to fall quiet: the Grande Armée was on the move. The martial glitter of bayonets and breast-plates showed in the wan morning sun as the dense columns of soldiers marched over the slopes like giant caterpillars. They converged on one vast open area in a sea of plumes, helmets and banners. More and more appeared over the line of hills to join the immense horde.

It was happening.

'Boat approaching, sir,' said Tawse, matter-of-factly. The little midshipman was clearly not about to be overawed by anything Frenchy.

It was a pinnace under a press of sail. It rounded to, hooked on by the side steps and a lieutenant bounded breathlessly on board. 'Captain, sir?' he said excitedly. 'From Cap'n Savery, his compliments and believes you should want to know what is afoot.'

'I do,' Kydd said drily. 'My cabin?'

'No need, sir, I'm hard pressed. Sir, this is the Emperor Napoleon and he's called the Grande Armée to—'

'We know this, sir. Get on with it, if you will.' Kydd ordered.

Hallum's apprehension was plain and others came up anxiously to hear.

'Well . . .' Kydd prompted.

'Er, sir, our agent was able to get out to us during the night with news of Bonaparte. Sir, he's called the Grande Armée to a parade only and—'

'To a parade!' Kydd choked. 'You're telling me he's mustered those hundreds o' thousands of soldiers just for—'

'Yes, sir, I am. This is no ordinary parade. It's something of an historical day, for Napoleon wants to be sure of the army when he's finally crowned, the people having had a revolution to get rid of the aristocrats, and he desiring to start a parcel o' new ones from his own family. More'n that, he's creating a whole new order o' chivalry to honour the new French Empire, as will have himself at its heart. This day he's to award a new medal to the soldiers to replace the Croix de Saint Louis. He calls it the Légion d'Honneur.'

Kydd's mouth dropped open.

The officer became animated. 'One hundred thousand men, captured banners, massed salutes and all the glory t' be wished for! And for his throne—'

'Hard pressed, you said?' Kydd reminded him.

'Um, yes, sir. And I'm to say that Cap'n Savery conceives that no action of any kind will take place these three days on account of no Frenchman would dare to risk being bested before the Emperor. He'll be falling back to the Downs and hopes to see us all in the Three Kings to raise a toast of damnation to the new Emperor.'

The shipwright had been right: the timbers for *Teazer*'s wounds were not so easily to be acquired. For days now Kydd had had the galling sight of the stripped-back bulwark with naked top-timbers protruding from the deck where new timberheads had been scarphed into the stumps, awaiting their cladding. As well, the fore-chains still lacked its channel and was unable to take the fore-shrouds.

Unfit for sea duties, *Teazer* could only lie to her moorings until she was made whole and was nominally transferred to the Downs defensive inshore division. It was now a matter of controlling frustration and preparing for the time when she would return to the offensive.

Meanwhile it was not good that seamen, keyed up for any sacrifice, were spending their days in idleness. Kydd was too wise in their ways to contemplate more harbour tasks of endless prettifying and pointless restowing, and allowed them relaxed discipline, with liberty from midday. However, it bore heavily on his spirit to lie stagnating while others sailed to face the odds.

There was a marked coolness about Calloway, but it was an ideal time for both the midshipmen to exercise their craft and Kydd saw to it that they were duly occupied.

On the fifth morning dawn broke on a falling barometer and a veering wind. The sea stretched hard and dark, like gunmetal, out to a luminous band on the horizon under a greying sky. There was no mistaking the onset of uncomfortable weather, but equally there did not appear to be any ominous swells heaving in massively to warn of the approach of a gale.

Kydd, not yet fully confident of his knowledge of sea conditions in the English Channel, crossed to Dowse. 'Foul weather, I think?'

'Aye. Out o' the east.'

This meant it would be one of the unaccountable continental blasts that could reach gale proportions within hours but because it had passed entirely over land would be given no chance to establish a fetch, the long, powerful seas induced by the same wind over hundreds or thousands of miles that were common in the Atlantic. It would be unpleasant but not deadly.

The sailing master sniffed the wind and stared upwards as he estimated its speed by clouds passing a fixed point in the rigging. 'A sharp drop in th' glass. It could be a pauler or it might pass. I'd say it t' be the first, sir.'

'Mr Purchet, we'll turn up the hands to secure the ship for a blow, I believe.' They were safely within the Downs, largely protected from anything in the east by the Goodwins, but Kydd was too respectful of the sea to leave anything to chance. They would lay out another bower, veer away cable on both and have the sheet anchor on a slip stopper along with the usual precautions.

'An' strike topmasts, sir?'

'If you please.' Even if it did turn out that it was a passing blow it would do no harm to perform the exercise. 'Oh, and let the first lieutenant know if we have any stragglers ashore, would you, Pipes?' Apart from needing a full crew on hand for any eventuality there was the requirement to have a tally of men aboard, such that any missing after the blow would not be assumed swept overboard.

By mid-morning the wind had hardened and steadied from the east-north-east and the first white-caps appeared. Snugged down, though, there was little to fear, only the endurance of *Teazer*'s endless jibbing and bobbing to her anchors as she lay bows to the seas.

'An easterly,' Renzi said, looking up from his writing in the great cabin.

'It is,' Kydd grunted. 'A fair wind for the French, but I have m' doubts that even for His Knobbs, Napoleon the Grand, they'll put to sea in this.'

His tea was now slopping into its saucer, a wet cloth on the side-table necessary to prevent it sliding off. It would be his last for a while, but with a bit of luck they should be over the worst by the next morning and could then get the galley fire going again.

Kydd wedged himself more tightly into his chair, which had been secured to its ringbolts, and reflected ruefully on sea life in a small ship.

After a tentative knock, Purchet looked in at the door. 'Er, a word wi' ye, sir.'

Kydd stood. This did not seem to be an official visit.

'Thought ye'd like to know of it first. See, Mr Calloway ain't aboard.'

'Does the first lieutenant know?'

'Um, not yet, sir.'

'Thank you for telling me, Mr Purchet.'

The boatswain waited.

'Er, I'll take the matter in hand m'self – no need t' trouble Mr Hallum.'

'Aye, sir. An' if ye wants . . .'

'Well, yes. On quite another matter, tell Mr Moyes and Mr Tawse to step aft, would you?'

The boatswain nodded and left. If it ever became official, Calloway was in deep trouble: breaking ship after a direct order from her captain was at the least desertion and would most certainly end in a court-martial with the destruction of his career.

Renzi closed his book. 'I, er, need to chase up a reference,' he said hastily, passing Moyes and Tawse as he left.

Moyes was a new-made master's mate and took his duties seriously, but when Kydd questioned him about one of his reefers he could throw no light on the disappearance. 'Thank you, Mr Moyes, you can go.'

'Mr Tawse,' he said, as menacingly as he could, 'I want you t' tell me now where I can find Calloway, and I'll not take no for an answer.'

The little midshipman turned pale but stood his ground. 'He's – he's not on board,' he whispered.

'I know that, you simkin! If he can be got back aboard before this blow stops the boats running, he's got a chance t' avoid serious consequences, so where's he t' be found, younker?'

Tawse flushed and stared stubbornly at the deck.

'I'm not talking about a mastheading, this is meat for a court-martial. Flogging round the fleet, I'd not be surprised.' At Tawse's continued silence he went on, 'I know about his saucy piece, his – his Sally, was it? He's gone t' ground with her, hasn't he? Answer, you villain!'

The young lad looked about miserably, then said, in a small voice, 'He's quean-struck on her, Mr Kydd, and – and he won't listen to his shipmates . . .' He tailed off under Kydd's venomous look.

It was the end for Calloway unless he could be brought to reason.

A memory came to Kydd of a shy thirteen-year-old painfully learning his letters with dockyard master Thomas Kydd in Antigua those years ago. Now that lad had turned into a fine seaman whom he had been able to set upon his own quarterdeck as midshipman, with a future as bright as any. But if he spared him, ignored the crime, every seaman in *Teazer* would expect their own offence to be treated in the same way.

Calloway must face the consequences and . . . No, damn it! How could he let young Luke be scuppered by some scheming wench? If only he could get to him, talk to the rascal, knock a bit of sense—

'Mr Tawse! You're guilty o' condoning desertion, failing t' inform your superiors,' Kydd bellowed.

The lad shrank back, his eyes wide.

'And I find there's only one thing as'll save your skin.'

'S-sir?'

'Tell me truly where he's at – and no whoppers or I'll personally lay on th' stripes.'

'I – I don't know, sir. She's – she's not o' the quality, I know. Luke – Mr Calloway – he won't say much 'cos I think he's worried we'll not approve her station.'

'Where?' Kydd ground out.

'Oh, sir, on stepping ashore we always must leave him at the top o' Dolphin Street. Mustn't follow or he'll give us a quiltin'.'

'That's all?'

'Why, sir, we've never even seen her, no matter where she lives.'

It was hopeless. 'You've not heard him talk of her last name a-tall?'

'I can't say as I remember – oh, one day I heard him say as she's got long hair like an angel, as our figurehead has.'

'I see. Well, duck away, Mr Tawse, and not a word t' anyone. D' you mark my words?'

'Clap a stopper on m' tongue, I will, sir,' the youngster piped.

Kydd bit his lip. The only chance Calloway had now was if someone went ashore and roused him to his duty before it became open knowledge and reached the ears of authority.

Should he send Tawse? And let the lad roam the streets of a sailor-town alone? Purchet or Moyes? No. It would compromise their standing aboard if ever it came out.

Then who? It must be someone he trusted but at the same time a man who had the power to give credible reassurance. Kydd heaved a sigh. It was crazy, but there was only one who could go about the darker side of town knocking on doors and entering taverns, then confront the looby and hale him back aboard. Himself. But he would need a trusted accomplice.

'Mr Hallum,' he said casually, after going on deck, 'I've just recalled something as needs my presence ashore for a short while. Call away the pinnace, if y' please.'

'Sir?' the first lieutenant said, frowning. It would be a wet trip, if not impossible, but a delay in returning would probably prevent his captain being able to get back at all until the storm abated.

'Of course,' Kydd added casually, 'should I be unfortunately detained then you've nothing to worry of. We've the safest anchoring in the kingdom.'

'Sir, may I ask what it is—'

'No, sir, you may not.'

A worried look descended on Hallum, but Kydd told him, 'I'll need to take the gunner – no, a gunner's mate will suffice.'

'That's Stirk, then, sir?'

'He'll do,' Kydd replied. 'Have him lay aft.'

While the boat's crew were being mustered Kydd retired to his cabin, tore off his captain's coat and breeches and pulled on an old pair of Renzi's plain trousers that he had borrowed. With his ancient grego he would probably pass as a merchant skipper on business ashore.

When a mystified Stirk arrived, Kydd laid out the situation before him. 'Young Luke's got himself in a moil.'

'I knows, Mr Kydd, sir.' Nothing could be read from the glittering black eyes.

'And I've a mind t' do something for him.'

No response came.

'Someone should go ashore an' bring the young scamp t' his senses. I've a notion that's t' be me. What d' you say ... Toby?'

Slowly, Stirk's expression eased into a smile. 'As I was a-thinkin' – shipmate.'

A rush of warmth enveloped Kydd. The years had been stripped away; the old loyalties of his days as a foremast hand had not been forgotten.

Stirk rubbed his chin. 'Won't be easy. We'll need t' describe 'em both without anyone knows the cut o' the jib of his dollymops.'

'Heard tell she's a head o' hair like our own figurehead. All we has t' say is, anyone seen a tow-headed youngster with a long-haired filly astern, somewheres south o' Dolphin Street?' Kydd chuckled, aware that his hard-won refined speech was wilting under the influence of the returning years.

'*I* has th' say.'

'Aye,' said Kydd, meekly. 'Well, boat's alongside and—'

'Poulden's coxswain,' Stirk said firmly, as though that explained everything. Kydd dutifully went down with his old friend into the boat, leaving a puzzled lieutenant watching.

It was a wet trip, the boat's sail under a close reef, and they surfed forward on the backs of the rolling seas until they grounded with a solid crash on the shingle. Kydd leaped nimbly overside before the recoiling wave could return and waited while the boat was brought up.

'I, er, don't know how long m' business will take, Poulden. Do ye wait for me here.'

Expressionless, his coxswain acknowledged, and Kydd set out with Stirk for Dolphin Street. It did not boast the lofty residences and courts of Middle Street, but a dark maze of interconnecting alleyways between the taphouses, chandleries and shanties of the boatmen and artisans of the King's Naval Yard.

The rich stink of marine stores, stale beer and fish hung heavily as they moved urgently along. The taverns were full of local sea-folk waiting out the foul weather – and they would be best placed to notice strangers coming and going. Rain squalls added to the wind's bluster and Kydd drew his old grego closer as he waited patiently at the door while Stirk entered the Farrier. He wasn't long inside. 'Some reckons they've clapped peepers on 'em but can't say where they's at. We're on th' right course, cuffin.'

Without Stirk to allay suspicions, there wouldn't have been a chance of laying hands on Calloway, who, as a child, had been a barefoot waif in London and knew all the tricks. They hurried on. The wind was rising and Kydd tasted the salt sea spume on the air.

The Brewer's Arms brought news: a fuddled man in the blue jersey of a boatman disclosed gleefully that not only was Calloway known but that he had taken up with the daughter of Jack Cribben, a hoveller who, it seemed, was none too happy about the situation. The obliging boatman was at pains to point out that Cribben could be found in one of the little homes towards the seafront.

'Spread more sail, Toby. We'll have 'im back in a trice.'

The windows of the house were barred, shuttered and wet with the constant spray. Kydd hammered at the door. There was a muffled shout from within and he realised he was being told to go to the back where it was sheltered.

The door was answered by a diminutive, furtive woman, who immediately called Cribben, a powerfully built older man. 'Yer business?' he said abruptly, noting Stirk's thick-set figure.

'We need t' talk to Luke Calloway, if y' would.'

Cribben stiffened. 'Who says—'

'We know where he's at, mate,' Kydd bit off. 'Take us.'

'Hold hard, there, cully! An' who's askin'? Are yez a king's man?'

'We're . . . shipmates o' the lad who wants him back aboard afore he runs afoul o' the captain,' Kydd said quickly. 'Y' see, we know you're not, as who should say, glad t' see him and y' daughter . . .'

'My Sally's not marryin' into th' Navy! She's a sweet lass as needs a steady hand on th' tiller an' one who comes home reg'lar each night. No sailin' away t' them foreign parts, havin' a whale of a time, an' her left wi' the little bantlings an' all.'

'Then we'll take 'im off y' hands, sir,' Kydd said briskly. 'Just ask him t' step outside, if ye would.'

Standing legs a-brace, Cribben shook his head and folded his arms defiantly.

'No?' Kydd spluttered. 'An' why not?'

''Cos I'll never be the shabbaroon as cravenly delivers up a body t' the Navy fer anyone, begob.'

A flurry of light rain came with the wind's growing bluster. 'Then we'll have t' get 'im f'r ourselves, cock,' Kydd said.

The man did not move. 'Y' won't find 'im here.'

'S' where *is* he?' Kydd demanded.

There was no response.

Stirk's fists slowly bunched. 'If'n y' don't give us th' griff, cully, an' that right smartly—'

Kydd caught his eye. 'No, drop it, Toby. Sea's gettin' up. We'd best be on our way.' Calloway would be tipped off about a Navy visit and would hide deeper.

As they turned to go a small boy raced around the corner, and burst out excitedly in front of Cribben, 'Old Bob Fosh seen a packet in trouble off the North Goodwins.'

Cribben's eyes glinted, then the light died. 'I thank 'ee, y' little rascal, even as it's t' no account.' He found a coin for the child, who darted off.

At Kydd's puzzled expression he said, 'All of 'em hereabouts is out after th' *Princess* draggin' anchor off the Bunt, seein' as how she'll pay over the odds, bein' an Indiaman. That's going t' leave me wi' no crew to go a-hovelling,' he said bitterly, 'Not as ye'd care.'

He turned to go back inside but Kydd stopped him. 'No hands? I'll work ye a bargain, Mr Cribben. We crew f'r you an' ye're going t' tell us where t' find our Luke. Agreed?'

'Ye'll want shares in the hovel.'

'No shares, should y' keep this t' yourself.'

Cribben hesitated for a moment. 'Wait,' he ordered, and snatched an oilskin from behind the door, then plunged off down the beach frontage. Kydd followed.

'Ye're breaking ship y'self, then,' Stirk said, with relish, as he caught up.

The lively seas were rolling in, with white-capped breakers here and there, the wind flat and hard from the east. If they left now they would make it out to *Teazer*, a wet and uncomfortable trip, but if they delayed . . .

Kydd chuckled. 'Well, we bein' held up ashore, th' ship's boat won't take seas like this, will it now? S' what we do while we waits for th' weather t' ease is no one's business . . .' They laughed together, like youngsters out on a prank.

Cribben disappeared inside a hut further along and came out with a weathered individual. 'Dick Redsull,' he threw over his shoulder. 'We needs another.' The man was clearly of some years and cackled a greeting at them, but Kydd recognised the wiry build of a seaman.

Cribben hurried along to another boat-hut, but without success. 'Long Jabber Neame?' Redsull suggested reedily.

'If'n he ain't betwaddled wi' ale,' muttered Cribben, but entered a small cottage and emerged with a large, bewildered man carrying sea-boots and trying to pull on foul-weather gear.

'Jack Neame, lads,' he said apologetically. His red-rimmed eyes probably owed more to grog than salt-spray but he steered a straight enough course.

'Get some foulies f'r ye,' Cribben said, and briefly ducked into his house, finding Kydd and Stirk sea-boots, jerseys and oilskins. They were well used, with the smell of tar, linseed oil and humanity.

Leaving the grateful pair to haul them on, Cribben went away to get further word on the ship. He returned with a satisfied grin. 'A three-master t' seaward o' the Knoll,' he said, to understanding nods from the hovellers. 'We'll go 'im I think. Oh – what does we call ye, then?'

'Ah, Tom's m' tally an' this here is Toby.'

Cribben nodded, then explained that the ship was probably a foreigner without a pilot, too much in dread of a notorious reputation to attempt the narrow channels through the treacherous sandbanks to the shelter of the Downs on the other side. And, with the easterly wind strengthening, so would be their anxieties over the anchor and cable that were holding them.

Daisy May was lying stem seaward with deck-covers whipping and hammering in the gusts, but already a large beach party was milling about in expectation of employment. Cribben waved cheerily at several men as he tramped over to the field past the King's Naval Yard.

Dozens of anchors of all shapes, weights and vintages recovered from the sands were laid out there; Cribben took his time and picked a stout piece nearly twice his height. 'This 'un,' he declared. It needed twenty men and a sledge to bring the awkward monster to the water's edge, the seas breaking heavily about it in a seething hiss.

The crowd held back respectfully while Cribben heaved himself up into the lugger and carefully checked the gear. 'Jack?' he called, and Neame joined him. The long fore and mizzen yards with sails already bent on were handed into the boat, clapped on to their masts and quickly rigged.

A steady stream of men laid square timbers down the shingle. 'Come on, let's be havin ye!' Cribben urged. Kydd heaved himself up over the high bulwarks and stumbled over a dismaying tangle of ropes and spars lying about in the capacious hull.

Fortunately a dipping-lug rig was the simplest of all, and by the time impatient shouts were going up from those outside, he had taken it in: two masts, a yard for each, tacks and sheets. Under the wet snarl of rigging, all around the bottom-boards, there were regular coils of substantial rope, with the left-hand lay of anchor cable.

'You, Tom, go take th' fore wi' Jack. Toby, aft wi' me.' Kydd did as he was told and glanced to seaward. It was a scene he had seen many times before – but from the deck of a well-found man-o'-war, not an open boat hardly bigger than a frigate's launch.

Under the hammering easterly the white-caps were increasing and now marched in on the backs of grey-green waves, setting the many ships in the Downs jibbing energetically to their anchors. But what drew Kydd's attention was an indistinct white line developing on the grey horizon: wild seas piling up on the hovellers' destination, the Goodwin Sands.

The tide was low, making it nearly a hundred feet down steep shingle to pull the craft to its native element. The beach party crowded round, every inch of the boat manned, and a double rope led out forward with willing hands tailing on.

Kydd looked down on scores of backs bent ready.

'*Alaaaawww!*' At the hoarse cry every man buckled to.

They were launching into the teeth of a dead muzzler, and Kydd knew they had to win their way against wind and the surging combers.

'*Alaaaawww!*' the cry went up again. It was answered immediately by a regular chant, and the heaving began. 'Alaw boat, *haul*, alaw boat, *haul, haul, haul, haaauuul!*' At first the straining saw no result, but then the boat shuddered and inched forward over the timbers.

'*Alaaaawww!*' The tons deadweight of the *Daisy May* picked up speed and slithered down the ways until she met the seas in thumps of spray – and they were afloat, the wet black iron of the big anchor left forlorn on the beach.

'Jack, damn ye!' But Neame had already leaned over the bluff bow and taken the dripping rope handed up to him, straightening and passing it rapidly to the waiting Redsull. Then Kydd understood: this was a haul-off warp, and he bent to help get it over the stout windlass so that they could heave their boat bodily out to sea past the line of breakers.

Daisy May reared and shied at the considerable seas now rampaging in, but with three men at the windlass they hauled out steadily in the teeth of the wind to the warping buoy and quickly tied off. Then the hard work began: lines had been taken to their beached anchor and secured around its peak, where the shank met the flukes, in order to drag it out without it digging in.

It was back-breaking work in chill bursts of spray and on an unsteady footing: six-foot handspikes were thudded into square sockets in the horizontal windlass drum; then came a heroic backwards straining pull, the rhythm kept up by having the holes offset from each other so each man could re-socket at different times.

Unaccustomed to the toil, Kydd's muscles burned, but there could be no slacking – he had seen Stirk's devilish grin. All four laboured until, when the anchor was near, Cribben called a halt. Then it was more work at tackles to align *Daisy May* before the last task – lifting the anchor bodily from under them until it hung suspended close beneath. Cribben ordered the jigger tackles secured and their tethering to the warp buoy singled up, then raised an arm.

Kydd had to concede it masterly seamanship, performed in the wildest conditions.

'Get on wi' ye,' Neame said good-naturedly. The long yard needed to be hooked to the foremast and hoisted. Kydd aligned the spar to the direction of the wind, seized the halliard and looked aft with concern. A dead foul wind blowing hard could drive them helpless back on to the shore to be cast up. There would be no second chance.

Redsull pushed his way past to the bow painter while Neame, at the sheet, looked steadily at Kydd, who in turn kept his gaze on Cribben. His arm fell: Kydd hauled furiously hand over hand and the heavy yard began to lift. The wind hustled at it until, at chest height, it caught the exposed sail, which bellied to a hard tautness, *Daisy May*'s bow shying away in response. At the same time Neame threw off the buoy slip rope, the mizzen briskly rose and took, and suddenly they were making way against the towering boisterousness of the onrushing seas.

Kydd hunkered down behind the bow with Stirk, trying to avoid the sheets of spume curling over as they met each wave with a crunch and smash of white spray. They were winning their way slowly to seaward. Light-headed, he felt a guilty thrill at the escapade but savoured the exhilaration of such seamanship. He flashed a grin at Stirk, who winked back.

They thrashed out through the anchored ships and towards the line of smoking white that now lay across their entire horizon, vivid against the dark of the storm-clouds. With her burden *Daisy May* made slow progress against the powerful seas but she was sure: this was her true element, and her high-waisted, broad lines felt sturdy and secure.

On impulse, Kydd abandoned his shelter and passed hand to hand down the boat to where Cribben sat at the tiller. 'Snug as a duck in a ditch,' Kydd offered.

'Aye, she is that.'

'We're going north-about, then?'

Cribben looked at him in astonishment. 'No, mate, we're goin' through in course,' he said, as if speaking to a child.

'Through! Why, we're—'

'F'r them as knows th' Goodwins it's no great shakes,' Cribben said. 'Ye'd have t' know that they's shiftin' all the time – ye have t' keep a trace o' every little spit and bay, where the swatchways run in a tide-fall, th' gullies an' scour-pits all a-changing, where lies th' deepest fox-falls, how the tide runs, an', b' heaven, we knows it!'

During their slow beat out he went on to tell of the sands themselves. In calmer weather they dried to miles of hard-packed grains on which the local lads would play cricket in bravado – but woe betide the laggard, for the returning tide could race in faster than a man could run. Then the water would transform the vast sandbar into hillocks that ran like hot wax, quickening the sand into treacherous glue to drag a victim under. And if a ship was unfortunate enough to be cast up she had but one tide to break free: when the sand became quick she would 'swaddle down' to be held in the maw of the Goodwins for ever – like as not, with her crew as well.

'More'n two thousan' good ships've left their bones t' rot here,' Cribben said soberly. 'It's bin called b' your Bill Shakespeare, th' "Ship Swallower" an' he's right an' all.'

They drew closer, and the effectiveness of the huge mass of the sands in arresting the onrush of the gale's heavy seas was becoming apparent: to the weather side, there was a broad band of hanging spray where the waves were in violent assault, while to its lee *Daisy May* was making her laborious way in perfect safety.

The Goodwins were now in full view with the ebbing tide – a long, low menace, not the golden yellow of a beach but the dark, sable sand of the sea-bed, stretching away unbroken into the far distance in both directions.

A gull landed on the gunwale, hooking in its claws and swaying under the battering of the wind. It was not the usual grey-white species but a big, flat-headed type with cruel yellow eyes that watched them with cold calculation. Every member of the boat flailed at it, sending it quickly up and away. 'Is a priggin' corpse eater,' cursed Redsull.

Then, ahead, Kydd saw their way: at a sharp diagonal through the main banks and therefore unseen before, it stretched away through to the violence on the other side. They went about for the approach. 'Kellett Gut,' grunted Cribben. 'Nothing to worry of – we's more'n sixty feet under us.'

Hundreds of yards wide only and churning with a tide-race, it seemed a fearful prospect for the plucky little boat but she won through, emerging into a quite different seascape – murderous combers crashing in to spend their fury in a bass thunder of breaking seas, their tops smoking with white spume, the stinging spray driven mercilessly downwind by the blast of the gale.

No more than half a mile to the north a foreign-looking barque was near hidden in the mists of spume. Cribben gave a soft smile and shouted against the wind, 'He's in a fair way o' takin' the ground where he's at – loses his holding there, an' it's all deep water t' the Knoll.'

Kydd understood: the barque was hanging on to an unseen narrow spit, and if her anchor tore free of the sand under the wind's blast, the deep water between it and the steep-sided Knoll would give no holding whatsoever – they were in dire peril. 'Go forrard then, Tom, where we needs ye,' Cribben told him. He pulled on the tiller and, crabwise, *Daisy May* came up with the deep-laden ship, passing into the small lee around her stern. Smart work with fore and mizzen kept her there, while Cribben stood and, hanging onto a stay, hailed the anxious faces peering down from her taffrail.

'Yez standin' into danger, that there sand-spit. *Compree?*' he bellowed.

'Ach, ve know,' came back a faint hail. 'But vot can we do?'

It was a Prussian barque, a Danziger with a valuable freighting, but when her master realised what was afoot he quickly turned cagey. However, Cribben had done such haggling many times before and did not have to mention how inadvisable it would be if, in the event of an insurance claim, it became known that the offer of a perfectly sound set of ground tackle had been turned down.

It was not long before they were lighter one anchor and cable, and the barque was in possession of a third anchor to windward. Taking advantage of their lee, *Daisy May* was put about for a rapid trip back before the wind. The absence of the deadweight of an anchor resulted in a lively roll in the beam seas before they were able to shape course into Kellett Gut, away from the chaos of the gale.

'Hoy, Jack!' cried Neame, urgently, throwing out an arm to seaward. At first it was difficult to make out what he meant, but then a passing squall lifted the mist and revealed the stark outlines of a small derelict – a coaster perhaps, dismasted out to sea and now driving to her inevitable doom on the Goodwins.

Kydd's heart went out to the unknown mariners who had suffered this calamity for he knew they could not be helped; *Daisy May* was too far committed into the narrow passage of the Gut and the wreck would be cast up well before others could come to their aid.

Nevertheless, perhaps out of some sense of brotherly feeling towards them in their extremity, Cribben luffed up and came to in the lee side of the immense sandbank. 'Killick,' he threw at Neame laconically. The man cleared away their little bow anchor, which plummeted down while all eyes followed the final act of the drama.

Figures on the derelict were jerking about in some sort of frantic activity, but the end could not be long delayed. Soon the huge breakers roaring in would rise up as they felt the solid bank under them, bear the derelict aloft and smash it to flinders on the unyielding sand.

As Kydd looked on, mesmerised, he realised that the activity on deck had been that of some hero who had fashioned a steering oar from a plank and had succeeded in wrestling the bow resolutely shoreward. And he also recognised the vessel, with her rakish lines, she was a *chasse-marée*, a French privateer.

Nobody spoke as a giant breaker curled and fell – and as the boiling surf raced up the sand, it sent the wreck shooting forward. The hero's final actions were rewarded, for as soon as the dark shape of the craft came to rest the figures stumbled from it on to the blessed firmness. The sea returned in a hissing roar and pushed the craft crazily broadside but the men were not running for safety: they were struggling with something in the wreck. It was a body – no, an injured seaman, and they were dragging him out, then making hastily for the higher ground.

Kydd felt like cheering but Cribben's look was bleak as he grunted, 'They've got t' come off of there – tide'll have 'em in a couple of hours.'

'Can't we close with th' bank an' take 'em?' Kydd asked.

'Why? They's only mongseers, is all. Let 'em take their chances.'

'They're sailors, jus' like us all.'

'No.'

Kydd felt his blood rise but held himself in check. 'Five guineas t' lay off the bank.'

Cribben looked at him in astonishment, then peered into Kydd's face as if for reassurance as to his sanity. 'Seven.'

'Done.'

The others looked at Kydd warily, but helped to pull the lugger in as far as was prudent and Kydd signalled to the stranded seamen with exaggerated beckoning movements. There was a distracted wave back but no sign that they understood the urgency of their situation.

Kydd swore; in a short time they would be beyond mortal help. He repeated the signal, then got everyone aboard *Daisy May* to join in, but the Frenchmen were not going to risk the tide-rips.

'Leave 'em be, the silly buggers,' Cribben said dismissively, clearly ready to leave.

Kydd said nothing but began to strip off to his trousers.

'What're ye up to?' Cribben demanded.

'I knows th' French lingo,' Kydd retorted, 'an' in common pity they have t' be warned.'

'We only gets th' bounty fer bringing back bodies, not live 'uns.'

Standing on the gunwale Kydd leaped clumsily into the cold shock of the sea and struck out. The current seized him and carried him along but after frantic strokes his toe caught the hard roughness of the sandy bottom and he staggered upright, looking for the castaways.

The chill of the wind's blast nearly took his breath away and when a Frenchman hurried up to him he could hardly control his shuddering. '*V-vous êtes i-ici dans un g-grand péril, m-mon brave,*' he stuttered, and tried to convey the essence of the danger.

It was surreal: he was standing on hard-packed brown sand that was about to plunge beneath the sea, talking to a French privateersman whom it was his duty to kill – and himself, a commander of the Royal Navy, taking orders from a Deal hoveller.

The Frenchmen chattered among themselves, then explained that for reasons of humanity they could not abandon their injured comrade – he had been the one to wield the steering oar – and besides, like many seamen, none could swim. There was such poignant resignation in their faces that Kydd was forced to turn away.

Staggering with the force of a vicious wind squall across the flat banks he tried to flog his frozen mind to thought. Cribben would not keep *Daisy May* among the leeward shoals for much longer. It was—

A faint shout drew his attention to the lugger. He saw Stirk jump into the sea and strike out for them, Redsull back in *Daisy May* furiously paying out a line.

Stirk splashed into the shallows and Kydd helped him up. A double line was threaded through his belt at the small of his back, which he released. Hoarsely, he panted, 'They hauls 'em out b' this rope. Cribben's in a rare takin' – but them others'll be good 'uns.'

The light line was handed rapidly along as an endless loop until a heavier line arrived and, with a piece of timber for flotation, the rescue was rapidly made complete.

'S' then, Mr Hoveller, where's our Luke Calloway?' Kydd demanded. Cribben was at the head of the beach with his arms folded, watching *Daisy May* hauled out of the surf and up the shingle in the fading light.

'Where's m' seven guineas?' snapped the man, keeping his eyes on the straining capstan crew.

'You'll get 'em by sunset t'morrow,' Kydd replied tightly.

Then Cribben turned to him with a smile. 'I don't rightly know who you is, Mr Tom, but youse a right taut man o' th' sea as ever I seen, an' I honour ye for it. Follow me.'

'I'll go, Toby – no need f'r you,' Kydd said.

Cribben stamped up the shingle and into the maze of alleyways. He stopped at the gaunt old edifice of a deserted maltster's and gestured contemptuously. 'I know they's got their heads down in that there loft. Take him an' be damned to the shab.'

Kydd eased open the ancient double doors and entered into the smelly darkness, the wind covering the noise of his entrance. As his eyes became accustomed to the gloom he saw dust-covered mash-tubs, long planked floors and, to the side, a flight of rickety steps leading up to the blackness at the top of the building.

Kydd tiptoed to the stairs, ears a-prick for any sound.

Halfway up he heard muffled giggling. He completed the climb, arriving at what appeared to be an overseer's office. Within it, he heard furtive movement and beneath the door saw dim light.

He crashed it open. 'Mr Midshipman Calloway! Y'r duty t' your ship, sir!'

With a horrified shriek, a naked girl snatched for covering. Calloway sat up groggily, and glared resentfully at him.

'T' break ship is a crime and an insult t' your shipmates, Luke. Why . . . ?'

'Er, me 'n' Sally, um, we're—'

'Y'r country lies under such a peril as never was. Are ye going t' tell me you're comfortable t' leave the fighting to others while ye cunny burrow with y' trug?'

Calloway reddened and reached for his clothes. 'I'm done with roaming,' he said stubbornly. 'I want t' cast anchor next to m' woman, an' she won't be found in a poxy man-o'-war.'

'Leave my Luke be!' screeched the girl. 'Him 'n' me's gettin' spliced, ain't we, darlin'?'

Kydd ignored her. 'Your duty calls ye, Luke,' he said remorselessly.

'I – I'm not . . .'

'I c'n have you taken in irons and haled aboard as a deserter.'

The lad stiffened.

'But I won't. I'm leaving – now. And if y' follows me, it's back aboard, no questions asked, all a-taunto. And if y' don't, then you'll have t' live with y'r decision for the rest o' your life . . .'

Chapter 6

Renzi contemplated the wind-torn seas of the Downs through *Teazer*'s salt-encrusted stern windows. Years in Neptune's realm had inured him to the motion and he knew he would miss the honest liveliness and daily challenges of the elements if ever he was obliged to go ashore for good.

For now, though, that was not in question and he blessed his luck in securing a situation that ensured food, board and the company of his friend while he pursued his scholarly quest. It was proceeding well: he had settled back into his studies after the catastrophe of the failed plot against Napoleon and, just recently, had reached a delightful impasse in his careful building of the edifice of support of his central hypotheses. the Nomological Determinist position was threatening the entire substructure of his 'Economic Man', but once again the sturdy pragmatism of Hobbes, two centuries earlier, was coming to the rescue. In fact, conflated with the naturalistic philosophies of Hume, the so-called 'Compatibilists' had—

The distant wail of the boatswain's call sounded. Kydd was being piped aboard after his enforced delay ashore. Voices echoed in the tiny companionway to the great cabin, then Kydd poked his head in, shaking water everywhere.

'I'll be with you in a brace o' shakes, old chap,' he said, and disappeared to change, then returned quickly to down a restorative brandy. 'A tolerably divertin' time of it yesterday,' he said expansively, 'and one young fussock back aboard as is considering his position.' He wedged himself in his chair against *Teazer*'s jerking at her moorings, which was her way of indicating her impatience for the freedom of the open sea. Eyeing the canvas dispatch bag, he added, 'I see the boats are running again – is that the mail?'

Guiltily, Renzi emptied the contents on to the table. Only one item seemed at all official; any concerning officers would be conveyed personally by a midshipman or lieutenant, so this was probably in regard to a member of the crew or yet another routine fleet order that *Teazer*, still awaiting repairs, would be unable to comply with. He passed it to Kydd.

'Why, I do believe you're found out, Renzi. Listen to this: "The ship's clerk, HMS *Teazer*, to attend at the flag-officer's . . . forthwith."' Kydd laughed, 'Don't worry. I'll send along a hand to bear a fist with all your workings.'

The trip out to *Monarch* was uncomfortable, wet and not a little irksome. The order had not specified which papers were due for a surprise vetting so Renzi had been obliged to take along as many as he could manage, carefully protected in two layers of oilskin.

His irritation increased when no one seemed to know why he had been sent for. Finally, the first lieutenant appeared and regarded him curiously. 'Ah, yes. It *is* Renzi, is it not?'

'Sir.'

'Then my instructions are to convey you to Walmer Castle with all dispatch. They're expecting you, I believe. Er, pray refrain from discussing your visit with anyone. That is, anyone whomsoever. Do you understand me?'

'Aye aye, sir,' Renzi replied, taken aback.

'Very well. I shall call away our own boat immediately. There's no need to detain yours. And do get rid of that raffle – I hardly think Walmer are likely to be interested in your weekly accounts or similar.' He chuckled.

This was strange indeed. Renzi had seen Walmer Castle from the sea, a low, round edifice like Deal Castle, also dating back to the eighth King Henry. He had heard that it was now home to the Lord Warden of the Cinque Ports, an honorary position under the Crown whose origins were lost in medieval antiquity.

The castle was near the edge of the beach at a secluded location a mile to the south of Deal. A tight-lipped lieutenant accompanied Renzi as they trudged up the shingle and approached the ancient bastions.

'Halt, an' who goes there?' It was the first of many sentinels who challenged them before they reached the round Tudor gatehouse and Renzi felt stirrings of unease. Army sentries at a private residence?

The lieutenant spoke to the gatekeeper sergeant, who took Renzi in charge, gruffly telling him to follow. They went through the echoing gateway and upstairs, eventually entering a distinguished residence with hanging pictures and velvet curtains: With kitchen odours and the distinctive serge and leathery smell of soldiery, it appeared well tenanted too.

They passed into a central corridor, then mid-way along the sergeant stopped and knocked at a door. It was answered by a well-dressed civilian. 'Renzi? Do come in, old chap.'

Warily, he entered the small room, with its single desk and

visitor's chair opposite illuminated by a mullioned gunport. 'Sit down, make yourself at home. Tea, or . . . ?'

Renzi declined refreshments.

'Hobson, Aliens Office. You must be wondering why we've asked you here,' he began mildly.

Renzi remained silent.

Hobson went on, 'We have the warmest recommendation from Commodore d'Auvergne in Jersey as to your probity and reliability, which leads us to consider whether in the matter of—'

'No!'

'—a particular and delicate service—'

'I am never a spy, sir.'

'—of the highest importance to the interests of this country, that you would consider—'

'Understand me now, sir. I find the practices of spying repugnant to my character and odious in the extreme. Should you—'

'Mr Renzi. No one has mentioned spying that I recall. This concerns an entirely different matter and I confess I'm quite at a loss to account for your hostile manner, sir.' He paused, then resumed stiffly, 'You will be aware of the humane and practical custom between belligerents of the exchange of prisoners-of-war, both of paroled officers and the common sort.'

'I am, of course,' Renzi replied.

'Then you will be as dismayed as His Majesty's government at the abhorrent actions of the French in detaining our prisoners with no hope of repatriation in any wise, contrary to the usages of war, which, until the present conflict, have always served perfectly adequately.'

Renzi knew of the unprecedented act of barbarism by

Bonaparte at the outset of the war in seizing every Englishman, high or low, military or harmless tourist, and incarcerating them, along with their women. Was this to be some crazy rescue attempt?

Hobson continued in the same tone. 'There is to be noted a marked imbalance in prisoners held. At the moment we hold some three or four times as many French as they do ours, and it is our belief that this may be the means to bring Napoleon to a more rational standing on the matter.'

'To negotiate?'

'Quite so. Agreement has recently been reached with the French government through an intermediary for a diplomatic mission to be sent by us to explore the question.'

'You wish *me* to—'

'No, Mr Renzi, we do not. The foreign secretary, Lord Hawkesbury, has appointed a Mr Haslip, lately of the Transport Board, to conduct the mission. It is his wish to be accompanied by one in the undoubted character of gentleman who, at the same time, might be relied upon to undertake the humbler – but nevertheless vital – tasks as they present themselves.'

Despite himself, Renzi could not smother a cynical chuckle.

'Come, come, sir. This is not an occasion for humour. Consider, if you will, the families of the unfortunates in the fortress prisons of France with no hope of release. The hardships they must daily face, the—'

'I thank you for your consideration, Mr Hobson, but I have to tell you I am perfectly content where I am.'

Hobson steepled his hands in thought. 'You do surprise me, Renzi. Clerk of a brig-sloop, now to be given the opportunity to visit Paris, the home of Diderot, Rousseau and Enlightened Man – and, while under diplomatic protection, to be quite free to take your fill of the sights and mingle in learned company . . .'

He had Renzi's avid interest now. This was another matter entirely. Savants of sufficiently adequate stature on both sides were – after considerable fuss at the highest level – sometimes given safe-conduct for the express purpose of furthering human knowledge and were thereby able to pass unhindered between warring nations. That he, unpublished and unknown, could enjoy the same privilege would be an *incredible* stroke of fortune.

'Er, there is no question of my abusing such a position to engage in activities in the nature of spying, of course.'

Hobson frowned in exasperation. 'Mr Renzi! This continual adverting to some form of espionage does you no credit at all. You have my word on it that no spying is involved. In point of fact, should you be so far in want of gentlemanly conduct as to undertake such on a private basis, then His Majesty's ministers will utterly condemn you. You will go openly, under your own auspices and with stated diplomatic objectives, while no doubt you will be, from the first, subject to a form of surveillance by the authorities. Provided you are earnest and diligent in the discharge of your duties and refrain from being seen near locations of a military nature, I can see no difficulties pursuant to an interesting and rewarding experience.'

'I shall proceed in cartel, as a full member of the mission to . . . ?'

'Mr Renzi, if you have a stated moral objection to assisting at such a level then please to let me know at this point,' Hobson said, with a touch of impatience. 'I shall then be obliged to find another.'

'No, not at all. I was merely—'

'Then shall we continue? An accreditation to the mission

requires more than a few diplomatic formalities, which should be put in hand without further delay. Mr Haslip has let it be known he wishes to depart at the earliest possible opportunity.'

'Of course,' said Renzi, hastily. 'I shall immediately put my affairs in order in my ship and—'

'There will be time for that later. Now, to the first. Do you wish to travel under your own name or another? Some feel it more congenial to their privacy to discourage curious prying by a foreign power.'

'Oh? Then, er, "Smith" will answer, I believe.'

'Certainly. There are other details we shall need to record, and then, under your signature, these will be sent to Whitehall by special messenger for your formal accession to the body of the mission. I suspect Mr Haslip will therefore wish to be aboard the cartel ship, departing this Thursday night from Ramsgate.

'There may be final matters to discuss before you leave, so perhaps we shall meet once more on Wednesday. Oh, and as no doubt you have already been told, the invariable custom in these affairs is that complete secrecy is to be observed. Not even your captain must know.'

He looked Renzi directly in the eye. 'You have no conception of the villainous creatures who inhabit the nether world, ready to take advantage.'

'Quite, quite,' Renzi said, with feeling.

'You're taking a holiday?' Kydd asked, in surprise, as Renzi assembled his bags in the larger space of the great cabin. 'Where will this be, old trout?'

Renzi fought with the temptation to mention casually that he intended to spend the weekend in Paris. 'It did seem the most suitable opportunity, *Teazer* being under repair for the time being.'

Light-headed with exhilaration at the prospect before him, he deliberated whether the old but finer blue coat would more suit in a Paris of fashion and gaiety, or was it to be the newer but sombre brown? In the end he decided that if he was to put up a decent showing as a diplomat then perhaps he would visit a fashionable tailor while he was there. After all, he was representing his country.

Kydd would not let it rest. 'Fine weather, just the ticket for a bit o' sporting in the sun?' He tried again. 'Do you have anyone to go with, Nicholas?'

'You mean in the character of a female?'

Kydd grinned. 'I see, you wicked dog.'

'No.'

'Then where?'

Renzi picked up one of the bags, as though checking its weight. Thwarted, Kydd stumped off to annoy the officer-of-the-watch.

The day before the cartel ship was due to sail Renzi made acquaintance of Haslip. He was a humourless, pompous bureaucratic functionary but Renzi knew how to handle such as him.

Hobson greeted him warmly. 'So you're leaving tomorrow for Paris? I envy you, Renzi. My position seldom allows me such diversions.' He closed the door. 'Now, one thing has come up, old fellow. Do see if you can help us. While you're in Paris there is one chap we'd like you to look up. He's an artist, portraiture and such, the duke of Devonshire and similar. Rather good, too – he's hung in the Royal Academy, no less.'

'Oh?'

'Yes indeed,' Hobson said smoothly. 'You see, he's an odd

kind of cove, head full of strange notions, but we'd like you to let him know that we're quite keen to see him back in the old country. I'll let you have a sum of money to that end – you'll sign and account for it in the usual way, of course, but we are rather concerned to have him return.'

'You mean – to smuggle him back?'

'Goodness gracious, no! He's a citizen of the United States, a neutral, and is quite free to go where he pleases. Name of Fulton.'

The cartel ship left the pier at Ramsgate in the anonymous darkness and was soon butting into a chill south-easterly. The passengers scuttled below to light and warmth, but Renzi stood on the foredeck, clutching a shroud and burning with indignation.

He had been well and truly hooked, caught and landed. Dazzled by the daring thought of Paris in the summer he had not stopped to consider why he, Renzi, had been plucked out of obscurity to perform the task. The real reason for his visit turned out not to be spying but something infinitely worse and more dangerous. The stakes for him and England could not have been higher.

This Fulton, or Francis, the code-name he sometimes went by, was an extraordinary man, possibly a genius. From childhood poverty in Maryland he had attracted early support for his painting talent sufficient to have him sent to England, where he had shone as a portrait painter. He had spent some fruitful years in Devon, then come to the attention and patronage of Benjamin West, the president of the prestigious Royal Academy. In the course of time he had been hung beside the great masters.

On the continent the hideous excesses of the French Revolution had turned to power struggles and thence a fragile

162

form of stability while energies were directed outward in war. With England convulsed in the bloody mutinies of Spithead and the Nore, Fulton had suddenly decided to leave and cross to France, where he had quickly taken up with the circle of expatriate radicals and friends of the Revolution who encouraged the blossoming of his growing republican idealism.

Then, within months, word had trickled back to England that, extraordinarily, Fulton had presented plans to the Directory for a 'submarine boat' for use by the French Navy against the British. Why and how a noted artist had turned his talents to such fancies was not explained to Renzi. Then, after a coup in 1799, Napoleon Bonaparte had become Consul for Life and his attention had been drawn to Fulton's schemes. He had advanced the inventor funding to produce his first 'submarine', *Nautilus*.

If reports were to be believed, Fulton had indeed built it and trialled it in the Seine, submerging with his crew for an hour before horrified witnesses, then triumphantly returning to the surface. It seemed a far from practical weapon of war, but when he later manoeuvred the submarine confidently about the entrance to Le Havre and then the open sea, and talked of fitting it with his new exploding 'torpedoes', there was no more doubt but that the sinister and deadly craft was about to rewrite the rules of war.

He had been granted a personal audience with Bonaparte and had energetically begun to prepare plans for a bigger and more destructive submersible, but peace had been declared and development stalled. When war resumed, Fulton was well placed to demand what he would for a weapon that could be aimed directly at the one thing that denied the French domination of the world: the Royal Navy.

Since Napoleon's seizure of power, his network of spies and secret police had clamped a tight hold on the capital so reliable information was virtually impossible to get – but it did not take much imagination to realise that any maritime nation would be helpless against the possessor of such an instrument of destruction, utterly defenceless against something that could not even be seen. Who knew what was being promised to its inventor as Bonaparte gathered his forces for the invasion of England?

Renzi's task was simple: locate Fulton, detach him from the French cause and conduct him to Britain.

The unfairness nearly choked him. Why should such responsibility be placed on *his* shoulders? On sober reflection, though, he realised he was uniquely qualified for the job. After his hard experiences in Jersey, assisting a spymaster, he knew what to expect of the French system; he was intelligent yet unknown to the French, and with considerable experience of sea service. Added to that there was his undoubted moral integrity, the demeanour of a gentleman and the fact that his naval record would even show service on the North American station. That was why he had been chosen.

And it was a job that demanded the guile of just one man, not a force, and still less a full conspiracy. With numbers came the chance of betrayal, and the French would be merciless to any who threatened their trump card.

In summary, his task was to find where the man was hidden in the great city and approach him with unanswerable arguments as to why he should betray and turn on his benefactors – after he had unavoidably revealed himself to Fulton as a British agent, of course. And this to the man whose intercepted letters had described England's Navy as 'the source of all the incalculable horrors' committed against the free citizens of the ocean and whose firm friend in Paris was Tom Paine, the notorious revolutionary.

It was the stuff of nightmares, a near impossible objective but one that had to succeed.

His mind reeled, his body oblivious to the cold and spray as they made for Calais and enemy country. He had no idea how he would begin: he was on his own with nothing but his wits and cunning.

A white flag prominent at her fore-topgallant masthead, the cartel ship hove to in Calais Roads to await inspection. To Renzi, dazed with lack of sleep, it was utterly unreal. So recently *Teazer* had been fighting for her life in these very waters, trying to prevent ships entering. Now here he was, on an English ship, about to be welcomed into that same port.

Soon they were making their way within a narrow staked passage through the mud-flats, past the forts and into the inner basins crowded with invasion craft and dominated by the louring Fort Nieulay. Then came the sight of sour-faced *douaniers* on the quay, the sharp tones of the officer conducting exchanges and the indefinable odours of foreign soil.

As his passport was minutely examined Renzi felt himself in an increasingly dream-like situation that was paradoxically insulating him against the dread of the reality into which he was being sucked.

He and Haslip were separated from the others and conducted to a quayside office where their papers were checked yet again, then taken outside to a waiting carriage. A *gens d'armes* lieutenant helped them to board and, without comment, entered as well, signalling to the escort of two horsemen behind.

It was the usual gut-rattling journey into the interior, relieved only by regular stops for refreshment and a change of horses. No one spoke. Haslip had not been made privy to the real reason for Renzi's appointment and ignored him in a lordly way, while the lieutenant was not disposed to be friendly to an Englishman. Renzi stared out of the window at the flat, boring landscape, prevented from dozing by the gritty jolting – and the thought of the madness into which he was about to be plunged.

His mind strayed to the last time he had been with Kydd before they sailed. It was soon after they had seen fit to inform Renzi of the true nature of his mission. Something in his face had sparked dismay in his friend: brushing aside Renzi's light prattle of holidays, Kydd had gripped his hands and wished him all good fortune for wherever it was he was going.

Villages became more frequent; here, little had changed in the years since, as a carefree young man, Renzi had passed through France on his Grand Tour, and as they neared the capital, he felt a surge of exhilaration at approaching the legendary City of Light.

The outer reaches of Paris were much as he remembered, and suddenly they were in the city. The same open spaces, narrow muddy streets and, rising above the stink of horses and coal-smoke, the enticing alien smell of garlic and herbs, always on the air. There were as many people on the avenues as before, but they were of a different kind, sombrely dressed and keeping to themselves as they hurried along. There were fewer shabbily dressed poor.

Renzi recognised the rue St Honoré and, close by, the ancient church of St Roche. Then the massive stone columns and classical pediments of the Hôtel Grandime came into view, and the carriage swayed finally to a stop. The lieutenant asked them curtly to remain and bounded up the steps. He returned with footmen, and they were ushered inside.

Conscious of a wary hush and hostile stares, Renzi completed the formalities, the eyes of the concierge flicking between him and the lieutenant. Their rooms were on the first floor, a larger inner suite and a smaller outer one, which he took for himself without comment.

'I shall dine alone, Smith, and shall not want to be disturbed,' Haslip said importantly. 'See that you're able to attend upon me at ten tomorrow. Is that understood?'

It suited Renzi well: from his rooms he could slip in and out quietly as he pleased, and that Haslip wished to remain in his solitary glory was even better. His meagre luggage arrived and, worn out, he flopped onto the musty four-poster and closed his eyes. He drifted off quickly but woke feeling stiff and cold. Immediately the dread of his situation rushed back but he did not allow it to take hold. He finished stowing his gear in the old-fashioned drawers and splashed his face with water.

He patted his waistcoat pocket, and was reassured by the crackle of his passport. Then he went downstairs, with an air of jaunty defiance, ignored the watchful gaze of the concierge and strode out into the evening. Hesitating, he turned right, then walked purposefully along towards the vast Place Louis XV.

He emerged into its great spaces and slowed. This was now the Place de la Révolution and he was making pilgrimage to the spot where, just a handful of years ago, the guillotines had slithered and fallen before screaming crowds to end the lives of so many of France's ancient nobility.

The sense of loss of the older world was overpowering here, and he closed his eyes in melancholy. The feeling passed and he walked on rapidly – he needed the comfort of human company.

Inside a nearby tavern it was warm and dark, dense with pipe-smoke. Low candlelight played on the animated features of couples and the babble of talk ebbed and flowed. Renzi found a corner table and settled quietly, letting the memories return. *'Garçon!'* The tapster seemed not to hear and he repeated the call more loudly. Astonished faces turned to him as the man stormed across. *'M'sieur, un demi de bière, s'il vous plaît.'*

The tapster came to an abrupt stop and peered at Renzi. *'Vous êtes anglais?'* he said disbelievingly.

Whether it was because of his square-cut English coat or his accent, Renzi did not know; but he was obliged to explain at length why an Englishman was on the loose in the Paris of Napoleon. In return he had to accept a scolding over his use of *garçon* and *monsieur* where now the egalitarian *citoyen* was expected.

A nearby couple made much of moving to another table and, behind him, a noisy incident was probably another pair ostentatiously removing themselves from the proximity of an Englishman, no doubt for the benefit of hidden watchers.

Alone, Renzi sipped his beer as the conversations started again and his thoughts turned to what lay ahead.

It was near impossible, but a start had to be made. The hardest thing of all would be to locate the American. He had his freedom to move about, but that did not mean he could simply go up and ask where the submarine inventor called Fulton was. Even the slightest interest in matters not directly concerning his official purpose in France would be reported and seized upon jubilantly as evidence that he was abusing his position to spy. The *Moniteur* would trumpet to the world such perfidy against 'his innocent hosts', and the worthy cause of the hapless prisoners-of-war would irrevocably be lost.

Renzi forced himself to concentrate: there had to be a way to Fulton if he had the wit to find it. Without question he was being followed. After Jersey, however, he was too wise

in the ways of spying to try to shake them off. Once iden-
tified, an agent was a known quantity but, more importantly,
a slick evasion would be the quickest way to guarantee the
attention of Fouché's secret police.

The safest course would be to appear to make the most of
his stay and move about, visiting and gaping. This would have
them relaxing their surveillance and make furtive meetings
more possible. He smiled wryly. Right at this moment he was
where duty called – openly tasting the night life of Paris.

There was movement under the candlelight by the far wall
as a raven-haired *chanteuse* with a darker central European
violinist bowed together and opened with a soaring peasant air
from the Auvergne which took Renzi back to long-past days
of gaiety and passion. The singer made shameless play of her
charms and held the room spellbound. Despite himself, Renzi
was caught up in the charged atmosphere and applauded
enthusiastically.

Then followed a sensual love lament. The tavern fell quiet
as she held the audience with her tale of longing and suffering,
loving and losing. Renzi couldn't help a sudden rush of feeling;
for some reason she was reaching him with a message of
humanity and grief that rose far above the gross distortions
of war. As the urgent, pleading harmony enveloped him, his
mind rebelled: he was furious with the pitiless logic that said
the ultimate course for nations in disagreement was to throw
themselves at each other in a struggle to the death.

He gulped at the intensity of his reaction but then an image
of *Teazer* assailed him – the graceful being in whose bosom
he had been borne while his theories had matured, destroyed
without warning in a cataclysmic detonation, prey to a lurking
submarine boat, her unsuspecting crew torn to pieces by the
explosion.

It was horrific, an unthinkable fate that might come to pass unless . . . In the warm darkness it was all he could do to prevent his helplessness coming out in a storm of emotion and overwhelming him.

It was stultifying in the room: Haslip had resorted to a lengthy legal argument and was presenting it in a monotone. The French were led by an arrogant young firebrand, an earthy scion of the Revolution who clearly despised both the English and what he had to do, and did not bother to hide his impatience.

The presentation droned on, and when they broke for refreshments Renzi went to Haslip to show him his notes and express support. He met nothing but self-importance and a pompous disinclination to listen.

In the afternoon the French deployed their own man, an arid word-grinder whose lengthy, many-tailed points were almost impossible to follow and summarise on paper. Renzi despaired. It was as if the opposite party was under orders to obfuscate and delay, and he was relieved when an appeal to an obscure medieval case-law finding was interpreted in opposite ways and it was agreed to retire for study and deliberation.

His offer of assistance acidly declined, Renzi felt able to take time to get a hold on the situation. But before he did so he would indulge himself – just this once. He had noted a bookshop of some distinction further along the rue St Honoré that it would be a sin to ignore, in this the Paris of Montesquieu and Diderot.

It was, in fact, a grand palace of learning, ramparts of books stretching away, alcoves and desks for enquirers and stiffly dressed assistants attending the browsing public. He reached for a Voltaire and was soon contentedly absorbed in its earnest and learned preface, written by another scholar, praising the author as an epitome of the Enlightenment.

An assistant came up to him. Renzi thought of his own studies. Clearly, now was the perfect opportunity to discover the works of lesser-known authors – and at source. In his best French he asked politely if it were known that the philosopher Johann Herder had published anything of note following the *Ideen zur Philosophie* which had so informed Renzi's earlier searches for historical origins.

'*Je suis désolé, M'sieur,*' the man said sorrowfully, clearly untroubled by Renzi's English appearance.

An older man nearby removed his spectacles and cocked his head to one side. '*Pardonnez-moi, Monsieur,*' he said. 'I could not but help overhearing. I rather feel he would be most offended were I not to make mention of his *Briefe zur Beförderung der Humanität* recently to print.'

'You are so kind, sir,' Renzi said, with a bow. 'I find Herr Herder at a refreshing distance from Goethe's classicism.'

'Are you then a scholar, M'sieur?' the gentleman said, with rising interest.

'In the slightest way, sir. I am as yet unpublished, still to mature my hypotheses on the human condition.'

'Then surely the swiftest way to an enlightenment is disputing with the author himself.'

'"*Was ist Aufklärung?*"' Then what is enlightenment? Renzi could not resist Kant's pungent epigram. Then he hurried on, 'And I should wish it possible, sir.'

The man's eyes twinkled. 'Tonight you shall. It is the first Thursday of the month so there is a lecture at the Institut and I am sure your author friend will be there. Oh, may I introduce myself? Pierre Laplace, astronomer and mathematician.'

Renzi was stunned. This was the very savant whose work

on celestial mechanics and advanced mathematics had earned him the title of the French Newton – and, if he had heard aright, he was inviting him to the famous Institut to mingle with the finest minds of the age. 'B-but I am English, sir,' he said faintly.

'You may be a Hottentot for all I care. This night you shall be my guest, Monsieur . . . ?'

'Oh – er, Smith, Nicholas Smith.'

'Quite so.'

Close by an anonymous individual continued to concentrate on his book – Renzi noticed it was upside-down.

The lecture, on the taxonomic peculiarities of seaweed, was persuasively delivered, and afterwards Laplace went in search of Herr Herder. However, it seemed that the elderly gentleman was ill and they dined alone.

For some hours Renzi had been able to throw off his feeling of hopelessness, and taste something of what it must be to reach a level of recognition that would find him welcomed into the company of great thinkers such as these. Would his own contributions to knowledge ever achieve such greatness? 'Sir, I must express my deepest sensibility at your kindness in inviting me here,' he declared sincerely.

'Nonsense, Monsieur. You will go from here with renewed purpose, a higher vision. This is what *la belle* France is giving to humanity – a world where all are equal, each may enter the Temple of Learning as a consequence of their gifts of logic and scholarship, never the circumstances of their birth.'

'Sir, our Royal Society—'

'Is prestigious but class-bound. In France we order things differently. Why, where would be your Genevan Rousseau, even your Pole Kościusko had they not slaked their thirst for philosophies at the fountains of wisdom only to be found here in Paris?'

Renzi murmured an agreement, and Laplace continued expansively, 'Why, there are sages and philosophers from *all* corners of the world flocking here to be recognised – I honour these savants – and even original thinkers, like the American who came here, desiring of all things to create a submarine boat.'

'A – a what?' Renzi could hardly believe his ears.

'A species of plunging boat that submerges completely under the water. A most amazing device. I have seen it myself, for I have the honour to count the inventor among my friends,' Laplace said.

'It – it immerses under the water and stays there?' Renzi's mind was flailing wildly. 'Come, come, sir, this is hard to accept.'

'No, it is true, Monsieur, you have my word. I was able to intercede on his behalf to secure the funding – I have the ear of the Emperor, you know, and he was concerned even in these busy times to allow the gentleman to realise his undersea dreams.'

'How generous,' Renzi said, as heartily as he could. 'Can you conceive of it? A boat that swims freely in the realm of the creatures of the deep and allows the brave Argonauts aboard to view their disporting in safety and comfort. This is a marvel indeed.'

'Quite so.'

'And it may remain under the water for a – a period of time?'

'I myself and three-score distinguished witnesses observed its disappearance beneath the Seine to reappear whole, the crew unharmed, after a full hour had passed. And later the craft was transported down-river to the sea and he repeated the miracle. The submersible – he calls it *Nautilus* – may be relied upon to navigate unseen, travel many leagues at sea and carry quantities of men.'

'A magnificent opportunity for science,' Renzi enthused. 'Does it have a window at all? And how might the brave sailors breathe for so long in such confines? This is a mystery that must seize the imagination of even the most hopeless dullard. How I wish I might see this wonder of the deep.'

'Ah. That may be difficult. I believe the inventor is under contract to our government for its development and, naturally, there is much discretion involved in such. It is tedious but governments being as they are . . .'

Renzi allowed his disappointment to show. 'I understand. Such a pity. In my old age I might have recounted how I set eyes on the first submarine boat of the age, and now my curiosity must remain for ever unsatisfied . . .'

'A vexation for you. The pity of it all is that the man himself is most probably in the library below us. It is his practice that when he concludes at the ministry he invariably spends time there. He does treasure it for its quiet.'

Catching his breath Renzi stammered, 'To be here, when . . .'

Laplace tut-tutted, clearly moved by Renzi's ardent manner. 'Sir, this at the least I will do. I will leave it to Mr Fulton whether or no he desires to be introduced to one who stands in admiration of his work and prays that he might learn more. I believe the proctor's office will be available to us at this hour, and thus you may discreetly satisfy your curiosity as he will permit. That is all I can promise.'

It was an incredible stroke.

Chapter 7

In the book-lined, leather-smelling proctor's office Renzi waited for Laplace's return with pounding heart. It seemed an interminable time but suddenly he heard voices outside, then two men entered the room.

Renzi got hurriedly to his feet. 'Th-thank you, sir, so kind in you to see me.'

The man was tall and slender, even graceful, but what caught Renzi's eye was the intensity of his features, the large, dark eyes, intelligent forehead and quick, darting manner. 'Not at all, my friend,' he replied, in a hardly noticeable American accent, then smiled. 'And if I'm not mistaken in my reckoning you're English, sir.'

'Oh – Smith, Nicholas Smith of, um, Plymouth in Devon,' Renzi stammered, hoping to appear overcome at being in the presence of such genius.

'I know where Plymouth is, friend. I spent three years in Devon at my easel. Fine place to be. Now, be so good as to tell me how an Englishman is here in Paris unhung?'

'Er, I'm assistant to the official mission concerning the

exchange of prisoners-of-war – and by way of a scholar, but in the meanest degree,' he added, with a shy glance at Laplace.

'A cartel man? So, not a son of Albion come to his senses and the Republican cause?'

'Ah, not as who should say, sir,' Renzi said, aware that any pretence to radical sympathies as a means of penetrating a tight-knit group of expatriates of the Revolution would never stand scrutiny.

'Pity. So what can I do for you, sir?'

'Mr Fulton, Monsieur Laplace was good enough to tell me something of your submarine boat, and I confess I'm quite overcome with the grandeur of your vision. To conceive of a craft that swims with the fishes, inhabits Neptune's world like the native denizens – it is truly magnificent.'

'I thank you, sir.'

'Do tell – for I'm on fire with curiosity – when under the sea, do you see by light from the windows or is it a lanthorn or similar? I cannot imagine how it must be, warm and dry but fathoms down in the pelagic gloom lit only by . . . ?'

'Foxfire, sir. Naught but your common foxfire!' At Renzi's look of incomprehension he gave a boyish grin and said, 'A lanthorn or candle produces vitiated air, not fit for a human. This foxfire, we get it from the woods after a season of rain. It glows in the dark, quite enough to conn our noble craft, sir.'

'And you speak of air. Do you take a – a balloon or some such with you on the expedition, to release when the breathing becomes . . . difficult?'

Laplace stood up. 'Forgive me, gentlemen, I must attend to another matter. Do feel free to continue your discussion while I'm gone but, pray, do not leave this office together. It would prove . . . inconvenient for me.'

Renzi could hardly believe his luck: was this his chance?

His whole being urged him to make the move while he could – there might be no further opportunity. Yet a tiny voice of caution insisted that until he knew more of this man he stood a good prospect of being denounced as a British agent.

Fulton moved to the proctor's desk and sprawled in his chair, fiddling with a quill. 'You're both fascinated and in dread of the beast, am I right?'

'Your *Nautilus* is a scientifical phenomenon of the first order and I'm finding it difficult to grapple with its implications for mankind,' Renzi said.

'It is that.'

'Then – then do you not fear that your wonderful creation might not be subverted to serve another, baser interest?'

'That of war?'

'It might be supposed.'

Fulton smiled cynically. 'Then, Mr Englishman, I have news for you. The entire reason for my inventing it is war.'

'Sir, I beg you to elucidate.'

'Believe me, Mr Smith, to be an enemy to oppression wherever it's to be found. And the only guarantee of liberty for the individual, is freedom for the nation. I see that there exists one tyrant, one oppressor, who sorely bears on the nations of this world, that has made perpetual war in my lifetime by bestridin' the seas and robbing the world of its ancient maritime freedoms. Sir, I speak of the Royal Navy!'

'Go on, sir,' Renzi said.

'The rest then surely follows. *Nautilus* and her sisters'll make it impossible for your damn navy to take to the seas. Their ships'll skulk in harbour, a-feared o' silent assassination, the people will rise up on their monarchy, and then the oceans will be free for all nations in amity to progress on their lawful occasions.'

Was there any sign of madness behind the triumphant smile? If so, Renzi couldn't detect any.

'And that, Englishman, will be the end of war as we know it. No state will ever more hazard to set a fleet of ships a-swim with the intention of dominating the seas, which will then oblige each nation to live peaceable within the bounds nature has set it.'

He spindled a paper lazily. 'In course, I've taken steps to place the whole on a sound commercial footing, as you'd expect of a Maryland farming boy – there's to be a bounty payable on every warship put down by my submarines and a royalty for each one built under licence. Self-funding, you see.'

Renzi struggled to reconcile the stern political radicalism with the artless words of a backwoodsman. Was this the raving of an unworldly visionary or was the future to be this horrifying reality? He asked respectfully, 'Sir, might we say your plans to this end are advanced at all?'

'Do you mean, sir, is *Nautilus* ready for her destiny? Mr Napoleon Bonaparte thinks so. He told me to my face to take her overland to Brest and there, before a quantity of admirals, I stalked unseen a ship – and blew her to smithereens with my torpedoes. That opened one or two eyes, I can tell you.'

'Out in the open sea?' Renzi said, chilled to the core. This submarine did not just work, it was now armed with a deadly explosive device and quite ready to strike wherever it chose. It had happened. The world he knew was fast ending.

'Of course. And I'll tell you something else.' He chuckled. 'In the end months of the last war I took her out myself on patrol and there's two English brigs alive today only because they sailed before I could see to 'em!'

Who was to say that one of them had not been *Teazer*, unwittingly hunted by an unseen assassin to within a moment of being blown to fragments? Renzi pulled himself together. 'A – a fine achievement,' he said faintly. 'I had no idea.'

'Why, thank you, sir. I didn't think to hear the same from an Englishman.' Fulton seemed genuinely touched.

'Er, it would gratify me no end if I were able to view your fabled *Nautilus*.'

'That will not be possible,' Fulton retorted, with a hard look.

'I did not mean to offend, sir.'

Fulton's features softened. 'Well, if you must know I'm right now in negotiation with the French Ministry of Marine for a larger, more potent plunging-boat and . . .' He tailed off and gazed out of the window.

'I do understand your position, sir,' Renzi said.

'The world will hear about 'em soon enough.' Fulton swung around in his chair and rose, extending his hand. 'Pleasure to meet you, friend. And good luck with your prisoners,' he added breezily, and left.

The situation had changed from grave to catastrophic. From future potential to present reality. Here was the truth of all the rumours: a submarine craft *had* been constructed, tested and fitted with weapons of irresistible destruction. Fulton had indeed the ear of Napoleon and was concluding a contract for a whole fleet of the submersibles. And very soon these would quickly break the stalemate and see the Channel cleared wide open for a grand concluding scene.

In an agony of helplessness Renzi sprang to his feet and began pacing the room. If there was going to be any time left for action he had to think of something now. But, for God's sake, what?

His frantic thoughts were interrupted by the arrival of Laplace. 'Ah – so Mr Fulton has returned to his work. Did you find satisfaction, sir?'

Renzi composed himself. 'Indeed so, Monsieur. A most fascinating gentleman.'

'Then I must bid you farewell, Mr Smith. *Bonne chance* in your negotiations. I shall see you to the door.'

Out in the street Renzi let the ceaseless flow of people and vehicles eddy past, trying to bring to bear a line of thought that would lead to a path of action, but there were too many conflicting elements.

The fortuitous meeting with Laplace would be seen as harmless enough in itself, for the academician had thoughtfully arranged his meeting with Fulton in privacy – no one would know and he was therefore unlikely to be under suspicion. Renzi still retained his freedom of movement and Fulton had shown himself not unfriendly, so it was reasonable to assume that he stood a chance if only he could think of *something*.

He paced slowly, forcing his mind to concentrate. The only way that Fulton was going to leave France was of his own volition. Therefore it was up to Renzi to create the elements that would lead to such a decision with arguments so persuasive that the inventor would see it overwhelmingly in his interest to abandon Napoleon to go with the British, no matter his political views. It seemed impossible and time was running out: who knew how much longer the talks about the prisoners would last?

Then, some hundreds of yards ahead, he saw Fulton walking down the street, carrying a large flat case, his head bowed in thought. Impulsively, Renzi followed – at the very least he could try to find out something more of the man.

Almost certainly Fulton was being trailed. Bonaparte had too much invested in him to do otherwise. However, Renzi had been seen publicly with the highly respected Laplace, who had obviously trusted him, so at the moment it was unlikely *he* was being tracked.

Deliberately Renzi stopped and gawped upwards at an imposing stonework façade, then wandered on, taking in the sights but alert for one thing. It wasn't long before he spotted what he was looking for: a man who found shop-windows very interesting, then hurried on, his quick, covert glances always in Fulton's direction.

Renzi eased his pace, letting Fulton pass out of sight ahead. As long as he had the tail in view he was being led after his quarry. They both disappeared to the right down the next street. Renzi lengthened his stride, moving faster without the appearance of haste. Round the corner Fulton was comfortably in sight again. He remembered this avenue led to the banks of the Seine – what was Fulton up to?

The American paused at the edge of the water. Then he made off up the river on the leafy *quai* that led to some of the grandest sights in Paris. With the red of the setting sun, the distant image of Notre Dame seemed to Renzi to lift ethereally above earthly dross.

As if in sudden resolution, Fulton stepped out faster. The evening promenaders drifting across the line-of-sight made it easy for Renzi to keep a discreet observation on his mark. It was puzzling, though: the further sights were grander but this was not a district noted for its residences. Then, suddenly, clutching his case close to him, Fulton hurried across the Pont au Change and on to the mid-river island that bore the great cathedral – and the blood-soaked Conciergerie prison.

He didn't stop and passed quickly across to the other bank. This was a mystery indeed. Fulton was now on the Left Bank and, in the gathering dusk, heading deep into the Latin Quarter of seedy, decaying tenements. Was he visiting a paramour?

Unlikely, given the kind of doxy to be found in this district. Or the rendezous place of some revolutionary band?

Finally it was down a short street and into a dead end where Fulton passed into a doorway. Renzi crossed the road but stayed by the corner, looking back diagonally across at the anonymous apartment building. If he was caught, there could be no pretence now of sightseeing – there could be only one reason for his movements.

Was this merely a visit, a delivery – a clandestine meeting? Nerves at full stretch, Renzi waited. There was no sign of the follower. He pressed back into the grimy brickwork as an infant squalled on a lower floor and cooking smells wafted out. At the top a light flickered into existence and steadied. A shadow passed in front of it, then another light sputtered on and Fulton passed unmistakably between them.

Yet another light appeared close to the first. Still no other figure. Fulton crossed back, and when all had been still for some time it became clear to Renzi that this was no secret rendezvous or other furtive assignation; Fulton's unsuspecting movements could have only one meaning. This was simply a man returning home after a hard day of work. The many lights meant he was probably working on his design ready for the next day's meetings.

This raised as many questions as it answered, but he now had the priceless secret of where Fulton could be found. His spirits rose. But there must be a reason for the man's living in such surroundings. Perhaps, as an artist, the Bohemian lifestyle of this *arrondissement* appealed? But why subject himself to the noise and stinks when he could no doubt demand a mansion?

Renzi shook his head at the conundrums and turned to go. From round the corner the follower stepped squarely into his path. In one terrifying instant Renzi had to make a decision to fight or run. Both courses would have the same outcome: his spying would be discovered. In a burst of desperate inspiration he plastered a foolish grin on his face and swaying towards the man, fell to his knees, pawed ineffectively at him, then keeled over and dry-retched into the filthy gutter.

The man stepped round him in disgust and Renzi crawled away, groaning, then staggered to his feet, trembling. It had been a narrow escape.

Haslip was waiting for him. 'This I could scarcely credit, Mr Smith! One in your position, daring to approach a gentleman of such stature as Monsieur Laplace, and at the Institut no less. The French government have rightly expressed to me their serious misgivings that a junior member of a diplomatic mission should so far forget himself.' He snorted in indignation.

So the French knew of his meeting Laplace and were nervous – but they had no idea he had spoken to Fulton or it would have been a very different matter. Renzi forced himself to an icy calm. 'Sir, I do sincerely regret the impulse that led me to such an action. In my studies I have often encountered the work of Monsieur Laplace and—'

'That is to no account, sir. As head of mission, I forbid you to engage in such scholarly pretensions above your station, which can only result in ridicule. Do I make myself clear?'

'Why, yes, Mr Haslip, you do. I shall not trouble the gentleman again.'

'Hmph. It seems to me there is little enough work to keep you occupied. I shall think on it.'

'Thank you, sir. Should I go now, sir?' Renzi wheedled. To his contempt, he could see that this had mollified Haslip, who sniffed and indicated that the interview was at an end. Renzi left and took refuge in his room.

He sat on the edge of the bed, head in hands. The situation was tightening. Without doubt he was now being watched; he could not count on freedom to act any more. And what *could be* the meaning of Fulton's living in such eccentric circumstances when he was the confidant of an emperor?

His feet hurt and the incident with the follower had unsettled him. To be at large in the Paris of Napoleon Bonaparte, who, no doubt, was preparing for the night in sumptuous surroundings less than a mile from where Renzi sat, was almost too fantastical for belief. Yet if he put a foot wrong – a lapse in speaking, an unlooked-for coincidence, recognition by one from his past – Fouché's secret police would pounce.

There was a bottle of brandy between two glasses on the dresser. He splashed himself a strong measure and tried to compose his thoughts. Everything hung on his conjuring an argument to detach Fulton from the French cause.

He felt the brandy doing its work and paced up and down while he considered his next move. He had to act quickly to prevent any suspicion growing. For the moment they would be presuming that he had been reprimanded by his master for straying outside set bounds. Therefore he must do something suitably predictable in the circumstances, and it must be a move that no self-respecting spy would make.

It came to him almost immediately, effective and credible, but with the grave drawback that if he could not pull it off to perfection he would end by being the instrument of his own betrayal. Only iron self-control would see him through – the prize, his freedom to act.

It was the only way forward. Tonight he would get drunk.

Not just flustered or even betwaddled, but completely cup-shot and maudlin, such that any sympathetic stranger sidling up to share his woes would not doubt for a moment what they heard.

Renzi made his preparations. He had not been lost to drink since his youth and the wanton excesses of the Grand Tour. Now he was determined to bring it to pass – there could be no studied pretence at intoxication: it could be only the real thing, convincing in its repulsiveness and gradual descent into incoherence. He examined his store of coins. How many of these new-fangled 'francs' would it take to achieve total drunkenness?

Carefully he went through his pockets: there was nothing incriminating. His precious passport was slipped deep within his waistcoat and he was ready for the night.

Outside it was dark but the traffic showed little sign of diminishing. He dithered at the hotel entrance, long enough to be seen, then turned left, ambling along in quite the opposite direction from the Latin Quarter, towards the more northerly faubourgs, Montmartre – or was that now Mont Marat after the scientist and revolutionary?

He resisted the temptation to see if he was being followed and kept his eyes ahead, but allowed himself to be jostled by a passing couple and swung about to glare after them. With much satisfaction, he saw guilty movement in a slightly built man a dozen yards behind.

He resumed his walk without a second glance back. As the larger establishments turned into a smaller, more intimate hostelry he looked about. Le Canard Sportif appealed and he went in. The noise, the glare of Argand lamps on brass and crystal and the smell of humanity, beer and Gallic cuisine assaulted his senses, but Renzi reminded himself he had a job to do.

His order was taken by a waif-like girl in an apron who, on hearing his accent, ran back to the *patron*, who came over to peer at him suspiciously.

But he had his story, and, with a suitably woebegone expression, then the ostentatious checking of francs, it seemed to persuade the man that he would be no trouble. What did he desire to drink? Why, *absinthe* would answer – he had heard of but never tried this newly fashionable tipple. So Monsieur has a taste for Paris? Then the *verte* would probably most appeal. *Mademoiselle – ici!*

An odd pinch-waisted glass was brought with an intense green liquor in the base and a narrow, spike-ended spoon placed across the rim. A lump of sugar was put on its slotted bowl and ice-cold water poured over it, clouding the result to an opalescent milkiness.

Fascinated, Renzi took it, inhaling the wormwood aroma appreciatively. He sipped: the complex of herbs took him by surprise but was, he concluded, very agreeable. Remembering his duty he downed it resolutely and, before long, felt the subtle tendrils of inebriation begin to spread.

Another? Certainly. A few curious glances came his way. The liquor had a lazy potency that was deceptive and even a fine onion soup did nothing to halt the muzziness stealing over him.

He became aware of someone drawing up a chair beside him. At last – they were making their move! But it was a girl. They chatted amiably but she pouted and left when he kept reaching for his *absinthe*. The spirit took a deeper hold. His inner being calmly noted a curious rotation of perspectives, a plasticity in objects as his mind gently separated from its corporeal existence.

He noticed a distraction to one side and drunkenly turned

in his seat – it was a man, smiling affably, who introduced himself as one who so deplored this unfortunate state of hostilities between two such great nations, and who seemed not to notice his befuddlement.

It took a convulsion of will to realise that the moment had come. Fighting lassitude, he fumbled for the elusive French that expressed his solemn agreement and hope that this fine city might soon be open once again to any English hearts seeking to pay homage.

The man agreed and summoned more *absinthe* for his new friend – his opinion on a clear variety, La Bleue, was earnestly solicited. Renzi allowed it a splendid drop and confided it was going far in helping him overcome his woes. His head swam.

Woes? Surely not! Another La Bleue persuaded Renzi to unburden and, to the man's sharp interest, he obliged passionately.

Rather than the loneliness of a foreign country, it seemed it was more the cruel fate of the prisoners-of-war that grieved him. They were getting nowhere in the negotiations and all the time men on both sides were spending their years in unjust captivity, merely for doing their duty to their country.

Renzi grew more emotional: to see the conditions of the prison hulks in Portsmouth and Sheerness, it would wring the heart of the devil himself – and now there was talk of building a massive fortress prison in the middle of remote Dartmoor. He struggled for words to describe the desolate heath, the hopeless pallor of the prisoners, families unseen whose grief at the separation . . .

To Renzi's relief the man's interest declined and, finding he had an appointment, he departed.

What was left of his rational being exulted – and, with a seraphic smile, he surrendered all and slid to the floor.

The next morning his plea of illness was relayed to Haslip – Renzi didn't care how it was received as, despite his hammering head, he was gloriously triumphant: by some mysterious working of the brain, he had woken with a glorious, vital inspiration at the forefront of his consciousness.

He now understood the real reason for Fulton's hiding away in the stews of the Left Bank – and with it he had the key to making an approach. He lay back in growing satisfaction, letting all the pieces come together. And they fitted as snugly as he could have wished.

It was the character of the man. His was a brilliant and fecund mind; in a few short years he had changed from an artist of the first rank into a self-taught engineer, able not only to conceive of but actually bring to realisation dread engines of war. But that very quality, his lonely genius and single-minded drive to achieve, had made him almost completely self-reliant, never needing the support and comfort of an organisation. And, like many deeply immersed in a project of their own conception, he was suspicious and wary.

The vital clue was what he had said about a business footing for his endeavours. Greed for gold did not figure in this: he was using a commercial mechanism to *control* the project and remain at its head. But thinking that Paris would agree to such a novel prospect – commercialising the art of war – was both naïve and futile.

However, if Fulton was holding out for a business relationship, that would explain both the conspicuous absence of the military about him and his humble lodgings. With the

French standing firm, the man was probably fast running out of money.

Was this, then, his chance? Despite his thudding head, Renzi felt a leaping hope. After his short talk with Fulton he felt certain that, for him, the bringing into the world of his creations stood above all else. He had almost certainly chosen to go with the French as having the greatest need for a war-winning sea weapon against the all-conquering Royal Navy, and the radical talk might be just that.

It was time to act – but was he prepared to stake everything, even his life, on one drunken insight? He had until that night to decide.

Slipping out of the hotel quickly, Renzi stepped down the avenue and into the darkness, pausing only at the corner to glance back. As far as he could tell, his previous night's debauchery had succeeded and no one was interested in him. He pushed on as if he was heading for the Bastille. Then he took a last precaution. At Le Marais he chose a narrow street, turned down it and hid in the first alley he could find. He had not long to wait: he *had* been followed.

As the man pressed past urgently Renzi was out and behind him. Hands clasped, he brought his fists down hard on the nape of the other's neck, then dragged his pursuer, senseless, into the alley. In the blackness he went through the man's pockets, taking a watch, money, papers. He stuffed them away and, for good measure, took the coat, a stout fustian, then left. Now free to move, he cut abruptly right and across the Seine by the Pont Marie, dropping the coat into the river as he went.

He headed directly through the Latin Quarter to Fulton's address, slowing when he got near. A watcher stood at the corner opposite. This was another matter entirely. Close in with the wall and at full alert, the man could not be taken by surprise. Lights showed in the top floor – Fulton was there.

Renzi's resolve hardened. Should he kill the man? But that would only awaken suspicions. Then he remembered something. He turned back to a small pile of old furniture. With a flap-sided table over his shoulder, he walked firmly towards the doorway. The watcher would probably know the tenement residents, but it was unlikely that a tradesman delivering goods would be challenged.

At the entrance he mimed to a woman that he was a mute, jabbing upwards. She let him in and he stumped up the dark stairs, leaving the table at the top landing. Then, heart racing, he knocked at the door.

Fulton's muffled voice demanded who it was. Renzi mumbled a few words until an exasperated Fulton flung the door open. 'Mr – Mr Smith! What in hell's name—'

Renzi pushed his way past, ducking out of sight of the windows. 'Forgive the intrusion, Mr Fulton, but my business with you is pressing and cannot stand on ceremony.'

'What business? And how in the devil's name do you know where I live?'

'Sir, I know you to be an inventor and genius of the first rank who will surely find a place in history. I am also aware that you're frustrated in your desire to see your creations born, to have them become a tangible reality.'

A long table at the end of the room was overflowing with drawings and other papers. Renzi thought he could detect the form of an undersea craft.

'Not only that, but you are being denied the fruits of your labours – even the means to sustain existence while you bring these wonders into the world. Mr Fulton, I'm here to—'

'By God, you're English and you've come to put in your oar with me and Emperor Bonaparte!' he gasped in astonishment. 'The barefaced hide of you, sir!'

A knot formed in Renzi's stomach: if he revealed his true identity he might court betrayal to the watcher outside, but if he denied it, he would have no standing by which to negotiate.

'It's true, isn't it? How can you know of my affairs,' Fulton snapped, 'unless you've agents in the Ministry of Marine?' His eyes narrowed.

'Sir, if your heart is set on this, you must see that your present arrangement will not be the one that achieves it. Napoleon's France will never agree to putting a military master-stroke in the power of a Yankee businessman, no matter what the terms. You should see this, sir!'

Time was slipping away: at any moment the watcher might realise that the deliveryman had not emerged and become suspicious. And if he had made an error concerning Fulton's true situation he was done for.

'Well, Mr Smith, or whatever your name is, I can tell you now, you're plain damn wrong in your reckoning. There's nothing stands between me and my arrangement save a little matter concerning the crew of the submersibles.'

'The crew?' Renzi said, mystified.

'If it's the barbaric custom these days to treat fire-ship crews as pirates and incendiaries, I want the French to stand surety that the enemy won't hang 'em – and take reprisals on their prisoners if they do.'

'Sir, I'd hazard they've been hanging fire over this for . . . a long time,' Renzi said quietly. For the canny French it would be an ideal sticking point to drag matters out. It was looking more and more certain that they were letting economic hardship do their work for them in forcing Fulton to hand over the plans and come to a different agreement.

'They'll get to it,' Fulton said uncomfortably.

'Perhaps,' said Renzi, seeing his chance. 'But in the meantime it would grieve me to see a mind as worthy as yours brought to such a needy pass.' He fumbled beneath his waistcoat and found his money-belt. 'Here – twenty English guineas.' He placed them on the table. Fulton made no move to stop him. 'They're yours, sir, with my best wishes. There's no need to account for them – no one has seen me give them to you, have they?'

They were part of a sum he had signed for in far-away Walmer Castle and he would have to explain later but for now . . .

Fulton gave him a look of indignation. 'If you're thinking I'd sell out for English gold . . .'

But Renzi had seen the gleam in his eye – the money meant decent meals, wine, a respite from creditors . . . independence. At the very least Renzi had bought his silence. The danger of betrayal had receded. 'Sir, I would not think to imply such a thing. Do take it as your due.'

Fulton picked up the coins and slipped them into his pocket. 'Accepted with my thanks – but I see myself under no obligation whatsoever.'

'Quite. I cannot help but observe that it's not without its merit to consider some kind of business relationship with Britain as will see your projects properly completed. I'm sure—'

'Are you an English agent?' Fulton asked.

Renzi caught his breath. 'I'm authorised to offer you a contract with His Majesty's government for the full realisation of your works in a sum to be determined, and all possible assistance from the naval authorities under your direction.'

This was breathtaking gall. Renzi knew very well he had no

such authority – in light of Fulton's commercial inclinations he had made it up on the spot.

'So it seems you *must* be an agent, Mr Englishman. Well, unless I did not make myself clear before,' he said sarcastically, 'let me inform you that my democratic and republican views are as—'

'Democratic? Republican? A singular position, may I say, for one who will now be seen as supporting the world ambitions of an emperor, no less, whose own views on—'

'Leave Mr Bonaparte out of this!'

'I cannot see how that is possible,' Renzi said smoothly. 'So long as you confine your labours to the cause of this French emperor the world must draw its own conclusions.'

Fulton's face reddened. He started to say something but thought better of it.

Renzi continued, in a brighter tone, 'For one in the character of a businessman, I'm surprised you do not see the opportunity before you of enabling a helpless and frustrated navy before the invasion ports to enter unseen and put paid to the flotillas skulking within. For this power they will pay much, I'm persuaded.' Renzi pushed the vision. 'In course, you will conjure such a fleet of submarine boats as will astonish mankind. Should you be paid by results, as you wish, then the elimination of two thousand invasion craft—'

'You're speaking for the British Admiralty?'

'Not at all. I speak for His Maj – the government of Great Britain, the prime minister, sir.'

Fulton paced about the room. 'If such a thing were possible, it could only be under a copper-bottomed business contract that sees me in charge, and be damned to pettifogging interference.'

'Can there be any other way? We speak of results – what

better way to secure them than to place the responsibility entirely in your hands.' Renzi smiled ironically. 'You will appreciate that the practice of business is not entirely dissimilar in our two nations.'

Fulton scowled but said nothing.

A thought suddenly struck Renzi, one that appealed to his romantic streak. The submarine: how fitting – how exciting it would be if they were to make their dramatic escape in it from Napoleon's clutches safely to the open sea beneath the waves!

'Er, incidentally, where do you keep *Nautilus* at the moment?'

'She is no more.'

'Oh.'

Fulton turned his face away. 'To keep myself I was constrained to break her up, sell the pipes and cylinders, all the ironwork.'

'I'm sorry to hear it,' Renzi said softly, the vision fading.

'The French were in a right taking when they heard about it.' He grinned sourly.

As well they might be, thought Renzi. Without a working specimen, everything lay out of reach, confined within Fulton's fertile brain. It explained why they had held off seizing what they wanted and were now applying more subtle pressures.

Renzi gave what he hoped was a look of sincere sympathy. 'No more than they deserve. A disgraceful treatment of a distinguished man of engineering. You will find that we British will—'

'You British!' Fulton snarled. 'Have a care, sir – I've said naught about toadying up to King George, as I remember.'

'Nor should you!' Renzi came back swiftly, 'As we both know, it is in the nature of a business arrangement only.'

Fulton stalked away and stood glowering out of the window.

'Above all things,' Renzi said, 'you will agree that while you remain here you stand small chance of seeing your sea dreams realised. A firm contract with my government means you could be building within the month.'

There was no visible response. 'Mr Fulton, if—'

'You're asking I take up with the losing side,' Fulton retorted acidly.

'Do you not have confidence in your own device of war, sir?' Renzi replied coolly.

'I'll think on it.'

'Sir, I must press you to—'

'I said I'd think on it, damn you!'

'An understanding, perhaps, that—'

'Get out! Before I tip off your friend yonder.'

Renzi drew himself up. 'Very well. Should you desire to discuss terms then, er, I shall be in touch. Good day to you, Mr Fulton.'

He turned to go, but Fulton stopped him and pointed to the ceiling. 'I'd advise you leave by that hole – it lets out over the roof,' he said, with a twisted smile. 'No point in letting 'em know who you've been to see.'

'Why, thank you for your concern, sir,' Renzi said.

Fulton grinned. 'Shall we say I've seen my share of creditors?'

It was not until he was halfway back that the full implications of what had happened dawned on him. In effect, for all his efforts and personal danger, Renzi had nothing to show for it. The best that could be said was that he had been right in his insight and that Fulton had listened. Whether this might be turned to advantage was another matter.

Now he was faced with a near insuperable problem: he had slipped his shadow and, for a certainty, would now be trailed closely wherever he went. With Fulton under observation as well, how would they get together to conclude anything, even if the man was receptive?

At the Grandime Hotel he took care to reel in happily, a foolish smile in place, nodding to the silent men at the desk before he hauled himself up the stairs.

He flopped onto his bed and tried to recruit his thoughts. It had all happened so quickly, but at the same time he had achieved only a reconnaissance and, worse, he had lost the ability to continue any negotiations with Fulton. Even if the man could be persuaded, there was still the matter of an exit strategy, an escape route that would keep them ahead of the inevitable hot pursuit – the French would spare nothing to stop them.

Staring up at the dark ceiling he tried to bring together all the threads, but always reached the same conclusion. So near and so far – he could see no way forward on his own.

There was one last move open to him, one that he had been warned was only to be made in extreme circumstances, which did not include personal danger. This was to make contact with the network of agents in Paris, the precious few who remained after the recent catastrophic failure of the plot against Napoleon.

The next afternoon when Haslip was taking time for himself, Renzi made his way to the broad open spaces of the Place du Carrousel. This was where the plot to assassinate First Consul Bonaparte had so nearly succeeded two years before. The Breton giant Cadoudal had barely escaped with his life to try again the following year. Renzi carefully pinned a revolutionary red, white and blue cockade to his left arm and, with his hat firmly under the right, strolled through the gardens, admiring the flowers.

In the pleasant sunshine he nodded to the ladies, trying not to think of his deadly peril. A covey of screaming children raced on to the grass with a scolding woman in vain pursuit.

'*Vous là! Oui, se tenir prêt les fleurs!*' challenged a gendarme, with a fierce moustache and red-plumed bicorne. '*Venez ici!*' he commanded, gesturing.

'Papers!' he demanded, when Renzi came up, one hand on his sword-hilt, the other outstretched.

Renzi fought down the impulse to run and fumbled for his passport, heart thudding. Passing promenaders gave them a wide berth.

'*Oui, Monsieur – les voici.*' The gendarme examined it closely, then looked up sharply. 'The wolf howls only at the moon!' He stabbed his finger at the passport.

'Th—then it is silent!' Renzi answered nervously. It was the challenge and response, and he was now in contact with a royalist agent.

'What do you want?'

'A – a delicate matter. If you can arrange, in some way, a privy communication with a certain person . . .'

'When?'

'Er, as soon as possible.'

'Very well.' He thrust the passport at Renzi. 'Be sitting at the park bench over my shoulder at four. Do you understand?'

Renzi nodded.

The gendarme smiled unexpectedly. '*Bonne chance, mon brave,*' he said, stepping back and folding his arms in dismissal.

In good time Renzi was sitting on the bench as instructed. At four there was no one, and at a quarter past the hour a young mother insisted on occupying the other end while she dandled her baby on her knee in the sunshine, cooing and clucking, inviting him to admire the now squalling infant.

It was a clever ruse and, within a few minutes, Renzi had been invited to impart the essence of the difficulty. In return he received a businesslike solution. A vase of flowers would later appear in his room. If it was placed in the window it would indicate that a message for Fulton was concealed under its base. Likewise, Fulton's message for Renzi might be found under the base should the vase appear again in the window. At the other end there would be different arrangements. How it was done was not his affair.

That night he wrote a short message, in anonymous block capitals, which simply explained how Fulton's new friend might be contacted and hoped that he would hear from him soon.

He placed the vase in the window and went to bed. In the morning when he woke it was still there, but when he returned from another morning of stupefying boredom at the prisoner-of-war negotiating tables, he found a different paper in the hollow base. Feverishly he tore it open.

'The matter is not impossible,' it read, in a beautifully neat and characterful hand. 'What can you offer?'

Exultant, Renzi paced up and down while he considered. In his body-belt he held eight hundred pounds in gold, intended for travel expenses and the like. Would this be enough to tempt Fulton to leave immediately, the form of the contract to be discussed in England?

The thought of quick acceptance followed by rapid departure from this fearful world of danger and deceit was intoxicating. Quickly he penned a reply, emphasising immediate payment and rosily reviewing the prospects he had mentioned earlier.

For the rest of the day he was forced to attend a legal

hearing and did not arrive back until late – but there *was* a reply. Renzi scanned it rapidly, and his heart sank. In lordly tones Fulton was demanding no less than ten thousand pounds to leave France. Carefully he composed a reply. It would not be possible to raise such an amount at short notice but the eight hundred would be more than sufficient to ensure a swift passage to England where all things would be possible. His overriding objective was to ensure his freedom to negotiate at the highest level he chose.

When the response came it was long-winded, hectoring, and demanded, as a condition to Fulton's considering any proposal, an undertaking that the British government form a plenary committee within three weeks of his arrival to examine the scope not only of his submarine craft but of other inventions. In return he would be able to offer the plans for an improved *Nautilus* and his torpedoes to the Admiralty for a hundred thousand pounds. Further, written proof of the offer from the British at cabinet level would be necessary before he would contemplate acceptance or leaving France.

It was an impossibility. The annual salary of a senior clerk for a thousand years? The man must be mad – or was he? Whoever stalked the undersea realm would surely command the seas, and it was plain that those who stood to lose the most were the English.

Renzi slumped. His first impulse was to promise anything at all, as long as Fulton left for England. He was living on borrowed time – and the stakes could not have been higher. But he knew he could not compromise his principles still further.

He sighed deeply and reached for his pen. With the utmost regrets he admitted he was not in a position to bind the

British government to the amount indicated. However, to keep faith with Fulton he would, with all dispatch, open secret communications with Whitehall to establish a basis for negotiation.

There was little more he could do, now that he was passing the responsibility to a higher authority – and, wearily, he realised that this presented a grave problem in itself. How the devil would he get messages of explosive content safely to England when he had no means to secure them? Trusting the agents to perform some kind of coding was asking too much – and, apart from that, they would then be privy to state secrets of the highest importance.

He had no cipher materials: possession of such in any context was *prima facie* evidence of espionage. Yet if the communications were not enciphered he could not risk divulging vital and necessary details. In any case, to meet Fulton's demands he had to obtain a written undertaking at the highest level, which must be secure. He was going round in circles. There must be a way.

Renzi was by no means ignorant of secret codes after his experiences in Jersey: could he find a method from first principles to encrypt the message? The gravest difficulty of all was that in virtually every case the key had to be known beforehand at the receiving end or it must be sent in clear by other means – with catastrophic consequences if compromised.

Despite everything, Renzi found himself drawn into the logical challenges of the dilemma. After the intense boredom of the prisoner-of-war negotiations, the danger and frustration of dealing with Fulton, this bracing intellectual exercise was congenial, and he bent his mind to the task.

Any cipher whose key could be discovered was by definition unusable. Classical ciphers, such as the famous Caesar Shift, with no key but letter substitution, were unsafe – code-breaking had moved on in modern times. The same applied to the transposition types and, without prior arrangements, more complex techniques would require a key or method-type to be sent on before in clear.

A book cipher? This had the advantage that the key was already in the possession of the receiver – the text of a pre-agreed book held by both. A word in the message was specified as a precise location of that same word in the book. The disadvantage was that not only was it essential for each to have precisely the same edition but it was laborious, and the resulting encipherment could be large in size. The Bible had been used many times, with its exact chapter and verse convenience, but of course it would be the first that code-breakers tried.

There was another method: the running-key cipher. This used a source book too, but at individual character level. From a given point the ongoing text was used as a continuous key-stream to yield coded values against the message contents. This was better – and if the book's title was protected the resulting encipherment was near unbreakable.

So, what volume was to be used, known precisely by both parties? The Admiralty's own King's Regulations? Or the Articles of War? But without them to hand he could not swear to accuracy. And if it was to be some other book, its name and edition had to be divulged first. He was back where he had started.

He lay down and closed his eyes. It was the separate transmission in clear of a key or decoding method that was the sticking point. If he could only—

He sat bolt upright. That was it! The method, the key-text – and a cast-iron secure way of transmitting the key!

Galvanised, he set to work. He would not be disturbed – he had uncovered some time ago that Haslip's concern to be left alone was on account of a certain woman, and the French could not trespass on diplomatic territory.

Snatching up paper and a pencil he began to set up his *tabula recta*, the encoding matrix. Not needing to consult a book, he was able to work swiftly, and at a little after midnight he had the result. Carefully he burned his workings, folded the papers as small as he could and sealed them tightly together.

He hesitated over the forwarding instructions but eventually settled on 'Foreign Office, per Smith, Paris'. It would find the right handler easily enough. Underneath, in smaller lettering, was the more important entry: 'Refer Cdr Thomas Kydd, HMS *Teazer*'. It was done.

Kydd stalked into his cabin in a foul mood. This was the third man flogged within the month for petty crimes, unavoidably in full view of the shore, and the spirit aboard was stagnating. When would the damned timbers arrive for the repair? He was keenly conscious of the fearful danger under which England lay and it went so much against his grain to lie in useless idleness. And Renzi – heaven knew what he was up to, and would Kydd ever find out?

Restless, he ventured on deck again. A fine sight, so many blue-water ships, particularly the big Indiaman to the south – as massive as a line-of-battle ship with, no doubt, a freighting aboard worth a prince's ransom, and soon to venture out to the open ocean where dangers lurked in wait every day of her six months, or more, voyaging.

Ashore, he could pick out the Deal hovellers. On this fine summer's day there was nothing to occupy them except the taking out of fresh provisions, passengers—

'Telegraph's in a taking,' Hallum offered, behind him, trying to make conversation. The shutter atop a bluff tower in the King's Naval Yard was indeed busy, clacking away furiously. The chain of signal stations stretched all the way to London and the Admiralty in a direct line.

Idly, Kydd wondered what it was signalling. Never used for routine messages it was how the first lord of the Admiralty, through his senior staff, was able to reach out and deploy the chess pieces that were his fleets to counter enemy threats. Incredibly, this signal would be here, in the commander-in-chief's hands, some fifteen minutes or so after it was sent from London.

He resumed pacing. It was no use worrying about his timber, which would come in its own good time. He must contain his impatience and be ready to throw *Teazer* into the fray the instant she was whole once more.

'Boat approaching, sir.'

Oddly, the vessel had been launched from the King's Naval Yard instead of the flagship, and with only a single officer in the stern-sheets. Kydd stayed on deck and watched it hook on.

The officer came on board. 'Commander Kydd, sir?' he asked respectfully, with more than a hint of curiosity.

'It is.'

'Then, sir, I have a message from the admiral. You are to hold yourself in readiness at his office immediately for a particular service that he will speak to you about – in person.'

'Er—'

'I know nothing further.'

'Very well.'

Admiral Keith was short almost to the point of rudeness. 'Kydd, I have just received a signal from the Admiralty concerning you that greatly disturbs me.'

'Sir?' The Admiralty?

'It asks – no, damn it, *demands* that you be taken out of your ship and made ready to receive a parcel o' rogues from the Aliens Office under circumstances of the utmost secrecy. Now, sir – this is intolerable! I will not be kept in ignorance. You will tell me what is afoot this instant.'

Kydd swallowed. 'Sir, I – I cannot. The Aliens Office?'

'Are you asking me to accept that a – a junior commander is to be made privy to matters considered too sensitive for a senior admiral? Have you been politicking, sir? I won't stand for it in a serving captain of mine, Mr Kydd, no, not for one minute.'

'N-no, sir.'

'And I intend to be present when those jackanapes arrive!'

'Of course, sir.'

'Most irregular!'

'Yes, sir, it is.'

'You'll wait here until sent for,' Keith rumbled irritably. 'You may not leave on any account.'

'Aye aye, sir.'

Sitting alone in the little side office, Kydd waited apprehensively.

Late in the afternoon he heard a commotion in the outer office: raised voices, scraped chairs and hurrying footsteps. Moments later, two travel-dusty men strode in, closely followed by a red-faced Keith.

'This is insupportable! I will not have it! This officer is under my command and—'

'Sir. We take our instructions from the foreign secretary directly, this being as grave a matter as any that has faced this kingdom.' The taller individual sniffed. 'You have a telegraph, sir. If you have any doubts . . .'

He waited pointedly until the admiral had left them, then addressed Kydd: 'From this point on everything that is said shall be at the highest possible level of secrecy. Do you understand me?'

'I know my duty, sir.'

'Very well.' He opened his dispatch case and extracted a small packet, the seal broken. 'What do you understand by this?'

Kydd took it and went cold. 'Why, this is from my ship's clerk and good friend. Where is he—'

'That will be of no concern to you. Can you say any more?'

'Er, unless I might read the contents?'

'No, sir, you may not,' he said, taking it back. 'Please answer me directly. Was there any arrangement between you touching on the transmission of privileged information?'

'None. He's in a – a difficulty of sorts, is he?' Kydd said uneasily.

The two exchanged looks. 'He is performing a mission of the utmost importance that is proving unfortunate in its complexity,' the taller man said carefully. 'You may know that what you hold is a form of communication that is strongly ciphered. We do not possess the key, however, and believe that his referring to yourself implies it may be found by reference only to you.'

Kydd was dumbfounded. 'We've never discussed anything in the character of spying – nothing! Renzi wholly detests it, you may believe.'

'Then this leaves us in a difficult position indeed,' the man continued heavily. 'If you know of nothing he has said, no paper to keep guarded, no locked cabinet . . . ?'

'I do not.'

'Nothing whatsoever that may lead us to a key?'

'Tell me, this key, how would I know it?'

The other man broke in, his dry voice calm. 'Mr Kydd, the practice of privy communications is a black art but has a number of inviolable axioms, one of which is that the receiver must be in possession of the same key that was used to encode the message, without which he is helpless.

'It is the usual practice to establish a key beforehand, else we shall be obliged to transmit the key by other means, a most unsatisfactory and hazardous proceeding. In this particular case we have no prior arrangement and the key not being onpassed therefore must exist here, and be alluded to. The only clue we have is what you see before you. Your name has been invoked and that is all. A masterly stroke, which is its own guarantee of security but, regrettably, leaves us in a quandary.

'As to its appearance, well, a key can be of many forms – an arithmetical formula, a grid of nonsense, a passage in a book and in fact anything – but without it . . .'

Kydd realised that the men would not have acted as they had unless the matter was vitally important, and Renzi would not have given his name unless he himself was the key.

'Show me the message,' he demanded.

Reluctantly it was handed over. Kydd examined it minutely: it was in his friend's hand but consisted of lines upon lines of meaningless letters in groups of five and covered several pages. A few mistakes were blotted out and there were one or two crossed-out sequences in the margin, but that was all. It was not signed, and the beginning was only a bare date on one side, with what looked like a doodle on the other. No doubt it had occupied lonely hours of danger for Renzi.

He looked at the little picture. It was a stylised open book and a fat exclamation mark next to it as though in exasperation at the tedium of the task. Was this a sign – or a pointer of some kind? A clue?

Then he had it! 'Why, I think I know what it is. A passage from a book, you said. Will a poem do at all?'

'Yes, damn it!'

The sudden tension in the room made Kydd think better of a grand gesture and he contented himself with the plain facts. 'By this little picture Renzi is reminding me of a poem he's got fastened to the bulkhead in his cabin above his desk. Taut hand with words, is Nicholas.'

'What poem?' the taller man ground.

'Oh, it begins – let me see:

> *"Up! up! my Friend, and quit your books;*
> *Or surely you'll grow double:*
> *Up! up! my Friend, and clear your looks;*
> *Why all this toil and trouble . . . ?"'*

Kydd tried to recall what went next but failed. 'I can't remember the rest.'

'Go out to your ship and get the doggerel! Now!'

'I don't see any reason why I should,' Kydd replied quietly, but at the man's reddening face he relented. 'We can find it at the bookseller just along by Beach Street here. It's by his friend Wordsworth, whom he much admires. Should you get an 1800 edition you'll no doubt find the poem in it.'

The proprietor was taken aback when three men burst into his shop, demanding urgently that precise volume of Wordsworth but hurriedly obliged. There was the poem: 'The Tables Turned'.

At the office the table was swiftly cleared and paper

produced. The taller yielded to the other, who drew up his chair, sharpened his pencil and opened the book.

'Priceless!' He chuckled and read:

> *"Books! 'tis a dull and endless strife:*
> *Come, hear the woodland linnet,*
> *How sweet his music! on my life,*
> *There's more of wisdom in it."*

'Damn you, sir! Get on with it!'

Patiently, a *tabula recta* for the tableau was constructed and the cipher-text applied. In a short time the man raised his head and, with a satisfied smile, said quietly, 'Gentlemen, we have a solution!'

Renzi returned to his rooms weary and depressed. It had been weeks of waiting and no reply – and the worst of it was that Fulton had disappeared. Renzi had sent him a short message saying that London had been contacted on his behalf but it had been returned unopened with the terse notation 'not at this address' and no further clue.

It had been maddeningly frustrating. Was Fulton taken by the authorities? Had he quit the field entirely, returned to America? Or was he in possession of a fine new contract from the French that now saw him in some palatial lodging and for ever out of reach?

As he flopped into his chair he noticed the vase back in the window. Nervously he lifted it – but there was no message. Then he saw a copy of that morning's *Moniteur* tossed carelessly to one side. And deep within it he found a substantial packet.

The superscription was in an unknown hand and, unusually,

the packet was secured with sailmaker's twine instead of the usual ribbon. Inside, there were two parts, both ciphered. One was short, no more than a few sentences, Renzi guessed. The other was boldly inscribed even if in coded groups and on stiff, expensive vellum.

There was no key, no little drawing or textual hint. However, he guessed immediately the significance of the unusual fastening, for that would surely be:

> *Age! twine thy brows with fresh spring flowers,*
> *And call a train of laughing Hours . . .*

He took the vellum first, a prominent 'I' indicating the key-stream was to start with it and continue to the other. He set out his matrix. Soon finding himself correct in his assumption, the two pages were swiftly deciphered and then he sat back, satisfied.

It had told him two things: the first was that Kydd, knowing his penchant for memorising poetry, had correctly divined his key. The next was that Whitehall had accepted his difficult situation and taken positive steps to help him, for this was in effect a counter-offer from the foreign secretary of Great Britain himself. Renzi could prove it by decoding the vellum in front of Fulton.

The offer was interesting, but would it be sufficient? He turned his attention to the shorter message and applied himself. This was a very different document – and Renzi was shocked to the core. It was terse and to the point: if Fulton did not accept the offer he was to be killed.

Mechanically he burned his workings and stirred the ash carefully. All he had feared was coming to pass. He was now being expected to perform the ultimate act of dishonour in this whole wretched business, that of mercilessly ending the life of an unsuspecting other.

Could he do it? He knew he must. This was the transcendent logical outworking of what he had undertaken to do.

The means? Silent but sure – a blade. He had none, but a quick foray produced a kitchen knife, thin-bladed but effective, the point honed to a wicked sharpness. There was, of course, the chance that he would never use it, for where was Fulton now?

The prisoner-of-war talks dragged on with no sign of an agreement, even though Britain held some four times as many prisoners as the French and was prepared to exchange at the rate of many for one. The unspoken obstacle was the reality that trained seamen were too valuable to return to duty in a navy that was so successful. There was every probability now that there would be no hope left to the wretches in Bitche and Verdun.

Utterly depressed by the futility of the situation, Renzi was unprepared for what met him when he reached his room after another week of tedium. As he entered, he was confronted by a grinning Fulton rising from a chair. 'Hail to you, Smith!' he declaimed dramatically. 'How goeth it?'

Recovering himself Renzi said, 'What the devil are you doing here? You're being followed, you fool!' Anger flooded over him at the careless attitude and jocular tone. Then he became alarmed. Was this part of a French trap?

'No, I'm not trailed,' Fulton said lazily, stretching. 'I'm only this day back in Paris, and nobody knows I'm here. Er, have you, by chance, heard anything from London?'

'Where have you been all this time, may I ask?'

'Oh, Amsterdam. Thought I'd like to see the canals – very interesting to me.'

Renzi bit off a retort and forced himself to be calm. If the French wanted to catch them together they would probably have made their move by now. 'Well, I'm pleased to tell you that I've been in contact with England – and at the highest level.' He moved to the other chair and smiled winningly. 'It seems that you've earned the attention of no less than Lord Hawkesbury, the foreign secretary of Great Britain. In fact I have a communication from him addressed to you.'

'Oh?' Fulton said.

Renzi drew a deep breath. 'Indeed so.' He went to a picture on the wall and felt behind it, detached the packet and opened it. 'Here.' He handed it over, letting Fulton feel the quality of the paper.

'It's in code.'

'Naturally. For your protection, should the French discover you are treating with the English.' Renzi took it back and smoothed it. 'However, I shall now decipher it before you as your assurance of its authenticity.'

'Don't trouble yourself. If you're fooling me we'll find out soon enough. Just tell me what he's got to say.'

Renzi's stomach contracted. It was the last throw of the dice. 'Well, in it the foreign secretary welcomes your interest and notes the terms you are asking, including the forming of a plenary committee and, er, your one-hundred-thousand-pound fee. I'm happy to say he sees no insuperable bar to any of your provisions.'

'Go on.' There was no reading anything in Fulton's face.

'Of course, he trusts you will understand that there can be no question of payments until your inventions have been properly examined and tested in England.'

Fulton wheeled about. 'That's it? No advances, no promises?'

'I do assure you, sir, that should you trust us with your naval secrets then the government will treat you with the utmost liberality and generosity in strict accordance with the importance of your inventions.'

'And that's all?'

'At the moment, it is.'

Fulton sauntered over to the window and looked out over the rooftops. 'Are you seriously suggesting I pack my bags and leave on the strength of *that*?' he asked, continuing to gaze out.

Dread stole over Renzi: Fulton was not going to accept the offer and therefore he was going to walk off for ever. He had his grim instructions. Fulton was facing away, unsuspicious, and it was not in public. Would a protest that he had had no idea Fulton was anyone but a common intruder fool the French long enough to buy him time to get away? He had so little time to think.

Rising silently, he tiptoed over to the bureau and eased open the drawer. The knife glittered up at him. With it he would end the life of one whose mind had dreamed of voyaging with Neptune, and had so brilliantly succeeded. Renzi reached for it but at that instant he became aware that Fulton had swung around. The man cleared his throat and said abruptly, 'Yes, I will.' He moved back across the room. 'I trust you. We'll go back to England together.'

Renzi went rigid, then his hand moved to the decanter. 'A drink, then, Mr Fulton?' he said huskily, and splashed cognac into two glasses. 'To brighter times.'

He'd done it! Against all the probabilities he had brought it off. Then despair flooded him. How were they to flee across France ahead of vengeful pursuers when he had only the sketchiest plan prepared? When they were seen together the conclusion would be obvious.

The solution, when it came, was an anticlimax. Renzi would find an excuse to return to England alone, using his diplomatic passport. At the last minute Fulton would arrive at Calais to join the cartel ship and they would leave together. Fulton's papers from the ministry gave him access to all the northern ports and, in any case, as a neutral he could not be prevented from leaving.

Renzi left it until the last possible moment. The tedious carriage ride with another petulant young lieutenant had been a trial – but finally, rising above the low Customs building ahead, he saw the upper yards of the cartel ship. His heart beat faster for it would mean the end to the nightmare.

He sat outside a nearby tavern in the warm sunshine where he was able to view the comings and goings into the building, and as time wore on for the evening sailing, he grew more and more anxious. There was no sign of Fulton.

It was impossible that he should return without him, but who was to say that Fulton had not arrived early and was at this minute in his cabin? Or that word had been sent from Paris to detain him?

They had let him alone to take his last fill of France, but when he passed through the gates and was processed aboard, there would be no turning back. In an agony of indecision Renzi waited until just two hours before departure; then he rose, paid the tavern-keeper and walked slowly to the hall.

There, he handed in his passport and other papers, which were notated, and after guarded pleasantries, he was escorted to his ship. He mounted the gangway and stopped to breathe in the familiar tang of tar, timber and shipboard odours, a poignant moment after his recent travails.

Nodding civilly to the dour captain, he enquired casually

if any Americans were on board. It seemed there were not and none expected. It was hard to take and, with a sinking heart, Renzi watched the lines singled up, the capstan bars shipped for warping out.

Two hours had become one: in despair, he allowed himself to be shepherded below with the other passengers in preparation for the the awkward manoeuvre out into the stream, hearing the clunks and slithers of rope-handling above, the business-like squeals of the boatswain's calls and sharp orders.

Then came the shuddering creaks as the hull took up after the lines were thrown off. It was all over. They were on their way out.

As the first dip and heave of the sea took the vessel, Renzi realised they were clearing Calais Roads. Shortly afterwards passengers were allowed on deck into a soft, violet dusk. The excited chatter of the others depressed him and he wandered forward to where the jib-sheets were being hardened in. The lines were belayed, the seamen dispersed, and then he became aware of another, standing in the shadow of a staysail. The man moved towards him.

'You – where . . . ?'

'Thought I'd come aboard at the last minute, just in case,' Fulton said casually.

'I didn't think—'

'As you would, Englishman. I'll have you know that an American is accounted a welcome guest in France, as would any true republican, which means I can come and go as I please.'

Renzi swallowed his anger. 'Just so. Now you are a guest of the King.' He regretted the words immediately, but it was too late.

'We won a war so's not to bend a knee to a king – and I'm not about to start now.'

Something made Renzi answer quickly, 'Then why, pray, do you feel able to stand with us now?'

'You don't see it, do you?'

'I beg your pardon?'

'As I said before, my inventions are for mankind – at one stroke to annihilate the present system of marine war by making it impossible for a navy bent on aggression to venture forth on the high seas. By this we create a guarantee of the liberty of the seas for all men and, where there is free trade, there we will find the true sovereignty of the people.'

'But—'

'Once the people have their emancipation they will throw off the yokes of oppression – your monarchs, politicians and other parasites with their standing armies – and at last stand free. Whoever makes my machines possible is of no account, so long as they are created.'

Renzi paused. 'Some would say that the submarine boat is a barbaric weapon that pits innocent seamen against a foe that can never be seen.'

Fulton's face shadowed. 'That may be true, but for the greater good it must be suffered. I have started a revolution in the minds of engineers that cannot now be stopped, and I must go forward to face my destiny, sir.'

Chapter 8

'A re we all assembled? Then we'll begin.' Although only in his forties the prime minister, the younger William Pitt, wore on his face the effect of years spent leading England in the long wars against the French. This capable prime minister had resigned earlier on a matter of conscience but the lacklustre administration that had replaced his had stumbled on from an ill-advised peace treaty, through a hasty declaration of war to the current crisis. Now matters appeared to be reaching their climax but that did little to lift the mortal weariness that lay so heavily on him. The others in the cabinet room regarded him with concern.

'Sir, I feel I must express my profound sense of deliverance in seeing you once more in the chair that so rightfully belongs to you, at the helm of state in these parlous times. I'm sure I speak for us all when I say—'

'Thank you, Lord Harrowby,' Pitt said, to the new foreign secretary, 'but business presses.' He looked meaningfully at the secretary of war. 'My lord Camden?'

'Our confidential agent in the matter of the French

216

plunging boat has just returned from France. I have to tell you he confirms the reports concerning its effectiveness as only too true, sir.' There was a general stir about the table.

'Go on.'

'It seems it is no mere philosophic curiosity. Before Napoleon and his admirals in Brest the inventor personally stalked a vessel from beneath the sea and exploded it to pieces before their eyes.'

'Melville?'

The first lord of the Admiralty leaned forward. 'Sir. If this device is ever perfected we stand under a near-insuperable threat. Our navy being unsafe even in its own harbours renders our entire strategic situation questionable. I cannot answer to the consequences.'

'It may not come to that pass, sir,' Lord Camden said quietly. 'This agent was successful in seducing the inventor from the French and at this moment he is in England awaiting our pleasure.'

'Ah, yes . . .'

'Foreign Secretary?'

'I have to bring to your attention, gentlemen, that my predecessor was in communications of a clandestine nature with this inventor in France. As a condition of his quitting the country, certain demands were made and agreed to that we are morally obliged to accept.'

'And these are?'

'Among others, that a committee be immediately convened to examine his plans for a greatly improved submarine boat to be constructed and deployed by us, with a form of assistance from the royal dockyards and the Navy to this end.'

'This seems reasonable enough,' Pitt replied. 'But I'll wager there's somewhere a price in gold being asked.'

'A considerable sum was mentioned but this is contingent upon his satisfying the committee in the particulars.'

'Then I see we have a way forward. Ask the gentleman concerned to prepare his plans for the craft, which he will then present in due course. This will satisfy the immediate problem.'

'Er, which is that, Prime Minister?'

'That while he is working for us, he is not for the French,' Pitt said. 'And we buy ourselves time to consider our position. I'm not altogether convinced that this is something we, a maritime nation of the first rank, should necessarily be involved with.'

He went on, 'We'll give him his chance, see what he comes up with. We'll have a strong committee – philosophers, scientificals, engineers of note and all of some eminence – to judge his work. Then we'll decide what to do. Agreed?'

At the polite murmuring he declared, 'I shall ask the Treasury to open a disbursement account against my discretionary funding for now, this to include some form of emolument, say a monthly subsistence draw, and desire the Navy Board to afford him access to the dockyards and so forth. Oh, and he's to have a place of work that shall be secure – we can't discount that the French will seek to interfere with our new submarine navigator.'

'And to keep him under eye,' Melville added drily.

'Of course. Dover Castle springs to mind, being convenient should he wish to try his toys on Mr Bonaparte's flotilla.'

'There is one more consideration, Prime Minister,' Harrowby said smoothly, 'It seems that Mr Francis – as he wishes to be known – is rather in the nature of an American with decided republican views and, er, somewhat novel, not to say whimsical, ideas on marine war.'

'Just so, Foreign Secretary.' Pitt reached wearily for the decanter of port. 'I'll bear it in mind. As well, he will be needing a form of regular liaison with the Navy in an operational sense. Don't want him getting our admirals huffy. A trials vessel too. Dover – that's Keith's bailiwick. Desire him to make a man-o'-war and crew available for both purposes, not too big.'

'Yes, Prime Minister.'

'And we'll have to find a commander who knows Americans,' he said sourly. 'Shall we move on?'

It had been more than a month but now *Teazer* was complete. Kydd looked up from his journal as the door to his cabin opened. It was Renzi. 'Reporting for duty, Captain,' he said, with a tired smile.

'Good God, Nicholas, you look dreadful. Sit down, dear fellow. Tysoe! A hot negus on the instant for Mr Renzi.'

'Pay no mind to me, Tom. I'm— It's that I'm out of sorts is all.' Renzi took the armchair and sank into it, turning his face to catch the sun streaming in through *Teazer*'s stern windows.

Kydd rose. 'So good t' see you again, even if a mort weather-torn!' He contemplated Renzi then continued softly, 'I don't wish t' pry but—'

'A rather disagreeable episode I would much rather forget,' Renzi said distantly, then added, 'But it was kind in you to remember the Wordsworth.'

'The commander-in-chief was not amused when I was hauled out of my ship by some rum coves from Whitehall to answer some strange enough questions. Er, they didn't say what it was all about?'

'Nor should they. I'm sworn to mortal secrecy still, else I

should tell you all. It was a singular enough experience. Perhaps later.' He closed his eyes, drained.

'And it has put you to some measure o' grief, I fear.'

Renzi opened one eye. 'It will pass, should I be granted the sublimity of a space of peace and quiet – and a good book.'

Kydd knew Renzi well enough to be disturbed by his manner. What was it that he had endured? More than a physical trial, certainly, for he was like a man returned from the dead. 'That you'll get, Nicholas,' he said warmly. 'For his sins young Calloway has been taking care o' the ship's books – if you find 'em out o' kilter, let me know.'

Kydd cleared his throat. Renzi's tiny quarters in an operational ship-of-war were not what was wanted to heal him after his nameless ordeal. 'We've lately been with the Downs inshore forces, another having taken our place in the flying squadron, so our days are not so exciting,' he said, as breezily as he could, 'but I do think you'll find you'll need more in the way of a constitutional.' He paused. 'Nicholas, there is a favour I'd ask of you.'

'Of course.'

'I want you to go to Bath for the waters. For as long as you need – not forgetting to hoist in some reading while you're there, of course.'

Renzi sighed, too tired to protest. 'I – that is, it is well taken, and I confess I'm in sore need of respite. I do believe I'll take up your handsome offer, dear brother.'

The next morning Kydd saw his friend safely off in the coach. They had been through so much together and he was grateful he had the means to do this for him.

Then his mind returned to the war. Sober estimates of the size of the invasion flotilla were now nearer two thousand than one, and the flying squadron had taken a recent mauling that had left two shattered wrecks on the dunes near Calais. Fortunately the battleships of the French fleet had not ventured from port but this was widely held to be their admiral husbanding his forces until such time as they would be called on to lock in mortal combat with the British at the grand climax of the invasion. The threat could not have been greater, but Kydd and *Teazer* were kept back on the shores of England in the second tier of defences and he felt the frustration acutely.

At last the summons came. A peremptory order to report to the commander-in-chief for redeployment.

Keith kept him waiting for twenty minutes, then called him in. 'Mr Kydd, you're of this hour relieved of duty in these inshore waters.' Why should the commander-in-chief himself tell him that he was to resume in a flying squadron? The usual order pack would normally suffice. Kydd felt uneasy.

'Tell me, does the record speak true? While you were on the North American station you were sent ashore in the United States to resolve some dispute that ended well enough, then spent a little time at sea in their new navy.'

'I did, sir.'

'So therefore it would be true to say that you know Americans?'

'Well, sir, I—'

'Capital. You and your sloop are stood down from active duty on this station. My condolences on the loss of opportunity for distinction, but we all have our cross to bear.'

'Sir! May I know—'

'Since you have shown yourself inclined to furtive

intrigue I have given you over to the Foreign Office in their service.'

At Kydd's evident shock, Keith gave a cold smile. 'Don't imagine you'll be out on some wild adventure. I gather it's to be acting as dogsbody to some American charlatan inventor. You'll remain in my command, Mr Kydd – as inspector of Fencibles.'

Surely not. The Sea Fencibles – a home-defence force of dabblers and seamen past their prime. At one stage the doughty Earl St Vincent, first lord of the Admiralty, had muttered dismissively, 'The Sea Fencibles are there only to calm the fears of old ladies, both within and without Parliament.'

What had he done as a fighting seaman that he should be relegated to this? Kydd bit his lip in frustration. 'Aye aye, sir,' he said bleakly.

Keith waved his hand in dismissal. 'Flags will tell you the rest.'

How things had changed. From service in the very front line of the war at sea to nursemaid of well-meaning amateurs and whoever the American was. The flag-lieutenant was unable to add much. Sympathetically, he explained that the commander-in-chief had received his orders from a higher level and had complied, with Kydd the unlucky choice. It was apparently a discreet affair, and while his line of responsibility lay with Whitehall, his appointment as inspector of Fencibles was to give him cover and keep him administratively within Keith's command.

A gentleman from London was, however, in attendance to explain. He was at pains to make clear the contractual arrangements between His Majesty's government and the American, a Mr Fulton, who also went by the name of Francis, which in the main appeared to be the production of plans for a contrivance of his inventing to be scrutinised in due course by a learned committee.

Kydd's role was to act as intermediary between the inventor and the Navy, providing assistance of a practical nature to include advice concerning operational procedures and administrative support at all levels. This latter was of particular importance, it seemed, bearing as it did on weighty matters, including the proper form of indenting for dockyard stores requested by Mr Fulton and lines of responsibility back to Mr Hammond, under-secretary of state with responsibility for the project.

This contrivance? The functionary was not certain, leaving it up to Kydd to pursue details as he wished with the contractor. All costs must be fairly accounted for and rendered in the proper form, and a journal to be kept.

Voice lowered, the man went on to inform Kydd that, the contract being of a confidential nature, all elements pertaining should be kept from public view. Security for the principal of the contract and his workings would not be his responsibility, however, except in so far as unforeseen events dictated.

Francis, not Fulton, was the name on the contract, he was a gentleman of singular views and would need sensitive handling. Work space was being provided in Dover Castle, any sea trials would probably take place locally and, other than that, well, Kydd was expected to work closely and supportively with the man, provided always that the interests and prerogatives of the Crown were upheld.

Numb with rage, Kydd made his way back to his ship. A sloop-of-war of the first rank and a commander, Royal Navy, at the beck and call of some money-grubbing projector – it was infamous. England needed every sail-of-war to face Napoleon!

He swallowed his bitterness. 'Mr Hallum, we have new orders.'

'Sir?' The man's grey subservience irritated Kydd. 'We weigh within the hour for Dover – and strike the blue ensign,' he snapped.

'S-strike?'

'God damn it!' Kydd roared. 'Take it down, I said. Hoist a red 'un in its place!' He went on grimly, 'As of now we're an unattached private ship so we fly a red. Hands t' turn to, unmoor ship, Mr Hallum.' It would be remarked all over the anchorage: HMS *Teazer* was standing down from the fight.

During the short trip south to Dover, Kydd brooded. He had no choice other than to do his duty, but all his warrior instincts were to face the enemy. What he had heard at the Admiralty had shaken him, and to be absent from the field in his country's time of trial was almost too much to bear.

He had never been to Dover; the harbour to the west of the town was small and had no naval presence to speak of, but brazenly atop the towering white cliffs was the mightiest fortress in the south: Dover Castle.

The town nestled snugly in a fold of the white cliffs. After he had taken one look at the roads winding up the steep hills, Kydd hired a carriage to take him to the castle. Despite his savage mood he was impressed by the sight of it: the giant central keep within near half a mile of protecting ramparts and bastions spoke of defiance and age-old puissance in a world gone mad. It had been a symbol of tenacity looking out to England's enemies for nearly eight centuries and, yet again, had come to be a major element in the forward defence of the kingdom.

Entering through the Constable's Gate his spirits rose.

The red coats of soldiers everywhere, others in fatigues with pickaxes and carts, more drilling at their heavy cannon showed it to be an active fortress of a truly majestic size.

Feeling conspicuous in his naval uniform among all the soldiers, Kydd was marched by a genial sergeant inside the walls and his pass was verified. Then an officer was produced who knew of the castle's distinguished guest.

It was not to the towering keep that he was taken. Instead they walked seaward over the grassy slopes of the hill and approached the edge of the cliff. Then, unexpectedly, it was an abrupt descent into the bowels of the earth and a dark world of medieval tunnels, passages and steps. Here, there were subterranean barrack rooms, kitchens, work places, storerooms, sleeping quarters and guard rooms. Then the blessed sight of sunlight – not above, but at the end of casemates, long, fortified chambers, much as Kydd had known in Gibraltar but this time, rather than a view across a dusty plain into Spain, he found himself looking out from a height over the sparkling sea.

Towards the centre of the complex of casemates the officer stopped. 'You'll find your Mr Francis in there,' he said, pointing to one.

Kydd entered the long cavity and made his way towards a figure arranging desk and drawers at the end. 'Mr Francis?'

The man turned abruptly. 'Who're you?'

It was odd to hear the American twang he had last encountered in Connecticut in such surroundings. 'Commander Kydd, Royal Navy.'

'And you're to be my keeper,' Fulton grunted, and went back to his sorting. The desk was well sited for detailed work, the sunlight streaming in through the iron grille at the end of the casemate.

'Not so, sir,' Kydd said. 'My orders are to furnish you with such assistance as the Navy can provide, and the services of my ship, the brig-sloop *Teazer*.'

Fulton paused. 'Why, that's right handsome of their lordships,' he said. 'I guess for passage, trials, that sort of thing.'

'As will promote the success of your work.'

'To be a victim.'

'A what?' Kydd said irritably.

'If I'm to be creating a submarine boat, it will need a victim to practise upon, wouldn't you say?'

Kydd stopped. 'A submarine boat?'

'You have no idea, do you? Your government is paying me thousands for a plunging boat and they don't see fit to tell their man.' He shook his head.

'Mr Francis, I was hauled off my ship in the middle of a war to be told I'm to assist a private contractor make a hill of money, not what he has to do to earn it.'

Fulton waited for the outburst to subside, then leaned towards Kydd. 'If I tell you how your Mr Boney will be stopped in his tracks by this one device – against which there is no defence – will that be enough for you?'

'The submarine?' Kydd said sarcastically. 'If you're going to tell me now that you're the only one in the world can design it . . .'

'I've built such a one and I've used it – against the British Navy.'

Fulton's cold certainty was disconcerting. 'Go on.'

In a short time Kydd had the sense of it, a submarine craft that was able to navigate silently under the waves, completely out of the sight and knowledge of men until it had delivered its death-blow, and against which there could truly be no defence. What gun could pierce to the ocean's depths?

As Fulton revealed more, Kydd fought off the unreality that was closing in on him. This was more than yet another crazy idea, it was a new reality that threatened the world of ships and the sea that was at the centre of his life. It promised to render useless the great fleets that were the bulwark of Britain's defences and . . . and he needed time to think, to make sense of what he had just heard.

Kydd took to his cabin, telling Hallum and Tysoe that he was not to be disturbed, and let his thoughts run free. Should he even be party to such a devilish scheme? If he refused the duty, there would quickly be another found and, in any case, the question hinged on deeper considerations. It was barbaric and not to be contemplated by any gentleman – but was it morally wrong?

Probably. But did that mean it should be immediately discarded by any civilised country? That was the nub: if all nations refused such weapons, the answer was yes, but if this were so, then any weaker that ignored the pact might easily prevail over a stronger by their introduction. Thus, logically, all should acquire them to preserve the balance.

It was a melancholy but irrefutable fact: the genie was now out of the bottle and could not be put back. What was invented could not be uninvented. The future of war at sea, therefore, would now be one of submarines and sudden death of the defenceless.

There was, however, one question that, to Kydd, put all others aside: was this going to be the means to get at the invasion flotilla skulking in harbour and put to an end the mortal threat that hung over England, once and for all?

If it was then, damn it, he would give it all he had.

Chapter 9

Kydd filed in and sat next to Fulton. Others took position around them and all rose when the chairman, George Hammond, under-secretary of state for the Foreign Office entered and took the head of the table.

'Thank you, gentleman, and especially you, er, Mr Francis, for affording us your valuable time.' He shuffled some papers, then looked up sharply. 'The purpose of this meeting – this informal meeting – I should remind you, is to discover how the committee for the examination of the submarine boat be most effectively constituted so as to give a true and fair view of its prospects in service.' A large man next to him gave an ill-tempered harrumph, which was ignored.

'I shall introduce you all. This is Mr Jackson, an engineer of some repute, Major Wardle, for the Ordnance Board, Captain Gresham, for the Royal Navy,' the large man nodded and glared around the table, 'and, of course, Mr Francis himself.'

Hammond looked enquiringly at Kydd, but before he could say anything Fulton said firmly, 'Mr Kydd, of the Navy, who's my keeper and liaison man. If needs be, he'll be advising me – that's so, isn't it, Commander?'

'Er, yes. In accordance with Mr Francis's conditions in coming to England I'm to assist in any way I can to facilitate his work by way of explaining our operational practices and arranging procedural matters on his request.'

'Very well,' Hammond said crisply. 'To business. Mr Pitt strongly believes that the importance of this project demands that only men of the highest eminence need be asked to sit on this committee. Therefore I ask that you do consider deeply your separate professions as to who might best be approached.' He paused. 'For instance, the name of Sir Joseph Banks has been mentioned as chairman.'

Kydd was impressed; the well-born naturalist who had sailed with Cook to the South Seas, president of the Royal Society and adviser to governments and kings – this was eminence indeed.

Hammond continued, 'Mr Jackson. Might we start with yourself? Who in the practice of engineering would you consider in this regard?'

The pleasant-faced man appeared perplexed. 'As I'm not well acquainted with what Mr Francis proposes to do, I'm at a stand, sir. If it's shipbuilding—'

'No, sir, it is not,' Fulton said energetically. 'This is a new departure in the marine arts. As such it—'

'Damn it all for a lunatic charade!'

'Captain Gresham?'

'Will someone please explain to me why on earth we're contemplating creeping about under the sea in these contraptions, like some verminous highwayman in the woods, when we've got the mightiest and best navy the world's ever seen?'

'Because the prime minister desires we shall,' Hammond retorted. 'Mr Jackson, please continue.'

'Oh, yes. I would think that—'

'Let me answer our salty son of the briny,' Fulton broke in abruptly. 'We're contemplating a submarine because not even all your king's horses and all your king's men can defend a battleship against even one of these. If ever you stopped to think—'

'Mr Francis, I have to rule you out of order, I'm afraid,' Hammond came in. 'You're here in an advisory capacity and may only address the meeting when called upon to answer a particular *technical* question. Mr Jackson?'

'As I was saying, you'd be well served by a dockyard engineer – they're a canny breed, quite at home with curious sea machines. I'm thinking of Mr Bentham – that's Samuel, not his brother. And, in course, Mr Rennie . . .'

'Thank you, sir. Major Wardle, who in the view of the Ordnance Board would be suitable?'

'Who has not heard of Thomas Blomefield? Or the younger William Congreve? There is a gratifying superfluity of persons of an ordnance persuasion, sir, ready to do their duty.'

'Indeed. I should perhaps at this stage make mention that Mr Henry Cavendish has indicated his willingness to allow us the benefit of his observations in the scientifical line.'

'Cavendish?' Gresham asked his neighbour.

'Rum cove – factitious airs, the electric fluid, Mr Lavoisier's hydrogen . . .' the man replied.

Fulton leaned back restlessly. 'These philosophical gents are all very well, Mr Chair, but your most significant man will be your seaman who knows the sea. A whole navy to choose from, sir – who will it be?'

'Hear, hear,' rumbled Gresham. 'Our American friend and

I are at last in agreement. We need one of weighty experience, knows the crackpot from the plain lunatic—'

'Quite so.'

'Not an admiral as is set in his ways, been at sea more'n a dog-watch, smelled a mort of powder smoke—'

'Rather similar, in fact, to yourself, sir?'

'If you insist, Mr Chairman,' Gresham said, with oily satisfaction.

'It will be considered in due course,' Hammond said, and turned to Fulton. 'Mr Francis, this committee is convened upon your request. Do you have any objection to the names mentioned as having the competence to adjudge your work?'

'Only one,' Fulton said, looking pointedly at Gresham.

'That is noted. The names, sir, will be put forward to the prime minister's office and selection made. You will be informed, of course. Thank you, gentlemen.'

With a shuffling of feet the meeting adjourned. In the hubbub following, Jackson crossed to speak to Fulton but Gresham stopped Kydd. 'A junior commander is it, then, Mr Kydd? I do hope you've wits enough to see through this crafty rogue. The Navy doesn't want his kind about when we've got more pressing engagements, if you see what I mean.'

'I have m' duty, sir, and that's to give Mr Francis a clear hawse in the matter of designing a submarine boat,' Kydd said pointedly.

'Don't take that tone with me, sir. You have your duty, and it's to the Service, not to some jumped-up Yankee projector who's got ideas as will bring about the ruination of the profession! The Navy expects you to stand by its traditions with courage and right-thinking, not go chasing after hare-brained schemes that—'

'Mr Kydd!' Fulton called loudly across the room. 'I find I'm hard-pressed and must leave – if you're ready at all?' In the street outside he pulled on his gloves savagely and jammed on his hat. 'God save you from all his tribe,' he said bitterly, 'else you'll be a-seeing Mr Bonaparte marching down this very street before long.'

'The committee's not yet selected, sir. It might be he's not on it.'

'He will be.'

'Let's wait and see.'

'No, we won't – I don't like waiting. I must get to work.'

A few days later Kydd returned to the casemate, this time taking in more of the details. Halfway up a sheer cliff, its slatted wooden decking was probably to guard against the damp and mould of the vast chalk cavern. The only entry apart from the one he had used, which was through an army barracks, was a small exit to the open air, barred with a grille. It was perfectly chosen for the purpose of securing Fulton and his plans from the outside world – or acting as his prison.

Fulton beckoned him in. He was trying to heave round his desk and Kydd hastened to take the other end, manhandling it into place as close as possible to the light and air streaming through the grille. 'It will serve,' Fulton panted. 'I've worked in far worse and time's not on my side.'

It was beginning to shape up: the drawing desk across the mouth of the casemate, shelves down each side and stowages resembling ship's sea-chests in strategic locations. This was where the war at sea was going to be changed utterly.

Fulton glanced at Kydd and seemed to come to a decision. 'Do you desire to see how a submarine is constructed, sir?'

'I do.'

Rummaging in his chests Fulton came up with a clutch of

long papers, which he smoothed out on the desk. 'Hmm – these are construction details for the workmen, each to his own and never the whole to be comprehended by one man.'

Then he took out a smaller drawing and spread it in front of Kydd. 'But with this you may see my *Nautilus* in all her glory.'

Kydd leaned over intently: his first view of what lay in the future for the world, and which promised to save England from Napoleon Bonaparte or plunge the realm of the mariner into unthinkable undersea warfare for ever.

Before him was a sectioned craft as unlike a ship as it was possible to be. Long and sinister, tubular with a conical bow and small protruding dome, it seemed to be filled with cranks and wheels and above it, like a giant bat's wing, an apparatus of rigging.

'There's no waterline marking on the plan,' Kydd said, searching for something to say, then cursed himself as he remembered that, for a submersible, waterlines had no meaning.

'On the surface she's nearly awash, only this little tower for conning the ship to be seen.'

'If – if she's made of wood, won't she just float?'

'Her hull is of ellipsoid section, copper sheeting over iron frames, but a fair question. I reserve space in the keel for ballast, and as she progresses under the sea, a crewman drives a horizontal rudder of sorts to send her deeper while two more turn the cranks, which operate this four-bladed propelling paddle here.'

'And this?'

'That's a window into the deep – I can see the minute hand on my watch at twenty-five feet,' Fulton said proudly.

Kydd tried to visualise what it must be to exist in the gloom and stench far beneath the waves, the immensity of the sea pressing in, the knowledge of the coming detonation, wreckage, torn bodies . . . 'Is it – what is it like, er . . . ?'

'Tolerable, tolerable,' Fulton said absently. 'I find it takes but two minutes only to unrig for diving, and when deep, I navigate by compass in the usual way, even in the open sea when it's a damn relief to get down to the peace of the abyss, where there's no hurry and rush of the waves.'

'C-can you see mermaids and such? Sailors set great store on such things,' Kydd said, his eyes widening.

'None seen by me – it's naught but dull green down there. It goes on for ever as you'd never conceive,' Fulton said. 'Black rocks looming up of a sudden – gives you the frights to see 'em close to like that.'

Kydd struggled for words as he grappled with the images. 'Er, do you not fear it when your air is, er, used up?'

'As to that, carbonic acid and lime has been promoted but I find a trusty copper globe of air as I've prepared under pressure answers better. Just tap off what we need. Four hours and twenty on the seabed with myself and three crew, and it was boredom that drove us up in the end.'

'So – so this is your *Nautilus* as—'

'As I constructed, trialled before Napoleon Bonaparte himself and used to blow to flinders a brig before the eyes of all his admirals,' he said grimly.

'And may I ask where she lies now?'

'In pieces, sold for scrap value. Don't worry, I've left nothing behind. You English have no fear he can make another.' He slapped the drawings together again. 'Right now, I've work to do. A seagoing *Nautilus* with double-sized crew, provisioned for a patrol of three weeks at a time, nine torpedoes. This'll make 'em sit up.'

It was a fearful and wondrous creation but Kydd was damned

if he'd show how awestruck he was. 'Well, then, shall I leave you to it, Mr Francis, or is there anything you need?'

'No. I crave to be left alone for a space, sketch out some thoughts. I'll be sure to let you know.'

A caustic letter arrived from Keith suggesting that as an inspector of Sea Fencibles – albeit not a regular-built one – perhaps it was time Kydd earned his keep. As a sea officer of some experience, possibly an active tour of the less-frequented posts, a revealing report to follow? It was not a formal order but, for all that, a call to duty – and, despite his feelings about the Fencibles, Kydd welcomed the chance to do something seamanlike, something he could understand, while Fulton worked on his plans.

He spread out the operational chart of the south. On it were marked the defences, including all those manned by the Sea Fencibles – harbour batteries, inshore gunboats, signal stations. And all his for the rousing! He'd make sure they'd hear of him and *Teazer* on the coast.

Where to begin? He could not stray too far from Fulton in Dover but a day's sail was half the south coast and even round North Foreland, if the wind was kind. And the south-east was both the closest to France and the most exposed to invasion. Perhaps . . . here, hard by the notorious smugglers' haunt of Romney Marsh. A small coast signal station on the flat, lonely shingle promontory of Dungeness, little expecting visitors.

HMS *Teazer* eased inshore off Dymchurch and hove to while her gig was put in the water and stroked briskly ashore. Curious onlookers were puzzled that when the sloop sailed away, two of her company were left there.

They wore plain clothing so there was nothing to alarm the sleepy little village, and Kydd, with Midshipman Calloway, found no difficulty in hiring horses. Soon they were clopping along the road between the marsh and the sea, but instead of following it as it curved inland to Snargate they struck out on a poor track across the stark bleakness of the promontory.

For several miles they crossed the flat landscape, not a rise, not a tree intruding until they came to the tiny settlement of Lydd in its centre. Then they followed a barely visible path through the salt marsh and shingle out to a distant solitary hut at the very tip of the promontory.

Their approach from inland was covered by the ceaseless muffled roar of the sea and they had time to note the old ship's topmast with its extended staff and gaff to suspend signal hoists a good eighty feet above. The hut was in rough wood, finished in tar and ochre with a liberal sand-dash.

Smoke swirled from a makeshift chimney and Kydd handed the reins to Calloway while he stepped over a tiny plot of greens.

At his knock the weathered wooden door creaked open and an old man in carpet slippers appeared with a steaming mug, looking at Kydd in astonishment. 'Why, gennelmen, what can I do f'r you?' he wheezed.

From within the hut a stronger voice called irritably, 'Who th' devil's out at this hour, George?'

Kydd held his temper and said levelly, 'Commander Kydd, inspector of Sea Fencibles, come t' visit.'

'We ain't heard nothing o' no inspection,' came the voice from inside. 'Bid the bugger begone!'

'That's enough!' Kydd barked. 'Fetch your lieutenant,' he ordered.

The old man paused, then drew himself up with pathetic dignity. 'I am he, sir.'

Kydd pushed past him contemptuously into the hut. A pot

simmered over a smoky fire in the corner and there were two rooms made snug with rickety furniture; a table stood across the single window looking out to sea, a well-worn telescope in brackets above it.

From the other room two resentful seamen appeared, one in underclothes. 'The other?' Kydd demanded. There should have been three manning the hut.

'As he's got his head down, ain't he?' one said truculently.

Wheeling on the lieutenant, Kydd ordered, 'Your log, if y' please.'

The man shuffled over to the table and found the book, but did not offer it. Kydd strode across and took it for himself. If it was not in order he would see the man dismissed instantly for crass incompetence. These old officers might be long retired from worthy service at sea but it was vital to the country that ceaseless vigilance was maintained when every hour could see an invasion fleet lift menacingly above the horizon.

He flicked the pages and was surprised to see it entered up with more than a score of vessels sighted that day alone. 'A busy day, then,' he said, mollified. Then suspicion crept in. It was a cosy billet: this ancient lieutenant, when closed up, was earning eight shillings a day for his trouble, near as much as Kydd's full naval pay, the men two shillings for every day on muster, the same as an able seaman facing the rigours of the sea and the malice of the enemy – and with it protection from the press-gang.

Was it impossible to believe they could have fabricated the only evidence of honest labour? A list of imaginary ships to justify their existence? He'd soon find out. He consulted his fob watch and noted the time with satisfaction.

Stepping outside he watched steadily to the left and, right

on time, *Teazer* came slowly past the point. 'So, what happens now, Mr Lieutenant?' Kydd said, with relish.

The man stood there, regarding him steadily.

'Well, that's number twenty-eight, is it not?' Kydd said testily. '"Name of Vessel Passing is Required", or am I mistaken?' A finite number of signals could be sent from a coast signal station in their own code, which *Teazer* also carried and with which she must respond.

The lieutenant glanced at the older seaman and nodded. The man turned and went outside to hoist the two flags, then came back to wait beside him.

'Well?' exploded Kydd. 'The log! Find out if the private signal is correct, the name of the ship. Then enter it up, decide if this is an alarm – get moving, damn you for a mumping set o' lubbers!'

The lieutenant folded his arms and said quietly, 'Yon ship is the brig-sloop *Teazer*, Captain Kydd, Downs Squadron, having been on the coast these last two months. If'n you wish me to make entry of our own forces as are already known to Admiral Keith, I will, or should you want an alarm raised . . .'

He was quite right, of course, and in a way that suggested Kydd had underestimated the ragged band. They were locals – fishermen, smugglers, whatever – and could be relied upon to know exactly what was afoot on their own doorstep. Could it be a much more effective system than bringing in highly trained man o' war's men who would have no idea of local conditions?

Only if they knew the rest. 'Tell me, an enemy flotilla is making t' land at Winchelsea beach. What is your action?'

'Red pennant at the masthead, three black balls at the peak,' the man said calmly.

'And?'

'At night, touch off the faggots in the fire-frame, lanterns and a blue light.'

'Where is it?'

He raised an arm and pointed to a twelve-foot post near the water's edge. It had a deep iron basket at the top, which was ready charged with combustibles.

A wave of contrition came over Kydd. These men had the loneliest task in the Navy, miles from any other humanity but at the very bullseye of the invasion's target. On this flat desolation, exposed to cutting winds and driving rain, there was no escape from the tedium of duty, noting details of ships interrogated as they passed, such that lesser evils, such as privateers and others, were caught out and instantly reported down the line, the source, no doubt, of so much of the cryptic intelligence that had sent *Teazer* and her sisters off in righteous pursuit.

'Quite right,' Kydd said, with a sudden smile. 'Well, sir, I find your attention t' duty a caution to us. I'll bid you good day.' He turned to go, then paused, fumbled in his pocket and found a guinea. 'God bless you all, and here's rhino enough to drink the health of that fine barky you see out there.'

Ramsgate was a bustling trading port at the south-east tip of England, well-favoured by those of means embarking on ocean voyages. Even the mysterious cartel ships returning from France disembarked on Harbour Parade.

This was no benighted, out-of-the-way exile for the Sea Fencibles. All the comforts of home and town were there, and no danger of being caught short by the weather, with the abundance of taverns on hand. Kydd saw what he wanted as soon as *Teazer*'s boat passed the stubby piers at the entrance and told Poulden to lay alongside the seaweed-covered steps on the inner side.

Watched curiously by idle promenaders he cast a professional eye over two prime pieces: a pair of twenty-four-pounders atop the wall each side of the entrance with a field of fire to seaward. He went to the nearer one. It was fitted with a tompion and a stout lead apron, promising gun-locks in action, and was finished in traditional sea-service black.

An official-looking small building stood where the pier joined the shore and Kydd strode over to it. 'Where are the Sea Fencibles? I mean to see 'em drill,' he said, to a man lounging at the entrance puffing a clay pipe.

Conscious of admiring glances at his commander's uniform from passing ladies, he asked again. 'Their lieutenant, then?'

The man looked at him then slowly removed the pipe. 'How in blue blazes would I know, Admiral? I'm th' Revenoo only.'

Customs and Excise men were immune to the press, or Kydd would have been sorely tempted. Stalking past, he entered and got the information he wanted, then dispatched his men – and waited.

It was nearly two hours before a sullen and resentful gun crew were all closed up, still in their shopman's aprons, sea-jerseys and tradesmen's smocks. An elderly lieutenant in morning clothes arrived red-faced in vexation.

'So kind in Mr Bonaparte to wait upon you, sir,' Kydd said sarcastically. 'And now may we see some action? Pray muster your equipment.'

One of the men turned on the lieutenant. 'An' it's Toosday and Sat'day only we drill. What's th' meaning o' this'n?'

'It's a special muster for the officer here, and you'll see your silver right enough,' the lieutenant snarled. By now a knot of people had gathered, the exercise promised a pleasing diversion for the Ramsgate sea-front.

Kydd pulled out his watch pointedly. The lieutenant called

them to attention and made the gun numbers sing out their duties. That done, the order was given to cast loose the gun and rig tackles. There was another wait while the side tackles and other equipment were located in store and brought out. It took some looking to find the ring-bolts to take the breeching and more for the training tackle before the gun was ready.

It was a hot day but Kydd was taking no nonsense and the gun crew bent to their labours.

'Out tompion!'

'Run out the gun!'

'Point your gun!'

'Fire!'

'Worm and sponge!'

The age-old orders rang out, but it was not an impressive sight, even without the heavy real twenty-four-pound shot and cartridges. The flat space atop the pier was not best suited to close exercise, but Kydd was merciless – if the French came they would be serving their piece whatever the conditions.

'Pity help you, sir, when we go to live firing,' Kydd said sorrowfully, to the lieutenant.

'Live firing?'

'Yes. I will have at least one round from you.' Kydd had noticed that the vent hole was blocked by a neat little spider funnel, proof enough of how much the gun had been used.

'Why, sir—'

'You object?'

'It's – it's not done, sir. The noise, it would frighten the ladies. And people would think the French to have come.'

'One round, if you please.'

The lieutenant looked about helplessly, then muttered stubbornly, 'I haven't the keys to the magazine as I must apply to the colonel of militia.'

Kydd could hardly believe his ears, but said, 'Then we can oblige you, sir. Poulden, send to *Teazer* for a twenty-four-pounder carronade ball, cartridge, wadding and gunner's pouch. There, sir,' he added genially. 'You shall have your fun.'

The expectant spectators were now several deep and an excited murmur went round. 'Mr Austen won't half be in a takin' sir,' one member of the gun crew said, fiddling with a tackle fall and looking anxiously at the lieutenant, whose face had paled.

'Sir, don't you rather think that—'

'Bonaparte's hordes could be upon you at any time, and you hesitate at a live practice?'

A grinning gun crew arrived with the requirements. 'Do you stand back, the Teazers. We'll be leaving it to these fine men to show us how to serve a gun. Are you ready, sir?'

'Well, I—'

'Clear the area, you men,' Kydd told his boat's crew, who shooed the interested audience off the pier to a safe distance. There was now a sizeable crowd lining the esplanade. 'The first time in dumb show,' Kydd said encouragingly. 'Then the real firing.'

The Fencibles gun crew mumbled to themselves as they addressed their iron beast, soon to bellow its defiance to the world.

'Come, come, gentlemen!'

In half-hearted show a dummy run was performed. Then, in deathly silence, the gun was loaded. Cartridge, wad, a gleaming black shot and another wad. Priming, quill tube – and the gun captain stood ready, looking unhappily at the lieutenant.

'Point your gun, then,' Kydd said impatiently. When the men with the crow stood about, looking confused, he added, 'At the French, you lubbers – there!' The coast of France was a grey line on the far horizon.

'Stand by!' The lieutenant's order sounded thin and nervous. The entire amphitheatre of the harbour went still.

A final glance at the implacable Kydd and the order was given. 'Fire!'

A fraction of a second later there came the bursting thunder-clap of sound and a vast gouting of powder-smoke. The crash echoed around the harbour, sending a dense cloud of seagulls screaming skyward as onlookers clutched each other.

The swirling smoke finally cleared, leaving a stupefied gun crew standing in horror at what they had achieved.

'There! So now you know what a real battle is like,' Kydd said happily.

It remained to make acquaintance with the sea-going Fencibles, and he pulled out the chart once more. It did not take long to find somewhere squarely within the invasion area but suffi-ciently small so as not to warrant too senior a presence. Rye.

Guiltily, Kydd knew that an element of his choice was his curiosity to see the place. It was an ancient town of the medieval Cinque Ports and therefore entitled to '. . . right of soc and sac . . . blodwit and fledwit, pillory and tumbril, infangentheof and outfangentheof, mundbryce . . . flotsam and jetsam . . .' and probably the oldest port in England.

So old, in fact, that the town lay far inland where centuries of silt from the river had extended the coastline out several miles into a flat, reedy estuary.

Teazer let go her anchor in a lively sea, pivoting immediately to meet the waves, but when her boat reached the narrow mouth of the Rother it grew quickly peaceful. The river was dead straight for more than a mile, the result of untold years of striving to keep the port open as the land extended itself. Rye harbour was at the first bend; a pair of gunboats should have been maintained there by the Sea Fencibles to throw into any last desperate clash off the beaches. Kydd braced himself for what he might find.

The boat swept round the bend but then he was confronted with the last thing he expected: along the gnarled old timber quay were lined up men in smart jackets and trousers that would not have been out of place in a man-o'-war at divisions, and as the gig glided in, an officer in full-dress Fencibles uniform called his men to order and swept off his hat. 'Welcome to Rye Harbour, Mr Kydd,' he said. 'I do hope we'll not disappoint.'

Collecting himself, Kydd suspected that word of his mission had been passed on – Dungeness suggested itself but, anyway, this was all to the good in the greater scheme of things. 'A fine body o' men, Lieutenant. I shall inspect them.'

They were a stout crew: fit, well turned out, direct eye gaze, capable seeming. All the signs of a good officer looking after his men. Satisfied, Kydd turned to their charges.

The gunboats were secured to improvised trots out in the stream and Kydd summoned them alongside. One was in a pattern of the last war but wonderfully kept; gunboats were numbered but this one sported a nameplate on the bow, with *Vixen of Rye* picked out in gold on scarlet.

Kydd dropped down into it. Double-ended and capable of rigging a lateen on a folding mast it mounted a respectable eighteen-pounder on a slide on the foredeck and a handy carronade aft.

He went forward to the gun, the officer hovering anxiously. He inspected the bore – it was an old pattern requiring a quick-match to fire it rather than a gunlock. Kydd used the old gunner's trick of reflecting sunlight from the back of his fob watch into the bore but there was no sign of kibes, the bright metal of a flaw made by a shot loose in the bore striking along its length.

The vent-work was in pristine condition, and the rest of the boat quite up to it, so there was little Kydd could find to criticise. The other vessel, of similar vintage and named *Wolf of Winchelsea*, was in the same fine shape. Sensing Kydd's pleased surprise, the lieutenant rubbed his hands together. 'They're to your satisfaction, sir?' he asked.

'Most certainly.'

'Then it will be my pleasure to invite you to our usual meeting at the George in Mermaid Street, sir.'

'Not so fast.'

'Sir?'

'I desire you should now attack my ship.'

'A-attack?'

'I shall be towing a barrel a cable astern. That will be your mark. You have powder, shot?'

The young man's face beamed with pleasure. 'Why, certainly!'

'Then shall we say half a league offshore in one hour?'

Out in the bay the seas were as lively as ever, but there would be no allowances: this onshore blow was ideal for a fast French crossing and they would have to cope.

Vixen emerged first, her plain lugsail set taut and making to seaward of *Teazer* in a swash of white bow-wave. The smaller *Wolf* remained inshore, but both bucketed along in the brisk seas. Kydd nodded approvingly.

When at the wind's eye to *Teazer*, the first lowered her long yard at the run and manned sweeps. Before long her single cannon opened up, the powder-smoke whipped away in the strong breeze. The ball, however, tore up the sea only a dozen yards ahead of the small vessel. 'Too much motion for 'em,' was the general opinion of interested watchers. *Wolf* was not much better: her shot went somewhere into the unknown and *Vixen*'s second passed close overhead with a vicious *whuup.*

Kydd winced, but these were keen and valuable men who could not be expected to know how a gun was pointed in the open sea with no one to show them. It was time to take a hand. 'Mr Duckitt,' Kydd told *Teazer*'s gunner, 'you and Mr Stirk each are to go aboard and teach 'em how to point a gun in anything of a seaway. Then, to spare *Teazer*'s hide, we'll set the barrel adrift and you lie off half a mile, a pistol-shot apart to await the signal.

'Then we'll have our sport. Shot b' shot you'll advance on the target and see who'll be first to hit.' As they drew closer it would be easier and thus one would eventually be sure to strike, with suitable effect on their confidence.

'Oh, and tell 'em that the winner will be presented with Mr Duckitt's very own gun lanyard as will, er, be worked with a three-way Turk's head and other proper ceremonials.'

The barrel was cast off, bobbing jauntily, and *Teazer* hove to at a safe distance to await events, her sides lined with seamen pleased at the entertainment and, no doubt, happily placing wagers on the outcome.

The two gunboats squared off and, at the signal, first *Vixen* and then *Wolf* let fly. It would not have answered in a prime man-o'-war but at least the sudden plumes arising were in sight. Trying to wield rammers and gunpowder in the bluster out to sea without injury was a triumph in itself – but Kydd had seen it done before, and by the French, off Calais . . .

'Some sort of fishing boat, I think, sir.' Hallum pointed to a small craft under a single lugsail emerging from the river.

'If the codshead can't see what we're about he soon will.'

Kydd laughed, watching one lucky shot skim the tops of the waves to miss the cask narrowly.

'I do conceive he wishes to speak us,' Hallum said apologetically, looking at the direct course steered and the dark figure angrily gesturing by the fore-stay.

'He thinks we're frightening th' fish!' Purchet chuckled.

On balance Kydd thought that *Vixen* was making better practice, for *Wolf* was gamely taking seas over the bow, which must have been making it hard to keep a footing at the gun.

'Er, it seems there's a naval officer aboard,' said Hallum.

'Give that t' me,' Kydd said, snatching the telescope. The gesturing figure of a hatless post-captain leaped into view. 'Man the side – we've a visitor.'

'You'll give me an explanation, sir, this minute!' fumed the officer, after he had heaved himself energetically aboard.

'I beg your pardon, sir?' Kydd said coldly.

'Austen, Captain Francis Austen. District captain of the Sea Fencibles, and I'll have your explanation as to why you're stirring up my command to no purpose.'

Kydd allowed his gaze to move to the final stages of the engagement where, to the raucous joy of the seamen, *Wolf*'s next shot smashed the barrel to flying wreckage. 'I have a roving appointment from Admiral Keith as inspector of Sea Fencibles, and—'

'Inspector? And you a commander?' Austen said, in disbelief.

'Shall we go below, sir? I'd be happy to explain.'

It took all of a bottle of Kydd's best claret to make good his position, that the inspectoring was no more than a cover for a deeper game but that he had to make a good show of it.

Austen made clear his conviction that the Sea Fencibles, by taking the second line of defence, were releasing the Navy for their aggressive first line at the French coast and, further-more, by being part-time were able to support themselves between times providing fish for the nation and at no cost to the government.

As to the business at Ramsgate – which had sent him after Kydd in hot pursuit – Austen pointed out that the Fencibles had their own range and gun for live practice safely out of the way near North Foreland. Any dilatoriness Kydd had seen in mustering at the harbour was because their instructions were that, in the event of an alarm, maroon rockets would boom over the town and each then would know his duty.

Only after it was discovered that both had fought at the Nile and shared an admiration for Horatio Nelson did the atmosphere thaw and Austen accept the convenience of a passage back to Ramsgate.

'And you'll oblige me exceedingly, dear fellow, should you now allow my Sea Fencibles to go about their business without alarums and anxieties. Please believe, they're a fractious crew if they see themselves practised upon.'

'Ceased as of this minute, and my report will be a warm one, you may be assured, sir.'

Idly picking up a book lying on the sideboard Austen raised his eyebrows. 'Descartes, *Regulae ad directionem ingenii – Rules for the Direction of the Mind* no less! I find I must admire your choice of literature, Mr Kydd.'

'Oh, er, that belongs to my ship's clerk and particular friend. He's a prime word-grinder, Renzi, and is now engaged in writing a book.'

'Goodness me. How curious! I wish he could meet my sister, Jane – she takes such satisfaction in scratching away and swears she will be published some day, bless her heart,' Austen said fondly.

Chapter 10

'Nicholas! Take a seat, m' friend. It seems the waters o' Bath are in truth a sovereign cure, you looking so well.'

Renzi sat in his usual chair by the stern windows and stretched lazily. 'Such a quantity of women, each with a tongue that simply could not be still. That a man must find peace in a man-o'-war is a singular thing.' Then he gave Kydd a quizzical look. 'Far be it for me to lay criticism at the feet of my worthy commander but did I not see a gaudy red at the ensign staff supplanting the pristine blue of our noble Admiral Keith?'

'Aye, you did. For now we are an unattached ship while I top it the inspector of Fencibles.'

'Oh?'

'Well, you should know this is b' way of a blind while we are on a secret tasking.'

Renzi jerked upright.

'Why, nothing t' remark,' Kydd told him. 'In fact, we're not to trouble the French in any wise.'

'The Irish?'

'No. Oh, I'm sanguine you'll hear of it in time, but I'll ask you t' keep it in confidence. Our real task is to act as trials ship and Navy liaison to an American cove who's been inventing a submarine boat.'

'Was this by any chance a man called Fulton?' Renzi asked, with a curious note in his voice.

'Er, yes, but here he's known as Mr Francis.'

Renzi's face tightened. 'I didn't think to see that man again.'

In dawning realisation, Kydd said, 'Then – then it was *you* conducted him to England?'

'Yes.'

'How did – you were *in* France?'

'Paris.'

Kydd's face was grave. 'Nicholas, now the French know you did—'

'There is nothing to connect my quitting the country with Fulton's departing. It's rather him that stands into danger. The French may now rue his leaving and take steps to silence him. Is he guarded?'

'Yes. In Dover Castle.' Then Kydd challenged, 'Why do you dislike the man?'

'Did I say that?' Renzi came back defensively.

'He's a genius who's going to give us the means t' get at Boney's flotillas,' Kydd said stoutly.

'He's a mendacious and deluded fool, who covers his motives for creating his evil machines with absurd nonsense about saving the world from itself.'

Kydd blinked in surprise at Renzi's intensity. 'He's said some strange things, I'll agree, but if he's going to provide us with—'

'Have you not considered the nature of what he is doing,

pray? He desires we send out these submarines, like assassins in the night, to fall upon unsuspecting victims who are powerless to defend themselves. This is never within the usages of war of any civilisation worth the name.'

'Well, Nicholas,' Kydd said lightly, trying to lift the mood, 'if it is so dreadful, no navy will want to put to sea, and there you'll have your universal peace.'

'Do not insult my intelligence,' Renzi said. 'In Earth's bloody history there will always be found those who place their lust for domination over any consideration of ethics or humanity and would, without hesitation, subject the world to a reign of terror for their own cruel ends.'

'Are you meaning that our employing this against Boney is immoral by *your* lights?' Kydd snapped.

'Damn it, I am! And I'm surprised – very surprised – that you should see fit to encourage such a means of waging war.'

'So, out of notions of honour we should lay aside the weapon that saves us from Bonaparte?'

Renzi did not reply at once, as if he were considering his response carefully. 'If we're speaking of honour, consider this little analogy. What is the difference, may I ask, between he who faces another squarely in a duel, and the one who waits until darkness to break into his opponent's house to slaughter him in his bed?'

'Desperate situations call for radical measures.'

'There must be limits to acceptable behaviour in war or we're lost as a species. And pitting a man sword in hand against an unarmed, blindfolded adversary is nothing but contemptible.'

'You are, of course, hoist b' your own petard, Nicholas.'

'Do go on,' Renzi said stiffly.

'Before, you said that there'll always be found those so lost t' honour who'd think to employ such a means. By logic, therefore, we must ourselves acquire the same, or the godly must surely be overcome by the unrighteous.'

'That's as may be, but it does not make it an acceptable course for an honourable nation.' He paused. Then, with a twisted smile, he added, 'And yet, you see, you have omitted one small matter.'

'Oh? And what's that?'

'If this should be the manner of war then where might distinction be won by the valiant? Where is the triumph, the victory, in the mass destruction of unwary sailors?'

'Be that as it may,' Kydd said tightly, 'but tell me this. If you feel as you do, why did you take such pains t' bring the man to England?'

Renzi sighed. 'So as not to leave him to the French, the main reason. And – and he has created a wondrous undersea chariot with which to visit Neptune's kingdom that might yet be of incalculable value to science.'

Kydd said nothing and Renzi continued, 'Since returning I have had time to consider, and now I've come to realise I loathe to the depths of my being what he is visiting on the world, I fear I cannot face him again. If he comes aboard I must tell you I will not sit at the same table with such a man.'

Troubled, Kydd could see that more than duty and morality had now entered his friend's thinking. But was there any other way to get at Bonaparte's menace?

Kydd found Fulton in his casemate, head in his hands. 'Is there a problem, Mr Francis? Are you not well?'

Fulton lifted his head and Kydd could see the ravages of fatigue in his face. 'I'm as well as I can be,' he croaked. 'Nothing to worry of.'

'Are the plans near complete at all?' Kydd ventured.

'Don't concern yourself, Mr Kydd, if that's the purpose of your visit. My calculations show a working depth of thirty-five feet and an increase to thirty in the number of submarine bombs she can carry in her deck compartments – and you cannot but admire my undersea observation ports in the dome.'

Before he could look Fulton pushed the plans to one side and swivelled round to Kydd. His eyes burned with a feverish glow. 'Tell me, Mr Sea Captain, what is it you're thinking? That I'm mad or a quack – that this is all a humbug to win gold from your king? Go on, say away!'

Kydd felt for the man. 'You've been at your scribbling for weeks now. Have you had any bear you a hand?'

'There's no one on God's earth that's in any kind of position to help me. I conceive of it, I test the idea, do the calculations and then the draughting. Who else?'

'So all this time you've been here . . .'

Fulton slumped in the chair wearily. 'I've worked every hour God gives, so help me. Night and day, meals brought in, don't wash, don't sleep much.' Then he sat up, energised. 'It's just so . . . damned breathtaking, dazzling to the mind working on the beast, I can't leave it.'

Here was a man entirely on his own in a foreign country, grappling with devices and concepts far beyond the wisest philosopher and conjuring into being a mechanical sea-beast to plunge into the depths so that man could for the first time be truly a child of Neptune. 'I'll tell you what I'm thinking about your submarine boat, Mr Francis, but not here,' Kydd said. 'You'll first hoist inboard a square meal, as we say in the Navy, then talk.'

'I can't—'

Kydd gave a friendly smile. 'I'm not without means. It'll be entirely at my pleasure, sir.'

The snug of the White Horse Inn was unoccupied, and Fulton devoured his steak and ale pie in privacy, expressing every degree of satisfaction with the victuals. He dabbed his mouth with his napkin, then prompted, 'So what, then, *is* your feeling, sir?'

'I've had space t' think about it, Mr Francis. Therefore I say to you . . . it's the most fearful and wonderful thing I've ever seen. And I'm persuaded it's the future, sir.'

Fulton gave him a penetrating look, then threw back his head and laughed until the tears came. 'At last – at last! A believer! And, dare I hazard, one who's ready to go with my *Nautilus* into that future whatever it brings, no matter that some name me a murderer of sailors, a charlatan and projector? You are to be congratulated, then, sir.'

Kydd was discomfited by his ardour and took a pull at his drink. He caught the eye of the potboy and signalled for another round, then asked, as casually as he could, 'Have you heard anything of the committee, sir?'

'Ah, yes. I meant to speak to you about it. They have constituted it and I'd be pleased to hear your opinions as to its members. We have Sir Joseph Banks its chairman, whom I met once, Henry Cavendish a scientist—'

'Banks, of course, is of some eminence. I know but little of Cavendish,' Kydd said. 'Who will be the naval representative? Gresham, I suppose.'

'Not at all! Note was taken, he's not on it. But I'd wager it's not the last we'll hear from the gentleman. No, it's to be one Popham, a high captain of sorts.'

'Popham! Then you've a right cunning fellow there – he

has distinguished service, and is a scientifical and inventor too. He's introducing a completely new method o' signalling into the Navy. If there's anyone to convince, it'll be he.'

'Umm. Then there's Rennie, dockyards, and a redcoat Congreve from an ordnance department of some sort.'

'Seems sound enough but I'm not sure I can add much.'

'Ah, well.' Fulton took a pull of beer.

'Do you have plans o' business as will see your *Nautilus* a-swim? One man on his own . . .'

'Yes,' said Fulton crisply, 'I do. The prime need is to get one party interested enough to fund my design. In this case, your Admiralty. She builds and off she goes under licence to my company and starts among the enemy like a tiger let loose. I will have a contract that says for every ship of size I put down there's a royalty – tonnage or guns I don't care. With these proceeds I build more and better. It's cheap, pays for itself, so other countries take a note and next thing there's submarine boats in every navy.'

'You said before as your intention is universal peace and liberty for all b' making it impossible for warships to put t' sea.'

'Just so. When all have my vessels, how can they? Some kind of mutual-destruction war? I don't think so. Therefore the high seas are made free for any and every man.'

'I see,' said Kydd. 'Then I should wish you good fortune, Mr Francis.'

'Look, my friends call me "Toot" – will you?'

'Oh, er, of course, um, Toot.' Kydd warmed to the man's need to reach out. He was alone in the country, yet with such world-shattering plans in his head.

'Thank you, sir. And you?'

'Well, I'm Thomas Kydd, Thomas Paine Kydd after the radical as charmed my parents.'

Fulton chortled. 'Tom Paine! I'll have you know, the old feller's been a good friend to me, living in Paris all this time. Returned to New York only a year or so past. So right readily I'll call you Tom, my friend.'

Kydd grinned. Fulton's enthusiasm was infectious and he raised his beer in salute. 'To *Nautilus* as will be!'

It was time. The plans were ready to present. Kydd and Fulton boarded the Canterbury coach to London. Kydd took rooms in the White Hart as before but Fulton rejected offers of assistance in the matter of lodging, insisting he preferred the independence and freedoms of more humble quarters in the Minories, on the pretence of it being close by America Square.

On the due day they waited together in a discreet ante-room of Somerset House, Fulton clutching his flat case of plans and in high spirits. 'Do you think one guinea a ton royalty an excessive figure?' he asked Kydd. 'Being a fraction of what it costs to build?'

'As you sense the mood of the meeting, I'd suggest,' Kydd replied, with what he hoped was a reassuring smile. No doubt the illustrious chairman would be taken with the novelty, the dockyard representative would be interested in the technology, the scientist with prospects for natural philosophy – but the one who stood capable of bringing down Fulton and his scheme was the representative of the Navy, Captain Popham. If, being creative and inventive in his own right he took against Fulton for reasons of jealousy, or perhaps adopted a high moral stand, then he had the power to ruin the enterprise. Kydd was well aware of what that would mean to the courageous inventor.

The door to the meeting room opened. 'The committee

will see you now, Mr Francis,' a secretary said quietly. Kydd rose as well. 'This is a closed meeting, sir,' the man said firmly, ushering Fulton in and shutting the door.

Kydd knew there was no real requirement for him to remain, his duties were mainly of a liaison nature, but he wanted to see the thing through and Hallum would be keeping *Teazer* in order for him.

There was not long to wait: in less than twenty minutes the presentation was over and the members streamed out, talking excitedly. Kydd stood – the major in regimentals had to be Congreve, a reclusive-seeming gentleman in thick glasses the man of science, and there was Popham, a strong-faced figure in naval uniform striding out and looking thoughtful, nodding gravely to Kydd as he passed.

When Fulton came out, he was beaming. 'A good meeting, my friend – they listened and learned, and when the sceptics opened fire I was ready. God, was I ready!' He chuckled.

'And?'

'I just told the fools that they're whistling in the wind – a submarine is not to be doubted for it's been built, proved. It's already happened. They'll be getting a much more advanced craft, is all.' He laughed again. 'Fair took the breeze from their sails – couldn't say boo to a goose after that.'

'So what happens now?'

'They go away and think about it, talk among 'emselves. Promised to get back to me without delay.'

'So you—' began Kydd, but a large, wealthy-looking gentleman walking painfully with an ivory stick had come out. It could only be Sir Joseph Banks.

'Interesting, damned interesting,' he said genially, regarding Fulton keenly. 'Not your common diving bell but a locomoting plunging boat. Fascinating.' With a quick glance at Kydd, he continued, 'It would gratify me much if you'd consent to come to my little gathering tonight. There'll be some present who'd be with child to hear of it – upon such short notice I know, but while you're in town?'

'Most certainly, Sir Joseph. Be glad to.'

'And your friend? I'll send my carriage. Where?'

'Oh, the White Hart in Charles Street, sir,' Kydd intervened, before Fulton could respond.

'Excellent. Shall we say six o' clock?'

It was only a small *soirée* but the Grosvenor Street mansion was of an intimidating quality.

'Why, Sir Joseph, your leg is still troubling you?' said a stately lady, solicitously, elegantly working her fan.

'The trials of age, my dear,' said Banks, then turned to Fulton. 'This American gentleman is Mr Francis, and this is Mr Kydd, his friend while in England.'

Kydd essayed his best bow – but Fulton's was deeper and more extravagant.

'Gentlemen, the Lady Broughton.' He continued, 'Mr Francis is here for a particular and quite diverting purpose, Bethany. I'm sanguine you'll never guess it in a hundred years.'

The fan stopped. 'Mr Francis, do tell. What is it brings you to these shores?'

'The conjuring of a submarine boat as will swim beneath the waves with the fishes, that will disport with the porpoise and sealion and altogether put a frightener on our Mr Bonaparte,' Fulton said, in lordly tones.

'I – I'm not sure I follow you, sir.'

Banks interjected: 'He means to say he is constructing a species of plunging boat that might creep along the seabed to rise up on unwary ships a-slumber at their anchor and explode them to atoms. Is that not so, Mr Francis?'

'Indeed it is, sir. At home both in the Stygian depths and ranging the oceans looking for prey. But as well the intrepid crew might peer through their port and be witness to sights in the depths until now seen only by drowning sailors and Neptune himself . . .'

'Goodness gracious!' Lady Broughton said, staring at Fulton through her quizzing glass in awe.

'Ah, Toot, perhaps we should not bore the ladies with such talk,' Kydd said uncomfortably. 'Er, and is not the character of your work to be accounted secret?'

'Quite so!' Banks agreed. 'But the Lady Broughton here may never be thought your common French spy, Kydd. I can personally vouch for her, may I not, Bethany?'

'Why, thank you, Sir Joseph.' Then she pressed Fulton, 'But does not your submarine boat frighten the fishes? Or do they not recognise such a – a thing, and then you open a little door and spring out upon the poor unsuspecting creatures?'

Fulton replied in ringing tones that echoed around the room. Others came over to listen to the new-found social celebrity. Eventually Kydd and Fulton left with firm invitations to the theatre, a *fête champêtre* in Hyde Park and various ill-defined assemblies – but Kydd was growing concerned by Fulton's flamboyant behaviour.

A note had arrived by hand from Captain Boyd of the Admiralty, remembering Kydd's earlier visit and cordially inviting him to an evening affair – his friend would be made welcome.

'These are the gentlemen you have to convince, Toot,'

Kydd told him seriously, as they arrived. 'They'll be the ones finding men for your submarine and sending them off to fight in it. They'll need to be confident in your plans, I'm thinking.'

The two mounted the stone steps into the Admiralty, Kydd, in deference to his companion, not in uniform. Boyd greeted him effusively. 'So good to see you again. I've heard you had a brisk time of it in the Downs?'

'May I introduce Mr Francis? He's undertaking some work for—'

'Yes, I've heard. Welcome to London, sir.'

A larger officer with a face of granite loomed behind. It was Gresham. 'We meet again, sir,' he said loudly, to Fulton. 'How convenient. I was just trying to explain to my friend Noakes here how you propose to pay for your little toy.'

'No mystery, sir,' Fulton said icily. 'They're self-funded after the first, as any who attended the *committee* now knows. Kydd, do explain to these worthy mariners if they're still confused.' He gave the smallest of bows and turned his back.

'Look here, sir—'

'Captain Gresham, Mr Francis is under pressure t' complete his design. I'm sure—'

'He'll explain to me *now* how an untried and unworkable gimcrack contraption is going to save us all from Boney or I'll—'

'Gentlemen, gentlemen,' Boyd said, 'this is a social occasion. Not the place to air professional disagreements. Now, can I press you both to a glass of punch?'

The elderly Noakes shifted uncomfortably but seemed determined to have his say. 'Nonetheless, I'd be obliged for a steer in the matter of the morality of all this. As I understand it, if the plunging boat works as advised, we're being asked to sneak up on the enemy like common burglars and—'

'Good God!' Fulton exploded, as he turned back abruptly. 'Do you want to beat the French or no? You think a bunch of cow farmers in red coats is going to stop Napoleon if he lands – there's two thousand invasion craft over there, stuffed to the gunnels with Boney's best! Your only hope is to top 'em in their harbours before they sail. I'd have thought it plain enough for any simpleton.'

He folded his arms and glared at Gresham, who said, with a sneer, 'But it's all to no account. Where are we going to find crews enough to man all these death-traps among our honest tars? They've more sense than to—'

'Come, Mr Kydd,' Fulton snarled, 'I find there's more important work I have to do. Captain Boyd, I'll thank you for your hospitality and we must leave. Goodnight.' He pushed his way to the door and out into the street.

'Toot, this is not the way to—'

'They were waiting for me. I'll not stand to be a punch-bag for all the doubtin' loobies in the British Navy! I'm away to do my work.'

'I'll call a carriage.'

'No. I need to walk.' He stormed off down the road and Kydd hurried behind.

At an ornate gate Kydd suggested they cut across the park, hoping the pleasant trees and shrubs would calm his mood. After a while Fulton eased his pace. 'You really should not provoke 'em like that, Toot,' Kydd told him. 'They have the ear of Popham, who's very senior and—'

Fulton drew a long breath. 'It's hard, damnable hard.' He sighed. 'I've worked on this for years and still I'm fighting to make 'em understand. When will it all end?'

Kydd had no easy answer. Fulton's hopes of his creation coming alive had already been dashed after months of French bureaucracy. Was the same thing to happen again? And would Britain's only chance to deal directly with Bonaparte's deadly threat vanish?

'The committee is a true one. It'll give you a good report, I'm sure. Just—' He froze. Behind them, tapping steps had broken into a run. Kydd spun round as two men rushed towards them. He threw Fulton to the ground and stood astride him, whipping out his small-sword just in time to catch the first attacker with his weapon. The man gave a howl of pain, dropped his knife and ran for the bushes.

The other stopped and drew out a heavy pistol, hesitating whether to kill Kydd first. A sharp crack rang out; he clutched his bloody face and fell kicking.

'What in hell?' Fulton said, brandishing his pocket pistol as he heaved himself to his feet. 'I've never seen robbers—'

'French assassins,' Kydd said grimly. 'I've got t' get you under protection, m' friend.' He looked round. It were better they were not found on the scene and he dragged Fulton through the bushes to another path.

Fulton pulled himself free. 'I'll not have a posse of redcoats at my tail!' he snorted.

'Then you'll have to stay somewhere a mort safer than your Minories. Until we get word from the committee, you'll be a guest aboard my ship.'

Fulton hesitated. 'Where's she at? Not London, I'd say.'

'In the Downs, only a few hours away. Have no fear, Toot. Deal is a gay enough town, with quantities of ladies to be entertained. However, I do believe you'll be safer in *Teazer* for the present.' Kydd had sensed his reluctance to leave the capital – the lionising and awe must be a heady brew for one so far from home and on the brink of fame and fortune.

'Mr Hallum, *Teazer* has an important guest arriving shortly. It'll only be for a few days, and your cabin . . . ?'

Renzi took the news coldly and announced that he would be detained by his studies.

Fulton arrived and immediately took over the great cabin, spreading out his plans and scratching away at new ideas for *Nautilus* and his other devices. He was a figure of mystery and excitement for the ship's company and lurid rumours flew about the mess-decks.

He appeared on deck only once in the next few days; Kydd followed companionably a few steps behind him as he paced with a distracted air. Men stopped their work and stared wonderingly at him, then broke into animated talk after he had passed.

When he reached the fo'c'sle Fulton stopped, bewildered. A brawny seaman took him gently, turned him round and, grinning broadly, sent him on his way aft.

For Kydd this little incident with the unsuspecting sailor in his act of kindness, secure in his wooden world, yet unaware that Fulton was planning its destruction, touched on all the elements of what was gathering pace and soon to break on the brotherhood of the sea. Did Fulton truly understand what was being wrought?

Kydd turned on his heel and went to his cabin.

The next day Fulton was full of spirit. 'Well, I've solved it!' He chortled. 'A torpedo detonation without human intervention. Yes, quite unseen and deadly certain.'

Kydd could summon little interest in the detail but asked of it politely. Fulton gave him a pleased grin, wagged his finger, then made a mysterious reference to a horn atop *Nautilus*'s conning dome.

Kydd persuaded Fulton to accept an invitation to a musical evening given by a marchioness in honour of the valiant defenders to be held at Downlands Hall. Nestling in the gently rising swell of the North Downs it was the prettiest country house Kydd had seen, above the sprawling village of Nethersoke.

It turned out to be a splendid affair, the scarlet and gold of regimentals vying with the dark blue and gold of naval uniforms among the most fashionable gowns of the age, all in the breathless heat of a still evening under the coruscating gold and crystal of the chandeliers. There were indeed quantities of ladies as the guests mingled before the performance, and Kydd saw Fulton disappear quickly into the throng. He accepted an iced confection and was just about to enter a conversation when he was startled by the distinct thud of a distant gun.

The noise of happy gossip and repartee tailed off and the officers looked at each other meaningfully in the sudden quiet. Another gun sounded, and a corporal of yeomanry burst into the room. 'The beacons!'

There was pandemonium as everyone struggled for the doors and flooded out into the garden. Strident shouts came from some, with the occasional well-bred female shriek and the hoarse bellow of command rising above the excitement. Atop the nearest hill the stuttering glow of a beacon strengthened, and in the far distance the orange point of another wavered.

Kydd's heart lurched. Was this Napoleon Bonaparte at last?

A trumpet sounded in the village below, an urgent *tan-tara* that had the soldiers girding their swords and hurrying away. The church bell began a continuous tocsin, unnerving in its dissonance.

A sudden shout drew all eyes seaward. In the dusky blue light along the edge of the horizon hundreds of pale sails could be seen, too far away to make out details but heart-chilling in their import.

The naval officers shouted for their carriages and, nearby, the nervous rattle of a drum indicated local volunteers beating to arms and forming up. Kydd was conscious that to be caught ashore was every captain's nightmare – but where the *devil* was Fulton?

Hallum would have the sense to send in a boat double-manned to get him back aboard, but he had to get through chaos to make Deal and the beach. Kydd cast about for Fulton, cursing that he had not kept closer to the man. Downlands Hall was still a blaze of lights; he went back inside and hurried through the deserted rooms, calling him.

A bugle quavered near the village – had he gone to see the militia turn out? It was out of the question to leave him on his own when *Teazer* sailed. Who knew when she would return and if fresh French agents would have their orders?

'Toot!' he bawled again into the evening, as the last carriage left at full tilt.

There was now nothing for it but to get to the village on foot, see if Fulton was there, then find a horse or some other conveyance.

Panting, he arrived at the square. It was packed with a milling crowd, tearful women saying their farewells to menfolk humping muskets, militia crashing to attention, fearful old people and children wailing. It was hopeless calling for Fulton against the bedlam, so Kydd reluctantly gave up his search and looked about for some means to get to Deal.

The militia marched off and a harassed clergyman implored the women with children to form groups for their speedy transport inland. Outside the Red Lion a straggly line of agricultural yeomen hefted pitchforks and scythes, growling defiance as a squire with a fowling piece joined them.

The first carts turned into the square and the children clambered up, mollified at the prospect of a ride, some mothers joining them with cloth bundles of food. Then, with a crash of hoofbeats on cobbles, a troupe of yeomanry thundered past. More followed, and Kydd saw his chance.

He stepped out and waved his arms. They slid to an undignified halt. 'In the name o' the King!' Kydd bellowed. The corporal in charge looked at his splendid naval dress uniform in astonishment. 'I demand you yield your horse t' me,' Kydd told him.

'Why, sir, I must attend at Walmer wi'out delay, sir!'

'Then take me,' Kydd replied and, without waiting, hauled himself up behind the man. 'Carry on,' he ordered. Fulton must now take his chances – if this was Bonaparte, there would be more important matters to attend to in a very short time.

The corporal rallied his men and they clattered on into the gathering darkness. The roads were choked with people fleeing and the horses shied at their presence, but they made good progress and wheeled onto Beach Street where Kydd jumped down, sore after the ride.

People looked with curiosity at his now dishevelled appearance. He ignored them and hurried to the King's Naval Yard where he found his boat patiently waiting – and, standing beside it, Fulton. 'Where the—' he began. 'I was worried for you, Toot.'

Atop the signal tower the semaphore clacked furiously in the last of the light. Fulton smiled sardonically. 'I thought to find a grand seat for the performance to come, Mr Kydd.'

Calloway came up to Kydd and politely removed his hat. 'Sir?'

'Well, an alarm, is it not?' Kydd said peevishly, aware of his appearance.

'Er, no, sir. Some farmer burning off his bean straw, a coastal convoy becalmed offshore, and the lobsterbacks got excited.'

Word came that a decision from the committee about future submarine plans was imminent. Fulton would not be held back, so he and Kydd posted to London the same day.

As soon as they alighted from the coach Fulton threw off his travelling cloak and hurriedly went to the hall-stand at the Minories. Three waiting letters were cast aside but he seized on the fourth. 'This is Banks's writing,' he said, tore open the seal and went into the poky drawing room to read it. Kydd followed.

Fulton scanned it. Then, with a set face, he read it again. 'See for yourself,' he commanded, thrusting it at Kydd and turning away.

It was a short but courteous note, thanking Fulton for his exertions and expressing every admiration for the genius of his design but thinking it only right to advise him in advance of the formal communication that the committee, while agreeing on the probable technical feasibility of the submersible, had decided that there would be insufficient time to develop the means to overcome its operational limitations, given the imminence of the invasion threat for which it was designed. It concluded with further warm compliments and the suggestion that an early approach to the Treasury for a settlement of accounts would be in order, given that, unhappily, this must be regarded as a termination of relations.

Kydd looked up in consternation. 'This means—'

'The fools!' barked Fulton, 'The benighted imbeciles! The cod's-headed, hidebound jackasses! Can't they see – don't they realise—' He broke off, pounding his fists and choking at the enormity of it all.

Fulton's world had collapsed on him. The two biggest naval powers in the world were locked in a death struggle, yet neither wanted to take further his invention. In effect it was a conclusive vote of no-confidence in the device. Kydd knew it was now unlikely that Fulton would ever secure further development funding and must—

'God blast 'em for a – a set o' stinkin' skunks!' Fulton croaked.

Anger gripped Kydd that such a gifted inventor should be so treated by the world. 'Toot, this is not the end, m' friend. We'll find out what it is ails 'em, then—'

Before he could finish, Fulton snatched a decanter of brandy, swigged deeply from it, then rounded on Kydd. 'Be damned to it!' he gasped, wiping his chin. 'I should have known this'd happen, I throw in with the British.' He took another gulp. 'That was why we cast off the shackles, damn it.' His face crumpled. 'God rot the villains. I need fresh air.' He pushed past Kydd into the street.

The ancient grey-white bulk of the Tower of London loomed to the south; he flew toward its rear wall where he beat his fists helplessly against the dark-weathered stone. 'Bastards! Fucksters!' he cried. 'I'll see you in Hades, you pigging rogues.'

Passers-by stared in shock, and Kydd tried to drag him

away but he pulled himself free and looked around wildly. The dilapidated timber edifice of the Royal Mint was on the other side of Little Tower Hill. He made to storm across but then, scorning it, plunged past into the maze of Smithfield's streets.

Kydd tried to reason with him but Fulton shook him off, pushing faster into the crowds of market porters, butchery stalls and stinking squalor. 'This is no place for us, Toot,' he shouted. 'Let's go back and I'll—'

'To blazes with it,' Fulton said savagely. 'You can go to hell – I'm after finding some real people. The company of common folk.' He tore away from Kydd and disappeared ahead. Jostling against the tide of humanity, vainly searching for a glimpse of Fulton's bright green coat, it became all too clear to Kydd that the man had vanished.

He tried to think. To the left was the haunt of the apothecary and chirurgeon – no commoners there. To the right was the high rear wall of the new London docks – or there. But beyond . . . Kydd hurried forward along the line of the wall to where it stopped abruptly and headed back to the Thames. This was where Fulton was going – docklands. The stews of Wapping and Shadwell. The maritime rookery that accompanied the greatest concourse of shipping on earth – the Pool of London.

Beyond the rickety tenements and streets of chandlery, sailmakers, slop-sellers and breweries there was a thick forest of masts and rigging. This was where ships from every corner of the globe found rest and could discharge their cargoes of tea, spices, cocoa, tobacco, cotton and goods of every conceivable description, whose pungency lay so heavily on the air.

The nature of the crowds changed: in place of the clerk

and bookseller, now there were wharf-lumpers, sack-makers, draymen and sailors, going about their business in the narrow cobbled streets.

Kydd thought he glimpsed Fulton's green coat and re-doubled his pace. Now he was coming to the Thames waterfront, the haunt of the crimp, the scuffle-hunter and mud-lark, and his fears for Fulton grew. Then he saw him, looking up at the faded sign of the Dog and Duck.

Before he could reach him he had gone inside. Kydd hurried to the door just in time to hear him declaim to the astonished topers on their stools that he was a friend to all the oppressed, the common folk, the honest labourer, and he was prepared to stand a brimmer with any who'd drink with him to the greatest submarine inventor ever made.

'What's it do, then, cock?' one called derisively. 'Make eggs o' brass or somethin'?'

'A craft as swims like a fish beneath the waves and can explode any of your Nelson's battleships to splinters any time it chooses.'

Kydd thrust into the taproom, heavy with the odours of liquor, sawdust and rank humanity. Heads turned his way. 'A grog for every man!' he roared, and threw the tapster two guineas. In the riot that followed he yanked Fulton out on to the street. 'What do you think you're doing, Toot?' he demanded, only too aware that they stood out in their quality garb and that his sword was with his baggage.

Fulton tore free and ran down towards another waterfront tavern, the Blue Anchor, but before he could reach it a hard-faced man in leggings appeared from a doorway in front of him, standing astride and smacking a cudgel into his palm. Kydd swung round. Another was moving on them from behind.

In desperation he glanced about him and saw a bundle of building laths among materials for repair. He dived for it and whipped one out. It was an absurdly thin and insubstantial piece of wood, but Kydd held it before him at the ready, like a sword, and advanced on the first man, who stopped in surprise, then lifted his heavy bludgeon with a snarl. That was just as Kydd had wanted. He lunged forward in a perfect fencing crouch, the point of the lath stabbing unerringly for the man's face. It gouged into bone and, with a shriek, his attacker dropped his weapon, staggering back. The other shied away, unsure of what had happened. 'Go! Go for your life!' Kydd bawled at Fulton.

They headed instinctively for the water. Running feet and hoarse shouts followed them as they plunged through the narrow, stinking passages and across clattering footbridges at the edge of the river. Suddenly the vista opened up but Kydd had eyes only for one thing – the stone steps of wherry stairs. A waterman, dozing in the stern-sheets of his boat, woke at their shouts and they shoved off quickly, leaving their frustrated pursuers behind.

Chapter 11

Fulton hung his head in dejection. 'It's over,' he said, in a low voice. 'I'll never see *Nautilus* swim in my lifetime.'

Kydd moved his chair closer. 'How can you say that, Toot? The committee haven't given it enough thought, is all.'

'So who will bring 'em to their senses? Gresham isn't alone, damn his soul, for it's in the nature of the mariner to distrust new things. No, I'm one man against a whole tribe of Noahs. Pity me, Tom.'

Kydd grimaced at the street noises outside Fulton's small rooms, loud and unceasing. They were a sad distraction for any thinking man. Fulton deserved better but obviously could not afford it. Then a thought came: could he himself fund the development? Fulton was proud and independent, and would allow it only under contract as a form of investment, shares in his company, perhaps. But as a venture the yield would be considerable, even as much as— What was he thinking? To *profit* by the murder of sailors, however logic-ally necessary? His mind shied away in horror.

However, he now knew that he believed in Fulton's ability

to bring to reality a war-changing weapon of historic significance. And if this were so, then standing outside the situation was not an option. If Britain were to possess it, and if he had any influence or power to bring it about, his duty was clear.

'Toot, we're going t' see this through. The first thing we'll do is find what made 'em cautious. I'm to see Captain Popham, I believe.'

'Wait!' Fulton stood up and went to the window. 'I – I don't think it'll fadge.'

'Pray why not?'

'My purse is now uncommon light – at low water, as you sailors will say. If I'm to—'

'Toot, you'll honour me by accepting a small . . . accommodation as will see you secure for now.'

'You'll have my note of hand directly, Mr Kydd,' Fulton said woodenly, and looked away.

Kydd was ushered into a small, tastefully ornamented drawing room. 'Why, Mr Kydd, a very good morning to you,' Popham said pleasantly. 'Do be seated.'

'Thank you, sir.' After the usual pleasantries had been exchanged, Kydd came straight to the point. 'Er, you'd oblige me much by gratifying my curiosity in respect of Mr Fulton – or should I say Mr Francis?'

'Oh? A very fascinating cove indeed. Challenging ideas. Not your common projector, if that's what you mean.'

'Would it be impertinent of me to ask what the committee found objectionable in his plans?'

Popham hesitated, then looked at Kydd quizzically. 'Do I take it you have an interest of sorts in the fellow?'

'As a serving officer it would be quite improper of me to take advantage of—'

'Quite so.'

If Popham was the one to have objected on moral or other grounds Kydd knew he was sailing close to the wind, but the man continued, 'Yet one might take a professional interest, don't you think?'

Did this mean . . . ?

Kydd pressed his case. 'It appears t' me, sir, that if there is anything of substance in the design then we're duty-bound to discover its limits.'

'It will set our notions of sea warfare on its head, should he be successful.'

'Yes, sir, but if this is going to be the future, do we have the right to turn our backs on it without we know of it at the first hand?' There was no going back now.

'Ah, do I see an enterprising and forward-looking officer not affrighted by the original, the radical? Then we are quite of a mind, sir.'

Relieved, Kydd went on, 'Then may I know who objected to the submarine?'

Popham gave a lopsided grin. 'There were several who did, but one who quite swayed the meeting and discouraged all further discussion.'

'And he was?'

'Myself. I had to, of course.'

'I – I don't understand you, sir.'

'Reflect, if you will. Mr Pitt is asking for a steer in the matter of saving the country from the invasion fleet of Mr Bonaparte. That, at this time, is his first duty.' He paused, then said, 'Do you know much of the *design* of this submarine boat?'

'Not a great deal,' Kydd admitted stiffly.

'In warfare the devil's always in the detail,' Popham said.

'The general consensus among us was that the design may be technically feasible, if not brilliant. No, Mr Kydd, the problem does not in fact lie with our friend's plan, which might well end in a formidable and deadly craft. It is, in short, workable. But the target is the flotilla in Boulogne. And, as *you* should know, the sea depths to be found there are scant and with much tide scour. Yet the design calls for the submersible to pass under the victim. I would suggest that even if this were possible, in such cramped conditions it would be to the grievous hazard of the craft, and I cannot find it in me to condemn its crew to such a horrible end.'

'I see, sir,' Kydd said. 'Yet it has to be admitted that such a weapon would give complete mastery of the sea to whoever is able to employ it.'

Popham eased into a smile. 'Which, at present, we already enjoy. No, sir, the remit of the committee was the destruction of the Boulogne invasion flotilla and none else. This *Nautilus* cannot achieve this. Therefore I cannot, in all conscience, recommend to the government that there be an expenditure on a device without specific utility to His Majesty's arms. That was and is my duty to say, sir.'

'Then . . .'

'I'm afraid so.'

'But in the future—'

'The future may take care of itself.'

Kydd stood. 'Then I can only thank you for your time, sir, and—'

'My dear fellow, I might appear to you unsympathetic, but this would be far from the case. I am a friend to any who can carry the war to the enemy, and if Mr Francis had come to us with anything but a submarine boat he might have been more fortunate. Perhaps we shall look at it with interest, but later.

'If you see him again, do extend to him my every expression of admiration for his achievement, will you, old fellow?'

'So, as you can see it, Toot, there's little can be done. Without it does for the invasion flotilla, *Nautilus* is not to be set a-swim by us – and that's the last word, I fear.'

Fulton slumped in dejection. 'All these years . . .'

'Are not t' be wasted,' Kydd said forcefully. 'There's still a chance.'

'No! I'm not spending what remains of my days wheedling dullards who—'

'So you're to have done with submarines? Cast all the work aside?'

'I'm going back to America.'

'Where there's a great need of such,' Kydd said tartly. 'Listen to me, Toot. You can have your *Nautilus* if first you can show 'em something as will stir their interest, give 'em confidence in your inventions. That will set 'em talking.'

'What,' said Fulton bitterly, 'can be more amazing than a submarine boat?'

'Your torpedo machines? Did you not impress Napoleon himself with 'em?'

'At Brest, with his admirals looking on,' Fulton conceded.

'Then I can't conceive of anything more prime to launch against their invasion craft.'

'But without a submarine . . .'

'Toot, you contemplate your torpedoes and I'll see what we can do to deliver 'em for you. But might I know why you call them "torpedo" ?'

'After the electric fish that strikes invisibly. That's your Atlantic torpedo of the *Torpedo nobiliana* family.'

'Well, putting the name aside, let's clap on all sail. The

Admiralty will smile on any who can show a way to deal with the menace at Boulogne. Your course is set. Work up plans for a superior species o' torpedo and I'll see it gets attention. No time t' be lost, Toot.'

The promise of a means to deal with the crouching menace at Boulogne was vital to securing the attention and interest Fulton needed – but the original arrangement had run out and the committee had disbanded. How were they to get a fair hearing on another invention?

Popham would be the key, Kydd thought. If he could capture the man's imagination, persuade him to take an interest, lead him on, perhaps, to a personal involvement, then he most surely could take it to the higher levels. Fulton had sketches of the device he had used at Brest. With a few modifications it would bring attention.

'Against Boulogne?' Popham said, with growing animation. 'If these "torpedoes" can be relied on to sink a ship in a single blow, we have an entirely new method of assaulting an enemy. No more hours of battering away with broadsides at the hazard of life and limb.'

'That's as it seems, sir.'

'He will find much of the Service arrayed against him, of course. There are not a few inclined to oppose anything that is ingenious or not hallowed by the centuries, including those who have a moral objection to the employment of such weapons. Well, Mr Kydd, if you ask my advice, I would suggest you should batten down for a long and stormy voyage.'

'It does seem worthy of further trial but in this we have a perplexity, sir. Mr Francis is without means if he works on, and feels he must on that account return to America.'

'I see.'

'It does occur to me, sir, that were his inventions to be put forward by one of unassailable standing in the Navy it would not be Mr Francis alone to be resisted.'

'You're very persuasive, Mr Kydd, but I myself am much taken up with business. In the last election I'm made the Member of Parliament for Yarmouth, but at the least I shall spy out the lie of the land for you.'

True to his word, a message of encouragement arrived not long afterwards, followed by another requiring Fulton and Kydd to take coach to Deal to meet Popham at an unfashionably early hour in the King's Naval Yard with as many illustrations of the projected weapons as were available.

Mystified, they waited at the appointed place as morning blossomed into day. Popham arrived punctually. 'Thank you, gentlemen,' he said, with a mysterious air. 'Do join my carriage. We are expected.'

It was only a few minutes along the foreshore before they drew up at the quaint rounded edifice of Walmer Castle. They were saluted by soldiers at the gatehouse, then hustled inside to the comfortable residence within.

Kydd supposed they must be going to meet the lord warden of the Cinque Ports, upon whom Popham clearly felt it worth his while to call. Kydd hoped the old gentleman would understand enough of what was being said.

The doors of a long corridor were flung wide and a striking young woman appeared. 'My lady,' murmured Popham, with a bow. 'This is Mr Kydd, and Mr Francis. Gentlemen, the Lady Hester Stanhope.'

'You've not come with bad news, I trust, Sir Home,' she said sternly. 'You know how Uncle always takes it so personally.' She was dressed for the morning, but in an individual white gown with a boldly coloured shawl.

'No, Hester, this is merely an entertainment.'

She looked at him distrustfully.

'Mr Francis is an American gentleman with diverting views on marine travel.'

'Oh? Then I believe I shall stay. Come in, and do remember Uncle's health is causing us some concern.' She ushered them into a small reception room cunningly fashioned within one of the ancient Tudor bastions.

The men waited politely in easy-chairs for the lord warden to appear. Lady Hester took firm direction of the arrangements as a small circular table was spread with various hot and cold dishes. Then the door opened and, almost apologetically, a lean, drawn man shuffled in, wearing a well-used corded green dressing-gown and red slippers. He nodded to Popham and waved down the dutiful rising of the others. 'Please excuse,' he said, in a voice not much above a whisper, 'you'll believe this is the only way I have to attend on you.'

'It's kind in you to see us at such notice, sir,' Popham said respectfully, then introduced Kydd and Fulton.

The two bowed.

'And this, gentlemen, is William Pitt, the prime minister of Great Britain.'

Kydd's eyes widened in astonishment.

'Hester, my dear, there's no need to tarry on my behalf.'

'No, Uncle, I want to hear—'

'Dear child, I rather feel they have a matter of some delicacy to discuss.'

After his niece had departed, Pitt brushed aside Popham's background introduction of Fulton. 'I know of you, sir,' he said. 'My condolences on the committee's decision, which, in all fairness, does appear to me to be the right one.'

Popham leaned forward earnestly. 'Mr Francis recognises that his plunging boat may be delayed a while but he has since been turning his mind to the presenting difficulty of the age, Mr Bonaparte's armada.'

'Oh?' Pitt toyed with a kipper, but listened keenly.

'He has produced a remarkable plan for submarine bombs, which may be launched unseen from a distance, requiring but one to sink a ship and which appear to me eminently suited to an assault on Boulogne.'

'Have you details?'

'Mr Francis has brought his plans to show you, sir.'

Spreading out the drawings over a *chaise-longue* Fulton launched into an explanation. The artistic quality of the illustrations and his colourful metaphors brought a smile to the ailing statesman. 'So these torpedoes might be prepared using existing naval materials and ready within no more than three months?'

'Indeed.'

'So, if we make immediate arrangements for a monthly stipend of, say, two hundred pounds while you are so employed, with a capital sum against expenditure of naval stores of, what, five to seven thousand pounds you would be prepared to begin?'

'Should I receive the unqualified support of the Navy and a satisfactory agreement entered into regarding my recompense.'

'Being?'

'The sum of one hundred thousand pounds to release the plans under licence to your government and a royalty payment of forty thousand for every decked French vessel destroyed by my weapons.'

'One hundred thousand? Your engines come dear, sir.'

'The loss of this kingdom the dearer.'

Pitt gave a tight smile. 'Very well. I shall instruct the Treasury to draw up a contract of such a nature and, er, agree the financial details with you.' Pitt broke off to cough into his handkerchief. 'Not omitting that His Majesty's dockyards and arsenals be charged with assisting where sought. And, Mr Francis, it is my fervent desire that you should begin without delay.'

Outside, Fulton's eyes shone, and Popham observed drily, 'You'll agree there are some compensations in being a Member of Parliament, Mr Kydd. However, it might be that in going above the heads of the Admiralty we're on a lee shore to them. But be that as it may, to work! I suggest that, in this, I shall be the one speaking with the Admiralty and Navy Board and you, Mr Kydd, do take station as before on our American friend. Admiral Keith will no doubt agree to your continuing with trials and close liaison. Agreed?'

Kydd stepped gingerly into Fulton's crowded casemate. It was now more a workshop than a design office with three benches and workmen with sheets of copper, an industrious carpenter and a cooper sighting along his staves.

Fulton was bending over his plans and turned to greet Kydd. 'Now we're getting somewhere.' He rubbed his hands together. 'I'm to start all over again. Before, I had my *Nautilus* with its horn, slowly rising under the victim to strike, now it must be another way. I have my ideas . . .'

'I'm sure you do,' Kydd said hastily. 'I came to know if there's any service I can perform.'

'There is. As you can see, I proceed cautiously, trying and

testing, for nothing will serve unless it can be seen nobly to meet the ocean's billows. Your stout vessel will have its hour at the final trials but for now I need to conduct experiments of a privy nature, explosions and the like.'

Kydd considered the request. Who better to ask about a quiet retreat for activities of a stealthy nature than a Revenue officer?

Over a friendly jug of ale, he had his answer. 'The coast t' Romney Marsh is the worst in the kingdom f'r smuggling. Reckon I c'n find you a tucked-away little spot as will meet y'r needs. How about Martha's Cope, just a little ways off?'

Kydd went to view it. Sure enough, at the base of the soaring chalk cliffs close to Dover there was a tall cleft and several lofty pinnacles standing out to sea, a flat area in their lee, and a dark cave into the rock, a token of its more usual visitor.

It would do admirably. The towering cliffs would deflect the sound and would ensure their security as only boats could approach the area. A mooring buoy laid offshore would make for convenience, and marines posted at either shore approach would keep all would-be visitors at bay. Let the trials commence.

Pleased, he went below to detail his intentions to Keith and found Renzi at his books in the great cabin. As Kydd entered he looked up. 'So, you've found a portion of God's good earth on which to test your infernal machines, then,' he said acidly.

'As you will see,' Kydd said neutrally, not wishing to find himself in yet another argument.

'And your Mr Francis is ready with his inventions?'

'He works like the devil himself, but they will need proving first, Nicholas.'

'Of course, you see the true reason for his industry.'

'To save us from Boney,' Kydd said shortly.

'Not as we'd recognise,' Renzi replied, with a measure of venom. 'He merely wants to see his diabolic devices created and cares not a damn who pays for them.'

'That is a reason why we should turn our back on 'em in our hour of need?'

'You are a gentleman. You've reached a level of politeness in discourse and delicacy of perception that are a shining credit to you. It escapes me why it should be that you do encourage the man in his mass destruction of sailors. It's an inviolable maxim of conduct in war that one's enemy is met on the field face to face, that the issue be decided nobly by courage, resolution and skill-at-arms. Failing that, the mastery of the profession of war is set at naught and we descend into a base hackery – or the promiscuous exploding of bodies unknown.'

Stung, Kydd replied, 'And it's escaped me why you will not see that it's *happened*. This is the future for all men now, whether you like it or no, and we must learn the new arts.'

'Not so, my friend.'

'Oh? Then there is—'

'Recollect. Before Fulton there was no one with a deadly submersible like *Nautilus*. He has attempted to interest the French in it without success, mainly on account of their distaste for it and what it represents. It has been turned down as well by ourselves, and I cannot readily see who else in this terraqueous globe might be moved to expend their treasure in order to exploit it.

'In fine, as we look around, in the absence of any other of such inventive persuasion, it would appear that Mr Fulton and his ingenious contrivances are destined to appear as a curious footnote to history, he the only one of his kind, and the world will, with a grateful sigh, revert to civilised conduct once more. That is, if the gentleman is not rashly encouraged . . .'

'You would not grieve it if he disappeared from the face o' the earth tomorrow?'

'Since you ask it, no.'

The first trial was simple. *Teazer* lay submissively to her buoy over on the seaward side and a strange ceremony took place. Under the interested gaze of her entire crew, Fulton prepared his first experiment with a short, stubby barrel, well caulked, canvas covered and heavy. It was lowered over the side on a marked line, which Fulton paid out slowly, observing it sinking lazily from sight into the bright summer sea.

At the first mark he hauled in. It seemed unaffected, but Fulton shook it carefully, listening for water inside. Satisfied, he entered something on his notepad and repeated the action to the second mark. It wasn't until the fourth that the dripping barrel came up ugly with imploded staves.

The buzz of conversation rose when a second barrel was produced, this time larger and tar-black. It lasted to the seventh mark. 'I'll trouble you now for a length of slow-match, Mr Kydd,' Fulton requested.

In another cask of the same type Duckitt, the gunner, coiled slow-match close down on the ballast inside. A flint and steel had the end settling to a red smoulder and, step-ping aside, he allowed the header to be thumped in.

Without delay Fulton lowered it rapidly over the side to the fourth mark before drawing it up again. The boatswain himself knocked out the header – but the match inside was dead. He looked up at Duckitt wryly. Fulton appeared unperturbed.

'This was not vitiated air,' he murmured thoughtfully. 'The candles lasted for hours in *Nautilus*. I rather think . . .'

The next day saw a successful submerging and a triumphant return. Fulton waved the glowing end about the air in great satisfaction. 'Lead lining and no condensation – that's the ticket,' he crowed.

It was only the start: the barrels elongated and grew, now the size of hogsheads and half the height of a man. Significant looks passed between the watching sailors as they considered the implications of such when crammed with powder and set off; several turned their backs, faces set, and went below.

The unwieldy beasts needed tackles to sway them over-side, and, in the water, required extra ballast. The first returned as an untidy clutch of splintered timbers, the second brutishly fighting the training lines. Submergence was not all that was expected: they should as well pass silently through the sea on their deadly occasions.

Fulton worked throughout the daylight hours at his experimenting or figuring in a corner of the deck. Kydd became impatient. He waited his moment and confronted him. 'Toot, answer me this: I heard you say that you demonstrated one of these in Brest before generals and admirals. Why do we start again when you successfully destroyed a whole ship even then?'

'Ah. Well, that was, as we must say, a demonstration only,' Fulton said cheerfully. 'As would meet expectations. A simple barrel on a rope over-stuffed with gunpowder and, um, suitably deployed. In our present contract we look to the palpable reality where men must strive unseen against others and will not stand unless their apparatus is without flaw. Agreed?'

Kydd nodded reluctantly. 'It seems reasonable, given that any future contract would be at hazard, were your engines found wanting on the field of battle, Toot.'

Later in the day a naval officer in plain clothes came aboard *Teazer*. 'Kind in you to see me, Kydd. I'm here dispatched by our lord and master to top it the spy concerning your infernal machines,' he admitted.

Kydd gave a wry smile. This way there was no official notice being taken of the activities of a private contractor, but as the commander with operational responsibility Keith had a moral right to be in the know.

'I'm not certain I can tell you much,' he replied. 'The trials are at an early stage only, what's watertight, ballast required, that sort of thing.'

The officer turned grave. 'As I feared.' He shifted uncomfortably. 'You see, old chap, Keith is put under notice by the politicos to make a sally against the French using these infernals to satisfy the mob that Bonaparte is being dealt with severely – you do understand, I know.'

Kydd thought despairingly of Fulton's painstaking progress. 'And when is this assault planned t' be?'

'Well, yesterday would best suit but any time close after will serve.'

'I'm not the one t' say, but you're asking for the moon.'

'Am I? Then, dear fellow, if you have any influence over the chap, do impress on him the need for celerity and that sort of thing, won't you? I have the feeling that Keith will press on whatever state the contrivances are in. Did you know that our new first lord of the Admiralty, Lord Melville himself, bless him, fully intends to take part in the assault, so consequential is the action believed to be?'

'We'll do our best for you,' Kydd replied strongly.

'Stout fellow!' the officer said. 'You get along splendidly with Americans, I'm told. Best of luck.'

It put a new and graver complexion on the situation: was

it a measure of desperation at the highest levels that the august head of the Navy – who was certainly not expected to tread a deck, let alone smell powder-smoke – should feel obliged to be a part of it?

Fulton took the news calmly but retreated to his casemate, demanding that a soldier's camp bed be placed next to his desk, and set to work. By morning he had sketches ready; his mechanics turned to and he requested that *Teazer* be made available again.

At Martha's Cope it became clear that the character of the trials had now taken a more serious turn. The gunner was asked to provide material for live charges and, after a nod from Kydd, assembled the makings into an arms chest and brought it up.

The impedimenta was rowed ashore in the launch and prepared. 'Over there,' Fulton decided. It was a low, flat rock, lapped by waves; close by loomed the pinnacles of chalk that gave the tiny cove its name.

'Post your men,' Kydd told the sergeant of Royal Marines, and two sentries were sent marching stolidly under the vertical white cliffs in opposite directions to seal off the approaches.

In complete silence the first experiment was assembled. A simple contraption was erected, a metal hemisphere pointing cup down at the end of a hinged arm twelve feet long, braced by two legs.

'What's this, then, Toot?'

'It gives a measure of the vehemence of a blast. Observe here, where there is a scale at the hinge. With exactly the same charge a variation in the confining of the igniting powder will result in a different force.'

He laid down a metal plate and lowered the cup over it. 'See here, first powder quite unrestrained.' A cascade of black grains poured from the measuring funnel and settled in a pyramid.

'Mr Duckitt, clear the range!'

Every man stepped back to a safe distance. 'Fire the charge!'

The gunner blew on his portfire and touched off the powder. It flared up high in a bright, firework-like glare, with a vigorous but impotent hiss. When they tramped back to the apparatus the gauge had not moved.

Without comment Fulton produced a coconut-sized sphere. 'Charge this, if you please,' he said to the gunner, and explained to Kydd, 'This is, then, the same amount, within a half-inch clay jacket.' Match was inserted and lit. The onlookers retired hastily.

It detonated with a satisfying flash and a clap of thunder that echoed back from the soaring cliff-face. After a moment pieces of the jacket were heard skittering about. Fulton plunged into the eddying smoke and inspected the result, noting down the reading. 'One inch clay,' he intoned, resetting the indicator.

This time the explosion had a vicious ring and the shattered clay whipped through the air overhead, falling into the shallows in myriad splashes. Fulton took the reading from the canted arm, then became thoughtful. 'I'd hoped the effect would scale, but it does not. This is not double the impetus.'

'Meaning?'

'To multiply this force and be sure to sink a well-found man-o'-war will take either a mort more powder or a jacket so heavy as to cause the torpedo to sink. I must think again.'

The next day a three-inch jacket was tested, which confirmed the problem: a larger charge in the same case had the puzzling result of a lower indication on the gauge than expected. 'I wonder if it's the greater bulk of the powder smothering the speed of burning?' Fulton mused.

'Beg pardon, sir,' Duckitt interjected, 'an' have ye considered corned powder a-tall?'

'What's that?'

'New, like. Sifted mill cakes, hardened 'n' rolled in graphite. Makes f'r rare consistent firing.'

'Have we any?' Kydd asked.

'Aye, sir. Costs a pretty penny – we keeps it f'r the chase guns only.'

Duckitt was dispatched to find it and Kydd asked Fulton, 'If the explosion is within the sea, will not the water pressing on your, er, container, act t' tamp it like the clay jacket?'

'Coffer. That's what we call 'em,' he replied, distracted. 'Why, yes, I'm supposing it will, but how do I take the measure of an underwater blast, pray?'

Nowhere in Kydd's experience in the Navy had he ever come across explosions occurring beneath the surface. His question, however, seemed to have sparked something in Fulton, for the next trial was with small submersible casks.

'From the boat, if you please.' The match was started and the cask head thumped home, then the whole was allowed to sink on a line to an improvised buoy, nervous oarsmen sparing nothing to make certain the boat was nowhere near the spot.

In a deathly silence all eyes were on the barely ruffled innocent surface of the water. A sub-sea thump was more felt than heard, followed a second later by the bursting upward of a white geyser, which subsided to an ugly, roiling scar in the sea.

'We take it by the height of the splash,' Fulton said defensively, selecting another, larger cask. 'We'll see if this scales up.' There was another tense wait, and once more the plume rose skyward.

'Better!' Fulton said, with relief, lowering his improvised quadrant. Kydd pulled out his pocket watch and consulted it pointedly.

'Don't worry, Mr Firebrand, I'm satisfied an' will now move forward.'

'So this means—'

At that moment a naval cutter was sighted, making her way prettily towards them. 'A very good morning to you, gentlemen!' Popham said breezily, when he had stepped onto the shore. 'Do I see your new curiosities performing to satisfaction?'

Fulton busied himself obstinately among the apparatus in the arms chest, leaving it to Kydd to answer. 'Mr Francis is moving forward this day, sir, on account he has achieved satisfaction in the matter of the, er, coffer.'

'Splendid,' Popham said heartily, 'as it will please their lord-ships to hear.' His tone became more serious. 'The descent on Boulogne has been sanctioned at the highest, and time is now of the essence. Is there anything whatsoever that I might do for your American?'

Kydd detected a note of anxiety and guessed that there was more to the question than had been said, but before he could answer Fulton swung round, his face dark. 'Yes, there is, Mr Englishman – perhaps you'd keep clear of the works. There's enough to worry on without we have sightseers.'

Popham gave a wintry smile. 'Do tell me your concerns. I'm no stranger to novelties of a mechanical nature, sir,' he encouraged.

Fulton hesitated. 'It's the fault of your committee. Without I have a submarine, how do I attack with a torpedo? If it's agreed that it be done unseen, do they propose I use ships' boats splashing along with oars in full sight of the enemy? Or like the ancient Greeks, by swimmers with a torpedo under each arm?'

'There are other ways of approaching a prey,' Popham responded.

'Flying over it in a balloon?'

'I'm reminded of my service off the coast of the Coromandel. There we encountered nightly the thievery of the native peoples—'

'Captain, I'm very engaged today, If you've—'

'– who could approach unseen to within close hail except in the brightest moonlight.'

'Swimming.'

'No, Mr Francis. In a species of native craft called a catamaran. This has the property that it lies very close to the water, being of two hull forms joined by a central bracing. I'm sanguine it can be made strong enough to deliver your torpedoes.'

'Low in the water?'

'Inches only.'

'Then we have a possibility.'

Fulton looked speculatively at Popham, who hastened to add, 'Leave it to me. I know an amiable shipwright who will be persuaded to produce one immediately for our consideration. In the meanwhile you shall be free to concentrate on your curiosities.'

'It won't do! I calculate we'll need all of thirty minutes, if not the hour, to make our approach by stealth. An' if that's with slowmatch it'll die of suffocation long since.'

'A different kind o' fuse, Toot?'

'There isn't any not using fire, damn it all to hell! If we were going in with a submarine, there'd be none of this.'

Kydd's heart went out to him: to be pressured so and in a situation not of his making was taking its toll. 'Can you not – a mechanical fuse o' sorts?'

Fulton looked up with red-rimmed eyes. 'There's no such. Not even . . . Wait! I have it.' He laughed. 'Why not? Mechanical – an automatic self-igniter.'

He pulled out his notepad and, with hurried strokes, sketched in a gear train and cams, then a striker plate and cocking detent. 'Yes! Does not consume air, and can do its deadly work in secret, deep beneath the waves until it knows its time has come. Then, without warning, heroically sacrifices itself in one hellish detonation.'

Kydd shuddered at the picture but he had to see things through. 'It must be made of brass or some such, else the seawater will turn it to rust in quick time, and that'll cost you not a little.'

'Hang the cost! Set the price of one squiddy bit of brass clockwork against that of a man-o'-war? There's no argument, my friend.'

Despite his disquiet, Kydd found Fulton's sudden enthusiasm infectious.

'I've some drawings to make,' Fulton continued, 'and I'd be much obliged should you scare up a watchmaker who'll relish a challenge.'

Kydd was later entertained by the sight of Fulton explaining to the bemused craftsman the operation of a delay mechanism that, at its culmination, instead of setting off an alarm actuated something that looked suspiciously like a gun-lock.

'So. We have figures on depth to tamping effect for a given charge, as may be scaled up. A form of watertight carcass has been devised, proof to the depths it will be used, and if our crafty captain is to be believed, a near invisible means of launching the beasts. Now, with our automatic fuse in construction we can turn our minds to assembling them all into a fearsome weapon of war.'

The first torpedo was impressively huge: more than twelve feet long, square sectioned and with symmetrically sharp front and rear. It was ballasted to ride just beneath the sea surface and had within it twenty watertight compartments ready to receive their lethal cargo of explosives.

'My friend, I do intend now to test its force. Just for this I won't be needing either the catamarans or the automaton igniter. However, the concussion will set up such a commotion that I'd rather be elsewhere than here, further away from the ladies of Dover in their parlours.'

It was eventually agreed that Shell Ness, a few hours' sail around North Foreland at the tip of the Isle of Sheppey would suit. It was low, scrubby and desolate, with nothing but one or two empty shepherds' huts.

Teazer's deck bore three torpedoes lashed down securely, long, tar-dark coffers that, in their deadly menace, made hardened seamen tiptoe nervously past them. It was necessary to wait at anchor while their promised victim, a decrepit fishing-boat, was towed into the bleak mudflats. It was old but of a size, and to Kydd seemed to assume a pathetic dignity as it was led to its place of sacrifice.

No time was wasted: the coffer was lowered into the sea, grappled by the pinnace crew and manhandled round to face the target. The men strained at their oars, the torpedo wallowing sullenly after them until they reached the vessel's side where it was left.

The gunner in the gig then gingerly started the match fuse

and hastily pulled away. An expectant hush fell over *Teazer* as all aboard waited and stared at the tethered victim in horrified fascination.

Kydd aimed his telescope while Fulton had his improvised quadrant trained ready. Time passed in breathless silence. Suddenly the sea at the waterline shot up in a huge pall of white, suffused with gun-flash and smoke, and a clap of thunder rolled round the bay, sending countless sea-birds to flight.

Fulton grunted in satisfaction as he noted the height of the plume and grinned sideways at Kydd, but when it had subsided, the fishing-boat was still there. Motioning the gig alongside, Kydd went out with him to inspect the result.

Part of the vessel's side was stove in and gaping, but otherwise only a large area of scorched timber gave evidence of the cataclysm – and she was still afloat.

'What in Hades . . . ?' Fulton said, almost to himself, as he poked at the scarified hull and peered up at the crazily hanging gaff-yard. Then he collected himself and added calmly, 'But, then, this is our sea in its tamping. It works to satisfaction yet directs its force in the main to the line of least resistance, which is to the vertical. Hmm – this is a setback, I cannot deny it.'

Yet by the time they had returned to *Teazer* Fulton had his answer. 'We use two torpedoes, one each side, and crush the ship between their vehemence.'

The two remaining coffers were swayed down and put in the water, but at the long-suffering victim, another difficulty presented itself. 'Mr Duckitt, they must explode together, as near as you please.' This was a tall order, but the gunner bent his best efforts in cutting the match to the exact same mark. He borrowed a boatswain's call to sound the precise time to the gunner's mate on the opposite side to light the fuse.

A double roar saw the vessel hidden in smoke and spray but when it dissipated, there was the satisfying sight of blackened wreckage settling beneath the waves. 'The coffer size must increase, of course, but with an automatic fuse we will have a good result,' Fulton said briskly.

The catamaran was as strange a craft as Kydd had ever seen: two long, slender hulls joined with an open framework. The two oarsmen would take position on a narrow bench running fore and aft, set well down – in fact, they would be sitting in the sea. Their silhouette would be inches high only, a cunning device to allow them to close invisibly with the target before launch. Popham was clearly pleased and accepted the flattering comments about his contribution, then motioned the vessel to be brought alongside.

'Shall we make trial of it?' Kydd said jovially. 'Come now, you men, who'll volunteer?'

As always in the Navy, the out-of-routine had instant appeal and this promised at the very least a skylark in the summer sea for the lucky pair selected. They settled into their sub-sea seats to much ribaldry, and it was quickly clear that, barely head and shoulders above the surface, they would be more difficult to spot even than a small ship's boat.

The testing time was as night drew in. For some reason the darkling sea took on a feeling of looming menace; unknown shadows moving restlessly.

'Who's to come forward then, you idlers?' Kydd called encouragingly, to the knot of onlookers. This time there were no takers. 'That fine pair of this afternoon, you've had your amusement, so step up, my lads, and see what it's like to earn your grog.'

The two detached from the others and came to the ship's

side, looking down in consternation at the flimsy contraption in the darkness. 'Come along, then,' Kydd said gruffly. 'Salt water never harmed anyone. In you go.'

Hand over hand, they lowered themselves, exclaiming aloud at the chill of the night water as they immersed.

'Good God!' spluttered Popham, leaning over the side. 'For the cold plunging pool at Tunbridge Wells you'd damn well need to find five guineas – the Navy's giving you your health cure at no cost.'

The oarsmen seemed not to appreciate the joke, but Popham turned to Kydd and said, 'Damme, that's what I'll call the beasts – my plungers.'

Kydd watched the shivering pair shove off and awkwardly ply their sculls to take them into the anonymous blackness. They were under instructions to circle *Teazer* out in the moonless night, then close in from a random direction.

'Keep a bright lookout, ahoy!' Kydd roared up at the men in the tops. Much hung on this, as everyone knew, and a wary silence settled.

Some minutes later there was a call from aft – '*Boooat ahoooy! Away t' starb'd!*' It was some time before Kydd could pick out the low form that the sharp eyes of a ship's boy had spotted.

'Around again!' they were ordered, and this time, coming in directly on *Teazer*'s bow, they penetrated easily within a ship's length.

'Splendid!' Popham declared. 'There!' he told Fulton. 'You have your means of delivery, sir.'

Chapter 12

It had been frustrating in the extreme. Hours spent in journeying to London, two days explaining, reassuring, promising, Kydd waiting outside, and the solitary Fulton sitting at one side of a long table, with the seniority of the Admiralty assembled along the other. Popham had assured Kydd and Fulton it was necessary, but in their eyes there were more pressing concerns.

And now more hours in a coach on the return. Kydd pondered the extraordinary turn of events, and the irony that he had now the wealth and the opportunity finally to take his place in higher society, but the grave situation in which England stood made it all but meaningless. Even a small estate was beyond his grasp: as an active captain he could give it no real attention – and he had no lady to rule it.

He watched the neat, rolling hills of the Weald of Kent passing by, almost garden-like in their loveliness. Next to him Fulton's eyes were closed, and opposite, a merchant and his prim lady kept aloof. His thoughts turned inevitably to the war: there was no question but that in a short time there would be a reckoning.

Would he play his part with honour when the time came? Of course. Then doubt flooded in. Did honour include the stealthy blasting to atoms of sailors? Was it so necessary to support Fulton as he did, or had he, as Renzi believed, crossed a moral Rubicon? Troubled, he crushed the thoughts. Did not the situation demand extreme measures? Was not—

The coach lurched to a grinding stop, the horses whinnying in protest. There were sharp voices outside, and Kydd leaned out of the window. Two horsemen stood athwart their path, both masked and each with a heavy pistol. One walked his mount to the window of the coach and leaned down, flourishing his weapon.

'The men – out!'

Highwaymen! Rage filled Kydd that these vermin were still at their trade when the country's peril was so real. His sword was in the rack above the seat, but it would be useless in the face of the big horse pistol pointing steadily at him.

'Now.' The voice was flat, with no emotion, and left little choice but to obey.

Kydd climbed out, looking tensely for the slightest chance, but these were clearly professionals. One stood back to cover the other while he dismounted. Kydd tried to peer into the mask but there was only the glitter of dark eyes.

The three male passengers stood together and faced the two riders. It was odd that they were ignoring the lady, for she surely had the richest pickings.

'I – I h-h-have a w-watch!' the merchant stuttered, reaching for his fob.

He was ignored. The highwayman still mounted trained his pistol on each in turn, then rapped, 'Which of you is Fulton?'

In an instant it became clear. These were French agents sent to find the inventor. Fulton glanced at Kydd with a lopsided smile. Neither spoke.

The merchant looked bewildered and afraid.

The rider motioned meaningfully at his accomplice, who threw open the coach door. 'Out!' he snarled at the woman, holding his weapon to her head. She screamed and the man cuffed her to the ground. Still with the pistol aimed at her, he cocked it.

'Which is Fulton?'

If the French took back the inventor they would know in detail what was planned against them and take appropriate defensive measures. Then they would undoubtedly build infernals of their own. It could not be risked. 'I am,' Kydd said, and stepped forward.

In French the mounted man demanded, 'Answer quickly. What rank does Gaspard Monge hold under the Emperor?'

Kydd was unable to answer.

'You!' said the man, pointing to Fulton with his pistol. 'Come here.'

His accomplice swiftly cut the traces of the coach horses and slapped their rumps, sending them galloping away over the heath. Then he resumed his horse but kept his pistol out.

'Up behind!' Fulton obeyed awkwardly. They cantered into the woods and out of sight.

It was a catastrophe – and Kydd was responsible. It had taken half an hour to catch one of the horses and now he was riding south, bareback, thrashing it as hard as it could go. Kydd knew that the agents would be in urgent flight to the coast to spirit Fulton to France.

At a village he hired the best mount he could find and

thundered madly down the road, hoping against hope to see the riders ahead. Then, under the goading of urgency, he headed instinctively for his ship. Tired and sore, he left the exhausted animal at the King's Naval Yard in Deal.

As Kydd slumped down wearily Renzi looked up from his reading. 'Is there—'

'I've lost Fulton,' Kydd said simply.

'Lost?'

'We were bailed up on the highway from London b' French agents, not three hours ago. They took Fulton. I have t' do something!' With every minute gone they would be that much closer to France.

Renzi put down his book. 'You will be considering alerting the admiral.'

'Damn it, o' course!' Kydd forced himself to concentrate. 'I'd wager they'll want to get him over just as soon as they can. The closest place is right here. I feel it in m' bones — they're about somewhere.'

It was an all-or-nothing throw: that they would have made for this place of all the possible escape ports and, additionally, that they were here still. If he was wrong, the consequences could not be more serious, but the same instincts that had made him a successful privateer captain were reassuring him coolly that he was not mistaken.

The typical late-summer calm was preventing their final flight to France — to the land that was so plainly in sight across the Channel — but in an hour or two an afternoon offshore breeze would pick up and they would make a run for it, if indeed they were there.

Restless, Kydd got up, went to the stern windows and flung one open. In the Downs it was a calm, placid day, the sun glittering on a glassy sea. Upwards of two hundred ships of all sizes were peacefully at anchor waiting for a wind, lifting to the slight swell, a charming picture.

'What better place to conceal but in the middle of all those,' Renzi murmured, over his shoulder. 'It will be hard to flush them even with every boat in the squadron out.'

Kydd came to a decision. 'No! I'm not telling the admiral,' he said firmly. 'There's no time t' rummage so many ships – and, besides, who knows Fulton to recognise him? No, we're to wait out the calm and when they make their run we go after them.' If he was wrong, it would be disaster for England.

He went on deck to make his dispositions. 'Mr Hallum, I want both watches turned up. They're t' keep a tight lookout for, er, any craft making sail towards the Gull passage.' That was the direct route past the Goodwins to Calais. 'Five guineas to the man as sights it.'

Time hung: the sun beamed down in a show of warm beneficence. The lazy slap of water under *Teazer*'s counter and irregular creaking below were the only sounds to disturb Kydd's dark thoughts. At noon he sent one watch for a hurried meal, then the other. He himself stayed on deck, unable to contemplate food.

Then, more than an hour later, the first zephyr touched the water in playful cats-paws, hardly enough to lift the feathered wind vane in the shrouds. *Teazer*'s moorings had long since been buoyed ready to slip instantly and her sails were in their gear, held only by rope yarns that would be cut to let them tumble down.

At a little after three bells there was a definite lift and flurry in the breeze, enough to set lines from aloft slatting in expectation, the shadow of wind-flaws ruffling the glittering sea surface as they moved forward. It died, but then returned to settle to a playful, warm offshore whisper.

Kydd longed to send men to the yards but this would give the game away to their quarry. The wait was agonising and, to make things worse, it appeared that the whole anchorage was stirring in preparation for departure. Inshore, small craft were putting off from the shingle beach and larger ones shaking out sails.

'The fishing-boat, sir?' Hallum said doubtfully, indicating a two-masted lugger that had detached from the main body of the anchorage and seemed to be heading for the Goodwins. It was the same as many seiners at this end of the Channel – high curved bow and perfectly suited to conditions where it could blow up so quickly—

Fishing-boat? 'That's him!' Kydd said savagely.

'Sir?' Hallum said, puzzled.

'Lay out 'n' loose, damn you!' he roared at the stupefied crew, then turned to Hallum in glee. 'What kind of fisher-folk think the fish are biting now? Nearer sunset's more the mark.'

In minutes *Teazer* had slipped and her every sail was set – but the breeze was sadly lacking in strength, favouring the smaller boat, which was also directly before it. *Teazer* needed to cover the half-mile to the Gull close-hauled before she could square away after the chase.

In barely a ripple they glided along at a slow walking pace in weather that would have the folk ashore bringing out a picnic. Kydd pounded his palm in frustration. 'Wet the sails!' he spluttered, and the clanking of the deck-pumps was heard as buckets were filled and swayed up. Water cascaded darkly down the light canvas from the yards but there was no real increase in speed.

The lugger was comfortably under way and beginning to shape up for the Gull, gaining with every minute and showing no sign of noticing them. Was it indeed their quarry or an innocent?

Tide on the turn and no current to assist – it would be a close-run thing. At last *Teazer* was able to put down her helm and fell in astern of the lugger but almost immediately it was apparent that they were losing the race.

Renzi appeared at Kydd's side; his face was grave. It was unlikely that the languorous breeze would strengthen in the near term, and by the time *Teazer* had sufficient wind to haul in the smaller vessel, too much lead would have been established in the race for the blue-grey line that was the French coast.

'We're losing him,' Kydd said, in a low voice, watching the lugger spread her wings for the open sea. His mind searched feverishly for answers. Rig *Teazer*'s sweeps and row? It was unlikely they could make much more over the ground than they were doing. Ditch guns, water and so on? These were moves more suited to a long-protracted chase when fractions of a knot could add up over the miles. No, what was needed was a miraculous intervention that would see them catching up in just the next few hours. A bow chaser skilfully laid to take down a mast? No: Fulton's safety could not be put at risk.

A stray recollection – and he had it. 'Put us about, Mr Dowse,' he said. 'Take us back this instant.'

There were disbelieving cries but Kydd was having none of it. 'Get those men moving!' he bellowed, ignoring Renzi's bewilderment.

Under the impetus of her rapidly spinning helm *Teazer* swung right round the wind until hard up, heading back for the Deal foreshore as speedily as she could. 'Boat in the water the instant we're within soundings!' Kydd ordered.

Sudden understanding spread around the deck. Their captain was going cap in hand back to the admiral. Disappointment replaced frustration, but Kydd seemed unaffected. 'I want a particular boat's crew,' he demanded, and named, among others, Stirk, Poulden and Mr Midshipman Calloway.

The mystified men padded aft. Kydd waited until they were mustered, a wisp of a smile playing on his face. Then he stiffened and snapped, 'Barkers and slashers!'

Answering grins surfaced – pistols and cutlasses could only mean Kydd expected to close with the French in the very near future.

As *Teazer* slewed to the wind and stopped, the men tumbled into the launch – but before Kydd could be the last to board Renzi pushed past and clambered in. 'Nicholas, this is not your fight, m' friend,' he said, in a low voice. In the past Renzi had been insistent on detaching himself from the naval hierarchy, reserving the right only to take up arms if the very ship was threatened.

'You've a fine idea as I'm sanguine will prove diverting, old fellow. You wouldn't begrudge me the entertainment?'

The boat shoved off and Poulden took the tiller. 'After him, sir?' he said, watching the lugger with a frown. Although the light breeze was only sending the vessel along at walking pace it was beyond even the stoutest hearts to come up to it under oars.

'No, take us in,' Kydd ordered, ignoring the puzzled looks.

The boat grounded lightly in the shingle and Kydd was away up the beach immediately. He knew where to go and quickly told the man what he wanted. 'Now or sooner, Mr Cribben, and it'll be three guineas the man.'

The lazy afternoon on the Deal foreshore turned suddenly

into a scene of activity: urgent shouts broke the stillness as small boys raced away, hovellers stumbled blinking from their huts, others from the grog-shops, all converging on one long shed amid the sprawl of shanties further along the beach.

Cribben muttered angrily to the knot of locals who stood glaring at the King's men suspiciously, eventually thrusting past them and throwing open the shed doors A surge followed, then from inside came the lusty call: 'Alaw boat, *haaauuul*!' and out from the gloom, under the urging of a score of men, appeared the dark-varnished sharp prow of a long, low, oared craft.

This was quite a different matter from the iron sturdiness of the hovelling lugger. There, in unaccustomed daylight for all to see, was the notorious Deal galley-punt. Low and mean in build, it could make the French coast in two hours with twenty men at the oars, in good weather, and was known to be much favoured by smugglers and others of like need.

When the vessel was afloat in the gently lapping sea, the Navy men were sent forward while the oarsmen scrambled in, and then they were off, with low, feathering strokes that were quick and efficient; at night these would leave no tell-tale white splashes. They skimmed across the balmy seas and Kydd dared hope.

The rowers had quickly fallen into a rhythm and the strokes lengthened to produce a breathtaking dash across the waters. But several miles ahead the fishing-boat had won the open sea and now nothing was between it and Calais, already in plain sight.

'Stretch out for your lives!' Kydd roared at the men of Deal, who made a show of increasing speed. Then, wise in the ways of sailors, he added, 'You catch 'em and it's a cask o' beer and another guinea each.'

Leaving England to sink into anonymity astern, the rowers laboured on and on in a uniform dip and pull that was regular to the point of hypnotic, studied blankness on their faces as they concentrated on the effort. There was no doubt that they were catching the fishing-boat but would they be in time?

When the rolling dunes and cliffs of Calais were in stark clarity it was nevertheless clear that the race would be won. Pale faces appeared at the stern and Kydd's men prepared themselves. Stirk had a wicked grin as he tightened his red bandanna around his head and eased the pistols in his belt.

Kydd waited for the right moment and bawled across the last dozen yards, 'In the King's name, come to or we fire into you!'

Faces showed again and raised voices were heard, but the lugger did not vary its course. 'Lay us alongside aft,' Kydd hissed.

The rowers panted and sweated but the freshening breeze now cooling them was at the same time their enemy. Under its gathering strength the lugger dipped and swayed daintily, then began slowly to pull ahead – it was agonising.

'Stirk! The grapnell!' Kydd barked.

It was a last chance – but at thirty feet? Stirk stood braced in the fore-sheets, coiling the line deliberately, the main turns in his left hand, the grapnel and flying turns in his right, and began his swing, casting wider and faster and then, at precisely the right moment, he flung out.

The grapnel sailed across – and clunked firmly on the lugger's plain transom.

'Well *done*, Toby!' Kydd gasped, watching Stirk complete his feat by deftly taking turns around the little samson post and belay, letting the rope take up to allow them to be towed by the fishing-boat.

'Haul in!' Willing hands leaned out and heaved, but as they neared the vessel a face appeared above the transom with a heavy pistol. It fired – and Renzi was flung backwards into the bottom of the boat. An instant later three pistols returned the shot, the man threw up his hands and slumped over the stern.

Kydd dropped to his friend – but Renzi was already pulling himself up, his lower thigh wet with blood from an ugly scoring along his side. 'Damn the fellow,' he said faintly. 'Ruined a good pair of breeches.'

Reassured, Kydd looked up to where the transom was being rapidly hauled in. Poulden was first over in a lightning heave and leap. Kydd and Stirk followed, landing on the cluttered after deck and scuttling over to the side to take in the situation.

It was deserted, except for right forward where Fulton was kneeling, bound and gagged. Over him a man stood with a cocked pistol at his head. 'Get back!' he barked harshly, jabbing Fulton with the muzzle. 'Get back in the boat – now!'

Kydd froze. To be so near to success! A dead Fulton would be a disaster – but perhaps that would be preferable to allowing Bonaparte to take possession of the inventor.

He hesitated but the decision was taken out of his hands. Behind him Renzi had hauled himself painfully on board. He drew out his sword, a lowly hanger, and hobbled forward purposefully.

'Nicholas – no!' Kydd blurted. Was he, through his beliefs, contemptuous of Fulton's life?

'He'll die!' the man shouted, the muzzle at Fulton's ear. Renzi took no notice and came steadily on. 'He dies – now!'

The pistol aimed and the finger tightened, but Renzi did not waver, still moving forward. Coldly he detached the weapon from the man's hand and tossed it in the sea.

Stunned, the others rushed up and seized the agent, releasing Fulton, who fell, retching.

'What in blazes – Nicholas?'

'No mystery, dear fellow. Their orders were to recover Fulton for Bonaparte's service. It stands to reason that no servant of the Emperor would dare destroy him out of spite if there's a chance he might be secured later.'

Kydd chuckled. 'You took a risk on it, Nicholas, m' friend.'

'Not so much,' Renzi said, with perfect equanimity, 'for if he killed me, with but one shot in his pistol, Fulton would still be safe, and I flatter myself he could be certain your vengeance was sure.'

'And if Fulton was not?'

'Then, alas, I could not forgive myself that the world would thus be deprived of a most terrible new submarine boat . . .'

In the deathly silence nothing could be heard but a tiny *tick, tick, tick*. It came from a neat but incredibly complex brass mechanism secured in a vice, which the three men were watching.

Suddenly with a loud *clack* a sear rotated to allow a hammer arm to spring forward, tugging a lanyard. There was an instant fizz of priming and a small column of smoke, which rose and hung as if to mark the passing of a moment of portent.

'There! I give you twenty-nine minutes, gentlemen,' Fulton grunted, lowering his fob watch, 'and can thereby guarantee a detonation timed almost to the very minute.'

Kydd glanced at the expressionless face of the old watch-maker and murmured, 'To time to the instant when an unknowing man must be launched into eternity – this is our achievement?'

Fulton looked at him sharply. 'We progress,' he said coldly.

'As we must,' Kydd said heavily, then pulled himself together. 'So, what's our standing in the venture now?'

Fulton first addressed the watchmaker. 'Thank you, Mr Jones. There'll be one or two small changes, then I'm content to recommend the placing of an order for, say, fifty mechanisms to be delivered without delay.'

'W-what? H-how many did you say?' he stuttered. 'It will – sir, I cannot possibly—'

'Then I must find someone who can.'

'No, no, sir, I – I will hire every watchmaker in Kent, if need be. But – but this will cost, um . . . It will be expensive.'

'No matter, leave it with our Mr Hammond,' Fulton said airily, and turned to answer Kydd. 'Well, now, we have all the design testing complete. There will be some adjustments to my plans and then you may inform your masters that the production of ordnance may begin.'

'Adjustments?'

'A few. I've decided we must field all three designs of torpedo: the large coffer, against which even a ship-o'-the-line cannot stand, a small coffer, for the lesser breeds, and a hogshead carcass, as will be used against the flotilla.'

He pondered a little and added, 'This is all supposing your friend's catamarans are equal to the task, of course. The extra charge weight is not insignificant.'

'But we may say *Teazer*'s task is complete?'

'For the moment.'

As soon as Kydd entered the Three Kings it was obvious that the atmosphere had changed. Dyer of *Falcon* and Mills of *Bruiser* were slumped opposite each other at an empty fireplace, and an officer he didn't know stood with a glass gazing moodily out over the anchorage. There was no sign of Savery.

'Ahoy there, the Bruisers!' Kydd called cheerily. The man looked the other way but Dyer nodded wearily. 'Captain Savery not at his Friday occasion?' he asked, signalling to the steward. 'A supernaculum for my friends as need a recuperative,' he ordered, looking about genially to mark their preference.

'Cap'n Savery is not here, Mr Kydd,' Mills said suddenly, swivelling to look at him.

'Oh. Well, I—'

'He's up agin the French coast.'

'I wasn't aware—'

'Where he's been at the last month without even he's hauled off for a purgation.'

The officer at the window turned to look curiously at Kydd. 'Are you new on the coast, sir?'

'Not so,' Kydd said, nettled at his reception. 'I've been lately detained with secret matters touching on Boney's invasion plans.'

'Secret! Hah!'

'Your meaning, sir?' Kydd asked Mills.

'All the world knows o' these wild motions wi' infernal machines, dammit! Not as if you was out o' sight over wi' the French.'

'Since y' know so much of my business, Mills, then you'd also know that Mr Pitt himself authorised 'em – on account that in one blow we can put the fear o' God into Johnny Crapaud as nothing else will!'

'Er, how's that, sir?' The young officer had come over to listen. He had refined, sensitive features. 'That is, if you're at liberty to tell. Oh – Lamb, out of *Locust* gun-brig.'

'Well, Mr Lamb, as we'll be going against the flotilla with 'em quite shortly you have a right t' know. A very ingenious American has invented a submarine boat – and built one, mark you – which can swim underwater until it reaches its victim, then reach out and explode the vessel above without warning.'

'Good God,' Lamb said quietly. 'And the sailors aboard it?'

Kydd flushed. 'In war they must expect casualties, in course.'

'But that – that's no better than massacre by assassination!'

'It's the future, Mr Lamb.'

'And we must subscribe to such practices? Sir, this is neither courageous nor honourable. I cannot—'

'We have Bonaparte to beat,' Kydd said. 'What would you have us do? Tell the inventor to go away, we're too delicate?'

Lamb did not respond, standing stiff and pale.

'But then it's to no account,' Kydd continued, 'as in the event we'll not have the services of a submarine. Instead it will be—'

'It'll be your infernals, o' course! *If* they work. Heard the fishermen in Shell Ness say as the flounder still haven't returned, you explodin' carcasses *under water*, for God's sake!' Mills spluttered.

'So, then, what is your suggestion, sir,' Kydd asked, 'as a twelve-month of war sees Napoleon's flotilla untouched by us in the usual run o' fighting . . . ?'

'Gentlemen, gentlemen,' said Dyer, with a sigh, 'We have enough to do contending with the French without we assail each other. For myself, if we are given any weapon that promises confusion to the enemy, then I vow I'll not hang back from using it.'

*   *   *

Kydd returned to his ship in a foul mood. It was not his fault that he and *Teazer* had been kept out of the fighting and he felt the implied slights keenly. There was one course, however, that would see them both to rights.

Later that afternoon he left Keith's cabin with the promise of active employment until he was required, and within the day had his orders: in view of his acquaintance with the ordnance central to the upcoming assault, HMS *Teazer* would be the one to carry out the necessary reconnaissance of Boulogne.

He remembered the sight from the sea of the Boulogne hills, stretching away under the sinister blanket of troop encampments, and the crush of craft in the inner harbour. This time there was nothing for it but to crowd in as close as he could, daring everything to bring back vital information for the attack.

The orders as well entailed the embarking of Major Lovett of the 95th Rifles, knowledgeable about Napoleon's military dispositions and requesting an observation of Boulogne.

Two days later, *Teazer* weighed in the morning, and stood out for France in an easy early-autumn westerly breeze. Before long they were shortening sail off the dunes of Boulogne. Kydd turned to his guest.'You've been here before, Major?'

Lovett – an older man with an air of detachment – lowered his field-glass. 'I have, sir, many times.'

'And you know the purpose of my reconnaissance?'

'Not altogether, I'm afraid.'

'We shall be assaulting the port shortly with experimental weapons, torpedoes we call 'em, which require we close with the enemy before we launch them. I'll be taking an interest in tide states, depth o' water over the Bassure banks, lines of sight into the port, that kind o' thing.'

'Quite so.' Lovett raised his field-glass again. 'Ah. I see that the Corps de Garde have increased their numbers – over to the left by the Tour de Croy.' It was raised ground a mile or two north. 'Do you know much of Boulogne, sir?'

'I've read the reports,' Kydd said briefly, scanning the ridges with his pocket telescope.

'May I give you my appreciation?'

'By all means.'

'Well, as you know, the salient feature is the river Liane upon which Boulogne resides, disgorging to the sea between the hills. A contemptible waterway of some fifty yards breadth only, it is nevertheless the main route for the invasion of England.'

From seaward it was easy to make out the narrow entrance, as well as to glimpse the forest of masts that was the armada in its specially constructed assembly basins within. What caused Kydd much unease was a quarter-mile-long endless chain of ships moored head to stern across the river mouth, parallel with the shore, guns trained outwards.

'Marshal Soult's headquarters is beyond the fort – Châtillon – on the rise to the right. His troops will be first to embark. Ney's corps is at Montreuil, also to the right, twenty thousand men alone, and Davoût, with his fourteen regiments and Batavians, to the left, embarking at Ambleteuse. That's a total of eighty thousand men within your sight, Mr Kydd.'

'And guns?'

'Marmont calls this "the coast of iron and bronze", and with good reason,' Lovett continued drily, 'for between Fort de l'Heurt there' – he indicated a squat round edifice atop an island to the right – 'and La Crèche there to the north the guns are waiting. The Bombardiers' monstrous mortars and howitzers at the water's edge, guarded in depth by the

Chasseurs, with the Grenadiers' twenty-four-pounder cannon mounted on special carriages at the foreshore, all in advanced firing positions and any number of field pieces deployed at will by the horse artillery – some several hundreds of significant ordnance within that single league before you.'

Kydd said nothing.

'Here, too, we have history,' Lovett continued expansively. 'The ruined tower of d'Ordre just to the left of the entrance and up was constructed by the sainted Caligula to save the souls of mariners.' He paused, 'But getting back to the present, Napoleon, it seems, has found more sinister uses for it. The Batterie de la République is a perfect nest of artillery set to play upon any who will make motions towards the egress of the flotilla or such as dare interfere with it.'

'And that is all?'

Lovett ignored Kydd's ironical tone. 'Well, we have the Railliement to mock our approach with six- and twelve-pounders, but beyond that there is only the concentrated musketry of those eighty thousand troops . . .'

Kydd's face tightened. It was utter madness. What were Fulton's 'curiosities' against this overwhelming strength? Would the men flinch as they were ordered into this inferno of fire? The future of the world depended on the answers.

'We shall attack at night, of course,' Kydd said, hoping his voice held conviction. The darkness might help conceal them but it made the task of the torpedo launchers more difficult. By eye, Kydd plotted an approach from the west-south-west – the critical five-fathom line at datum was a mile offshore, according to the chart. Of all possibilities it was the least discouraging: there was the fire of the Fort de l'Heurt to be endured but . . .

'Place us with Le Portel at sou'-east b' east, Mr Dowse,'

Kydd ordered. There was one way to find out what they faced and that was to track down this approach and see what came their way.

'Aye aye, sir,' Dowse replied tersely.

The first guns opened up on *Teazer* as they crossed the five-fathom line under cautious sail on a line of bearing for the narrow estuary of the sluggish river. From various points along the sand-hills and beaches a lazy puff and thump announced a battery taking the opportunity of exercising on a live target.

Kydd had Calloway and the master's mate, Moyes, noting the precise position and estimated weight of metal of each, notwithstanding the likelihood that the heavier guns would be reserved for worthier targets.

The plash of strikes appeared in the sea, but Kydd was too experienced to let it worry him; most were close but all around them, and he knew that the only ones to worry about were those in line but short – they revealed a gun laid true and the likelihood that they would be struck on the ricochet.

How close could he go? Only a fraction of the guns were firing: a brig-sloop would be a common enough sight as enterprising young officers tried to steal a quick glimpse at the threats within.

Suddenly there was a sharp slap and a hole appeared in *Teazer*'s foretopsail. Their angling approach had the advantage of reducing fire from the further coast but at the cost of an increasing tempest from the nearer, which now showed in its true numbers. In the continuous rolling thunder, roils of powder-smoke viciously pierced by gun-flashes and the tearing *whuup* sound of passing shot, it became clear that nothing more would be accomplished by daylight.

At least they could return with their personal report of

what faced the attackers. 'That will do, Mr Dowse. Do you now bear away for—'

He never finished the order for, with a sudden thump and an appalling long-drawn-out splintering crash, *Teazer* came to a sudden stop, slewing drunkenly sideways and throwing everyone to the deck. The fore-and maintop-gallant masts tumbled down in ruinous confusion, smothering men in canvas and snarls of rope.

There was an instant's terrified incomprehension, then cries and shouts erupted from all parts of the ship. Kydd fought his way from under the mad, flapping folds, knowing what must have happened. A collision. In broad daylight and fair weather.

It was baffling – inconceivable. Kydd did not remember another ship within miles of *Teazer*. He discarded the last of the torn sail and looked round wildly. Where was the other vessel? Was it sunk?

'Throw off all tacks 'n' sheets,' he bellowed, frantic to take the strain off a motionless vessel under full sail. Purchet stormed about the canted deck with a rope's end, bringing back order while others picked themselves up from where they had been thrown.

Ignoring the imploring Hallum, Kydd tried furiously to work out what had happened, but then he saw the wreckage alongside – dark sea-wet timbers, planks over framing welling up sullenly that could only have come from another ship's hull. And alien to *Teazer*'s build, older – proof that they had collided with another ship and crushed her underfoot to be mercilessly swallowed by the sea.

His mind reeled. There had been no sighting, no sudden cries from the doomed ship – why had they not—

Then he had it. Traces of seaweed on the timbers, an even

scatter of barnacles – this was not another ship they had collided with but a recent wreck lying off the port they had piled into. There was little time for a moment of relief, though: Kydd became aware of redoubled fire from the shore. 'Clear away this raffle,' he threw at Purchet. 'I mean t' get away before the French come.' There was nothing more certain than that gunboats, galleys, even, would be quickly on the scene. These could stand off and batter the immovable sloop to ruin in minutes.

With icy foreboding, Kydd tried to think of a way out – traditional moves such as lightening by heaving water leaguers overside would not work in time and if he jettisoned his guns he would be rendered helpless. Should he tamely surrender? It was the humane thing to do in a hopeless situation such as this.

There were things that must be done. 'Moyes – duck down and ask the cook to get his fire going.'

'Sir?' he said, blinking.

'To destroy the signal books and confidentials!' Kydd rapped impatiently.

And what else must he do in this direful extremity? Find his commission: this would be proof to those taking him prisoner of his officer status. But what was there to say to his crew? They were certain to spend the rest of the war in misery, locked fast in one of the prison fortresses.

A rising tide of rage threatened his reason. This was not how it should be! *Teazer* had a destiny in the coming final struggle . . .

'Two foot in the well.' The carpenter had broken in on his thoughts. 'Could be much worse'n that,' he said, without conviction, but if the sloop was shattered they would have been swimming for it by now.

'They're comin', sir!' The ship was directly opposite the river entrance and, through the outer line of moored ships, beetling shapes of oared gunboats now made towards them.

'The tide, Mr Dowse?' The holding was good, and if they were granted time to stream a kedge they could conceivably haul off, if only . . .

'It'll be falling in a half-hour, Mr Kydd.' It meant they were in slack water at the height of the tide and then a settling on the wreck below. And the gunboats were clear of the line of ships and on their way. Bitter thoughts came, but Kydd knew that very soon he had a decision to make – to fight hopelessly or haul down his flag?

Then, as if by a miracle, *Teazer* stirred, a protracted groaning from deep within her bowels and a jerking realignment that saw her shifting by inches to be more parallel to the shore. Could this be . . . ?

'We're being shoved off – an' it's b' courtesy o' France itself,' Dowse said gleefully, and pointed to the port entrance.

It took Kydd a moment or two to grasp it, but then he laughed. 'Why, so we are. I should have smoked it! Hands t' set sail, if y' please.'

'Sir, if you'd be so good to explain,' Hallum said plaintively.

'Of course, Mr Hallum. You see yonder? That's Boulogne, and the river Liane. We're directly opposite so the current from the river is pressing us to seaward. We cannot resist, it will have its way, and soon we will be carried off our place of resting and then we're homeward bound.'

Chapter 13

To the intense satisfaction of her captain, and the relief of her crew, HMS *Teazer* sailed from Sheerness dockyard two weeks later, the shipwrights there proving more than a match for the damage sustained. The town was much as Kydd remembered from the time of Great Mutiny seven years before: bleak, windswept and far from any civilisation worth the name. Even hardened seamen were weary of the squalor of Blue Town and the stink of the marshes.

The sloop rounded the promontory for the Nore, then sailed south for North Foreland and the Downs. Kydd's blood was up: production of the ordnance must be close to completion and now *Teazer* was ready to play her part. In a fever of anxiety he made his number with the flagship and lost no time in reporting aboard.

Keith seemed preoccupied but acknowledged *Teazer*'s accession to his forces – and disclosed that production of the munitions was at such an advanced stage that staff planning had begun for the operation. Kydd should hold himself in readiness for a council-of-war, at which he might expect a role.

It was on. His charge as nursemaid to Fulton was at an end and now he would rejoin the war, a very different one from that of the past. Torpedoes, submarines, stealth, destruction – if this was the future, he was duty-bound to prepare himself to be a part of it.

The operation was to be led by Popham in view of his interest in the new weapons and his role in developing the catamarans. He had gone to the Admiralty to discuss strategy.

Kydd felt left in suspense, but then was called to a conference with Keith. 'Gentlemen,' the admiral said flatly, to his officers around the table, 'I have been apprised that the ordnance is ready, sufficient to make an initial descent on the flotilla. I have no doubt you realise that time is not on our side. The season is far advanced, and the weather cannot always be relied on to be in our favour.' There was a murmur of agreement. 'And, besides, it may well be in Bonaparte's mind to launch his invasion before the weather closes in and prevents it. Any means to deter this until the spring may be accounted worth the attempting.'

Kydd was one of three commanders at the conference; the others, eight post-captains, were far his senior, only two of whom, Popham and Savery, he recognised.

Keith continued, 'Like it or no, we must make our move at the next favourable time – a strong spring tide on the flood in the early darkness and no moon, the next of which being in eight days' time.'

This left precious little time for preparation.

'To the operation itself. I have to inform you all that, as a consequence of the gravity of the situation, the first lord of the Admiralty, Lord Melville himself, is to be present at the engagement and I myself will take personal command in *Monarch*.'

Popham's head jerked up. 'Sir? I have to say—'

'I shall be in command and that's an end to it, sir.' Clearly Keith was under pressure at the highest level. 'Now, this action has clear and definite aims. The reduction of Bonaparte's invasion flotilla by any and all means. After an eventful reconnaissance by *Teazer* I have come to the conclusion that a direct assault against the port is not to be considered.'

There were murmurs of heartfelt agreement. Nelson's bloody failure at the same task had been all too recent.

'But a further investigation by *Locust* has shown that the ships moored across the entrance are not a defensive squadron. They are the overplus vessels of the flotilla unable to find room within the port.'

The formidable barrier was only troop-carrying transports with makeshift armament. This was a different matter entirely.

'One hundred and fifty sail – and these shall be the target of the first onslaught from our new weapons, gentlemen.'

A babble of interjection arose, put down firmly by the unsmiling Keith. 'I go further. This entire action is to be considered a proving of the torpedoes and coffers. No engagement is contemplated of the regular kind.'

Astonishment and jealousy in turn showed on the faces of those assembled as it became clear that any distinction won would be with torpedoes, other weapons merely defensive – their keepers.

'The attacking force will be in three divisions: the torpedoes in the centre defended on either side by a strong force from my squadron, myself in *Monarch* to seaward, three sixty-fours and two fifty-gun ships, with five frigates flanking them at depth.'

If there was enemy interference with the cumbersome craft in the act of launching their torpedoes it would turn into a bloodbath.

'The torpedoes in turn will be in three divisions: the centre with catamarans of Mr Popham's invention, which are near invisible and have the chance of penetrating to the closest, and these shall be armed with the, er, hogsheads. In column on either side will be launches towing the coffers, the largest of which I have been reliably informed are now of two tons weight with the colossal charge of the equivalent of forty barrels of powder each.'

He ignored the gasps of incredulity. 'Further, to complete and make certain our descent, we will employ four explosion ships, which will carry similar amounts and will be set on course to intersect the enemy line before they are abandoned. These, with all our engines of destruction, will be fitted with the new mechanical timing machine that will be set to detonate the charges at precisely the right position.'

This was as unlike any pre-battle council that Kydd had ever experienced and the glances of consternation among the others revealed that he was not the only one to feel as he did. There had been no appeal to lay one's ship alongside the enemy, no talk of conduct becoming the traditions of the service, no detail of complex signals enjoining complicated manoeuvres. And, worst of all, it promised to be a battle in the night, the defenders not even brought face to face in the encounter, the torpedoes doing their work unseen. It was unreal and disturbing to many in a navy whose traditions were resolutely to close and grapple with an enemy until the issue was decided.

Keith seemed to sense the unease and his tone took on a stiff joviality. 'I leave it to you, gentlemen, to conceive of the terror in the hearts of the French at the destruction wrought in their midst by unknown and superior weapons. Thus I do confide in you my hopes for a good success in this enterprise.'

Queries and doubts were voiced, concerning responsibilities, timing, command, but all responses came down in the end to a single task: of getting the torpedoes to their target.

When the questions had tailed off, Keith resumed. 'I have mentioned the three divisions of torpedoes. At the seaward head of each column a dispatching sloop will be responsible for sending them in. The central, being the catamarans, will be in overall command, with responsibility for pressing home the assault.'

He looked round grimly, then settled his gaze on Kydd. 'As the only one of us with experience of these devices, this task is assigned to Commander Kydd.'

Exultant, but more than a little fearful, Kydd considered his position carefully. In effect he was a mini-commodore, placed above another two commanders in the most important job in the operation and under the direct eye of the commander-in-chief – not only him but the first lord of the Admiralty too. Under no circumstance must he fail.

He retired to his great cabin and began his planning. But as the list of priorities and concerns grew, so did his anxieties. The Articles of War required whole ships of men, officers included, to obey his every order without question – even if they were mistaken or ill-thought-through. And once the deadly machines were put into motion they could neither be summoned back nor even signalled to. His orders had better be the right ones . . .

The first vital matter was to establish the characteristics of the weapons, handling, firing or whatever. This would form the basis of the training and operational orders, and would give him time to think.

'Portsmouth, Mr Hallum. It's there we'll make trial of our

infernals, the catamarans now being at Lymington, the torpedoes produced at Priddy's Hard, o' course.'

The overnight voyaging saw *Teazer* enter the familiar harbour early the next day, but this time passing beyond the great dockyard into the large, enclosed expanse of shallow water beyond. It was deserted, but for a line of ships in ordinary in the deeper water along the western side, well suited for trials of a secret weapon.

Teazer sailed on as far as she could in the shallowing water and picked up moorings at the head of a channel through the mud-flats, Horsea Island. She waited patiently but it took some hours for a dockyard hoy to bring the weapons across the water from Priddy's Hard. An interested but wary ship's company had their first sight of the new weapons of war.

'Ugly beasts!' Kydd murmured to Hallum, who seemed lost for words as he stared down at them. Low in the water alongside, and within a canvas screen, they were dormant in the evening light, submerged until the upper surfaces were nearly awash, one of each type, black, deadly and evil.

Fulton arrived as the sun was lowering, in a fluster after some disagreement with officials of the Ordnance Board. He and Kydd, with Duckitt, went over the side and into a low punt. 'This is your hogshead,' Fulton said, and slapped its swelling bulk affectionately. It reverberated sullenly, a black parody of a large barrel of beer. Next to it floated a low cylindrical device, its exterior smooth black-painted copper but much bigger than the first, with a single line and grapnel. 'The small coffer.' Then, outside them all, lay a crocodilian shape all of twenty feet long, its dark menace barely visible under the surface. 'The large coffer,' Fulton said lightly, and stepped on to it from the punt. It barely gave, betraying its tremendous weight.

'Er, how heavy is it, Toot?'

'No more'n two tons. Get him going at the enemy, there's nothing on God's earth will stop him.'

'Sir,' Duckitt asked quietly, 'an' how do we, er, fire 'em?'

'Good question. You've to throw aside all notions o' *firing*. These don't mess with slowmatch – we use a modern mechanism.'

'An'how c'n we be sure—'

'See here?' Fulton pointed out a slightly recessed indentation. 'Inside is your timing engine. Screw in the plug and, for every turn, the explosion takes place five minutes later.' He demonstrated, twisting deftly.

Kydd started. Surely Fulton had not initiated the detonation . . .

'Three turns, fifteen minutes. This handsome machine is charged and armed and will explode in a quarter-hour.' Duckitt caught his breath. 'Were it not for this.' Fulton flourished an object very similar to a miniature belaying pin. 'The safety peg. It comes from here –' he pointed to a tiny hole next to the timing screw, fortunately occupied by an identical one '– and so long as he sleeps in his hole, all is tranquil. Withdraw it, and whatever is set on the timing will be the moment of destiny for the coffer.'

No one spoke, but Fulton grinned inanely. 'A contrivance of beauty and perfection, don't you think?'

Kydd needed time – much more than the days he had. Keith's orders were clear and sound: he was keeping back his conventional warships on outer guard tasks to allow the torpedoes clear sight of the enemy, a prudent and sensible measure given the disaster that would eventuate in the fog of war if a ship in the night chaos were to plough through the slow-moving and near-invisible catamarans.

But it meant as well that he alone was responsible for

devising the technique that would see them to the launch point and a successful conclusion. The first worry was the size of the beasts: the large coffer would need the biggest of ship's boats to get it going against inertia and water resistance and he could not see how a 'small' coffer could be brought aboard the catamaran. Even the hogsheads were huge and unhandy. It would be asking a lot of the crews.

A soft sunset had finally faded into the advancing night. They could begin. 'Pipe the launch's crew to muster,' he ordered.

Expecting the order they quickly appeared. 'Poulden,' he said, to the coxswain, firmly, 'this is not a time for volunteers. They'll be called on the night we're to attack. At this time I want a measure of how well these infernals swim.' It had slipped out – it couldn't be helped. 'Take the large coffer in tow six fathoms astern. When you reach a cable or so off, slew it around and, at the bo'sun's pipe, lay out with all your heart. Clear?'

Poulden could be relied on to get the best out of his men but he dropped his eyes and mumbled, 'Um, sir, is it, as who should say, *tender* in its motions?'

'If you're worried about it exploding precipitate like, don't. The safety peg is in. However, er, do keep clear of its hawse. It's armed and has a full charge.'

Uncharacteristically muted, the boat's crew tumbled into the launch, secured the coffer and bent to their oars. Straining and tugging produced only the slightest movement, and it was long minutes before they were able to heave it off into the darkness.

It was a clear night and a quarter-moon was rising. At a cable's length when the boat made its turn gingerly Kydd was dismayed to see its beetling black shadow clearly against the glittering moon-path. As promised, though, the torpedo was all but invisible.

He took out his watch and held it to catch the light from the binnacle lamp. The boatswain raised his call ready. 'Pipe!' he said. The distant rowers started in a flurry of strokes but slowed immediately to a near stop. Poulden's frenzied hazing could be heard floating across the water – it made Kydd smile, but on the night it would not do.

Twenty minutes on the return: this was dismaying. 'He's a pig t' steer, sir,' Poulden reported, after returning aboard. 'Worse'n a bull in a paddock as is shy o' the knife.'

A catamaran was available now and it was brought round. As Kydd had suspected, there was no possibility that the small coffer could be raised and carried on the flimsy gratings fore and aft. It would require ship's boats as well.

'Load with hogsheads,' Kydd said, after the two reluctant oarsmen had taken their place at the stubby sculls. One was swayed across and lashed in place. The catamaran settled at an angle until the other was aboard and then, with a heavy reluctance, the ungainly craft shoved off. 'Same as the others, if y' please,' Kydd told them.

They made slow progress, but this was due to their near comic performance at the sculls, so close to the water. They turned and started back. This was more encouraging – inches above the water only, it was difficult indeed to make them out. But it was hard going.

Helped aboard, the two oarsmen, soaked from the shoulders down, shuddered uncontrollably. 'Every man as pulls a plunging boat is entitled to a double tot, if he wants it,' Kydd ordered. 'Get 'em dry and see it's served out immediately.'

Too much hung on their efforts for rest and the remainder of the night was spent in timed trials, with two boats on the coffer, then three; the smaller with the pinnace at an angle to the launch and the carcass between, and, of course, the procedure for recovering the operations crew after the launch.

It was done: he had the facts, now for the figuring. But when he awoke later in the morning doubts and anxieties flooded in. Send them in as a broad wave or in stealthy column? The coffers first or the catamarans? Request some kind of diversionary tactic? Would volunteers step forward when the time came?

And the orders. *His* orders. The first he had ever given as a squadron commander as, in reality, he was. He bent to the task, nibbling his quill. So much to plan and decide.

'It's madness, is what I say,' exploded Mills. 'Settin' these vile contraptions afloat wi' a quarter-ton of powder an' two men sailing t' meet the enemy! I've never heard such—'

'Have a care, Mr Mills!' Kydd barked. 'These are my orders and I mean them to be obeyed! If you have objections, I'm sure Admiral Keith would like t' hear them.' With men's lives in the balance, only trust and teamwork would see it through. He resolved to catch Mills privately later.

Teazer's great cabin seemed an incongruous setting for such a briefing. Kydd had seen this room dappled by water-reflected moonlight from warm and exotic Mediterranean harbours; it had been the scene of his hopes and fears – and now was to be the place of his disposing of so many destinies.

Containing his emotions, he resumed his orders. 'The large coffers will have two boats each and will set off first on either side of the designated channel. The faster catamarans will then move forward and past the coffers, being able to penetrate unseen up to the French line where the torpedoes will be launched.'

He paused, conscious his words had rung with false

confidence, then went on, 'The recovery of the catamaran crews will be the responsibility of Mr Lamb and his little fleet o' gigs. The whole operation should take less than two hours.'

'How do we give coverin' fire if we're laying off t' seaward?' growled Mills.

Kydd bit his lip. Now was not the time for a confrontation. 'You don't. The whole point is to stand clear of the channel of approach and let the torpedoes go in and do their work quietly. You're a dispatch vessel, crew the catamarans and boats and send 'em on their way only. No play with the guns – is that clear?'

Lamb seemed troubled and Dyer's face showed resignation, but they paid attention while the remaining details were laid out – elementary signals concerning the start and others for cancellation of the assault, provision for an assembly-and-dispatch sequence, launch timing, accounting for munitions expended, the order of night mooring.

Kydd tried to end on an upbeat note. 'In the morning there's to be practice with the catamarans, and my gunner, Mr Duckitt, will instruct on the timing engine and other. Now, gentlemen, this is our chance t' give Boney a drubbing as he can't be expecting. Let's make it a good 'un, shall we?'

It seemed so thin, so fragile, but was this because he didn't really believe in the infernals – or himself?

The final conference was in *Monarch* and Keith wasted no words. 'I'm sailing at noon to anchor before Boulogne at sunset. I want the assaulting division to be ready for launch three hours after sunset, namely nine p.m. Mr Kydd?'

'Aye aye, sir.'

Savery coughed. 'Er, sir. To appear in force in full view of the enemy before sunset? They'll surely know something's afoot.'

'Can't be helped. The torpedo craft need to know where we are in the darkness, so they will fix our position while daylight reigns. They won't do that if we're tacking and veering about all the time. And it hardly needs pointing out that we've not been strangers to this coast, and while we'll be arriving in force, the enemy has no conceiving of the nature of our assault. We attack as planned.'

Weighed down with anxieties, Kydd returned to his ship. Now there would be the call for volunteers, an advisement to his dispatch sloops – it was all but committed. He swung over the bulwark, touching his hat to the boatswain at his call.

Renzi stood there, his face grave. 'Then we sail against the flotilla,' he said quietly. He was using a cane to support his wounded leg.

'We do,' Kydd said, then added, 'Nicholas, this is not your war – I want you ashore.'

'Ashore? Of course not! There's—'

'You'll go, and that's my order,' he said harshly, staring his friend down.

'Very well, then I must do as I'm bid,' Renzi said softly. He slowly held out his hand. 'Can I – may I sincerely wish that you do fare well in what must come?'

Kydd's bleak expression did not alter. He took the hand briefly then turned and hurried below.

HMS *Teazer* led the torpedo squadron to sea. For Kydd the overcast autumn day had a particularly oppressive and lowering undertone. Some five miles off Boulogne the fleet assembled about the flagship – frigates, minor ships-of-the-line, sloops, cutters and, at the centre, what gave it its purpose.

Before sunset the fleet had formed up opposite the port. The approach channel for the catamarans was resolved, the dispatch sloops positioned to seaward, and aboard each the process of arming the torpedoes was put in train.

Locust moved up between them, put its borrowed cluster of gigs in the water, and suddenly there was nothing further to do.

A sombre dusk fell; among the hills the campfires of Napoleon's host twinkled into existence, their myriad expanse a feral menace that seemed to reach right out to them. The last of the day's radiance hardened into a moonless night, a dark almost dense enough to touch. Surrounding ships lost their outline and were swallowed in the blackness, leaving only the single riding lights of the British fleet and the red and gold dots along the hills.

Kydd could only wait. His plans were straightforward enough but what were they next to the reality before him? The catamarans were already in the water but not the hogsheads, which must be swayed aboard fully armed and struck down on their gratings by feel – no lights could be allowed to betray warlike activity.

The watch mustered, and the volunteers. Sailors who had willingly stepped up when called upon that afternoon, who had trusted him in the matter of riding these infernal machines to victory against the foe or . . .

A lump rose in his throat. Would any of them survive the night? With false jollity, jokes were cracked in the age-old way as they pulled on their black guernseys, laced on dark caps and rubbed galley soot into their faces. Some yawned, a sure sign of pre-battle nerves.

'Sir – flagship!' The usual three riding lights in the tops of *Monarch* were replaced by four. As they watched, the fourth was dimmed. The signal.

'Into the catamarans, the volunteers,' Kydd ordered crisply, trying to conceal his feelings.

Without speaking the first two went down the side and, with gasps at the cold, took their places in the catamaran scheduled to lead the attack. 'As I live and breathe,' Hallum whispered, 'this is something I could not do, I confess it.'

It was too much: in a rising tide of feeling Kydd leaned over and called hoarsely, 'Timmins! Out o' the boat – I'm the one to lead the catamarans.'

The group on the quarterdeck fell back in shock; Kydd wasted no time in stripping to his breeches, and when the dripping Timmins appeared on deck, he took the man's guernsey and cap, then went hastily over the side, only remembering at the last minute to throw at the open-mouthed lieutenant, 'You have the ship, Mr Hallum.'

The sea was shockingly cold as Kydd settled into the little underwater seat and oriented himself. So close to the water the restless wavelets now held spite and *Teazer* loomed in the darkness, her barnacles and sea-growth so close.

There were voices; then Stirk was claiming the place of the other in the catamaran. He clambered into the forward seat, cursing vigorously at the cold.

'Thank ye, Toby,' Kydd said, in a low voice.

'If'n ye're going, Mr Kydd, ye'll need one as knows th' buggers, like,' Stirk grunted, and signalled up to the deck. As gunner's mate he had helped Duckitt instruct the others.

The first hogshead came, to be grappled by Stirk and struck down on the gratings. He made an expert slippery hitch, then gave another signal to the deck. The other came down aft, and Kydd struggled to ease the monstrous bulk onto its grating. Numb fingers passed the lashing and finished with the hitch to release it. 'Shove off,' he growled, pushing at the huge ship's side with his light scull. Almost sub-surface the catamaran was a heavy, awkward thing and he panted with the effort of getting it going. This was going to be near impossible, he thought, in despair.

They cleared *Teazer*'s side and pulled out into the channel. Low hails came from others in the vicinity. Kydd looked about carefully, shivering all the while with the bitter cold. There seemed no betraying noise or bustle in the anchored fleet and, turning shorewards, he saw no sign of any French alarm. Then he peered into the blackness towards the distant and barely visible line of ships that were their target. No indications of suspicion – but, then, the French had every reason to suppose that if there was an assault it would be at dawn in the usual way.

He looked behind – nothing. Ahead, the line of ships. 'We go,' he hissed, and dug in his sculls.

It was an unreal and frightening world of cold, darkness and beckoning danger. Stroke after stroke, double feathered and as silent as possible, onward towards the target. Muffled splashes from behind told him that the others had fallen into line with him. Stroke, pull, return, stroke. On and on.

Then, quite suddenly, they were close enough to individual ships that they needed conscious alterations of course to head towards them – they were nearing the launch point and still no alarm. It was time to select a victim. Curiously there was no feeling, only the calculated judgement of range and bearing.

'*Hssst!*' Stirk stopped rowing.

'What is it?' whispered Kydd urgently.

'I thought I heard— It's a Frenchy!'

Then Kydd made out a regular creak and splash of oars in the blackness to the left. The enemy was rowing guard on the moored ships in a pinnace. 'Get down!'

They bent as low as they could, faces slapped by the cold sea, and waited. Should he give orders to retreat now while they could? Kydd wondered. If they were discovered it would be slaughter with no mercy. Shivering violently, he heard the sound approach, then cross and, with no change of rhythm, move away to the right.

Apart from the ceaseless rustling of the night waters there was nothing more than a far-away peal of merriment, a shouted hail between sentries, anonymous sounds.

It was time for the climax. 'Cast off the line, Toby – it's secured to the other.' It was part of Fulton's plan to squeeze a ship between two explosions by connecting the two hogsheads with a line and cork float, which, on the incoming tide, would fetch up on their victim's anchor cable and inexorably draw in the charges on both sides.

'Set for twenty minutes, Toby,' he called softly, and waited while the turns were made. 'That'll do,' he said, as casually as he could. 'We'll launch now. Pull the peg, cuffin.'

There was a jerk and Stirk turned and handed him the safety pin. Kydd's orders were that all pegs should be returned as a surety that the torpedoes had been launched properly. After a quick tug on the hitch and persuasion with both feet the giant carcass plunged into the sea with a shattering splash.

They dug in their sculls to move out the requisite hundred feet – but a sputtering and popping of muskets started urgently from the line of shore. They had been discovered. The sound grew and was joined by heavier guns.

'*Pull!*' Kydd gasped. They were moving parallel with the shore to launch the second hogshead but the firing grew steadily in intensity. The timing mechanism was already primed so he fumbled with the safety peg and footed the monstrous thing clear to splash weightily in the sea.

They had done it! Torpedoes away, nothing could stop their rapid retreat. But they found themselves stroking into a strong flood-tide. The riding lights at the mast-head of the flagship were just dimly visible but now the shore artillery had added its weight to the barrage, and the entire foreshore of Boulogne was alive with gun-flash. It was only a matter of time before they were spotted – and the venom of a hundred guns unleashed on them.

They passed another catamaran going in the other direction, resolutely pressing forward into the inferno to its launch position, with others on their way behind. Kydd's eyes pricked at their bravery.

It was some minutes before he realised that, surprisingly, with all the blazing guns, there was no shot-strike nearby. Miraculously they had a chance: the gunners were night-blinded by the flash of their own guns and without a knowledge of what their targets were, even with fixed lines of fire, they were aiming high, presuming a usual form of attack.

'*Go to it, Toby!*' he bawled, stretching out until his muscles burned. Then, blessedly, they were up with the gigs and being pulled into the boats with words of rough, sailorly sympathy. They fell back on the dispatch sloops.

Kydd was hauled aboard his ship utterly exhausted, but insisted on remaining on the upper deck where he sat in a chair shivering under a cloak. It should be at any time now. With the sky and sea a fiery pandemonium it was difficult to make out anything. The French were firing wildly into the night, not understanding what was going on.

They would soon find out, thought Kydd, grimly. Then something clutched at his heart. So many brave sailors would, before long, be blasted to pieces – at his hand.

The rage and fervour of battle ebbed a little. Was Renzi right that this furtive creeping and stealthy detonating were no better than cold-blooded murder? With a dull spirit Kydd waited for the first cataclysm – but none came. Perhaps it was asking too much of the delicate watchmaking art to function in this wet chaos. But then the sudden thump and roar of a colossal explosion tore at his senses, its flash lighting the sea in sharp relief for miles, the firing dying away in awe at the spectacle.

Another – this time an even larger one, which seemed to be on the far side of the defensive line. More – then a gigantic roar in the centre. And more. Fulton's infernals had worked to perfection but at each detonation Kydd's heart wrung at where man's ingenuity and creative spirit had led him – and that the world must now change.

The last explosion died, the guns petered out and suddenly there was nothing left but to return to the Downs and home.

When *Teazer* had picked up her moorings opposite the slumbering town of Deal and sea watches had been stood down Kydd went to his cabin and collapsed into his cot. Exhaustion and reaction made sleep impossible and his thoughts raced on into nightmare – battles in the future fought under water and England's mighty ships-of-the-line replaced by swarms of catamarans. And for ever the fear that any stout ship, brought to her rest after hard voyaging, might without warning be blown to splinters with all her crew.

He drifted off, but was gently woken by Renzi. 'Dear brother, I'm desolated to intrude on your rest but Admiral Keith does require your attendance.'

'Er, what o' clock is it, then?' Kydd asked, struggling awake. 'Eleven.'

Kydd pulled himself up. 'Then this is the first reconnaissance now returned. I must go.' He would soon be faced with the product of his night's work, the tally of blood that would hang about his neck for the rest of his life.

He slipped to the deck, catching sight of himself in the mirror – grey, drawn and old.

Teazer's boat bore him to the flagship, the bright morning a mockery of what had gone before. Gravely welcomed by the flag-lieutenant he was shown to the great cabin with the others. There were few pleasantries and Keith entered grim-faced.

'I've first to thank you all for a stout and bravely executed action of the last evening – being as it was in the best traditions of the Service.' He paused, letting his gaze move about the seated officers. 'Further, I've to inform you of the results of the first reconnoitre now to hand.'

A ripple of interest went round, but Keith's bleak countenance did not change. 'Gentlemen, the torpedo contrivances exploded to expectations – each and every one.'

The chill of dread stole over Kydd as he steeled himself for the news.

Keith leaned forward. 'And I have to tell you they did so to no effect. None. Nothing whatsoever. The flotilla remains as it did before.'

Kydd's mind reeled. None? He had personally—

'I find that, at great hazard to our seamen, the torpedoes were launched to order and, further, that they were correctly armed and prepared, resulting as we've seen in their successful exploding. What was not in expectation was that the method of their delivery to the target has signally failed us and, quite frankly, I cannot readily conceive of any other.'

The sudden buzz of talk was cut short by Keith, who went on, 'And now the French are aroused and no doubt preparing a mode of defence to meet them. This can only be construed as nothing less than a catastrophic failure of the weapons. Gentlemen, as a direct result, we'll not be troubling you with such contrivances any further. That is all.'

The meeting broke up in a babble of noise but Keith called, 'Mr Kydd, a word with you, sir.'

Still shocked, Kydd made his way through the hubbub. 'Sir?'

'You should know that I believe your part in last night's action was entirely to my satisfaction.'

'Thank you, sir.'

'But now it is over. Done with. You are forthwith relieved of your duties with the American and will rejoin my Downs Squadron. Flags will attend to the consequentials. Understood?'

'Sir.'

Stumbling out into the bright sunlight, Kydd in his tiredness did not notice the lonely figure waiting by the mainmast. All he knew was that he had failed. His brave little fleet had achieved a derisory nothing. The enemy was untouched. No greater condemnation of a warrior's endeavours could be made.

'Tom? Tom, old friend.' Fulton took his shoulder and swung him round. 'What have you heard? Did you give the French a quilting?'

Kydd looked up dully. 'No. Nothing . . . touched.'

'Y-you mean . . . ?'

'They exploded, but without effect. We did our best – but I'm to be taken off duties with you, Toot. Your contract will be at hazard, I'd believe.'

Fulton staggered back. 'They – they can't! I'm promised . . . Tom, my friend, if you'll stay with me, speak with your high and mighty friends in the Admiralty—'

'I'm sorry. You tried your best – I tried. It wasn't enough.'

'Wait! I've some new – some ideas as will stretch the mind, will change everything. You'll see!'

'I wish you well, Toot, but it's finished. I have t' go now.'

'The world hasn't heard the last of me! I've only *begun* to conjure ideas. Listen . . .'

But Kydd had reached the side and, with a last wave, left to return to his old existence.

'You knew!' Kydd said, when Renzi hobbled into his cabin with a brandy.

'I did. Your sailor is not a retiring sort when stepping ashore after a hard action.'

Kydd said nothing, holding his glass and staring unseeingly. 'Nicholas, I have to live with this failure for all of my life,' he said, with a catch in his voice.

'Not at all!' Renzi began, but Kydd cut him off.

'Is there any more disgrace than a commander of men who leads them on into – nothing?' Savagely, he drained his brandy and slapped the glass down. 'I'll be a laughing stock.'

'It's not you they'll laugh at, brother.'

'What do you mean, Nicholas? Speak up!'

'The men ashore, they're singing glees about the infernals – about frog-toasters and catamarans that can do no better than entertain the enemy to an expensive fireworks show.'

'That's unfair! Fulton tried—'

'They are right, dear fellow,' Renzi said firmly. 'He tried – and failed. The time is not ripe for such dread weapons. The wit is there but the substance to work with is too frail. It is too new, the mechanicals not so advanced in sophistication.'

He regarded Kydd with an odd smile. 'There will be a time, I'm persuaded, when a submarine boat will be a common sight – and, no doubt, huge and with a steam engine to boot. Your torpedoes will probably come with paddle-wheels that allow them to seek out the enemy at a far distance – but not now. Their moment is not yet.'

Kydd closed his eyes in thought, then opened them. 'You're in the right of it, Nicholas, m' friend. Yet while there was a chance to hammer the invasion flotilla, we had to try.'

Renzi gave a half-smile. 'And I now concede there was no other course – for England's sake.'

Kydd knew what this admission meant for someone of Renzi's moral code. 'He's a genius, is Toot. Give him the chance and he'll conjure infernal contrivances as will make the world stare—'

'It's time we don't have,' Renzi interrupted. 'Even with all the resources of a plundered continent, Napoleon Bonaparte cannot maintain his colossal army in idleness for much longer. He must make his move, and this will be to clear the way for the invasion by overwhelming force. To this end he will assemble the greatest fleet ever seen on this earth to crush our battle squadrons with such numbers as we cannot prevail. Then the world will witness such a clash of giants as will ring down the ages to resound in the history of nations as the day of destiny for all.'

He continued relentlessly. 'I cannot say when, still less where, but in my very bones I feel that, within the compass of months, the issue will be decided for all of time.' The solemn pronouncement hung in the silence for long moments and neither friend looked at the other.

Then Kydd sprang suddenly to his feet. 'Ha! So it's no more the enemy skulkin' away where we can't get at 'em. Boney'll have t' step into the ring and fight it out man to man.'

He gave a wolfish grin. 'Bring 'em on!'

Author's Note

INVASION is somewhat of a milestone in my literary career, my 10th book in print – one million words! When I look back to that day in April 2001 when I held a copy of *KYDD* in my hands for the first time, I can only wonder at the enrichment Thomas Kydd has brought to my life since then. My wife Kathy and I were able to give up the day jobs and work together as a creative team and we've travelled the globe delving into the captivating world of the eighteenth-century sailor, at sea and on land. We've met thousands of readers and book-sellers and people from all walks of life have enthusiastically shared their specialist knowledge. These range from Professor Jack Lynch in the US, an authority on Georgian speech patterns, to expert knot-tyer Ken Yalden in the UK, to Joseph Muscat in Malta, with his deep understanding of Mediterranean sailing craft.

I have seen the Kydd books translated into Japanese, French, Russian and many other languages, and published as e-books, in Braille, as audiobooks and in large-print. I greatly enjoy interacting with readers through my various social networking sites – Twitter, Facebook, Goodreads etc. – and my regular blog BigJules. By the way, you can sign up for this via my website and have it delivered straight to your email address.

I'm often asked whether my original conception of the series and its characters has changed much as I've gone on – and the answer is no, with the exception of perhaps two things. When I first put pen to paper I thought the series would run to 11 books; now I can see it reaching at the very least to 20. As I've delved more deeply into the period I have found there's just so much rich material in the historical record to stimulate an author's imagination. The other main change is the character of Renzi. Initially he was just to be a means of articulating in a way that the uneducated sailor could not, and act as a foil to Kydd. However he's grown into his own character, in some ways as interesting as Kydd himself. Kathy actually tells me I am half Kydd, half Renzi. Just how much an author's personal experiences influence his writing is of course very hard to say, but she may have something there . . .

Writing about the sea in all its moods gives me special pleasure. I take great pains to ensure my prose is as accurate as possible and make daily use of ship's electronic sea charts and my now-vast reference library, as well as regularly consulting the various experts I've discovered over the years. Of course having been a professional sailor myself helps enormously in bringing to mind the sights, smells and sounds of deep sea. When Old Salts tell me they've really felt the heave of a deck under their feet as they read my books, I feel especially chuffed! And whenever I can, I take the opportunity to get in a bit of sea time, whether in tall ships or putting to sea with the modern Royal Navy, whose ships may be steam and steel but many of the traditions from Kydd's day are still honoured aboard.

Although I have rough outlines for all the books, the period of research and fleshing out of the plot at the beginning of each writing year is especially enjoyable. Often one tiny obscure fact will suggest a nice twist in a particular aspect of the story line – and the hunt is on to find out more. About half of the year is devoted to this initial work; during the other half it's down to solid writing, in my case about 1000 words a day. Kathy keeps a watchful eye on this as I go along and is always on hand with invaluable insights if required. We sometimes go for a walk in the lovely woodlands along the banks of the nearby River Erme to toss around ideas if I find I am writing myself into a corner – and it's never failed me yet.

Would I like to have lived in the eighteenth century? I think the answer must be yes. It was a far more colourful and individual time than it is today. The kind of characters who walked the Georgian stage will not be seen again and some of the great naval feats of the Napoleonic wars will never be repeated. It was also a more romantic and personally fulfilling time, I feel. I'm always taken with the soft effects of candlelight around a dinner table, of the art of conversation, of making your own musical entertainments in the evening. These the Georgians did very well!

In doing my research on historical people I have been fascinated by what has been discovered by modern scholarship – but at times what we *don't* know about some of these personalities is more intriguing. Robert Fulton, the maverick American inventor who appears in this book, is certainly a good example of this. There are several biographies of Fulton which I consulted extensively but he was one of those larger-than-life figures whose persona generates more questions the deeper you dig.

Fulton's nickname of 'Toot' was widely used but I can find no definitive reason for it. Some have suggested it derives from the whistle of the steamboat for which he's known, but it seems his nickname was used before this. Fulton was very gifted but difficult to penetrate as a person, naïve but intense. A Maryland farm boy, he came to England by invitation, and for a time lived as a portrait painter in Devon, near where I live. He reached the status of having his work hung at the Royal Academy so he was no amateur, but then went across to revolutionary France, and extraordinarily, within a year he was working on his incredible submersibles. It's on record that he actually met Bonaparte face to face and demonstrated a working submarine, the first *Nautilus*. It remained on the bed of the Seine for an hour to the horror of the assembled dignitaries; Fulton later took it out on several armed war patrols against the British. He destroyed it when the French delayed in making a commercial arrangement along the lines I spell out in the book.

Fulton's proposed machines were the first weapons of mass destruction – deliberately designed to blow up humans without warning or a chance to fight back and caused as much stir then as WMD does today. Did he really believe in what he said about freeing the world's oceans with the threat of mutual destruction or was this to assuage his feelings of guilt? The record is not clear and I can only guess at the answers to these questions.

And we'll never know whether *if* Fulton had been given full backing, he would have succeeded. It took another century before the world saw the first practical submarine but his terminology (submarine, torpedo, conning tower) is still in use today. How did it all end for him? He scraped together resources for one more try and succeeded in frightening the wits out of Admiralty officials gathered for a demonstration off Deal, but a fortnight later the Battle of Trafalgar took place and effectively ended his dreams. Fulton returned in penury to the US but went on to become famous with the first commercial steamship there. Ironically, he later began building another submarine, this time against the British who were blockading New York in the war of 1812, but he died before it was finished.

Other characters in this book may seem at first reading to be the product of a vivid imagination but there really was a mysterious 'Mr Smith' who detached Fulton from Napoleon to transfer his allegiance to England. There is very little known on this episode so I took what I felt was likely to have occured, and put Renzi in Smith's place. Likewise, the famed Parisian savant, LaPlace, was indeed a friend of Fulton's . . .

I enjoy Jane Austen's works and it was on a literary whim that I decided to mention her in *INVASION*, via her brother who actually was in post there at the time. She in fact had two sailor brothers: Francis, whom Kydd meets in the course of his acquaintance with the Fencibles, and Charles. Both later advanced to become admirals and Jane no doubt consulted them when she created William Price in *Mansfield Park* and Captain Wentworth in *Persuasion*.

As usual, I owe a huge debt of gratitude to many people. I cannot acknowledge them all for space reasons but deep thanks are due to Rowena Willard-Wright and Joanne Gray of English Heritage, who arranged special access to Dover Castle, Fulton's base while he was working on his inventions, and Walmer Castle, where Pitt lived and used as a secretariat for his clandestine operations against the French. And of course I would be remiss not to mention my literary agent Carole Blake and my new editor at Hodder & Stoughton, Anne Clarke.

Read on for the first chapter of *Victory*,
the next book in the Thomas Kydd series . . .

Chapter 1

At a hesitant knock on the cabin door Thomas Kydd's servant paused in shaving his master.

'Sir – Mr Hallum's duty an' Ushant is sighted to the nor'-east, eight miles,' blurted the duty midshipman, a little abashed at seeing his captain under the razor.

'Thank you, Mr Tawse,' Kydd grunted.

Nicholas Renzi looked up from the papers he was working on by the early morning light. He and Kydd were friends of many years. Both had achieved the quarterdeck from before the mast, but while Kydd had gained command of his own ship Renzi now pursued scholarly interests and acted as his clerk. Peering out of the stern windows of the little brig-sloop he said hopefully, 'And a fair wind for the Downs – I so yearn for a dish of Mistress Butterworth's haricot of mutton.'

Teazer had been taken from her patrol line along the French coast near the invasion ports and sent with dispatches, passengers and mail to the blockading battleships off Brest. A small ship had to expect such lowly employment but on her return, she would have a short spell in Deal, then be back on station, playing her part to thwart Napoleon Bonaparte's plans for the invasion of England.

It was the nightmare that haunted every man, woman and child – that the moat would be crossed and the staunch island nation must then taste the horrors of war. All it needed was for the emperor to wrest control from the Royal Navy for a few tides and, with half a million men under arms and two thousand vessels now in the invasion flotilla, he could flood the country with the armies that had conquered all Europe.

Kydd shifted restlessly. 'Thank you, Tysoe. A breakfast when it's ready.' The towel was expertly flicked away and he was released to take up his lieutenant's reworked quarters bill. They had lost two men to death and wounding and five to sickness; it had been made very clear that there would be no replacements, for the country had been stripped of trained seamen and *Teazer*'s humble station did not warrant special treatment.

He glanced at the paper irritably. Hallum had no doubt done his best but to rate up the pleasant but diffident Williams to full gun-captain was not the way to fill holes. Even now, after months in *Teazer*, his first lieutenant seemed not to know the men, their character, their individual strengths and weaknesses.

Kydd circled Bluett's name in the gun-crew and scrawled, 'to be GC' then realised that as a sail-trimmer the man could not be expected to absent himself just when his crew would need him. Damn. Very well, he'd make young Rawlings sail-trimmer. Barely more than a ship's boy, he was nevertheless agile and bright – he'd soon learn to swarm up to the tops with the best of them. But would he cope under savage enemy fire?

Imperceptibly the ship's angular rhythm of pitch and roll changed to a smoother rise and fall as she rounded Ushant, the lonely island that marked the north-west extremity of France. Now, with this fair south-westerly, it was a straight run up-Channel for home.

The masthead lookout's hail cut through Kydd's thoughts. '*Saaail hoooo!* Sail t' the larb'd quarter!'

He snatched up his grego against the autumn chill and joined the group on the quarterdeck. 'Mr Hallum?'

'Two points abaft the beam, sir, and steering towards us.'

Kydd nodded: the unknown ship was inward bound from the Atlantic Ocean. A lone merchantman? But every British merchant ship had by law to be a member of a convoy. Then was it a daring Frenchman breaking the blockade? If so, his luck had just run out . . .

'I'll take a peep, I believe,' he said, and swung easily up into the main-shrouds, mounting to the main-top. His pocket glass steadied on the speck of paleness away to the west. Smallish, but unmistakable with its tell-tale three masts, it was a *chasse marée*, a lugger, and the favoured vessel of the infamous Brittany privateers.

A smile of satisfaction spread across Kydd's face: he was perfectly placed to crowd the luckless corsair against the unfriendly Cornish coast, and in any chase the rising seas would favour the larger *Teazer*. He hailed the deck below, ordering the necessary course change to intercept.

Almost certainly the vessel was returning after a voyage of depredation from somewhere like St Malo, a notorious nest of privateers, but now it had found *Teazer* athwart its hawse. Suddenly the image foreshortened, then opened up again – it was putting about, back to the open ocean.

It would be to no avail: *Teazer* held it to advantage and

would converge well before it could escape. Kydd descended quickly and stood clear as the guns were cast loose and battle preparations made. The privateer was making a run for it. It was unlikely to take on a full-blooded man-o'-war but it was armed and dangerous with plenty of men so nothing could be left to chance.

The wind was veering and strengthening; there would be reefs in its soaring lugsails soon and, with the quartering fresh breeze as *Teazer*'s best point of sailing, he could rely on an interception before noon.

Within a few hours the sombre dark grey of the English coast lifted into view and they had gained appreciably on the privateer, which would soon be in range. Apart from a far-distant scatter of coastal sail there did not appear to be any other vessels and Kydd would shortly make his move.

'Bolderin' weather,' said Purchet, the boatswain, staring gloomily at the approaching change. Curtains of white hung vertically against sullen dark cloud banks. *Teazer*'s open main-deck in a line squall was not best placed for play with the guns; it was a challenge to try to keep the priming powder dry on heaving wet decks while rain hammered down.

The squall accelerated and then it was upon them, a hissing deluge of cold rain that blotted out everything beyond a hundred yards.

Suddenly Kydd snapped, 'Three points to starb'd!' The group about the helm looked at him in astonishment but hastily complied.

Teazer swung back before the wind, seeming to have abandoned the chase and wallowing in the temporary calm behind the line squall. But when the rain thinned and cleared, there was the privateer, not half a mile distant – and dead ahead.

Kydd had instinctively known that the captain would reverse course in the squall with the intention of slipping past him.

'Quarters, Mr Hallum,' Kydd ordered. 'We'll head him, I believe,' he added. 'And when—'

'Company, I think.' Renzi had come up beside him. While others were more interested in the unfolding action ahead, he had spotted a frigate emerging from the drifting curtains of mist a mile or two away in the wind's eye.

'T' blazes with 'im,' growled Purchet. Admiralty rules dictated that all on the scene would share equally in any prize-taking, no matter their contribution.

'Don't recognise she,' muttered *Teazer*'s coxswain, Poulden, at the wheel, his eyebrows raised.

'Private signal,' Kydd ordered Tawse.

Their flags soared up. After a short delay, fluttering colour mounted the frigate's mizzen, with what seemed very like the blue ensign of Admiral Keith's Downs Squadron accompanying it.

'Can't read 'em!' the youngster squeaked, training the signal telescope.

The flags were streaming end on towards them, but who else other than a roaming English frigate would be this side of the Channel?

The privateer had gone about once more in a desperate bid to evade capture but there was no chance for it now with a frigate coming up fast to join the fun. Kydd judged the distance to the privateer by eye and decided to make his lunge.

'A ball under his forefoot when within two cables,' he ordered, then glanced at the frigate. If it interfered, disregarding the unwritten rules of prize-taking that as Kydd was first on the scene it was his bird, the commander-in-chief would hear about it. He couldn't recollect ever coming across the vessel but it was not unknown for recent captures to be put into service without delay and this was clearly a frigate with distinct French lines.

The forward six-pounder cracked out: a plume arose not an oar's-length from the privateer's bows and precisely on range. The gunner straightened and glanced back to *Teazer*'s quarterdeck with a smirk of satisfaction. The lugger held on but it would not for long . . .

Then, in an instant, all changed. The frigate, now within just a few hundred yards, jerked down her ensign and hoisted another on the opposite halliard. After the barest pause it slewed to a parallel and guns opened up along its entire length, a shocking avalanche of destruction.

Aboard *Teazer* a man dropped, shrieking in agony and one of the marines fell squealing. Kydd forced his mind into the iron calm of combat. The frigate had not achieved its goal: it had obviously aimed for their rigging, intent on disabling *Teazer*, so it could then range alongside and accept their surrender under the threat of overwhelming force. But *Teazer* sailed on obstinately, capable of fighting back, albeit with sails shot through and lines carried away aloft.

Kydd knew it was no dishonour to flee before such odds, and he would have to let the privateer go as his first duty was to preserve his ship. He looked around quickly. The frigate was in a dominating position to weather and he had noted her swift approach before the wind. Was she as fine a sailer close-hauled as *Teazer*?

'Down helm, as close as she'll lie, Poulden,' Kydd cracked out. *Teazer* surged nobly up to the wind. The frigate, taken by surprise, was forced to conform also. They'd established a precious lead on the larger ship.

It was taking them in a hard beat back out into the Atlantic but it couldn't be helped. Kydd bit his lip. If they were overcome, Napoleon's newspapers would make much of one of Britain's famed men-o'-war humbled, captured in glorious combat on the high seas and paraded into port for all to see, with no account taken of the odds. The frigate's captain would be well rewarded by his new emperor.

The frigate, trailing by barely a couple of hundred yards, had only to make up the distance and the guns would speak once more. At the moment the gap stayed. And the privateer had not fled: it had curved around and was beating resolutely after them. Then Kydd realised they were working together.

Straining every nerve his little ship thrashed away over the miles, out into the wastes of ocean, in a desperate race for life. Speed was being dissipated with the loss of wind through the rents in the sails but it would be suicide to pause to bend on new.

Slowly the privateer overhauled *Teazer* and took position on her defenceless quarter, confident she could not break off to deal with it.

Meanwhile Purchet, watching the frigate, said in a low voice, 'She's fore-reaching on us.' Out in the open seas the broad combers that rode on the lazy swell were meeting *Teazer*'s bow in solid explosions of white, each one a tiny brake on their progress, while the larger frigate was throwing them aside with ease.

Kydd felt the creeping chill of doubt. The privateer was easing closer under their lee, the masses of men it carried clearly visible. It had few guns – but on a slide on its foredeck there was a twelve-pounder, double the size of *Teazer*'s biggest carriage gun. Suddenly this crashed out with a heavy ball low over her quarterdeck. The vicious wind of its passage made Kydd stagger.

It was now deadly serious. With the privateer to leeward and the frigate coming up to windward, they would soon be trapped. Another shot sent powder-smoke up and away to leeward. The ball threw Dowse, the master, to his knees with a cry and smashed the forward davit. Their cutter hung suspended aft, splintering against *Teazer*'s pretty quarter gallery until it fell away.

Kydd saw it was the helm the lugger was aiming at. With that knocked out, the frigate would be up in a trice and it would all be over. But there *was* a card he could play.

'Ready about!' He was gambling their lives that the brig-rigged *Teazer* was handier in stays than the three-masted frigate, but if any fumbled his duty . . .

The privateer could do nothing to stop them, and the frigate must have thought their motions a bluff for it carried past as *Teazer* took up on the other tack. There was a price to pay, however – its other broadside thundered out at the sloop's stern-quarters as she made away. Two shot shattered *Teazer*'s ornate windows and erupted through her captain's cabin, slamming down the length of the vessel.

It was a stay of execution. Now on the opposite tack, *Teazer* was being forced back towards the French coast and would be lucky to weather Ushant. The privateer resumed its station off their ruined quarter and continued its slow but relentless fire as the frigate went about and took up the chase again.

There would not be another chance. They could only hope for the deliverance of a stray warship of the Brest blockading squadron having occasion to go north-about as they had done. *Teazer*'s luck had finally turned and there was every prospect that before the end of the day the tricolour of Napoleon's France would be floating aloft and Kydd's precious fighting sword would be in the proud possession of the unknown frigate captain.

Kydd's eyes stung. *Teazer* – his first and only command. To be taken from him so cruelly, without warning and on her way home. It was—

A twelve-pounder shot struck an upper dead-eye of the main-shrouds with shocking force, setting the lanyards to a wild unravelling. The heavy rope jerked away, then swung dangerously free to menace the quarterdeck. Poulden gripped the wheel-spokes defiantly – another ball had nearly taken his head off before chunking into the hammocks at the rail and sending them flying to the wind.

With the privateer now redoubling its efforts to destroy the helm, Poulden continued to stand fast, doing his duty. Kydd honoured him for it as he balled his own hands in frustration. Then he decided: there was one last scene to be played. He knew his men were behind him in whatever must be done.

'Mr Hallum,' he said, to his lieutenant, in a calm voice, 'I'm going to hazard a move at the privateer. If we can put him down, we've a chance – a small one – with the frigate. Post your men quickly now.'

The older man's face lengthened. For a moment Kydd felt for him: he should be quietly at home with his grown daughters, not at the extremity of peril out here in the wild ocean. Then he realised that, although the lieutenant had no deep understanding of his men, the stolid and unimaginative officer was determined to do *his* duty as well in England's time of trial. He added warmly, 'Never forget, sir, we've the better ship.'

'Ushant again,' Renzi murmured. The grey smudge gratifyingly to leeward was token of *Teazer*'s weatherliness, but they dared not ease away south towards the blockade, for the frigate had already shown her qualities before the wind. It was time for the final throw of the dice.

Warned off, the men hauled furiously on the lines as *Teazer* wheeled on her tormentor, her carronades crashing out – but the privateer was clearly waiting for such a move. Instantly it put down its tiller and bore away, the pert transom offering the smallest of targets.

Kydd saw that the move had failed and, alarmingly, he now felt the weight of the wind more squarely on the battle-damaged fore-topsail. Then it split from top to bottom, each side flapping uselessly.

'Ease sheets,' he said dully, conscious of the many pale faces looking aft, waiting to hear their fate. What could he offer them? Surrender tamely? Fight to the last? Think of some ingenious stratagem that would even the odds?

It was no good. The end was inevitable: why spill his men's blood just to make a point? He raised his eyes to the frigate coming up. It seemed in no rush – but, then, it had all the time in the world to finish them.

Should he haul down their colours before the broadside came? 'Mr Tawse . . .' but the order wouldn't come out. The frigate altered course and made to run down on them, the row of black gun muzzles along her side probably the last thing on earth many of his crew would see.

But the cannon remained mute. '*Ohé, du bateau!*' came a faint hail from the frigate's quarterdeck.

Kydd cupped his hand: '*Le navire de sa majesté* Teazer.'

'*À bas le pavillon!*' demanded the voice, in hectoring tones – Strike your colours!

Feeling flooded Kydd. This was not how it was going to end with his beloved ship. He would not let the French seize and despoil her. It would be like the violation of a loved one. Fierce anger clamped in.

'*Never!*' he roared back, and braced himself.

The shock of the expected broadside did not come. Instead there was a brief hesitation and the frigate's side slid smoothly towards *Teazer*'s.

'Stand by to repel boarders!' Kydd bawled urgently, drawing his sword.

It was crazy: a frigate carried several times their number and their own guns were charged with round-shot, not the merciless canister that would sweep their decks clear. It would all be over in minutes – one way or the other.

They closed. Now only yards separated them, the milling, shouting mass on the enemy deck jostling with naked steel amain in anticipation. Kydd heard a hoarse order in French and shrieked, '*Get down!*'

He flung himself to the deck just as the murderous blast of grape and canister lashed *Teazer*'s bulwarks. Choking on the swirling powder-smoke he heaved himself up. A swelling cheer rose about him as *Teazer*'s carronades smashed back, adding to the thick smoke-pall and screaming chaos. Then, through the clearing reek, Kydd saw the high side of the frigate bearing down.

'Stand t' your weapons!' he roared. Around him Teazers hefted cutlasses, pistols and boarding pikes. There was an almighty shudder as the two vessels touched and groaned in unison, the movement sending several to their knees.

The seas were high, producing a corkscrew effect on the two vessels that made them roll out of step with each other. The yells of triumph from the Frenchman's deck tailed off quickly at the sight of a dark chasm between the two ships and the boarders hesitated. Some stood on the bulwarks poised to leap and were hit by pistol shot and musket fire from *Teazer*'s marines. They dropped with shrieks between the grinding hulls; others held back at the sight of the lethal points of boarding pikes held by unflinching British seamen.

A swivel banged from *Teazer*'s rail, another from forward. The French boarders' hesitation was fatal for at that moment the frigate caught a wind flurry and surged ahead and away, snapping the grapnels that held the ships together and spilling three men into the sea.

A storm of cheers went up from the Teazers at the sight of the frigate sheering off, but Kydd didn't join in. As the frigate readied for another attempt the privateer was manoeuvring to close and it was obvious to him that this time there was the awful prospect of a boarding from both sides simultaneously.

He hastily summoned every man aboard to join the lines of defenders, sending some into the tops with grenadoes to hurl at the massing boarders, with swivels to mount that could bring fire down on them, but it was so little against such odds.

The frigate had backed its mizzen topsail and was slipping back in a stern-board to lay itself alongside *Teazer* – the privateer was cannily matching its movements on the other side, a crude gangway hoisted in readiness to lower over the void between them.

Kydd stood in the centre of the deck with drawn sword and turned to face the massing privateers. In seconds the screeching horde on the vessel would be flooding on to their deck – but dogged courage like a man-o'-war's man's would not be their style. If they met with too much resistance they would falter and break, the effort not worth any gain. If by naked courage the Teazers could sustain the fight until . . .

'I shall attend on the frigate side, brother.' It was Renzi, with a plain but serviceable sword that, since he had taken up his scholarly quest, he had sworn to draw only in the last extremity. Their eyes met, then the frigate bumped and ground into the hull as the privateer's gangway crashed down on *Teazer*'s bulwarks.

A roar of triumph went up and Kydd sprang forward to meet the rush across the improvised bridge. The first corsair had a scimitar and a pistol that he fired left-handed as he jumped – it brought down Seaman Timmins in a choking huddle but before Kydd could face him the man took a pike thrust to the chest and he had to kick the squealing body away to confront another with a tomahawk and cutlass.

There was no science in it: Kydd lunged viciously for the eyes and, when the man recoiled, turned the stroke to slash down at the wrist. The cutlass clattered to the deck, but before he could recover, a flailing body from behind catapulted him on to Kydd's blade, which did its work without mercy.

Beside him, Kydd was subliminally aware that Poulden was being overborne by a brutish black man and, without thought, swung his blade horizontally in a savage backhand slash that ended in a meaty crunch in the man's neck. With a wounded howl he turned on Kydd, but Poulden saw the opening and thrust pitilessly deep into the armpit.

Kydd turned back to fend off a frenzied stab from a wild-eyed man – the crude flailing had no chance against Kydd's skill and experience and, with one or two expert strokes, he had forced him to a terrified defensive. The man slipped and tried to ward off Kydd's straight-arm thrust to his throat, but in vain – he went down gurgling and writhing.

Suddenly there were no more opponents: he saw that the makeshift gangway had clattered down between the ships and many were left impotently on the wrong side. He whirled round. Renzi, in a practised fencer's crouch, lunged up at a frigate officer in a blur of motion. The man stood no chance.

Defenders from the privateer's side righted the gangway, then sprang across the deck. The smoke-wreathed chaotic mêlée, wreckage, stench of blood, groaning bodies and frayed cordage whipping about was a scene from hell.

The frigate was in heaving movement with the high seas, the vertical motion making it a trial for those dropping down on to *Teazer*'s deck from its higher bulwarks. The attackers had to time their move, unavoidably signalling this to the defenders, and when they landed, stumbling and off-balance, they were easy meat for the pikemen.

A trumpet bayed from within the frigate above the clash of battle – and then again. The retreat? With swelling exultation, Kydd saw the attackers left on *Teazer*'s deck fling down their weapons in despair, knowing the penalty for turning their backs to return to their ship.

It was incredible, glorious, and Kydd's blood sang. They had repelled the enemy and *Teazer* was made whole again. Inside, a cooler voice chided that in large part they owed their success to the restless seas.

The frigate pulled away and cheers were redoubled again and again from the smoke-grimed and bloodied Teazers. But in a cold wash of reality Kydd knew what was coming next.

'For y' lives! Hands to wear ship!' he bellowed, stumping up and down to get the men from their guns and to the ropes. *Teazer* began her swing – but was it too late? The frigate was wearing about as well, but Kydd was gambling that their own turning circle was less.

It was – but it was not enough to escape. The frigate now no longer saw *Teazer* as a prize but an enemy who must be crushed. And against the unrestrained broadsides of a frigate the little sloop had no chance.

When it came the punishment was hideous. Quartering across *Teazer*'s stern the bigger ship's cannon blows brought a cascade of ruin and devastation, a tempest of iron that smashed, splintered and gouged, brought down spars, turned boats to matchwood.

In the blink of an eye Purchet, who had been with the ship from the first, was disembowelled and flung across the deck, his entrails strung out into a bloody heap against the waterway. The inoffensive sailmaker, Clegg, huddled by the main-hatch, was frantically trying to stitch repairs when he simply dropped, his head dissolved into a spray of brain.

From all sides came shrieks of pain from cruel, skewering splinters.

Shaken by the destruction, Kydd shouted hoarsely for sail of any kind on the fore. If they could just . . .

The frigate completed her veering, but she had another broadside waiting on her opposite side and she took time to tack about, a manoeuvre that would end in her coming up alongside the wreck that would be *Teazer*.

He felt a cold wetness: a grey advance of drizzle brought a soft misery that seemed to shroud the scenes of dying and ruin from mortal eyes. It fell gently, dissolving the blood so that Englishman and Frenchman mingled in fraternal embrace before trickling together through the scuppers into the sea.

Kydd pulled himself together. There was now no alternative to yielding: he must therefore face— But, *no*, he saw one last move . . . As the frigate completed its turn and took up for its final run he wheeled the wounded sloop off the wind and steered straight for the privateer to leeward. By feinting at it and causing it to run directly from his ship, Kydd was bringing it into the line of fire from the frigate chasing *Teazer*. They would not fire on their own: for the moment *Teazer* was safe.

But they did.

The broadside erupted without warning. The storm of shot that broke over *Teazer* was cataclysmic, smashing into her with an intensity that numbed the senses. A series of unconnected images flashed in front of Kydd. The fore-hatch bursting upwards a split second before a ball ended its flight with a colossal clang against an opposite gun. A ship's boy snatched from the deck and flung like a bloody rag into the scuppers. Hallum's face turning towards him in horror and pain, his mouth working as the splinter trans-fixing his lower body turned in the wound. And then came the deafening timber-cracking of the main-mast as it fell in dignified but awful finality, taking what remained of the fore-mast with it in a tangle of cordage, ruined spars and canvas.

It had finished. It was defeat. The end of everything.

As if in a dream he watched men slowly emerge from under the wreckage, go to the wretched bodies, stare in haggard disbelief at the passing frigate – and then from forward came the single crash of a gun.

Squinting past the heaped ruin of spars and canvas he saw it was his gunner's mate, Stirk, dragging a foot behind him but going methodically from gun to gun, sighting carefully and banging off defiance at their nemesis – whatever else, *Teazer* would be seen to go down fighting.

Eyes pricking, Kydd had not the heart to stop him. The frigate began its final turn to take possession of them – and, extraordinarily, one of Stirk's shots told. At the precise point of the slings of its crossjack there was a sudden jerk, tiny pieces flew off and the spar dipped awkwardly, then fell, rending the mizzen topsail above it and engulfing the driver.

The frigate – name still unknown – fell back on its course. Disabled and unable to turn back, it eventually disappeared into the grey mists of rain. The privateer stayed with it and suddenly *Teazer* was alone and desperately wounded in the desolate expanse of the Atlantic.

Dizzy with reaction Kydd mustered the Teazers. They seemed dazed, the petty officers half-hearted in their actions, the men shuffling in a trance. Kydd didn't waste time on words: if they were to survive it needed every man to rally to the aid of their ship. The time of grieving would come later.

Teazer wallowed sickeningly broadside to the seas, her foremast a three-foot stump, her main a giant jagged splinter. It was a deeply forlorn experience to see nothing aloft but empty sky, and with the loss of steadying sails, the vessel lurched to the swell like a log.

The first urgency was for a party of men to find the wounded and carry them below. The dead were heaved over the side. Hallum was dragged with rough kindliness to the lee of the capstan where he died quietly. Another party was sent to find the few Frenchmen still aboard who had hidden in fear of their own ship's broadside.

But the main chore was to clear the deck and try by any means to get sail on. All hands turned to, including Renzi, who stood in for Purchet and led the fo'c'sle party to set a series of purchases on the main spars and haul them clear before starting work on a species of sheer-leg. Even a rag of sail set to the streaming oceanic winds would serve.

Kydd forced his mind to coolness as he reviewed their situation. There was just one thing in their favour: these

Atlantic winds were south-westerlies that blew directly for England. If they could keep sail on *Teazer* they would eventually make an English port, however long it took.

The carpenter brought welcome news. He had sounded the wells and made his rounds and could confidently say there was no hurt to *Teazer*'s stout Maltese hull that he could not deal with – in a jet of warmth, Kydd realised that it was more than possible his command would be able to lay her before long to the tender care of a dockyard, her grievous wounds to be healed.

'Pass the word for the purser's steward. He's to see every man shall get his double tot.' There would be inhuman effort required to cut through the maze of ropes and canvas and shift the heavy spars, and little enough time to do it for it was now well into the afternoon.

Other thoughts intruded. Would the frigate return? Their fallen crossjack would have torn down much of the mizzen's ropery and would not easily be mended, not this day – and by morning *Teazer* would be well away from the scene of the action. Kydd thrust away the possibility that the frigate captain could calculate their uncontrolled drift and lie in wait for them.

And where were they in this immensity of sea? Their desperate slant across the Channel and out into the Atlantic had been only hazily marked, the dead-reckoning tentative at best and their last frenzied moves not noted at all. The leaden sky offered no hope of a sextant sight – they were to all intents and purposes lost and adrift.

The day wore on. At three bells in the first dog-watch the young Seaman Palmer choked on blood and died. No longer in action, *Teazer* saw him buried at sea in the hallowed way. An early dusk put an end to their efforts to show sail and for the long hours of night they were left with their thoughts and weariness, awaiting the dawn and what it would bring.

With the tendrils of morning light spreading, there was hope. The sheer-legs took a boom lashed to the summit and a reefed fore-topgallant spread slowly below to the cheers of *Teazer*'s company. Poulden hurried aft and took the wheel again, feeling for the life that was now filling her.

A fore-and-aft staysail rigged from the jagged main gave control and purpose in their creeping progress – until a dreaded call came from a sharp-eyed seaman forward. The grey cloudbank ahead had firmed. Ushant.

If their crazily lashed-up sail could not allow them to double the wicked northern headlands they would end driven by the same wind inexorably into the iron-hard cliffs.

Kydd tried everything: sweeps on the starboard side, scraps of sail everywhere they could be set, manhandling the guns aft – but it was not enough. In the dying light of day *Teazer* touched once, then again, before lurching to a stop on the dark, kelp-strewn Chaussée, a series of sub-sea reefs in the shadow of the ominous craggy heights of the Île de Keller.

Slewing sideways immediately, she lifted, then sagged, with a jarring, grinding finality, canted immovably over to larboard, the surf passing to end in hissing white rage on the further crags. It was so unfair! Nearly choked with emotion, Kydd fought against hopelessness and rage.

'Get forrard, y' chicken-hearted rabble,' he snarled, at a terrified crowd of seamen who were scrambling for the higher reaches of the after part of the crazily angled ship. But for a space his heart went out to them: this was how so many voyages ended for sailors, in terror and drowning on a hostile shore.

And Ushant was the worst: an appalling mass of rock

flung out into the Atlantic with surging ocean breakers and wild currents of ten knots or more, a place of nightmares for any mariner. The Bretons here had a saying, '*Qui voit Ouessant voit son sang!*' – He who sees Ushant, sees his blood!

Kydd crushed his desolation. 'Find the carpenter and send him below,' he snapped at the nearest seaman, who stared back at him in fear. 'Damn you, I'll do it m'self.' He pushed through the mass of men now on deck. The loss of the boatswain and his only lieutenant was a crippling blow: with just a single master's mate and the petty officers he had to take control of the fearful, milling men before they took it into their heads to break discipline and run wild.

He found the carpenter, broken at hearing of the loss of his friend Clegg. 'On y'r feet,' Kydd said brutally. 'Take a look around below, sound the wells an' report to me instantly. Now!' Without waiting for a response he stormed back to the wheel, collecting all the petty officers he could find.

'We've a chance,' he said urgently, shouting down the nervous cries from the back. 'Do your part, an' we'll swim again – don't and we'll be shakin' hands with Davy Jones afore nightfall.'

As if to add point to his words, a seething surf broke and thrust rudely past them, surging the hull further up with a deep, rumbling scrape that brought cries of terror from some.

But *if* they could get off the Chaussée and *if* they were not badly holed – there was hope.

'A strake near th' garboard forrard weepin' an' all, but nothin' the pumps can't clear,' the carpenter said woodenly, breathing heavily.

Kydd rounded on the haggard faces watching them: 'Hear that, y' lubbers? Next tide'll have us off! So clear this lumber and stand by!'

There was one thing he refused to think about: this was French territory. To his knowledge they had a form of military outpost, a signalling telegraph, on the western arm of Ushant, half a dozen miles to the south, probably tasked to report naval movements. If so, their situation would be known and . . .

'Get moving, y' shabs!' he roared, shoving men to their posts. The tide would return some time in the afternoon and they had to be ready. All wreckage overside, lighten the ship by any means – but not the guns. Not so much that they could defend their poor ship but to deny the enemy the opportunity of later grappling them to the surface.

A boat was lowered and fought to seaward, a small stream anchor slung under, the vessel rearing and plunging as it struggled out past the combers. When it was at a distance, the lashings were cut and the killick dropped away into the depths.

The tide receded hour by hour, leaving them still and silent on the wet rocks. 'They's come!' shrilled a voice, suddenly, and all eyes turned to the skyline above the black cliffs. Two figures stood looking down, and as they watched, others joined them.

'We ain't got a fuckin' prayer!' a young sailor blurted, eyes wild.

Stirk turned to him and scruffed his shirt. 'Shut y'r mouth, y' useless codshead. How're they goin' to come at us over that there?' He jerked his head at the sea-white cleft separating them from the cliff. 'They has t' come in a boat, an' when they do, we've guns as'll settle 'em.' He thrust the youth contemptuously away and turned to Kydd.

'Sir,' he said quietly, 'an' the carpenter wants a word. He's in th' hold.'

Kydd nodded. It was less than two hours to the top of the tide and then they could make their bid – pray heaven there was no problem.

They went down the fore-hatchway and Stirk, ignoring his leg wound, found the lanthorn. Without a word they went to a dark cavity at the after end of the ship. Moving awkwardly with the unnatural canting of the deck, Kydd dropped into the black void, filled with terrifying creaking and overpowering odours.

Stirk passed down the lanthorn and, bent double, they made their way to the lower side, where the carpenter and his mate stood with their own illumination.

No words were necessary. Evil and malignant, a wet blackness smelling powerfully of seaweed obscenely obtruded through the crushed and splintered hull for six feet or more, a fearful presence from the outside world breaking in on their precious home.

Kydd turned away that the others would not see the sting of the hot tears that threatened to overcome him at the unfairness of it all. 'Don't say anything o' this,' he said hoarsely. 'We'll – we'll fother, is all.' He nearly wept: for *Teazer*, to leave her bones in this break-heart place . . .

There was nothing the carpenter could do with a breach of such magnitude. There was a forlorn hope that fothering, dragging a sail over the outside, would give the pumps a chance.

Trusted men sat cross-legged in the gloom below, frenziedly sewing oakum and weaving matting into the sail, until it was obvious that the tide was ready to lift. It had to work: Kydd made sure the petty officers and others knew the stakes and personally selected the brawniest seamen to man the capstan that was to haul them off towards the anchor.

They had mounted the reef at about an hour before high water. Husbanding the strength of his men, Kydd waited until the ship shifted and moved restlessly, then drove them mercilessly.

Sobbing with the pain of the effort the men threw themselves at it, straining and heaving – and won. A sudden jerk, an odd wiggle like an eel, and *Teazer* was afloat and alive in the surging waters. Like a madman, Kydd roared his orders. Sail on the jury rig, the pumps manned instantly, parties ready at every conceivable point of trouble and the anchor cut loose just in time.

As they wallowed in clear water the fother sail was hastily produced, hauled into place and secured. Everything depended now on a clear run for England.

The wind was veering fitfully more westerly, fair to make an offing – but it would take them perilously close to that improbably named headland, Le Stiff. However, it was a bold coast, steep to with deep water, and in the brisk winds *Teazer* was making respectable way and within the hour had it laid astern.

Kydd had his two midshipmen positioned to relay any news from the hell below. He knew the chain pumps were beasts to drive, the rubbing of the many leather flaps of the watertight seal creating an inertia that was bone-breaking to overcome. It was not unknown in extreme circumstances for men to fall dead at the endless brutal exertion. 'Mr Tawse?'

'Holding, Mr Kydd.' The youngster was pale, his set face giving nothing away.

The hours stretched out. Kydd stood motionless on the quarterdeck, willing on his ship. After what she'd gone through . . . but they must be nearly halfway by now. In just hours more they would make landfall, say Plymouth or further on at Torbay. Rest for his sorely tried ship.

The carpenter broke into Kydd's thoughts: 'Sir, I'm truly sorry t' say, we're makin' water faster'n we can get rid of 'un.' Kydd could feel it now. A terrible weariness, no reaction to the bluster and boisterous play of the seas, a—

'*Saaail!*' Without tops to mount a lookout at a height, the stranger could not be far off.

'The Frenchy frigate,' Kydd said dully, as it smartly altered towards them. Fury slammed in on him – how could he give up his brave, his infinitely precious ship to the enemy after all this?

'No, it ain't!' Poulden said excitedly. 'That's *Harpy*, ship-sloop!' A friend! Glory be, they had help – they had a chance.

The sloop came alongside and hailed. In a whirl of feeling Kydd saw a tow-line passed and the men below on the pumps spelled. All the while, with a terrible intensity, he urged his wounded ship on.

With fresh men and new heart they laboured unceasingly, but the tow proved a difficult haul. At a little after one, a tiny blue-grey line was seen ahead: England. As if relenting, the seas and westerly began to ease and the unnatural wallowing softened as they struggled on.

But Kydd could feel in his heart that a mortal tiredness lay on *Teazer*. Like a dog in its last hour trying to lift its muzzle to lick its master's hand, she could no longer respond to please him. She was dying.

He hurried below in a frenzy of anguish. The men, in every stage of exhaustion, were fighting the pump to work amid as deadly a sign as the buboes on a plague victim: ankle-deep water, which was sloshing unchecked from side to side across the decks.

A lump in his throat threatened to choke him as he went back to the quarterdeck. The land was close enough to make out individual fields, the calm loveliness of Devon. And it was now so cruelly apparent that *Teazer* would not now make her rest. He could do no more for his love, his first command, she who had borne him on the ocean's bosom for so many leagues of both adventure and heartache.

It was time to part.

The tow was cast off, the men released from their Calvary and set to transferring their pitiful belongings to the boats. Such stores as could be retrieved were taken aboard and then, with the seas lapping her gunports, HMS *Teazer* was abandoned, her captain the last to leave with a final caress of her rail.

In mute sympathy, *Harpy* stood by as *Teazer* lay down and slipped away for ever from human ken.

THE
ADVENTURES
CONTINUE
ONLINE

Visit julianstockwin.com

Find Julian on Facebook

 /julian.stockwin

Follow Julian on Twitter

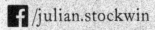 @julianstockwin